Hangfire Hill

Lee got to one knee and reached down to his right boot as the man jumped. He was just standing with his knife in his hand as the man landed half against him, knocked him staggering, and followed him, swinging a leather-clad slung-shot — a "jack" some people called it.

Lee took that blow on his left shoulder. He had felt nothing there since the other man hit it with the length of pipe. He took that blow and stepped back, trying to keep his balance. If he fell, he thought, this long-haired man would beat him to death...

Crossfire Country

Lee heard a grunt, turned and saw a grizzly bear — a big bear the color of cinnamon. It was up on its hinds not forty feet away, its paws folded to its chest, and was looking at him, weaving its head slowly from side to side.

The Indian girl shouted, and Lee knew what she would do next. He turned just as she was hauling her brand new Winchester repeater out of its scabbard at the paint's shoulder.

We'll get out of this, Lee thought, if that squaw doesn't start shooting. Might as well send Surrey a telegraph message as start firing rifle shots in these mountains!

The BUCKSKIN Series

RIFLE RIVER
GUNSTOCK
PISTOLTOWN
COLT CREEK
GUNSIGHT GAP
TRIGGER SPRING
CARTRIDGE COAST
BOLT ACTION
TRIGGER GUARD
RECOIL
GUNPOINT
LEVER ACTION
SCATTERGUN
WINCHESTER VALLEY
GUNSMOKE GORGE
REMINGTON RIDGE
SHOTGUN STATION
PISTOL GRIP
BUCKSKIN SPECIAL EDITION:
     THE BUCKSKIN BREED
PEACEMAKER PASS
SILVER CITY CARBINE
CALIFORNIA CROSSFIRE

Buckskin Double Edition

HANGFIRE HILL /

CROSSFIRE COUNTRY

Roy LeBeau

LEISURE BOOKS NEW YORK CITY

A LEISURE BOOK

Published by

Dorchester Publishing Co., Inc.
6 East 39th Street
New York, NY 10016

Printed in the United States of America

Buckskin Double Edition

HANGFIRE HILL /

CROSSFIRE COUNTRY

HANGFIRE HILL

Lee Morgan had found, somewhat to his own surprise, that he no longer believed in heros, and not much in the bravery of any fighting man. Gunmen, prize-fighters, soldiers who charged into cannon fire in battle and were appropriately killed—even the memory of his father . . . even the memory of that gentle man-killer . . .

He found not much real courage in any of them, not much more, say, than a brave dog might show, in a backyard fight.

He had seen real courage—seen it in action close to, and for many months, and thought it unlikely he would mistake the truth of it again.

Catherine Dowd, as much his mother as any woman could be who wasn't actually his mother . . . Catherine Dowd, who had walked away from her marriage with a cattle-king, and all for love of Lee's father, Buckskin Frank Leslie.

Catherine Dowd was dead.

Had been seven long, long months dying of a

cancer at her breast. And had uttered not one word of plea, or complaint, or anger in her monstrous pain and hopelessness. She had cared for the happiness of those who loved her, and had, perhaps, been grateful at the end to die, to go to rest beside her lover's grave in the grove of pines.

Lee and the neighbors and the men of Spade Bit had seen her off there, and planted her deep by Leslie's side. The next morning, for reasons of their own, Lee and the men had shot a handsome, dancing little dapple mare named Rapids, and had buried this animal at the foot of Catherine Dowd's grave. And with the horse, all tacked out, saddle-bags with clothing chosen by her Indian woman, an oil-cloth of trail food; a large canteen of spring water, and a small silver-plated pistol.

These things were done without off-ranchers knowing about it—then, or ever.

Ten days after she was buried, a little man on a big horse came riding with two hard-cases riding flank, asked to see the place, and was taken there by Lee. The hard-cases were left at headquarters house, with mugs of beer.

Mathew Dowd had aged more than a little in the few years since Catherine had left him to be with an over-the-hill gunman and killer.

Dowd had let them be, then, and had left the country for Canada where he'd come from. Dowd owned more land than most men had strength to ride over; but he had not owned Spade Bit. This pretty high-country horse ranch

10

had been Catherine's.

She had left it to Lee.

"I understand," Mathew Dowd had said to Lee, stopping for coffee after his visit to her grave, "I understand that you inherit this ranch."

"Yes."

"Well," the little man said, "I suppose that's fair enough." He'd sat in one of Catherine's rocking chairs—so small a man that only his toes could touch the floor as he rocked slowly back and forth, sipping at a cup of McCorkle's black mud brew. "I understand," Dowd had continued, the lenses of his spectacles reflecting the parlor windows opposite. "I understand that you own property elsewhere."

"Part of another horse ranch, Mister Dowd, in Montana—on the Rifle River, if it's any of your business." Lee found he did not like this little cold-eyed man.

Hadn't cared for his hard-cases, either. One of them, a man of some reputation named Tom Horne, had tried on some tough with Sid Sefton down by the corrals—and had received an earful from Sefton, who backed mount for no man.

"Listen, Cloudy," Sefton had said, referring apparently, to Horne's height, "how would you like to kiss my ass?"

As Lee had heard the tale from his foreman, Ford, Horne had colored up and looked danger-ous, and had drifted his hand to his gun belt.

"You surely aren't goin' to touch that

revolver," Sefton had said to him (Sefton mounted all this time on a gray gelding named Roger), "because if you do, I'll provide you a second ass-hole in no time at all." He had put his hand on his gun-butt, his thumb on the hammer-spur. At which, Horne, a very tall, handsome, somewhat mournful man, with a great reputation as an Indian scout, and a later, more dubious one as a barroom drunk and bully, had scowled fiercely, turned, and stalked away.

After that, Dowd's two guards had stayed off to themselves in the cook-shack, drinking McCorkle's home-brewed beer, waiting until Dowd was ready to leave. The second guard, a short, wide-shouldered man named Barney McAffee, had seemed more agreeable than Horne, but went to the cook-shack to drink beer with Horne none-the-less.

Lee had thought it an insult for Dowd to have brought such people — hired body-guarders—onto Spade Bit, as if Lee and four gun-handy wranglers (and simple hospitality) were not guarantees enough for his safety—millionaire or no.

Dowd had not, apparently, missed this.

He sat and rocked back and forth a while. Then, "Bad back," he said. "Rocking helps it." And continued to do so, the bright reflections in his glasses shifting up and down with the motion of the chair. After a few moments, he set his coffee cup down on an occasional beside him.

"I would like to ask you," he said, "I would like to ask you a personal question—two personal questions, in point of fact."

More silent rocking, up and down . . . up and down.

Lee saw that statements and silence were a habit with the little man. Likely a way he'd found to manage men in conversation, for business or whatever. It occurred to Lee that the West was a difficult place for a little man with weak eyes, however much money he might have.

At last. "What I would like to ask you is, first, is it true that you are Frank Leslie's son? And second, was my wife—was . . . Catherine . . . happy?"

There was nothing about Dowd to like. But Lee found himself feeling sorry for the man, for what he had lost in Catherine Dowd. And lost years ago, years before her death. It must have damn near killed him to have had a treasure like that, and been careless with it.

"Frank Leslie was my father—the ranch at Rifle River was his; he left it to my mother."

Dowd stayed rocking, looking at him.

"Who was *your* father?" Lee asked, nettled at that silence.

Dowd smiled; it was the first time Lee'd seen him do it. Poor little icy circus midget of a man. "Not as illustrious as yours, I'm afraid. My father was a lumber merchant, in Victoria. Successful, in a modest way."

Back and forth in the rocker, toes barely touching the hooked rug on the down-swing.

"Mrs. Dowd was very happy here, I think,"

13

Lee said. "From what I saw of her and my father together, I would say they were very happy. I never heard either of them say a word against you, sir." (Lee was surprised by the 'sir.'—it had just popped out. After all, this was an old man, must be in his fifties . . .)

"No," Dowd said, put his toes to the rug and kept them there, stopping the chair's motion. "No, I'm certain they did not." Lee thought he sighed. "Catherine was every inch a lady. Your father, that extraordinary man, was, in his way, a gentleman." He peered at Lee through his spectacles, as if seeking a resemblance. "Happy . . ." he said.

"Yes."

"And she suffered greatly in her illness?"

"Yes."

The little man suddenly took off his spectacles, pulled a handkerchief from his coat pocket, and polished them. There were tears on his cheeks.

"You will find, young man," he said, "that there are many, many things in life that do not bear thinking about." He finished polishing his spectacles, wiped his eyes with his handkerchief, and put his spectacles back on. "I understand," he said, "that Catherine has also left you some copper-mine shares in the Dakotas, at Hangfire Hill." The toes of his polished boots—boots small enough for a child—gently spurned the rug, and Dowd began to rock again.

Lee said nothing.

Dowd nodded. "Very proper reticence—espec-

14

ially considering the situation. A half-interest in the Golden Penny, I believe. A good working, I understand. Though, now, of course, it is not my business. Those shares were a wedding present to Catherine, when we were married. I have not busied myself about them since." He reached out to pick up his cup. "This is the worst coffee I have ever drunk—yet I found, in my time, McCorkle to be a redoubtable cook."

"He lets his wood-boy do the coffee, now. McCorkle's brewing beer."

"Ah," Dowd said. "I would suppose my Myrmadons are regaling themselves." He rocked slightly faster. "My apologies for foisting them upon you. Some, some difficulties up in Canada. Men of that sort have their uses." He glanced directly into Lee's eyes. "No offense, I hope, taken. I was not referring to your father."

"My father hired out his gun," Lee said. "That was his choice—I'm not ashamed of it."

"No . . . no, of course not." Dowd put his coffee cup down, waited 'till he came to the low point of his rocking, and abruptly stood up out of the chair. They were almost eye to eye, and Lee still seated.

Lee stood up. "You'll stay to dinner? You're welcome here, Mister Dowd."

The little man stretched out a child's hand, and Lee shook it. "No, no," Dowd said, "but thank you. I have a train to catch up in Parker, if they've remembered to put my car to it."

Lee walked with him out to the front porch.

There, to his surprise, Dowd put two fingers to his mouth and whistled shrilly, as if he were calling in a dog. A few moments later, first McAffee, then Horne came trotting out of the cook shack—very like watch dogs, in fact. They came over to their tethered horses—Ford had seen to it the animals had been grained and watered—and swung up. Dowd stepped down off the porch, hopped nimbly up into his hired rig, untied his reins and shook them out.

"You seem, and I can only say 'seem,' to be a fitting son to your father, Mister Morgan," Dowd said. "A word of advice, if you care to hear it."

Lee nodded.

"Copper," Dowd said. "Copper is booming—and the Dakota works are shallow mines. The profit may be great but it will not be lasting. I understand that a Mister Sean McGee has purchased the other shares to the Golden Penny. I understand that Mister McGee is a very interesting man." Dowd rested a small, gleaming boot on his dashboard. "I understand that there is practically no law in Hangfire Hill to speak of and no order, whatsoever." He clucked to his horse, touched it off-shoulder lightly with the whip, and rolled out of the headquarter's yard with his gunmen trotting at his back.

Lee stood on the porch, and watched them until they were a quarter mile off, down on the draw road, and out of sight.

Catherine Dowd had retained the best lawyers

16

in Boise. "The best protection money can buy, in civilized matters," she'd said, "are good lawyers."

The good lawyers hadn't minced words with Lee, when he'd gone to their offices after the reading of Catherine Dowd's will. It had been a tedious trip up to Boise, and the wrong time of year for it—the mares were foaling, and he was needed on the Bit. Ford was as good a foreman as there was; the small man, lean and quick-tempered as a jockey (and with some owl-hooting in his past, likely) could, and did, run Spade Bit by his lonesome, given Sid Sefton, Charlie Potts, and old Bud Bent to back him. Ford was more than capable. Still, Lee didn't like leaving at foaling time. The future of the Bit was marked in those foals.

But he left, and went to Boise to see the lawyers.

"As to the ranch property, I see no problem there at all," the junior partner, a tall, freckled-faced man named Padmore, had said. "You are in possession; the deed is not contested. You know the land, the stock. Above all—you are in *possession.*" He'd rolled the word over his tongue like cold beer on a summer day. "The same, regrettably, can not be said for this . . . mining property." He'd poked the little paper sheaf of mine-shares with a long, freckled index finger.

"You are not in possession of *that* property— except on paper. And, I am given to understand, the nature of the . . . political and legal system presently prevailing in that section of the Dakotas is reminiscent, I'm told, of the situation generally some ten or twenty years ago in most of the western territories." He'd flipped his finger at the sheaf of papers again. "And, there is a *partner.*"

"Are you saying, counselor, that I might lose that part-ownership?" All this beating around the bush was costing Lee some confidence in this particular lawyer of Mrs. Dowd's.

His confidence was swiftly restored.

"You're damn right," Padmore said. "The fact is, if you don't get out there and nail down your share of that mine—well, you can just kiss it good-bye."

"I've got a ranch to run."

"And I," Padmore said, "have heard a few clients say that they couldn't be bothered to go and do this or that business because they had this or that to run. It always cost them."

Lee had sighed, and shifted in the hard seat horsehide chair. "When, in your opinion, do I have to be out there?"

"Were I you," Padmore said, "I would have left yesterday—and taken a tough friend or two with me."

"Hangfire is that grim a town?"

"They like to call it 'The Hill', I understand. We have a banking correspondent in the south of that territory; his information is that the town is wide open, and about as dangerous as an active field of battle. Which," he added, "it is, in a way. They took just over two million dollars worth of copper out of that ground last year. Now, your judgment is as good as mine, what hard men will do for that sort of money."

Lee left Spade Bit four days later.

He'd said his good-byes at the ranch, and had likely driven Ford and the others half crazy with detailed instructions on this and that, and how to dose the roan mare, and patrol north every now and then to keep the rustlers staying put up in the Roughs, and repair the fences down by the Little Chicken (something in the dirt there seemed to eat fence posts), and to slap some white wash on the cook-shack and stables and tool shed—the horse barn, too, if they found the time—make sure that McCorkle got in his seventeen sacks of Champion Red Beans when the shipment got to Pete's in Grover, and cull out the geldings—but only for show-faults and continuous splints; he'd shuck them for conformation and wind when he got back, and, and, and . . . and a hundred and fifty other matters, great and small.

Ford listened to all this for some time, with patience; then, when Lee got to instructing about mending the buggy harness (not the black harness, the old brown), Ford had leaned politely to one side, spit some tobacco juice, then strolled away, leaving Lee with a good deal left to say.

Lee got the point, sighed, and left the ranch to Ford and the others, and the hell with it. He shouldn't be gone more than two or three weeks in any case.

* * *

He'd said his good-byes to Catherine Dowd and to his father, lying together in the shady grove of pines above headquarters. Then, he'd ridden north, to Parker, to catch the railroad train to the Dakotas.

In Parker, he'd gone to say good-bye to S'eon.

He'd walked out March Row, past the yards, and out into the beginnings of the country. The winter had broken; green, light sun-struck green flowed over the fields like running water. The new season's sun was hot on Lee's shoulders as he walked. Might have ridden, waited to stable the horse—but he hadn't. He felt like walking . . . walking to her.

The cottage stood at the edge of a pasture, a flowered cow pasture where a farmer named Macreedy ran a small herd of white-face.

The little house was hers, and three acres of ground with it. Lee had bought them two years before. Two years . . . Had brought a little Chinese whore—a slave girl with whip-scars on her back—back to the mountains with him from San Francisco. Had brought her, and some memories along with her. Memories of another girl . . . an actress . . . weeping, struggling beneath his weight. Memories of a one-eyed girl . . . a long, long alley . . . a straight-razor flashing in the moonlight . . . and, in the dirt, a brave hoodlum, sliced wide open, trying to die.

And the memory of a handsome man, tall, strong, perfectly dressed . . . joking as he died, knifed in the back by Lee's Chinese girl.

Memories . . . and a Chinese girl.

Worth walking for.

Lee kept down the path alongside the pasture. Honeysuckle was just budding along the farmer's split-rail fence. A midday breeze, cool under the blaze of the sun, came floating from far down the distant slopes of the Rockies. Lee could smell the spring in it.

The little buggy he'd given her was parked in the stable barn. The neat bay pony grazed its lot beside the house.

She'd be here.

There'd been two Chinese families in Parker when Lee'd brought her—the people who ran the steam laundry, and a family of railroad workers and their wives. These Chinese people had been cruel to S'eon at first, knowing her for a whore, a slave.

Lee had changed their minds—had at least changed their behavior toward her, by having a little talk with the men heading both families. A little talk first, then a little money. It had answered well enough. They were civil to her, now, the women coming out sometimes, to her small house to take the air, to gossip. This had, Lee thought, made her happier.

There'd been some other trouble. Two men— young men—town roughs named Bud Stitt and Harold Woolman, had loitered near the cottage, made gestures at her, said things to her in the street when she went to town. Lee hadn't heard about that for several weeks. S'eon had said nothing. Then, a woman named Molly Corday, a seamstress who gave S'eon some fine sewing to do sometimes, had sent a note down to Spade Bit with Charlie Wattress, when he delivered some freight.

Lee had read the note, and left that hour, riding to Parker as if the devil was chasing him. He was just wise enough not to take his gun to the two men, and kill them.

Two nights later, Bud Stitt and Harold Woolman, with another friend, had ridden out to the Chinese girl's cottage, dismounted at her stable gate, and, drunk, had walked past a lattice of vine to peer into her windows, and then started barking like dogs, and calling vile things out to her from the darkness.

There, Lee, who had been waiting since dark, came out from behind the stable building, and upon them.

He wielded only his black snake whip, and did not touch his Bisley Colts at all.

The third man, a boy, really, named Lloyd, turned and ran. The other two fought.

. They had no chance at all; and what happened then was bad. Bud Stitt's face was hacked by the lash as if a madman had come out and struck him with a saber. One side of his nose was sliced away, and his cheek was split wide open, so that his back teeth showed clear back to the hinge of his jaw.

Woolman, a tougher young man, was damaged worse. The bones in both his arms were broken by the long, weighted handle of Lee Morgan's whip. And his forehead was beaten in.

Woolman was never to fully recover from that beating. Would, in the long, long years left of his life, never be good for anything more than to stable-hand—and that, only at the simplest tasks.

From that night, there was no man in the town of Parker who dealt with the Chinese girl other than courteously, and tipped his hat to her as if she'd been a lady when he met her on the street.

But Lee, triumphant, his anger spent, had gone into the little house to find S'eon crouched and weeping, her hands pressed tight over her ears—trying, perhaps, to shut out even the memory of screams and the hiss and crack of the whip. Then he wished he'd called them out elsewhere and shot them down. He had, in his pleasure, forgotten the long white whip scars that laced the small girl's back. Had forgotten the cage he'd found her in.

Still, the work was done. White or yellow, no man treated Lee Morgan's Chinese girl ill. Even the wives of the town were civil when she called at their back doors for the fine sewing to be done. The word had been passed at the bar rail of the *Bull*, the lounge at the *Variety*, the feedstores and feedlots, the stables and saloons, the dry goods, mercantile, and banks.

What a man's wife does—the man will answer for.

So, by fear and force, and here and there by friendship, and by the power of the Spade Bit purse, Lee had made for S'eon a golden fence of

23

respect and careful manners. Though it remained a fence, never-the-less.

Lee climbed the three steps to the narrow front porch, stepped across it, and rang the door-pull. He had never kept a key—that would have made it less S'eon's house.

He saw her shadow through the lace at the glass door panel, then she opened to him. Unchanged, always the same. Small, sturdy, cool, dark-browed and silent. Not a very pretty girl, really. Lee had seen prettier Chinese girls in Boise.

She had a fold of blue silk in her hand—some of her needlework for Molly or some lady of the town—and lifted her face up to be kissed. S'eon had learned some English, but spoke it rarely, and then almost always to her customers, to merchants where she did her small shopping, to those who did not matter.

She had little to say to Lee but 'yes' and 'no.' The rest was gestures, smiles, occasional frowns.

So it was, until she was naked before him. Naked on the wide brass bed in the back bedroom. Then, twisting, stretching, convulsing with pleasure, her small sand-colored body spoke all the speech of love.

Even after years in a brothel cage—years of accepting what seemed unacceptable, suffering what seemed impossible to suffer—even after those many years, S'eon had required to be taught to kiss. The men and boys who had used her in every way they chose, had whipped her, urinated or shat on her if they could spare the two dollars that those things cost, none of them, not one, had dreamed of putting his lips to hers.

It was Lee, therefore, who taught her kissing. Which was not to say that he loved her—and certainly not to say that he knew her. It was only that she had become necessary to him.

Lee kissed her, walked with her into the sunny little parlor to sit beside her on the sofa, admiring the fine sewing, the delicate embroidery of which she was so proud, and to kiss her again.

She went to the kitchen and brought back Canada tea and cakes, and they ate and drank off of a black laquered table he had bought for her in Boise. It was one of the few things Chinese in the house. While they ate, Lee told her he was leaving on a journey, taking the railroad a little east, to the Dakotas. The reason being property, business. This S'eon understood very well, herself now being, in a small way, a businesswoman. She understood he would be gone, and for some time—Lee doubted she understood where. The strangeness of America to her was shown in S'eon's inability to imagine any place in it, other than where she was. San Francisco had been real enough, and the country they had passed on the railroad trip back to the mountains. And now, Parker was real to her.

The rest of America—the great expanse of it, its details, its variety—was only a dream to her, an odd map that might contain dragons, tigers,

25

emperors.

She had asked him about dragons in Kansas. Someone, playing a joke on her, had told her there were dragons in Kansas. "I doubt it," Lee had said. "Just long noses like me, and Redmen, and some fat old ladies even uglier than dragons." Which reply had pleased her enough so that she laughed, which she did very rarely.

So, though property meant something to her, the Dakotas did not. And, as to his being gone from her for a while; he had been gone from her before.

They ate her cakes, and drank the rough Hudson's Bay Company tea, and Lee stroked the blue silk and then her cheek, and made faces to show he was more pleased with the smoothness of her cheek. Then he kissed her, and they stood up together, the top of her head just above the level of his heart, and he kissed her again.

The back bedroom was flooded with sunlight. The bright brass at the bed's head and foot glowed with sunlight, shone with it. So, her skin shone in the golden light.

Once they were naked, Lee turned her, as he always did, and gently kissed along the scars across her back, as if he might kiss them away. S'eon sighed, and leaned against him, and stretched slowly and voluptuously as a cat as he kissed her. Lee knelt on the sun-dappled carpet to run his hands down her scar-ridged back—the scars alternating with skin as fine and smooth as running water—down to her solid, round little buttocks, firm with muscle, and on . . . on down sturdy, smooth-muscled legs to her ankles and feet.

She was like a living mechanism made of warm gold.

Kneeling, Lee took her small hip bones in each hand, and pulled her buttocks gently to him. S'eon spread her legs, and slowly bent forward until her long hair, black as hot tar-pitch and falling loose, its combs all gone, swept the carpet.

Lee gripped her round buttocks in either hand, and gently pried them apart. Below the tiny soot-rose of her ass, the girl's neat cunt gaped slightly open at this pressure—a narrow scarlet slice in a dark-furred fruit. Lee leaned into her, his face buried in her, his mouth fastened to that scarlet pout.

He ran his tongue up into her as far as it would go, and felt the muscles in her thighs tense as he did it. He licked at her, delicately, spreading her small cunt wider, wetting it with his tongue. Slowly, carefully, he licked and sucked at her, began to sip her juices.

The girl moaned, and thrust her buttocks back harder into his face, and Lee gripped her, his fingers denting the smooth flesh of her hips, and drank from her while she moved in his hands, bending lower, spreading her legs, reaching back anxious fingers to grip at herself, to clutch at her own buttocks, to spread them for him.

Lee began to gently bite at her, licking and sucking harder. When she moaned again, he moved up against her, and, still kneeling, licked at her as a mother cat would lick its kitten, getting his tongue deeper into her cunt, licking and sucking at it, then licking up and up into the warm crack of her ass, sucking at what she held spread open for him. He licked her ass for her, sucking at it, working at it with his tongue until the Chinese girl cried out and sank slowly down to her knees, her face to the carpet, her small buttocks high in the air.

Lee's cock was up and out, stiff and aching.

He straightened up, trembling with need of her, reached down, set the tip of his cock against the bud of her ass, and slowly . . . slowly, drove the thick, swollen length of him up between her buttock cheeks, up into her bowels.

The girl cried out, screamed softly with pain and pleasure as it went up into her. This was a thing she had taught him, had caressed him into doing with her on those days when she had been bleeding with the curse. Lee had not minded this blood, had wanted to love her just the same, but she would not have it.

Now, not bleeding, with no excuse but pleasure, the girl groaned and twisted with pleasure on the rod that impaled her, her strong back curved and hollowed, then humped, as he drove deeper into her, and hollowed again as she grunted with the effort of accepting him.

Lee, sweating, gasping as he labored over her, glanced down and saw the last inches of his cock, the stretched little mouth of her ass clasped around it as he drove against her. He felt the cool of her buttocks against his hips, groaned at the squeezing pressure on the length of him—and then was in her all the way. The girl cried out, her face buried in the carpet, veiled in the black cloud of her hair.

Lee slowly pulled it almost out of her—and S'eon grunted as he did that. Lee's cock gleamed with the dull oils of her bowels, a streak of brown along its side. Then he thrust back into her—faster this time. Harder. Holding her hips still as he drove it in. As his loins struck her buttocks, his cock buried deep inside her, Lee felt the girl raise her ass higher, presenting herself like a mare, opening herself to him, accepting it all.

Lee pulled out of her suddenly, and she squealed as he did it—then he began to thrust in and out of her . . . faster . . . harder . . . hearing their flesh smack together in the silent room. Hearing S'eon's moans as he fucked into her. She was sweating now, was slippery with sweat as he screwed into her, her thighs quivering as his weight struck her, as the full length of his cock slid back up inside her.

Lee felt a sort of pain begin to grow and grow at the roots of his balls. It was a pain of such sweetness that he could hardly bear it. It grew until he felt it rise up to overwhelm him.

S'eon screamed something in her pleasure as he thrust into her once again; an odor of sandlewood, shit, and sweat rose off her as she labored beneath him.

Lee gasped . . . tried to catch his breath . . . and lost it, lost everything. Everything. It all went into her . . . up into her. It pumped into her as if it were his heart's blood. It seemed to him he was dying with the pleasure of it. Lee fell forward across her back, his cock still thrust deep into her, and supported himself for a few moments on stiffened arms, then slowly collapsed to the carpet with her. Hugging her . . . cradling her . . . loving her.

CHAPTER TWO

S'eon didn't come down to the Parker station to see him off on the 4:55. Crowds of people troubled her.

Lee picked up his baggage at the *Bull*, had a cool beer with some friends there, Billy Pearson and Bob Clay, walked down to the station, and went aboard.

The only good thing about that train, was that Mister Harvey had set up the dining car on it—and that marvel of modern thought and technical skill served some of the best food Lee had ever eaten, fancy food, too. Partridges, elk steak, iced cream. Lee ate his way clear down that menu—dinner, breakfast, lunch, and dinner again. And he sat by the window, lounging as comfortably as he could on the dusty green plush seat, and spent the long hours watching the world go by.

For the last few years, Lee had never been at his ease on a railroad train. The sounds, the smells, the motions of the train brought back memories to him—especially at night, when the dim oil lamps flickered and swayed as the train thundered down its track into the darkness. Then, late, when the other passengers sat swaying in their restless sleep, Lee would sometimes think—just for a moment—that he saw a huge shadow thrown hulking down the aisle, as if, just then, a giant, insane, murderer, had entered the car. An Iroquois in an eastern suit, his eyes glittering black.

Gone, of course, when Lee twisted in his seat to look back at the car's door. And the shadow gone, as well.

Other times—once already on this trip—Lee had looked up from a book he was reading, a book about fishing for whales, and had thought —for the barest instant—that a man was smiling at him from the far end of the car. A small man, very well dressed in a banker's suit of clothes. A small man with big hands, and a humorous eye . . .

Railroad trains. Lee would never, in all his life, be perfectly at ease upon them—no matter how many of Mister Harvey's fine dinners he ate. No matter how wide, how pretty the country rattling by. No matter the sleep he managed in the early morning hours, when dark was deepest. Sometimes, in these sleeps, it seemed that gunfire came crashing . . . and men's screams . . . and he tripped and slipped somehow on bloody steel plating—and came awake with a gasp, his heart hammering, his right hand curved to the butt of an old converted Remington cap-and-ball .44.

Lee had that dream on his second night out traveling, woke from it sweating . . . and cursed himself for not making the long journey on horseback. Would have taken him near two weeks instead of days, but they would have been free and easy weeks, horse backing, sleeping trailside by his lonesome—not cooped up like a farmer's chicken in an iron coffin rocking through the night.

If he'd been more of a man—had dared Kid Curry to do his worse . . . If he'd been more of a man . . . his father . . .

But he hadn't been a man. He'd been only a boy. Lee wondered how he would ever learn to forgive that boy. Catherine Dowd had borne him no grudge for leading that small smiling monster to Spade Bit, though it cost her the man she loved.

His father had borne no grudge, either, had seemed, in a way, to be glad to face Harvey Logan across a few feet of cook-shack floor. Had seemed glad . . .

Not my fault. And, if it was, not one God damned thing I can do about it now.

Lee shifted on the seat, wide awake and waiting for morning. He'd eat another damned big breakfast—three or four eggs, over easy, bacon and ham and sausages. Some of those fine hot rolls—as good as best beaten biscuits for breakfast. He'd have a big breakfast, and then go and sit out on the observation platform at the back of the train, and read about the fellow fishing for whales with his cannibal companions, and, with the other passengers, look out over the plains—over those endless carpets of green and yellow grass, the soft swells of low hills rising beneath the grass and small wild flowers like great animals—like Mister Melville's great whales, in fact, just rising to the surface to breathe.

Looking for the herds of buffalo, where the great herds were not, and would never be again.

"There's one!" some fellow would shout, and throw his cigar away and go run to get his rifle. But the train would have traveled far past that single animal by the time he came puffing back to the platform, rifle raised and ready. That single animal, or two or three together at the most, would have been left behind, to wander alone in their ocean of grass.

Then, as the day grew even hotter, and the sun beat down like brass, Lee would finish up his chapter, share a swig of some Omaha drummer's rye whiskey, and then walk, balancing to the motion, up the train to the dining car, and get his lunch. Pork chops, likely, today. And baked apples. Spring peas . . . asparagus . . . white bread. Rice pudding, or cherry pie, or strawberry iced cream. He'd eat all of it he could hold, then go back to his seat and clean and oil the Bisley Colts, run some neat's-foot along the length of the black snake whip. Clean, oil and sharpen the broadblade dagger that lived in his right boot. Do these things, while kids watched him over the backs of their seats, watching, saying nothing.

That sort of thing made him feel better, riding on the train.

Morning of the third day, they pulled into a flat cow town named Shivaree. Had been a bad town, in its day, Lee'd heard, tamed now by a marshal named Asa Potter.

From the passengers' complaints—those who made this run regularly, for business—Lee gathered that they were near a day late, getting in. A small locomotive engine, the numerous water stops, took the blame for that.

Lee didn't give a damn for that, now—nor that he had a day's stage ride still to sit through, heading north, up into the hills, the mine workings. He was glad to be off.

"One stage a day for the Hills," the station boss said. "You don't have an inside seat punched out here, Mister Morgan," fingering down the length of the stage ticket Lee had bought in Parker. "Sorry, but you'll have to wait 'till tomorrow, you want to ride inside." He glanced sideways out his office window, and seemed pleased by the castles of black cloud gathering over the prairie to the north.

The station boss was a tough-looking old coot —a pot-bellied lantern-jawed fifty or sixty, Lee figured. And figured the old man did a good business in extra bucks slipped to him for inside seating among the drummers and mine clerks, and the ignorant Irish miners going up to Hangfire Hill.

His ticket was an insider, and properly punched and paid for.

"If there's anything I hate to see," Lee said, smiling at the man, "it's the sight of a range-wise old mossy-horn making a fool of himself."

The big old man cocked a cold water colored eye at him.

"This ticket ain't right," he said. "Yo're ridin' outside, Mister, if yo're ridin' today."

Lee set his big leather *portmanteau* down, leaned down to unfasten the buckles, lifted the lid, and pulled the coiled whip out. He swung his arm, and shook the length of leather free. Two drummers, standing just behind him, their tickets in their hands, skipped back and away across the little office floor, their cracked patent leather shoes tripping back along the sandy boards like goat's feet.

"I surely never thought," Lee said, "that I'd ever have to slice a chunk of rump meat off a man old enough to be my daddy."

The whiplash whispered along the floor.

The old pot-belly flushed an angry red, like a turkey-cock, and for a few moments said nothing.

Lee stepped back and cocked his wrist. Have to be careful not to really hurt the old fool.

"All right—all right!" The old man's eyes were popping with rage. "I was mistook—this is a inside ticket." His big, mottled hands were trembling as they tore the company's copy off the bottom. He handed Lee his half.

"Thank you kindly," Lee said, coiled the whip,

bent and tucked it back in his case, buckled that shut, turned, and strolled out.

He'd gone down the steps and to the street when he heard the office door bang open behind him. "You damn young pup, you! You young son-of-a-bitch! Were I ten years younger!"

Old man sounded furious. Would teach him, though, to choose his marks with more care. Sounded more like words than buckshot, anyway.

The stage office door slammed shut.

"What in the world?"

Lee looked around, expecting to see some old lady in black bombazine, bothered by the cursing. He saw, instead, a short fat man in a wrinkled gray suit, leaning against a telephone pole smoking a pipe. The fat man looked at him with mournful brown eyes. He was very fat; his voice had a wheeze to it.

"Old Efraim sounded mighty put out."

"I guess he was," Lee said, nodded to the loafer, and started on his way. He had time for a drink before the stage pulled out.

"Hold on, there," the fat man called after him, and Lee sighed and turned. When he did, he saw the glint of bright metal beneath the fat man's open coat jacket.

A badge.

"Tried that inside-outside dodge, did he?" The lawman looked amused, likely at Lee's surprise at such a soft-seeming fellow to be carrying a badge. "Efraim's been tryin' that one on for years. Got to be kind of a joke around here, and, to tell you the truth, Mister, it's never seemed my business to stop it."

"I guess not," Lee said. "A fool will be a fool."

The lawman grinned. He looked like a variety show comedian, fat as he was. He stayed where he was, leaning against the telegraph pole, and put out his hand to shake. "Asa Potter," he said. "What's yours?"

Lee had to walk over a few paces to shake hands with him, which, apparently, was what the marshal wanted. The broad, fat hand was very strong; the marshal's eyes, up close, not quite so mournful. He smoked a strong smelling pipe tobacco.

Lee looked for a pistol on the fat man, and found it, a small bulge at the right side of his jacket. Nothing there for a fast draw of any sort; Lee assumed that Potter was too clever a man to let himself get fish-hooked into a fast drawing situation.

"You'd be?"

"Morgan, Marshal—Lee Morgan."

Potter was short; he had to crane his neck a little to look up into Lee's face. "Morgan." The plump, sweating brow wrinkled like a puzzled baby's. "Hmmm . . . seems like I've heard that name." He stuck out a pink tongue to touch his upper lip. "You was mixed up in that Logan shootin', weren't you?"

"I was."

The marshal nodded, multiplying his chins. "It was your daddy killed Harvey Logan—and you was there."

"Yes." Lee wasn't surprised Potter remembered that killing. Few lawmen west of the Missouri who wouldn't remember it, for all that it was years ago.

"You the hand with a revolver your daddy was?"

"I'm handy—but not that handy."

The fat man nodded and made his extra chins again. "Just as well, boy. Some things . . . it don't pay to be too good at. You goin' up to the Hill, huh?" He took Lee's silence for a 'yes,' looked away down the dusty main street, and straight out over the prairie. It was a long look —and had to be, considering.

"My writ don't run up in the Hill," Potter said, still staring away. "Wish it did." Then he looked back at Lee, smiled a pleasant smile, and said, "I saw your daddy once, in Fort Smith. He wasn't hurtin' nobody, though. Just dealin' faro. One of the sights of the town, your daddy was. Nice lookin' man." He held out his fat hand again, and Lee shook it, then Potter turned from his telegraph pole, and slowly waddled away toward the center of town.

As Lee was watching him go, his eye was caught by some movement across the street. He looked over there, through a white-yellow haze of prairie heat, into a set of short coal-black shadows cast by the frame buildings opposite. A man had moved there—a narrow built man with a checkered shirt and work pants held up by red galluses. He had a badge on his shirt, and was cradling an army carbine in his arms. He'd

41

caught Lee's eye, shifting that piece from side to side, perhaps had meant to catch Lee's eye. The deputy stood in the shadows, staring across the sun-filled street at Lee, until fat marshal Potter had waddled a fair way away. Then the deputy turned, and staying on his side of the street, followed the marshal along.

It appeared to Lee that Asa Potter was a better lawman than many a lean rough with a cold eye and a fast gun might be. Potter was a man who took care.

The stage left on schedule—apparently, the old station-boss didn't fiddle the departures depending on bribes. Lee'd spent an interesting hour previous at a barrelhouse called *The Prairie Oyster,* watching a black widow spider fight a vinegaroon bug in a pickle jar.

The vinegaroon had won, and cost Lee three dollars.

A good bunch of boys at the *Oyster.* Drovers, four Mexicans up with a herd, as well. And two miners down from Hangfire Hill. The miners had much to say about their poor wages, and the abuse that working men had to suffer under Capitalism. They hadn't worked the Golden Penny mine, and knew little about it, save it was rumored rich. These miners had been turned out of town as agitators, and from the tone of their talk, and the relief expressed by the smarter of the two, they were lucky to have gotten out alive.

"Stand between those men and money, you're

as good as dead," the smarter miner said. He was a burly, bald-headed man, and wore eye-glasses. "They have no notion of fairness at all—as well preach fairness to a snake or a beetle, as talk it to them owners."

"Engels said—" the other miner started to say.

"Shut up," his smart friend said. "You said enough back there. Almost got us skinned alive. You can just shut up about Engels. Were Engels up here, you can damn well bet he'd have shut up, too."

"We should have brung up a scorpion," one of the Mexicans said. He was the only one that could speak English. He'd lost money on the black widow, too. "A little brown one. Would have killed that damn thing, quick." The vine-garoon was doing an odd dance in the pickle jar. It seemed to Lee that the bug had killed a lot of black widows in its time.

"Has a spider ever killed one of these damn bugs?" Lee asked.

The owner of the *Oyster,* a man with an eaten away nose, smiled and shook his head. "Never," he said, and grinned. His missing nose made his voice sound strange. Put a sort of buzz into his words. "Them'll take a spider ever' time."

So, that much wiser, and three dollars poorer, Lee walked to the stage station, collected his *portmanteau,* lugged it outside (the old station-boss paid no heed to him), and passed it up for the guard to strap on, up top.

He stood in the station dust, taking a last,

uncrowded breath of air, listening to a distant
mutter of thunder to the north, and the nearer
muttering of six or seven men perched up on the
roof as they settled in among the baggage and
shipped goods and mail sacks, all the while
eyeing the long mountains of black clouds
lowering along the horizon. Overhead, the sun
still burned white-gold, but the breeze from the
north was cool.

Lee stepped up on the footboard, and pulled
the coach door open. The vehicle was an old
Concord, and looked to still have Hunkpapa
Sioux arrowheads buried in its panels.

Lee's ticket had been for forward-facing, but a
lady and an Indian woman had got there before
him. The empty fourth seat faced back, beside a
bulky man with a pock-marked face. Lee tipped
his Stetson to the lady—a long drink-of-water in
a rust-colored dress and white linen duster. Big
black picture hat and a veil to match. Nothing
much else to be told about her as Lee hipped and
elbowed himself some room beside the pock-
marks. A lady, though. No perfume or toilet
water on her. A little smell of soap and clean
woman; that was it.

The same couldn't be said for Pock-marks. He
looked prosperous enough; apparently didn't
care to waste cash on hot water or laundering.
When Lee'd elbowed for sitting room, Pock-
marks had elbowed back right smartly. Lee had
turned to stare at him, to see if the fellow meant
to have trouble, and Pock-marks had dropped
his eyes, then turned his head away as if he'd

44

found something interesting to see out of his window.

Lee'd left well enough alone, and so as not to stare at the lady, glanced at the woman with her. Dressed in black, this one was, and as red an Indian as ever born—and a handsome one. A Cheyenne, Lee thought; perhaps a Crow. Some handsome, lofty built tribe. She was a woman in her late thirties, tall as a man and inky-eyed, with a nose on her as high-arched and proud as the bow-sp'rits of sailing ships Lee'd seen in San Francisco bay. In her grass-time, the Indian woman must have been a beauty . . . still was quite a looker, in her way, if you liked them grim.

The lady's servant, she appeared to be, had a jewel case on her lap.

Outside the coach, there was the usual palaver and fussing before a start—some more than usual, maybe. The horses were put to; no damn reason for a delay that Lee could see from his window. A small man in a stovepipe hat was talking to the guard, over by a trough. The driver shouted something to the both of them; Lee couldn't make out what, but the guard waved back impatiently, talked with the Stovepipe some more, then came marching over to the coach, shotgun over his arm, stood up on the step, and tugged the door open, Lee's side.

"There she is," the man in the stovepipe hat called after him. "She's in there sitting front!"

The guard, a short, broad-shouldered man with a flat face, stuck his head into the coach

45

and said, "Sorry, Ma'am," to the lady, "but that woman of your'n's goin' to have to ride top."

For a moment, the lady said nothing to that, and Lee wondered what sort of a voice she'd have behind that veil. The Indian woman appeared not to have heard what the guard had said at all.

"She'll ride with me," the lady said. Gentle, low, and positive. Lee could make out blue eyes through the material of the veil. The woman's eyes caught the light.

"Don't make no never-mind," the guard said, "what you say. She's not ridin' inside. We got white people out here want in outa the weather; ain't no red nigger goin' to ride dry while they get wet."

"Did you pay for two inside tickets?" Lee said to the lady, and hoped he wasn't about to play some sort of foolish Sir Walter Raleigh.

She raised her head, stared at him through the veil.

"Yes," she said. "I purchased two tickets for inside."

"They've got their tickets," Lee said to the guard, "why not let it go."

The shotgun guard turned on Lee with the quickness of a tough man who liked to fight. "You listen here, pilgrim," he said, "how's about you keep yore trap shut! Or else I kin kick you a new ass-hole—how'd you like that?" His face was flat as a plate, and his eyes were the color of a horse's hoof.

"Heavens to Betsy!" Lee said, "you sound

mighty hard!" And he reached out, wedged his left arm in between the guard's neck and the barrel of the shotgun, got a grip on the man's jacket collar with his other hand—and hauled him half into the coach.

The guard was a powerful man, and only surprised for an instant. Lee did his damnedest to use the instant well. He wrestled the man, using his left arm to keep the shotgun barrel up and clear, then suddenly lunged forward and butted the fellow in the side of the head. It hurt Lee as much as it must have the other but it kept the guard off balance for just a moment longer.

Then, just as the man gathered himself and twisted powerfully to be free, to turn on Lee punching, Lee let him go, fell back into the seat, doubled his legs, and kicked the fellow hard in the head. His left boot heel struck the man fair; the guard fell in between the seats—and immediately started to struggle up again.

Lee reached forward with his left hand, seized and held the shotgun barrel, and, with his right, reached down, drew the double-edged dagger from his right boot top, and set the point of the knife just under the guard's right ear.

The point of the blade went in a good half-inch before the man froze, silent and still as a spring fawn, hiding.

"I believe," Lee said, "that you owe the lady an apology for starting this ruckus." The guard lay still, half inside the coach, half out, his head down between the seats. Blood was running in a bright fine line down the side of his neck. "And I

47

believe," Lee continued, "that you'd be well advised to climb on out of here, to get on top of this rig, and keep your mouth shut from here on out. If you don't—"

Lee bit down on the words trying to force themselves out of his mouth. *If you don't—I'll kill you.* He bit down, and didn't say it.

But everyone heard the words anyway. They heard them in the silence.

The two women must have been mussed and shoved in the short fight right there against them, but they showed no sign of it. No sign of fear or upset, either. They both, the veiled lady and her tall servant, sat as still and upright as statues of what Professor would have called "attendant Goddesses," and stared across the guard's bent back at Lee, at the broad-bladed knife held, point down, to the back of the fellow's neck. The guard made no sound, and didn't move. The pock-marked man huddled to his side of the seat, and stared out of his window as if his life depended on what he saw through it.

The white lady's eyes shone faint blue through the gauzy material of her veil. The Indian woman's eyes were brighter, and black as number one molasses.

Lee found himself looking into those women's eyes in an odd way—as if they knew him very well, and had just learned more. He felt that the expression on his face was that of a man needing help. It was a strange feeling, since he needed none, and it embarrassed him.

Thunder thumped softly, a long way away.

The driver, high on the box, was calling, "Sim, Sim!" Another man shouted back. The guard's legs must have looked peculiar, sticking out of the coach door.

Lee took the knife away from the man's neck. It left a wound there—but nothing serious. He wiped the blade on the man's shirt, then put the knife away.

"You," Lee had to clear his throat. "You get on out of here. Do your work."

For a moment, the guard, still crouched down, his chest and shoulders jammed into the narrow space between the seats, didn't move. Then, he slowly hitched himself backward. The blood from the side of his face smeared across Lee's trouser-leg. The blood from the man's neck had run down his cheek onto the shoulder and front of his shirt.

The man glanced up at Lee as he crawled back out of the coach door, holding himself up on his hands like a crawling baby. He still had the shotgun leaning up across his right arm and shoulder, and the barrel of the piece knocked on the door frame as he backed out and stepped down into dirt.

The coach rocked a little on its springs as his weight came off it.

"Go on," Lee said to him, in a kinder voice, and reached out to grasp the door handle and swing the door shut.

The driver called down something from on top, but the guard didn't answer him.

Two men on top of the coach—outside passengers—called down as well, but the guard didn't answer them, either. From his window, Lee saw the man walk across the yard to the station office, go up the steps, open the door, go inside, and close the door behind him.

No one came out, and, after a few minutes more, and some shouting, Lee and the others heard the driver call to his horses, heard the sound of his whip—and the big coach lurched, slid slightly in the dust, then rattled into motion with a lunge and sway, and rolled out of the station as fast as a dog could trot.

For nearly an hour, no one in the coach found anything to say. It was rough riding; heading north into the Dakota badlands, creaking up one sloping rise after another, trailing billows of white dust and thrown yellow sand.

The driver sounded to be using a lot of whip to keep his horses up to speed. A lot of cursing, too.

It was on their way up yet another of these slopes—this one so steep that Lee expected he and the others would soon have to climb down, along with the outsiders, and maybe do some pushing—that the veiled lady seated opposite him said something.

"I would like to thank you," she said, Lee trying to make out what he could of her face through the sun-struck veiling, "for supporting us in that . . . difficulty, at the station."

"My pleasure, Ma'am; I regret the fuss, hope it didn't upset you."

"It didn't upset us."

She appeared to have nothing more to say, and the four of them swayed and jolted and rocked from side to side as the coach team—laboring mighty hard, Lee felt—hauled the Concord along.

Laboring too hard.

Lee touched the brim of his Stetson to the lady, then opened the coach door, climbed out, and jumped down into ankle deep sand, under the bright weight of the sunshine.

It was a hard grade. The team was plunging, heaving at the harness. As Lee put his shoulder to the coach's frame, just below the driver's box, he heard the whipper shout the outside passengers down, and they came scrambling, climbing down to push. The man in the stovepipe hat came down on Lee's side, gave him a quick glance, bent his head, set his shoulder to the spokes of the tall rear wheel, and shoved along, in time to the driver's *gee-yaps*.

Lee turned his back to the frame-edge, and dug his boot heels into the sand for better purchase. The work, the effort, was enough to bring out the sweat on him under the buckskin jacket. It felt good, though, shoving, bearing up under the weight. Thunder muttered along the ridges high to the north, but the sun still felt hot as a laundry iron on this slope. Lee set himself at the driver's shout, and dug his heels in and braced his back against the coach work and heaved hard, the other men scrabbling and grunting with effort around him.

The Concord lurched and groaned, the harness

creaking as the team took new strain, and then the coach suddenly eased on the trail, the wheels rolled free, and it took the slope, rode to the top —leaving Lee and the others staggering for footing, resistance gone—rattled to the crest, and braked to a stop to wait for them.

Lee walked alongside the others to the crest, reached the coach side, stepped up to swing the door open, and ducked inside, with an apology to the lady as he brushed past her legs settling into his seat.

They didn't have to push again. Looking out his window—as Pock-mark continued to look out his; Pock-mark hadn't gotten out to help shove—Lee saw that they had breasted a series of tableland rises, and now wheeled along a stony track that seemed to circle slowly higher and higher into the hills. There was nothing living to see but buzzards—no game of any sort, no trees to speak of, no running water.

Harsh country, steadily rising, covered —where it was covered at all—with a tall yellow grass looked as dry and rough as grass could be. Poor country for horses, Lee thought. Maybe not so good for men, either.

Almost an hour after that sandy slope, they came to the company's re-mount station. The passengers all piled out and off, heading for the station for whatever stuff was being dished for a meal, or to the privies for relief.

The lady went that way, toward the necessary, her tall Indian woman stalking after her, the jewel box tucked under one long lean arm.

Lee, watching them go, thought he wouldn't mind being a fly on that privy wall. The lady had a fine figure, a butt on her—or so it appeared in that long dress—like one of those New York society women's.

He stood watching the two women walk—the lady with an easy swaying gait, a fine mare's gait, the Indian woman stepping straight-legged and pidgeon-toed right behind her.

They went inside the privy together, and shut the door behind them.

"Choice viands, that." The man in the stove-pipe hat stood beside Lee, staring off at the privy with him.

Lee cut him a cold glance—didn't care for sharing a daydream with this fellow.

The man, thin and red-headed, with a straggly red beard to match, took the glance as referring to something else. "Say, now," he said. "No hard feelin's about me tryin' to get inside back there? I sure didn't intend that shotgun to go bullyin'." He stared at Lee like a red-headed bird, his head held to one side, waiting to see which way the wind was going to blow.

"No offense," Lee said, and walked off toward the station and some chow-chow. S'eon called any scrappy meal 'chow-chow.'

Scrappy was the word for it.

A pot of worn-out red beans, some fatty chunks of overripe beef, and bread not worthy of the name. There was a lot of it, was all that could be said in favor. The fellows that had been riding outside seemed pleased enough with the

53

mess, and went at it with a will, sitting at benches along the table, spooning the stuff up out of tin bowls as if someone was going to snatch it away from them momentarily.

The two women looked, and then stood and went outside for a walk, the tall Indian pacing behind her mistress like a fine-bred hound. Lee, not quite so finicky, managed half a bowl of it, before he, too, got up and strolled outside for a breather and a smoke. His appetite, and, no doubt the women's, had not been sharpened by the food having been served out by the stationer's idiot boy, who seemed likely to drool into the pot as he ladled it. The boy had a head the size of a bushel basket—though apparently no sense in it at all.

Lee stepped outside the station shed—glad to be away from the smell of the food—and strolled a little way off, digging in his jacket pocket for a stub of cigar. A Grover House smoke, pure fine-leaf Havana.

He lit up, and stood, rocking a little back and forth in his boots—a habit he'd picked up from old Bud Bent, who did it all the time—and drew in a mouthful of the fragrant smoke, looking the countryside over. It wasn't much to see. Big, of course, covered now with the great moving shadows of the clouds sailing down from the north. Big, and sparse of living things—a yellow-brown country, with only traces of spring green here and there amidst the gullies and rolling hills.

They'd come up fairly high, though. Could see a considerable way.

Lee's butt hurt from the coaching. Damned if he could see why they couldn't soften those seats. Hurt a man like a child's spanking to spend the day in one of the rattlers. One thing had to be said for the railroad. A lot easier on a man's backside.

He looked around for the women, and finally saw them some distance away across the ridge the station'd been perched upon. They were strolling together, talking like friends. The Indian woman taller, the white woman walking with that sauntering motion, that slight swing to her hips that even ladies didn't seem to care to prevent in their walking.

As he watched them, a cloud shadow came running over the ridge like a tide coming in. Lee had seen a tide coming in just once, into San Francisco bay. This was like that. And a cool, sudden breeze came on with the shadow. He thought about his share in the mine, The Golden Penny. Might be sensible to sell that share out, rather than stay stuck in Dakota forever, scrambling and butting at the trough for his part of the takings.

Then the rain started with a sudden spatter, the drops big enough to knock up little kicks of dust as they struck. Lee reached up to keep his Stetson on in the gust, hunched his shoulders, and ran for a privy.

He made it just as the rain swept in and began

to pound in off-rhythms across the rusty tin of the toilet roof. It was noise enough so that Lee couldn't hear his own farting as he crapped. Surprising, how cold the rainy air was, blowing through the slab planking. The wind and rain would buffet, sweep in, and be gone for a moment. Then come again. The tin roof leaked, just over Lee's left shoulder, and he leaned sideways to the right, to keep the water off him as he finished, and lifted a bunch of Sear's Catalogue pages off the nail to wipe himself. People were shouting outside, their voices high over the hissing rain. The driver calling the passengers to.

Lee was about the last one to the coach, stepped up and climbed into the cramped seats, and smells of wet wool and old sweat—Pockmarks—and wet women. The lady and her servant had been caught out and near soaked. As he settled back, the woman sitting opposite threw back her veil, and reached up to unpin her hat. Her arms up, then, in that most graceful of all women's gestures, she raised her head and looked full at him, and Lee saw that she was no lady after all, but was a whore.

It was not that she was painted; she wasn't. Nor were her looks spoiled, as so many whore's looks were spoiled by marks of old beatings— missing teeth, or broken noses, or a blind eye.

None of this. Her face was in every way a lady's—frank and open, smooth skinned, with not a trace of paint or lip rouge on her. She was beautiful, in a wide-faced, high cheek-boned way. She had a wide mouth, a bit too wide, her lips barely a shade darker than the pale white-pink of her skin. Her nose was short and broad as a child's, and her eyes were the color of a child's eyes, a clear and depthless blue.

She stared into Lee's eyes, stared at him as she unpinned her big hat, its brim wet and drooping from the rain, and then lifted it from her upswept hair—hair as black, but a finer, softer texture than her Indian servant's. She looked at Lee with a look he knew very well. A look of secrets shared. It was a look that said: I've seen the elephant—and fucked him, too. That said: I know what you want—and I've done what you want.

For money.

There was nothing nasty in her glance; it was more humorous than otherwise. She knew, of course, that he had taken her for another sort of female; and knew as well, that Lee would be as pleased as disappointed at finding her to be what she was. Her private parts, the softness, secretness of them, their wetness, hairyness, all this, that had seemed remote from him or any other strangers as the mountains of the moon, might now be available, if he would pay for it.

All this was in her look, and no man who had sampled the gay life could have missed it.

Lee felt Pock-mark stir against him, and saw that the man hard turned from his window to see her unveiled. He knew too, of course. There was a new understanding between all of them inside the coach. Only the Indian woman seemed

57

not to notice or care. She took her mistress's ruined hat from her, and twisting awkwardly on the cramped seat, gently rearranged the white woman's hair, neatening it with dark long fingers, red-brown against soft black.

The trail ran smoother now; the rain, so violent a few minutes before, had eased, only spattering the coach—and the cursing outsiders above—from time to time. The new team seemed stronger than the old had been, even at the start, and pulled together evenly, steadily.

The woman, her handsome face bare in the shifting afternoon light, gazed out of her window, and paid no more attention to Lee. Her throat, white as milk, looked strong for a woman's, round, delicately veined. Smooth as marble stone.

CHAPTER THREE

They wheeled into Hangfire Hill just before dark.

It was a stiff climb up into the main street of a town that looked like a part of the huge hill itself. Shelf after shelf of jerry-builts jammed and jumbled along the slopes, criss-crossed by steep streets pitted with small pits and ditches, signs of the endlessly busy workings beneath.

There was a haze of dust in the air, despite the small creeks of mud that ran in rivulets down along the gutters from the recent rain.

It was a crowded town, as well as a steep one. The old Concord had to thread and rumble through a crowd of workmen, miners, most of them, dirty and bearded, work clothes packed with sweat and rock-dust, their shoulders stooped from fourteen hours of labor completed, or yet to do. Some of these men had little oil hat-lamps already lit, so that they walked through the dust in crowds, the tiny flames winking as if they'd been swarms of fire-flies. They were, for the most part, silent, just walking along, climbing the sloping streets (none of those much more than tracks cut out of the hillside).

If the people, the workmen and townsfolk, were a quiet bunch, the traffic was not. Huge ore-drays, goods-wagons, delivery carts, coaches, buckboards, buggies, all rumbled and rattled, jamming the narrow ways in both directions, their drivers yelling curses at people in their path, shaking their fists and long-lash whips to clear enough room to move.

A rich, hard-working little mine town, it seemed to Lee. Not such a hellhole and roughhouse as he'd been told. He saw two uniformed policemen strolling one of the boardwalks. It was unusual for a camp like this to have uniformed officers—seemed they were putting on big-city airs at Hangfire Hill.

Lee saw a saloon's sign board down a side street they jolted past—no resorts on this main drag, though. All stores and warehouses, shops and small manufactories. All money-making, decent businesses—at least on Main Street. Unlikely such obtained throughout the camp—not with thousands of miners needing a rip, or to have their ashes hauled for them. There'd be other sorts of money-making ventures, on other streets.

The Concord slid briefly on a patch of soft mud—Lee heard the driver's whip as he collected the team and hauled straight—then shouldered past an ore-dray longer than a Conestoga, turned a rattling right, and rolled into a wide livery yard and on, under a two-story roof, the livery's stable and stores.

Lee swung the door open on his side, got down, and helped both women out; the Indian woman's slender arm was wiry as a man's. There was a great deal of bustle—outside passengers climbing down, hostlers unharnessing the team, a few bystanders leaning on rough cut pillars, chewing straw or plug tobacco, watching to see what the stage had brought in, and passing remarks accordingly.

"Good evening, Mister—?"

"Lee," he said to the handsome whore.

"Mister Lee. Again, our thanks."

"Pleasure to be of service."

The whore shook his hand, and her Indian woman gestured for their luggage, reached up as the case was handed down, and set it gently on a heap of straw—one of the few places surrounding the Concord not currently being trampled by the stage people, or piled with previous horse apples.

One of the loafers came ambling over, then, said, "Howdy, Early Evenin'," bent and hoisted the case to his shoulder. Then he held out his hand, and the Indian woman—apparently 'Early Evening'—put a two-bit piece into it. The loafer then walked off with the case, seeming to know well enough where the women were headed, and the handsome whore and her companion followed him out.

Lee looked up for his own *portmanteau*, and was just in time to catch it as one of the stable boys pulled loose the lashings, hoisted it up, and tipped it over the side. The falling weight of it spun Lee half around, and he caught a glimpse, then, of the coachman, his whip still in his hand, standing on the steps leading up to a glass-windowed office, talking to a tall man with long grey mustachios, and a lading book under his arm. The station boss, it seemed.

Both men were looking at Lee, and both turned away when he looked at them. Talking about the shotgun guard, and the trouble at Shivaree.

"You for the Continental?" Another loafer, the straw still in his mouth, looking for a porter-piece.

"The hotel?"

"That's her." The loafer looked to be a drunk, red-eyed, his cheeks laced with broken veins. He stared Lee up and down, taking in the fine boots and gray wool trousers, tooled gun belt, white shirt and string tie, fine fringed buckskin jacket and gray Stetson, curled and creased Rocky mountain style. "She's the best in town—"

"You're a liar, Philpot!" The voice, in a rich rolling brogue, came from behind Lee. "The Continental is a damned fleabox, a ditch, an infernal pit of unaired bedding, drunken hooligans, watered beer, and a band of the ugliest women in creation just out back."

Lee turned and saw a small, short, burly man with a face as rosy and clean as a girl's, belying the gray hair at the spit-curled temples, the neat businessman's belly tucked in beneath a green silk vest, a massive red-gold watch chain. The short man had eyes as gray as granite.

He held out a small square hand, washed white as linen, and fat with muscle.

"Sean McGee, at your service. You'd be Lee Morgan, or I'm much mistaken."

"That's right." McGee—his partner, and, despite the green silk vest, no tenderfoot.

"Philpot," the short man said, "take Mister Morgan's traps up to the Coffee Club." The gray eyes twinkled as McGee glanced up at Lee. "I reckon my partner can abide a bed with no bugs in it—as well as the best food served west of St. Louis!"

"Sounds fine," Lee said.

"A man of few words," McGee said, and put his hand on Lee's elbow to guide him out of the stage line stable, "a useful trait in a business partner—in ordinary circumstances." Lee glanced back and saw Philpot shouldering his possibles, and concentrated thereafter on not stepping in any of the manure littering the stable straw. McGee strutted on ahead in that prancing swagger so many short men adopted as their walk, and Lee followed, and watched him.

Partner.

McGee had known enough to meet the coach. Had known the day Lee would be arriving, had known what Lee looked like. Had, obviously, taken some trouble to find out, had corresponded with someone in Boise—or sent someone there.

Gone to a good deal of trouble, and for more of

a reason than simple curiosity about a new business partner. Curiosity would have been satisfied in the natural course of things.

McGee had been more than curious.

He'd been concerned.

Out on the boardwalk the short man led Lee over to a fine one-horse shay, all polished black and brass, with what appeared a fine chestnut stepper in harness.

"Neatest rig in town," McGee said with satisfaction, stood back while Lee climbed in, then mounted beside him, tossed a five-cent piece to a rag-dressed boy holding the chestnut's head, gathered his reins, and *hi-yupped* the horse off in a spanking trot. The shay was sprung like a sofa; and even so, it swayed and tipped in the Main Street ruts like a canoe in rapids.

"You'll be pleased with the Coffee Club," he said. "Mind if I call you Lee?"

"Be fine," Lee said. "Sean." McGee smelled of Cuban tobacco and Bay Rum, and the shoulder brushing against Lee's on the buggy seat was hard as oak under the fine wool suiting.

McGee reined his horse up around a street corner, and on up a steeper street climbing north, toward the distant rounded peak of Hangfire Hill. The short man was a good whip; he threaded the rig uphill through a slow grinding flood of drays and ore-wagons rumbling down into the town.

Lee noticed that none of the teamsters cursed McGee as he wheeled and angled them, and McGee made no noise himself, except to mutter at two young men on bicycle-wheels, who came rolling down the side of the street, drunk and singing as they peddled.

Not many women in the town, Lee noticed. At least, not out walking or shopping on the boards. Seemed to be even more a man's town than most mining camps were.

"Should have let you come to me," McGee said, out of the blue, as he steadied the chestnut for another climb up another muddy street; track, would have been a better name for it. "Fumbled a face-card, showing up at the station that way—let you know I'd been checking."

Lee said nothing. McGee had a crisp way of talking, for all his brogue.

"Truth was, I thought you'd be some straw-foot horse rancher never saw the elephant. Fellow of mine on the coach—that noisy stick with the stovepipe hat?—he set me straight. Said you'd made Sim Thorsen eat some mud in that coach, shotgun and all. Said he'd heard some tales from Potter's deputy about you, as well . . . fierce fellow—son of a fiercer fellow— and a sport who'd been here and there." McGee reached out with his whip and just touched the chestnut on its right shoulder. The animal threw as neat a left turn as a soldier, trotted down a narrow alleyway for a stone's throw and more, and eased to a stop with no reining at a broad green painted double door set into the side of a red brick warehouse.

Lee thought there just might be trouble here, and leaned a little away from McGee to clear a reach for the Bisley Colts.

McGee was quick.

"The Coffee Club, Mister Morgan," he said, "and no row expected unless one of the members, mine owners most of them, is unable to hold his liquor."

A black man in a checkered cap came out of the double doors, said, "Good day, Mister McGee," and went to hold the horse.

McGee climbed down, waited for Lee, and led him up two steps, through the double doors, and into a room—a sort of lobby—as rich as any that Lee had seen. It looked, in its red velvet hangings, Turkey carpets, brass cuspidors and lamps, sofas and cushioned chairs, like some result of mating a whorehouse to a bank—and polishing it fine.

Ten or twelve men were scattered about the room, some reading newspapers or journals of some sort or other, and three or four of them talking in a group at a neat, brass railed bar along the room's far wall. These all looked to be men of affairs, running to stout bellies, fine whiskers, patterned vests, crossed by considerable watch-chains, and faces as watchful and tough as any Barbary Coast crimp's.

Two or three of these men lifted their glasses to McGee as he and Lee walked in, and Lee saw them stare hard at him, measuring him, finding a certain place for him in their minds.

"McGee!" one of them called over. "You should have bet—I'm not sold out yet!"

"Daley," McGee called back, "you're a

horse's ass!" to some applause from the others at the bar. And steered Lee to two leather-backed wing chairs by a casement window. The window glass had been painted white.

McGee saw Lee noticing it. "We have fine dinners in here—having one Friday night, in fact —and then have the ladies in. Wouldn't do to have some trash peeping." He settled himself in his chair with a grunt, swung his short legs up and crossed his ankles, his feet resting on a fine foot stool covered in some rich blue cloth. McGee wore neat black boots, low-topped, that laced like brogans. They were polished so that the oil lamp chandelier shone in reflection in their depths. "So," McGee continued as if there'd been no interruptions, "it's just the slightest bit of an ass I've made of myself, coming down to greet you, pushing to bring you here, trying to impress and overawe, as if you'd still had Idaho mud on your knees." He sat, watching Lee, his stone-gray eyes considering.

"I like making a fool of myself, sometimes. It can help if a man thinks you're clumsy. Makes him careless. For all you know, I blundered deliberately, deliberately let you know I'd had you watched, had checked up on you in Boise. All this so you'd be sure I was a fool. There's no greater advantage in business, than to be thought careless—when you're not."

A Negro in an old black suit came over to them, and McGee ordered whiskey. Lee asked for a beer.

"But I'm not really so inept," McGee said.

"For example, I would say that right now, you're asking yourself, 'Is this fellow trying to hide profit—or loss—where the Golden Penny is concerned? And if profit, does he intend to have me murdered, or to do me out of it in some other way?' "

Lee said nothing; he watched McGee, and enjoyed him.

McGee sighed. "I can see," he said, "that you've decided that the best way to get the truth out of old McGee is to give him his head, and let him spin out enough rope to hang himself. You have, if I may say so, fallen victim to the notion—mighty prevelant in the West—that silence is strength; that talk is weakness."

The black man came back with their drinks on a small silver tray, and McGee took them, passed Lee his beer, and said, "Thank you, Donald," to the Negro.

"Couldn't be more wrong," McGee said, when the servant was gone. "Dead wrong. Nothing worth accomplishing in this nation—or in all history, either—but was commenced by talk, and a good deal of talk. Common grunts or simple silence may suffice for cow-prodding or ditch-digging, but I believe you'll find that more serious matters require *talk*. And the more of it, usually the better."

"You may be right," Lee said, and sipped his beer. It was a fine, chilled, rich home-brew, with foam as yellow as cream.

McGee laughed, a deep-chested laugh that sounded like a horse coughing. "And there's a

70

lawyer's answer. I can see I'm going to have my hands full with you, boy." He put back his head, and swallowed half his whiskey, neat. Then he put the glass down on the broad arm of his chair, and licked a drop of whiskey off his lower lip. His tongue was as pink as a child's.

"I'd like to see the mine," Lee said. "And the books."

McGee smiled at him. "You'll see the mine, then. And the books. But you're wrong about liking it—you won't be liking either one."

The Golden Penny had been dug deep into the crest of the Hangfire Hill. McGee's fine chestnut had sweat streaking its flanks by the time they drew up a steep track to a narrow, yellow painted two-story building. The Golden Penny was printed across a curving sign hung down along its high eave. The letters were painted in gold leaf, on a background of blue.

"Can't say it doesn't look fine," McGee said, climbing down from the rig with a grunt. "And by God, she was fine, up to last year."

"That so?"

McGee lead the way up the flight of wood steps to the building's front door. "You take a look at the books, young Lee then, if you know how to read books, you'll see what's gone wrong with the Penny."

As McGee unlocked the door, Lee saw ten or twelve men—miners coming off shift, it looked like—file out of what appeared to be an outhouse door, and hang picks, shovels, sledgehammers and kerosene lanterns on hooks alongside the small shack's wall. They were tired-looking men, stoop-shouldered, mud-caked, blinking like owls in the early evening light.

McGee paused with the door open. "Look at those fellows," he said. "You'll hear men, mine owners, will call those people the 'scum of the earth,' and mean it. But not me." He raised his hand to the men across the yard, some of them staring at the rig, at Lee, and one of the men lifted a hand in return.

"Not to me," McGee said, turning to lead Lee inside.

"To me, those fellows are the salt of the earth —and not trash in any way at all. I'm an Irishman," he said, bending to put a lucifer to an oil lamp on top of a big roll-top desk. The desk was crowded into a corner in a big room filled with stacks of canvas sacks—ore-sample bags, Lee thought—and bits and pieces of machinery, wheels, levers and gears (some of the iron-work as tall as a man, and heavy as a horse). "I'm an Irishman, and I well know how it feels to be called a white nigger. I've never treated a man who worked for me any other way but on the square."

He turned up the lamp, and winked a bright gray eye to Lee in the warmth of the light. "Doesn't mean I spoil them, of course." He pulled open a drawer, reached in, hauled out a two-foot ledger and dropped it on the cluttered desk top with a thump. "I call ninety cents a shift fair wages—seeing that there's only fourteen hours a shift to work. Now, Mister Morgan—*partner*, I should say—just you take a gander at those figures, and if you thought to be rich off the Penny, my apologies."

Lee pulled out the desk chair, sat down, and opened the ledger, thanking Catherine Dowd as he did so for seeing to it he learned something of business beside the raising of horses. Hours of tallying, figuring, feed-costing, tack-costing, expenses, wages, credits, payments and loss— and all double-entried. Lee didn't fool himself he was a banker's clerk, but he could damn well read a set of books. Whether the books were honestly entered, well, that was another matter.

"I'll just leave you to it, partner," McGee said. "You'll find it something more complicated than the horse business. I'll be getting us some gear to go down in . . ." He walked to the back of the room and up a narrow flight of stairs there. The room was left to silence, except for the rustling of pages as Lee read steadily through the ledger, and the faint moth-rustle as the wick in the kerosene lamp was consumed. It was getting dark, and evening coming on fast— what little of it showed through dusty dirt-streaked window panes.

As Lee read through the previous months' entries, he felt a faint prickle of excitement rising along his spine. The Golden Penny had produced a fortune—a clear post-production profit of one-hundred and sixty to two-hundred and some thousand dollars for four of the winter months. Continuing, the sums must amount to millions, or soon would. *A rich man . . . a very rich man.* That would damn sure take some getting used to, it if proved to be the case.

If it proved to be the case.

It didn't.

Not according to McGee's book, it didn't. For the past several months, the last three months in particular, the production of copper-bearing ore had slacked to half, then less than half of what it had been. Lee was no auditor, but even he could see, running his finger down the long columns, the gradual increase in red ink, the decimals moving to the right in the loss columns . . .

The Penny looked to be running dry.

Lee shuffled through the scattered papers on the roll-top, found a sheet of foolscap, a steel-nib pen and pot of ink, and began to note some summary figures down, with their entry dates.

The production figures remained the same in tonnage up 'till about six weeks previous; but the ore grew less and less rich (and those figures from the refinery at Fargo). The Golden Penny was now producing just enough copper to cover its running expenses—which meant, according to the ledger, not quite enough to cover its long-term expenses.

A rich man . . .

A laugh, as they said in the Life. Something he likely would not have to worry about. Unless McGee had cooked his book, but that wouldn't explain the refinery figures. No refinery would falsify an ore report—that sort of thing would ruin them for sure.

"I gather you *can* read a ledger, then, partner." McGee had come quietly down the stairs, must have been watching Lee work for some time. "And you've taken your notes, I see." He came and stood behind Lee, looking over his shoulder. "A sad little list of numbers, is it not? Nothing to ruin me, of course; I've made my pile from the Penny; and of course you're due a few thousand of that." He sighed. "Still, I would have enjoyed earning a few million. Cruel fact is, the damn vein gave out. God's fault."

Lee folded the note paper, put it in his pocket, and stood up. "Here you are," McGee said. "Gum over-boots that should fit well enough, I think—a slicker, and a lamp for you; I don't believe in those damn hat-lamps. It's wet, as well as dark down there." McGee had already put his gear on, and looked an improbable figure, the long, worn yellow slicker draped over his fine suit of clothes, his neat belly and gleaming watch-chain, falling down to the loose tops of huge gum-boots, apparently several sizes too big for him.

McGee caught the glance. "I don't as a rule, make a habit of going down into the works. The fellows, after all, are paid to do that; I'm not. And I find that giving one of them two or three dollars additional a week produces any confidential reports that I might need." Seeing Lee dressed—the gum over-boots were too big for Lee as well—McGee led the way to the shed door. "I don't hold with the Calvinistical notion that men are not to be trusted; though I wouldn't trust some workmen myself, any further than I could pick up and pitch them—damn lying, lazy, trashy creatures—but I do find a spy answers better than the Pinkertons, considerably cheaper, too." And so, down the steps, and into the yard.

Lee hardly listened. He was thinking about the ledger, the worn-out vein of ore.

He was a stranger in McGee's kingdom—how was he to discover the truth? "No law in Hangfire Hill . . ." except those uniformed policemen —present to serve the owners and to break strikes, if Lee was any judge. More regulators than lawmen. And bound to be in McGee's service, and his friends' service, not some drover's come poking his nose in from outside.

Mines did go dry. Ore ran thin. These things often happened. Still . . . still . . . damn convenient for McGee for a rich mine to become a poor one, just when a new partner came on the scene. Easy, then, to persuade the fellow to sell his shares and clear out, frightened of being burdened with a dead mine's debts. This was a thing that might be done . . . with enough care . . . enough planning, if the real value of the mine made the trouble worthwhile . . .

McGee, his lantern-light bobbing along through the near dark across the yard, was leading toward a distant shack door entrance, further across the hillside than the one the miners had come out of. "Don't think I'm gulling you, partner," McGee turned, smiling; Lee could see the round face glow in the light of his lamp. "We'll come out that other drift door." He turned his head and continued on his way. "You won't find any trouble seeing copper down there. It's plain as red hair on a woman—what there is left of it."

It occurred to Lee that accidents were common in mine workings—almost natural events in such dangerous conditions. *Accidents* . . .

He reached under the slicker to touch the butt of the Bisley Colts then, as he walked behind McGee, swiftly bent, found the handle of the double-edge dagger in the top of his right boot (the flopping gum over-shoe made it awkward) drew the knife, and slipped the blade up into his left sleeve, grip down. A little readier, there.

McGee went up to the plank door, produced a large key, twisted open a heavy padlock, swung the door squealing wide, and ducked inside, plunging—as Lee did, right after him—into utter darkness outside the yellow circle of his lamp-light.

Of course, accidents might happen to anyone. To McGee, for example, this pleasant, civilized, humorous man. He, perhaps now at the very start of a most clever plot, of deception, possibly violence. Right at this point, with all the aces in his hand—presuming the fellow *was* a thief— McGee might be check-mated by the oldest gambit of all.

Lee could kill him, now. Could, in that fashion, perhaps produce what the electrical professors called a "short circuit.' Could cut the Gordian knot, by cutting Sean McGee's throat, by smashing in his head with a timber or a stone. Lee felt the oddest feeling, and not for the first time. A sort of urge, almost sexual, to perform that act—to put McGee out of this race of life. To clear him out of the way.

A convenient thing. And not likely that the "law" on the Hill would object too strenuously. Lee, then, after that, would be legal owner of the Golden Penny, with all the cash necessary to arrange what he chose.

The dagger, short-bladed, heavier than his father's Arkansas toothpick had been, rested cool as a streak of snow along Lee's forearm.

Ahead of him, McGee labored along, stumbling every now and then over some small pile of scree, walking carefully in the ragged, moving nimbus of his lamp-light. "Copper," McGee said, his voice echoing shortly off the tunnel's arm's-length walls. And Lee saw it, a delicate spider web of gold-red etched into the rough-cut stone. He put out his hand, and ran a finger along the tracing of metal ore. It was damp with the tunnel's wet, and seemed to feel smoother under his finger than the stone.

"Not worth digging at," McGee said, not bothering to turn around. "That'd assay out to four dollars a ton. Trash." Shadows swung wildly about them both as McGee suddenly

78

stepped down into a deeper, narrower ditch. Here, along one side, the tunnel was almost filled by a long rock-fall. Half the tunnel ceiling seemed to have cracked and given, and fallen in. McGee's voice came quietly back over the crunch and rattle of their boots on the stones. "Good fellow hurt when that came down. Merwin. Busted both the poor tyke's legs."

They had entered now, a long, long corridor, very narrow, the walls so close they brushed Lee's slicker-sleeves as he walked, and the tunnel roof so low it knocked the Stetson off his head so he had to carry it under one arm and suffer the light drops and drizzle that the shaft roof drained from time to time upon his head.

A few drops of this water ran down his face; he tasted some. It tasted of metal . . . pennies . . . rust. And the coarse, clear taste of stone.

Somewhere in this long burrowing, perhaps in the consideration of the thousands of tons of rock that lay above them, Lee had, without deciding it, decided not to knife Sean McGee to death here underneath the ground. And not, in fact, to kill him at all—unless he had to.

Wait and see . . . *wait and see* . . .

The man might, after all, be honest—and the Golden Penny be golden no more, but only a wound in the earth.

Wait and see.

It was a long walk down. And a crawl for the last three hundred feet. Lee felt his trouser knees fray, his skin abrade as he crawled over the stone, the patches of mud. His arm ached from holding his lamp high enough so the mantle wouldn't smash on the rock as he crawled one-handed after McGee. The stout man was making good time for a pot-belly Capitalist —for a man who rarely went down in his mine. Making good time, and appearing to know his way very well . . . Lee wondered whether McGee had not done some mining work himself, when he was younger, before he made his pile. It seemed likely; the damned little man was scooting along through this warren like a gopher.

The tunnel ceiling was getting lower and lower. Just above Lee's shoulders as she crawled. The knife handle was sliding down his wrist, and Lee pushed to slip the blade out of his sleeve and into the sheath of his boot. It seemed to him that the roof of the shaft was slowly pressing down and down upon him, weighted with all the mass of the hill. Sweat ran down Lee's face with the dripping mine water; it seemed hot down here, difficult to draw a decent breath of air . . .

Appeared these poor miners deserved a better wage.

A damn sight better.

"Coming up here, now, Lee, place the men are still working. A damn little good they're doing by it." As Lee crawled over a slide of broken rock sharp as damn ditch-thorn spines, he saw McGee's lantern light bob and waver, vanish for a second, then reappear a distance off. Occurred to him that McGee might do worse than try to strand him here, deep in the Hill. He likely would, of course, find his way out in time. Then again, he might not . . .

The rock slide ended in a steep pitch, and Lee slid down most of it head foremost—until he felt solid stone beneath his hand, held his lantern higher, and saw McGee standing a little way away, his lantern up, looking around him. Lee got to his feet with a grunt of relief—feeling aged about ten years through the back and knees—and saw they stood in a decent-sized chamber, rough-hacked an almost round. Low-ceilinged, but high enough to stand and swing a pick.

Then he saw the copper, and more than a tracing. This was a twisting vein, thicker than a hawser, that ran and scrolled across the chamber wall like a painting of a giant snake. A painting in red-gold.

"Looks fine to you, son, I'll bet," McGee said, sounding not at all winded by the crawling. "But that is a paltry vein—perhaps eight to nine dollars a ton, and too damn deep. Takes time to haul ore up out of here; takes a damn fine vein of ore to be worth laying rails to wheel the ore up." He hawked and spat. "Price of these damn little cars would break your heart." He swung his lantern to the right, and Lee saw a narrow stretch of track with a heavy steel-wire cable running down it. Six, seven small open rail cars —push-cars, they looked like—lined up at the end of the track.

"Two hundred and seventy dollars."

Lee saw McGee's face, gold in lamp-light, turn to him. "Well, by God, boy; you *can* read a ledger." He cleared his throat and spat again. "Truth is, I got three of them second-hand and cheaper."

The two of them stood in silence for a while, each in his flickering aura of yolky light. It was quiet enough for Lee to hear the older man's breathing, brandy breathing, and beer and Port wine. Cigar breathing, too. Innumerable Havanas. It seemed, after a while, that Lee could hear the stone above them creak, groan softly with the strain of not instantly collapsing upon them to fill this empty space, to pack it full of rock, and mash the two of them to paste.

"Nasty business, mining," McGee said, his brogue thicker than it had been. "Only a fool would work at it—and only a greater fool would invest in it."

"Did well enough for you for a while, you said."

"Yes, well enough, for a while." McGee shifted where he stood; Lee heard his gum-boots squeak. "I understand that your father shot Kid Curry; is that so?"

"Yes."

"Then he must have been a hell of a man," McGee said. "I meet Curry years ago at Rosie Hugh's place, in New York. He was there with a Texan named Kilpatrick. That Texan was a tough cookie—but nothing to the little fellow. Scared the girls silly, the little fellow did."

Lee said nothing.

"Sorry if I spoke out of turn, concerning your father. Meant nothing but respect by it."

"No apology necessary, Sean," Lee said. McGee liked the Life, then, and occasional rough company. More than possible he knew some fairly rough company here in Hangfire Hill. Perhaps more than fairly rough country.

"Well then—you've seen the best the old girl has left, and damn well not good enough it is!" McGee spun his shadow down the cavern wall as he turned suddenly and trudged to the narrow freight tracks. "Come on—we'll follow the rails up; makes an easier climb."

Lee swung his lantern for a last look around, a last look at the red-gold snake of copper ore twisting through the stone.

CHAPTER FOUR

The night air was cool, and sweet as a drink of water. The climb up through the trackage shaft had been less unpleasant than the long climb and crawl down through the other entrance; but still, it had been no joy. Lee had felt more than a little relief when McGee had shoved the shaft door open, and they'd stepped out into the dark, and a slow night wind. The men's tools were lined hanging on the shack wall beside them, and a man with a lantern was waiting. A one-armed man with a lantern held high, a heavy revolver stuck down into his belt.

"Evening, Frank," McGee said.

"Evenin', Mister McGee. Everythin's quiet as can be."

"You see it stays that way. And Frank—"

"Sir?"

"This is Mister Morgan; he's a partner in the Penny now. He can come and go as he pleases. Understand?"

"Yes, sir." The one-armed man held the lantern closer to Lee's face, and stared at him to remember him. The watchman had the attentive caution of a good ranch dog. Lee had seen many men like him, who took wages and made a little kingdom of their chores. A good night watchman.

"O.K., Mister Morgan," the watchman said, and took the light out of Lee's face.

"Come on, boy," McGee said, "let's get this gear off." And strode away through the dark toward the company office.

"Now, this is what I figure," McGee was struggling with his over-boots in the big first floor storage room. "I figure you'll want a couple of days to make up your mind whether you want in on the Penny as she stands now—debts, running expenses, and all—or whether you'd just as soon pass the shoe with the twelve or thirteen thousand I figure you're owed to date." He wrenched an over-boot off with a grunt. "Up to you, young Morgan; no skin off my butt either way, except I'd appreciate splitting closing expenses, which is what it would amount to if you decide to come in." His other gum-boot came off easier. "Damn things!" He threw the pair into a corner.

Lee, sitting at the desk, got his own over-boots off, and tossed them after McGee's. "I'll think about it," he said.

"Well, don't think too damn long. You're a nice behaved boy, and no fool, but Sean McGee gives free rides to no man." McGee pulled a cigar case from his suit-coat pocket. "Claro?"

"Be pleased."

McGee waited until both had their cigars clipped, lipped, and lit.

"Now, I have to be traveling north for a day or so—farm properties, thank God. I tell you, Lee, it's wheat that's the future of this country— not silver or gold, nor copper neither, unless they make some strike big enough to open-pit it. *Wheat*—here in the Dakotas, and up in Canada, too, damn their British-loving eyes!"

That last was ground out in an unpleasant way, and Lee saw the Irish rise angry in McGee for a moment.

"You may be right."

"I am right, boy. This mining business—un- less you're in Pennsylvania coal—is a side-show, and not a damn thing more. Cheap food is this country's ace-in-the-hole, as those rebels found when they tried eating their coon-grown cotton. Cheap food, boy! *Wheat.* A man owns a few thousand acres of that black dirt country up there—"

"The winters," Lee said, watching McGee's flushed face by lamp-light.

"The winters . . . !" McGee tossed the Dakota winters aside, one-handed. "If we don't have a fine winter wheat ready to be planted in just five years, you can call me Cromwell. Burbank and those others aren't just wasting their time, you know! They're bright men! That Burbank can twist a seed to something else as easy as I'd twist a stick of licorice—and to hell of a lot more profit, I can tell you."

"Sounds good," Lee said. "If they can do it."

"They *will* do it. And the men who own the land, who've bought up their sections from those dumb Swedes and such, well, those men will have the country by the throat—in a manner of speaking." McGee subsided, breathing harder than he'd had to climbing down and up the shafts of the Golden Penny. Lee did not for a minute think that McGee was any sort of fool. It was, he supposed, possible that some professor might find a breed of late wheat. More than likely they were trying. And, once that was done, more than likely the Dakota land—and the Iowa land, too, come to that—would be worth a fortune. It would take a wait, though, and a great fortune spent while waiting.

By the ledger, McGee had taken a fortune from the Penny over the past years. But not such a great fortune as he seemed to need.

"Well, then," McGee said, in a quieter voice, and puffed on his cigar, "I'll be gone a day or two." He looked Lee hard in the eye, and rocked back and forth on his feet as Lee had seen impatient school masters do. "When I get back, you be certain you've made up your mind. *In . . . or not.* That's what I'll want to know, Master Morgan." He leaned over the desk to blow the lamp out, then walked through the dimness to the hat-tree, Lee following, and plucked his top-hat off to plant it on his head. Then he ushered Lee outside, and shut and locked the building door.

"If you'd like another look at the ledger, just you have Frank One-arm open up for you."

"All right."

"Now then, I've business to do; can I be running you down to the Club?"

"I guess not. I'll walk the town a little bit, I think."

McGee shook his head in admiration. "*Youth.* A fight, a day's stage ride, serious business to do on arrival, go down a mine, and what after that? Dinner and bed? Never! Now, Master Morgan will 'walk the town a little bit.'" McGee looked Lee up and down, smiling. "Well —you go to it, boy-oh! But mind you don't step on your pecker while you're about it!"

"I'll take care."

"Do that." McGee stepped to his horse's head, slipped the tether from a slanting post, then trotted 'round, climbed up and gathered his reins, and wheeled the chestnut lively out of the yard.

"In a day or two, then!" he called over his shoulder. And was gone.

Lee started across the Hill, first to see the high streets where most of the mines appeared to headquarter, then to work his way slowly down to the lower town, the Coffee Club, then food and sleep. Perhaps take a beer or whiskey as he went, if he found a likely place. Perhaps take a girl, too, if he came upon some flash ken or open house.

For now, he was glad enough to be in the open

air, breathing that air in. Hadn't cared for being down in the mine at all, was the truth. McGee, on the other hand, hadn't minded it—almost certainly had done that sort of work as a young man. A good way to persuade a greenhorn he wouldn't be comfortable in the mining business —take him down in one first thing. Take him down the hard way. Then, when the fellow has just surfaced, and is damn glad to be on top of the ground, talk down mines altogether. Talk up wheat. Open rolling lands, blue skies. Golden wheat in the blowing wind, sunshine.

Enough to make a young man lose his taste for copper mining, if that was the notion.

And so free with the ledger. There, wide open as a whore's knees, any time Lee cared to look. First businessman Lee'd heard of so eager to let another man—who might, or might not become a partner—look all he pleased at that business-man's business.

Only a dead-honest man—or a crook . . .

They had put street lights, of a sort, on Hang-fire Hill. Pitch-pine torches flickered and flared at every track corner and street turning along the slope. A group of about twenty miners passed Lee as he walked—stooped, as all in that trade appeared to be, and just off shift, from the weariness on their faces. They were quiet for a bunch of working men, tired or not, and it seemed to Lee that McGee and the other owners held Hangfire Hill in a tighter grip than most— and held the men tighter, too. Likely no miner's court here, no Marxians, either.

Did he take his share, Lee would be one of those owners, holding tight.

Pleasant in one way. Not so pleasant in another. It would be no joy to set the Pinkertons onto a working man, or these uniformed police onto one, either. Though he might have to do it, just the same, if he meant to have and hold the Penny, and get his profits out of it. If any there was to be had.

No unionizing on the ranges, thank God. But Lee knew what he would have done to hold the Rifle River ranch, to hold Spade Bit for Mrs. Dowd.

He would have done what had to be done— and God help the drovers who stood against him! Difficult to blame these mine owners for doing their same.

No singing in these streets, though. He remembered the Barbary Coast as he walked along the rutted ways in the torches' flickering light. Singing in those streets, by God. Singing and murder . . .

Lee saw another bunch of miners, somewhat livelier, trooping into a mine yard under a weathered sign reading *The Plum Perfect Copper Mine.* Lee watched them going in, and tugged his watch out of his vest pocket. Near nine o'clock. Night shift going in; no worn out vein down the Plum Perfect. He stood in the shadows across the narrow, muddy street, and watched the last of the miners filing in, and a man in a billed cap swing a narrow gate shut behind him. Some chatter between this guard and the men—not all sullenness and submission, then. Not all, but enough. Lee saw more lamp-light up ahead, a long line of men with picks and shovels over their shoulders (these with their own tools, then—McGee must lease his tools to his miners, make them leave them when the shift was done. Clever; it would mean an extra penny or nickel out of their wages, day by day.) Clever, if you cared for that.

Lee found himself tired of looking at mines, saw a street corner (or at least what passed for a corner on these mired and stony slopes) and turned down it, heading to his right, down for the lower town. This street, named Pickens Street on its board, was a tad wider than the hill track had been, was bordered here and there by pine torches, and had, at last, some people out for night walks and pleasure strolling its board-walks.

Not many, to be sure—a couple, two stagger-ing drunks further down, and three young ragged-trousered boys out ranging the town for mischief.

The boys came trotting like a dog pack up out of shadows and torch light, took a quick glimpse of Lee to see if he were small enough, or drunk enough, to be some sport—decided not—and trotted on by, one with a polite "Evenin', Mister," as they passed.

Better than the silent lines of exhausted men further up the hill. At least some spirit. Lee thought he heard piano music further down.

Some sort of sporting life. There had to be something like that.

"*Boy . . . Are you a saved soul?*"

Voice like a bass drum. It had rumbled out of shadow to his right.

Lee peered hard into the gloom, stopped walking, and saw a cloud of white hair and beard, glittering light blue eyes—and all towering seven feet, or near it above the sidewalk boards.

"I asked you a question," the old man said, his voice so deep and resonant it seemed to ring off the shuttered fronts he stood against. It was hard to make the old man out, except for his height, the blue eyes shining in shadowed torch light. He seemed to be wearing a brown sack suit that had seen better days. "*I asked you a question!*" Bullying tone to that—that street corner preacher had seen better days, like his sack suit.

"Damned if I know whether I'm saved or not, Dad," Lee said, and went on his way.

"Then you are not," the old man said after him, not having to raise his voice at all, "and I must and shall pray for you!"

No need to answer that. The two drunks stumbled off the boardwalk across the way; one called something to Lee and they both came staggering over the ruts and puddles toward him. Called something again, damned if he could make it out. Seemed friendly enough, though. Might know a good resort for a drink and so-forth.

The lead drunk, a big round-faced man in worn jean pants and shirt, called up, "Settle a bet, Mister?" and climbed the boardwalk stairs with some difficulty, waving at Lee to wait to hear him out.

His friend, even drunker, came up the steps behind him, stepped wrong, slipped, and saved himself a fall by a neat bit of balancing.

Too neat.

Except for that single blunder—that too nice recovery—they would have had Lee dead meat; the round-faced man was already up to him, breathing whiskey, smiling and pulling a length of lead pipe from the back of his belt.

Too close to draw.

Lee's skull would be cracked just reaching; would be cracked dodging back, too.

The round-faced man, still smiling, grunted with effort, stepped in, and swung the short piece of pipe to beat Lee's brains out.

Lee ducked and stepped right into him and took the blow on the back of his left shoulder. The shock of it went through him to his spine, and he ducked further, swung his right hand up into the man's crotch, gripped the fellow there, nuts and whatever, as hard as he could—and clenched his fist with all his strength.

The man whooped in a breath and shouted in agony as Lee crushed his nuts, breaking them in his grip. Lee set his shoulder into the man's belly, took another blow from the lead pipe across his back as the man flailed at him, staggering back howling. Lee drove the man, drove him back and back into the other one trying to get by, to get a chance at him. Lee didn't know what weapon the second man had. He began not to care. He felt good, despite the pain as the round-faced man struck at him, screaming. Lee felt all right.

He suddenly let go of the man's privates—his hand cramped from the force of his grip—spun away from him as the second man reached around his friend and hit Lee alongside the head with something black.

Light flashed in Lee's head as if he'd seen the sun, had been staring into it. All he felt for a second were the boards under his boots. He felt that, remembered where he was standing, and stepped far to the right and fell from the high boardwalk into the dark street below.

He could see better after he hit the ground and rolled deeper into darkness, the stones and slippery mud. He could see much better, and he saw the second man, a tall fellow with long, dark hair like an Indian's, come to the edge of the walk, then set himself to jump down where Lee was.

Lee got to one knee and reached down to his right boot as the man jumped. He was just standing with his knife in his hand as the man landed half against him, knocked him staggering, and followed him, swinging a leather-clad slung-shot—a "jack" some people called it.

Lee took that blow on his left shoulder. He had felt nothing there since the other man had hit it with the length of pipe. He took the blow and stepped back, trying to keep his balance. If he fell, he thought, this long-haired man would beat him to death.

The man jumped after him, quick as a cricket, and Lee stepped to meet that, took a blow that cracked him hard, grazing the top of his head— wondered when he'd lost his Stetson in the fight —and stuck the dagger into the jacksman's side as the fellow turned with his blow, following through.

The long-haired man was brave, or stupid. Instead of pulling away, so badly hurt, he grunted with effort and swung again, back-handed, so that Lee's knife—without his having to do much—sliced the fellow right across his belly, and opened him up completely.

The man dropped his weapon, arched himself back like a fellow doing a fancy dive into a stock-pond, and fell out full length in the street. He wore a dark shirt, which, with the darkness of the street, hid most of what was coming out of him at the middle.

Lee left off watching that one, got his footing and turned reaching under his coat for the Bisley Colts, looking for the round-faced man.

He didn't see him for a moment; then he saw him sitting down across the boardwalk, doubled up, his head on his knees. He was sitting with his back against one of the buildings. Likely didn't know that his friend was out in the street, dying.

Lee's left arm was stinging and prickling as if it had gone to sleep. He couldn't feel his fingers on that hand. Couldn't feel the hand, for that matter. He walked to the steps, feeling sick to his stomach. He had felt pretty well, but he felt terrible now. He climbed the steps; his left leg worked fine, got up to the boardwalk, and went across it to the man doubled up against the building.

He hit the man on his bowed head, fairly lightly, with the barrel of the Colts. "Whose idea was this?" Lee said.

The man didn't answer, didn't seem to notice, so Lee hit him harder. That seemed to wake him, and he looked up, his face white as chicken feathers in the torch light. He was weeping in agony. Lee could hear the man panting. His face was wet with tears.

"Whose idea was this?" Lee said again.

But the round-faced man wouldn't answer him, or couldn't, perhaps was too deep in his pain to think of the matter. Lee felt a great impatience seize him. It rolled over him like a wind, and swept him up.

He raised the Colt's revolver high and struck the man over the head with it. Once. Then again. Then hit him a third time. The blows made heavy socking sounds, like a baseball being hard hit. Lee wanted to hit the man again, and more than that—it seemed the right thing to do—but he was afraid he would damage the Bisley Colts if he did it. Had known men to ruin fine revolvers, hitting them in the head. So he stopped.

The round-faced man sighed and slid sideways

down the building front. He had manured his trousers, and the smell came up stinking as he fell over. There was a white chunk just above his ear. When Lee leaned over, he saw it was a bit of the man's brain showing.

"*Now I know you,*" the bass voice said, startling Lee so he jumped a little, turning. The old man stood a ways down the walk, staring at him, his white beard, and white hair foaming about his face in the torch light. "*Belial,*" the man said. "*The beast! And for you must I prepare . . . strengthen my soul in the Lord.*" Turned, then, and stalked away like a tall ghost, walking.

CHAPTER FIVE

It was one of the new zinc bathing tubs, big enough, almost, for a man to lie in full length.

Lee lay back into the steaming water—water almost too hot—and felt the heat soak into his bones, begin to soak and soothe the aches out of him. His back hurt him savagely whenever he moved too suddenly, or twisted, and he'd seen in the dresser mirror a sooty pattern of bruises running down from his left shoulderblade, where the lead pipe had struck him. No bruise on his head, where the long-haired man had clipped him with the slung-shot. A headache there, fierce enough to blur his vision when he moved his head too quickly.

A little more luck for them—for either of them —and he would have been done with his skull cracked like a boiled egg. Just a little luck, for either of them. If the long-haired man hadn't slipped on the muddy steps, hadn't recovered that shade too neatly to be drunk . . .

If the round-faced man had shortened his blow with the pipe, had chopped down, instead of swinging . . .

If . . .

Lee lay back in the tub, sighing at the water's touch. The colored man who'd served drinks to him and McGee earlier had not appeared surprised to see a lodger at the Coffee Club coming in late, and ruffled and bruised from a fight. Apparently, the mineowners and other businessmen occasionally did their rowdies like any drover or hard-rock miner.

When Lee had gone down into the street for his Stetson and his knife, he'd found that the long-haired man was breathing, was making a sort of snoring sound. He'd curled on his side, and his vitals were out in a small pile from his sliced belly. Lee was glad enough that the light was dim. He found his knife, pulled it free, and wiped it on the man's trouser leg and sheathed it. His Stetson had fallen almost beneath the boardwalk, and the brim was dirty with muddy water.

Looking up as he put it on, Lee saw a couple—an older man and woman—standing a good ways off, down at the end of the street, watching him. Lee could hardly make out their faces in the shifting torch light. When they saw him staring at them, the two of them turned and hurried away. They didn't look back.

Lee supposed they might be going to the uniformed police to report the fight. Or, they might decide to stay clear of the business. Damned if he cared, right then, what they did. Unlikely they'd know him for sure in broad daylight, anyway; not the way that crazy old preacher would know him.

The old man would know him forever.

The colored man had opened the Coffee Club doors to him as if he were the Duke of This or That, come in from a grand ball, had shown him upstairs to his room—some men drinking at the bar had not seemed much interested in McGee's new partner coming in drover-drunk—had taken Lee's order for a beef steak dinner and a tub of hot water, had provided both, and seemed more than satisfied with a half-dollar tip.

Lee had eaten fast as a lobo wolf. Felt starved, was the truth, and then had fallen into the hot bath—put down on a canvas tarpaulin in the center of his room's carpet—and now rested in it, feeling the slow easing of his pains.

Lee thought of many things, but not of the . He thought a good deal of what had needed doing at Spade Bit, and hoped that the boys weren't slacking while he was gone. Any workman, even a good one, will slack a bit while the stud-duck is off the lash-up. Human nature.

Lee thought about that sort of thing for a while . . . thought about elk-hunting—he and Sid Sefton had gone hunting mid-winter; had knocked over a beautiful young buck, big as a horse. Shot him down in the snow on the southern slopes of the Old Man. A running shot. Three hundred yards, if it was a foot, and made with a Sharp's rifle, heavy as a timber to swing on sight. The elk was a fourth-year buck, running, churning through the deep white powder, sending sprays of it up as he ran, the snow glittering bright enough to hurt the eye under the high mountain sun.

The snow foaming up like ocean water around that buck as he ran.

"You won't hit him," Sefton had said.

And Lee had shot him down. Sent him plowing down into the deep snow, until only the branches of his antlers showed, the long dark-brown line of his shoulders and back. The only darkness on a field of white.

He'd been dead when they'd snow-shoed out to him, to slice out his tongue and liver, to cut out the gall and sprinkle that juice on the raw liver and cut off bites of that and eat them, the blood steaming in the cold as they ate.

Then they'd butchered him out, hide-wrapped the meat, and sledded it off the field, over to the trees and the horses.

Lee couldn't remember enjoying a hunting shot since. Had made them, and eaten the meat, but had not enjoyed them. He thought it might be that that had been a perfect shot, on a perfect animal, on a perfect day.

No need to enjoy it again.

Perhaps. From that day on—some two years ago, now—hunting had been for meat, and for the ride. And for nothing else.

Not so, he thought, what had happened tonight. Had enjoyed that, right enough. Scared and all. Had enjoyed all of it. Blood will tell . . .

perhaps had told too much. Should ought, perhaps, to kill McGee for his scheming—if those had been, as seemed likely, his hiring. Might kill McGee if that was so, for no better reason than he had made Lee enjoy himself in such a fashion.

"Rein your passions," Professor Riles had said, and more than once. "Rein your passions—or they will surely rein you." True enough. But Frank Leslie had not seemed to enjoy his killings! Had not seemed . . . though blood, they said, will always tell. And may have told tonight . . .

Lee thought of it that much, and no more. He sat up in the tub, and reached for the bar of soap. Sleep, he thought. I'll think of sleeping in this room's big four-poster bed. I'll think of that, and dreaming of some whore or other. What's done is done. No need to think of it right now.

No need to think of anything, right now.

Lee woke slowly . . . slowly . . . like a man rising gently from the deeps at the bottom of a lake. He seemed to lift up through green to brighter green, and figured he was still dreaming as he woke. He dreamed his back ached, stiff and sore as a fresh-sawn plank—and as he woke, realized that it was so.

He didn't care to recall how he'd been hurt, so didn't recall it for a little while, as he lay still in the big linen-sheeted bed, cool and clean as fresh fallen snow. The room's ceiling was white-painted fine stamped tin, impressed with scrolls and flowers, angles and scalloped lines, all in fine detail, bold relief. White bed-linens . . . white ceiling. Lee lay drifting between them, slowly hearing more and more of the faint sounds of traffic out beyond the Club's alley. Men laughing, calling out. Whips cracking. The thump and rumble of heavy drays rolling.

He thought to roll over on his side and reach for his watch, propped up on its hunter's spring-cover on the small bedside table where the Bisley Colts also lay.

That seemed a great chore.

He had a pleasant discomfort at his root . . . a cock-stand that thrust the top sheet up like tenting. Couldn't remember any dream of a woman that might have produced it. It seemed to him that he had dreamed of a straight stage road running south, perhaps into Arizona. Dry washes . . . dry hills . . . cactus and *cholla*. That's what he remembered. That and some gambler— a washed out blond-haired man with a humorous, hollow face. A .38 revolver in a neat holster at the fellow's side. "Knew your daddy," the dream man had said. Violets on gray silk in the material of his vest. Dusty gray suit. He had a gray-blue, merry and menacing eye. Bit his nails down to the quick, Lee had noticed in the dream as they bucketed along. "Apache country," the man had said, "At least it was, before that lying dog, Sieber, roped them in. You'd have damn sure seen some doings out here before that." Southerner's accent. "Baltimore," the dream man had said, before Lee thought to ask him. "In my mis-spent youth. Alabama, before that."

"Your daddy," the dream man said, "and I, met over a game of cards. Honest cards, as it happened (probably fortunately for both of us) and, following that, attended a chicken fight, bet and won there, both of us, on a Red-spike cock mean enough to chew railroad rail. I still recall that bird, and honor him."

The stage coach had rolled more smoothly than any waking Concord ever had.

"I will confess, I didn't know quite the dandy your old man turned out to be. If I had, no doubt we should have been enemies, rather than friends. He never cared for Wyatt, for one thing —saw only his coldness, not the decency that impression shielded—and, for another, he was too damn fast with a pistol. Not hasty to draw, mind you; I didn't say that nor mean it. I mean quick at the *mechanics* of the matter! A special curse for your father, I believe, that handiness with any sort of a weapon. The knives and pistols seemed to come alive in his hands. I'll truthfully say I never saw his equal for handiness at killing. But too slow to start! That was his trouble. Too damn slow to open the ball! Why, in his place, I would have had whoever already shot through-and-through and lying on the sawdust bleeding out. Hell, I'd already be back to my game!

"Not your daddy. No, he must talk and try and reason the whoever fool out of his play. And always wasted time. Fight comes to that, it will go all the way. Most men—and it did not take me forever to figure it out—most men who braced the likes of us, did so in order to die. I understand there's a Jew doctor in Europe explaining the whole. And it's true; I've seen it more than once—and provided the service. Speaking of the Hebrew persuasion, by the way, John Ringgold is the only murderer—for that's what we were, however you like to gild it—was the only such that I know that your father avoided. He thought Ringgold mad, you see, and had a sorrow and horror of mad people. That Dutchy doctor might say he feared for his own reason . . . a gentle man killing so many . . .

"In any case, avoided Johnny Ringo like the plague. Ringo, of course, was not crazed at all, but simply too brainy for his own good, with his pocket Testament in Greek, his Old Testament in Hebrew. Forever trying to confound the Christians, forever drowning in a sea of them. Couldn't kill them all. Which is what he told Luke Short once, when they were drunk together. "Too many of you Christian swine to kill," he told Short. Short, no daffodil himself, but also a sensible man, agreed that there were a passel, and could likely use thinning . . ."

Lee had dreamt the hollow-faced man leaned back in his seat and laughed at the picture this tale recalled to him. Lee lay in his bed, hearing more and more of the sounds of Hangfire Hill, and trying to recall the man's talk, his memories of Lee's father. But those tales, that talk was fading fast, blotted from Lee's waking memory as if by the brightness of sunlight streaming in tiger stripes through the room's window shutters.

He remembered the man had talked of dentistry in his dream, had offered Lee his card, should a toothache assail him. Fellow had said he was dead, too, had died in a foolish sick bed fashion. "Not like Frank Leslie, by God. Your dad made a proper *adieu!*" And had said, while smoking a cheroot and gazing out the Concord's window at Arizona, that death was nothing much. "Not much to it," he'd said.

Lee tried to recapture more, tried too hard and woke all the way up, hungry as the devil.

He rolled to his side, grunted at the stiffness in his back and read his watch. It was past noon-time. He'd damn near slept the clock around. Dreaming most of the time, he supposed. His father . . . that odd, phantom dentist.

Damn foolishness to sleep half the day away. But he'd needed the rest. Needed those extra hours. Needed not to think about the fight.

No uniformed policemen had come pounding on his room door. No deputy or other come up to have a talk . . .

Seemed the law wasn't going to be a problem. Appeared that killings weren't all that uncommon in Hangfire Hill, tight run or not. Likely the miners tended to take their angers out on each other, in saloons and in the streets. Likely, too, the mine owners and police didn't much care.

Lee lay thinking about his dream—would have supposed he'd have dreamed about those two he'd killed. Who had damn near killed him. Would have made sense to dream about that . . . to have a hell of a nightmare ride about that. But he hadn't. Dreamed instead of a talkative dentist who said he'd known Buckskin Frank Leslie. Getting to be too old to be dreaming of his daddy or his daddy's friends. Was getting sick of it—sick of the questions, too, the remiscences (like McGee's about Harvey Logan in some New York sporting house). People seemed to get near Lee as if that way they'd gotten nearer to his father. It wearied him and was distastful.

For himself, Lee felt he would be happier to be a little further from his father. A little further from whatever it had been that enabled Lee that made him want to fight and kill those two hoodlums. That gave him pleasure about it.

He lay restless, conscious of the discomfort at his groin, his swollen cock beneath the covers. S'eon. A great pleasure it would be, to have her beside him in this big bed. Her smoothness, her warm mouth. A woman of some kind, anyway. But especially her.

She'd be stroking him, she'd have her mouth on him right now. Those black eyes watching him, watching his face as she licked at it. Kissed it. Sucked at it, gently.

Lee slid his hand under the sheet, grasped himself, began slowly to stroke the stiff swollen

112

length. She might have kissed and sucked at it, then sat back naked in the bed, her small breasts, her flat brown belly bare. And watched. Watched what he was doing. Watched his moving hand, the swollen cock like a club in his fist. Watched him, and then sat back further, brought up her rounded thighs . . . slowly . . . slowly spread her doubled knees to reveal the small triangle of dark down, the damp thin line of scarlet. And reach down and spread that gently open for him to see, to look into as if it were a flower, deep and wet and richly colored as any flower ever grew. And put her finger there, and stroke it. Then, after a while, when her finger was wet and glistening, sliding deep in and out, when her head was thrown far back, her long black hair flowing over snowly linen . . . then, she would make the sounds he made . . .

Lee sat half up, cursed, and then wiped himself with a wad of the bed linen. He lay still a few moments, his heart hammering. He'd made a damn mess of the bed sheets. Likely, though, the colored women, or Indian women, who cleaned these fine damasked rooms, the big four-poster beds, had felt stiffened sheets before.

He groaned, rolled onto his side, then slowly sat up, favoring his back. Still stiff, still bruised black and blue for sure, but not as bad as he'd feared. The long hot bath the night before and the long night's sleep had done him good.

Lee reached for the Bisley Colts on the bed-side table. There was a scrap of something, a dried shred across the blade of the front sight. A

113

dry smear of something on the ejector-rod guard.

Lee wiped the revolver clean with a corner of the sheet. Would have to clean and oil the piece tonight. He finished wiping those things off of the blued steel, then lifted the pistol and drew a fine bead on the finial cap of the dresser mirror. Sight seemed straight enough, barrel set straight in the frame. Hadn't had to kill that round-faced man. Hadn't had to do that at all. Would sure as hell be feeling better, not.

Lee set the revolver down, stood up from the bed, and went to the basin to wash. The carpet felt comfortable against his bare feet, the cool water, lifted up to his face in double handfuls, seemed cold as snow to his face, heated by hours of hard sleep in the dark, velvet-curtained room.

He washed his face, lathered and shaved, washed his armpits with palm-cupped splashes of water, then shook some bay rum into his hands, and rubbed himself with that. He was feeling hungrier as he washed. Damned hungry for a missed breakfast, and a due lunch.

As he dressed, Lee considered why McGee would want him killed—and not yet knowing whether Lee might just pick up stakes (convinced the Penny was worn out) and roll on back to Idaho. Supposing those head-crackers to be McGee's hiring, and not just drunk-bashers out for a poke—what in hell would the man gain? Might, of course, simply have decided to save himself the trouble of further persuasion. Might —and this more likely—have decided Lee had already made up his mind to stick, whatever.

And if that, of course, the Irishman was right.

Lee was sticking—had already decided to stick, down in that mine, without knowing he'd decided.

A man didn't care to be frightened of something—and that only a hole in the ground. McGee had blundered, tried too hard—the talk, the ledger, the dark crawling underneath the ground. Tried too hard, harder than a man needed to, when the truth would soon enough make his point for him.

The Penny might be at the end of her rope, and she might not. Either way, for a while, Lee would stick. And if those hoodlums had been McGee men, which seemed damn likely, Lee could count on the natty Irishman coming up with another hand of poker—this time, with aces in it.

Lee found his clothes from the night before neatly hanging in a press beside the window. Someone had been into the room while he slept, taken his things to be sponged and pressed. Whoever, had done their best—good service at the Coffee Club—and the buckskin jacket might do. The gray trousers, the shirt, were finished—stains there no cleaning would get out of them. Mud and blood. Lee didn't doubt the Coffee Club servants knew the difference.

Lee dug in his suitcase for fresh duds, found some tan trousers and a white lawn shirt, and dressed.

His boots had been cleaned and polished, too, and the Stetson cleaned and steam-blocked. The men who owned Hangfire Hill appeared to receive a fine level of service from their people, and likely happily paid what that cost. Useful— service like that—when you'd had a fight in a dark street, and put two men under.

Hadn't dreamed about it, either. Not a bit.

CHAPTER SIX

"Well, sir, now, we can serve you a fine brunch right here at the Club." Different colored man from the ones last night. This one was younger, with some white blood in him.

"I guess not." Lee wanted out of the place, out into some daylight, and away from oil lamps and red velvet and damask silks. Away from that fat-vested crowd at the bar, too. Some of the men having their nooners had nodded and lifted their glasses to him—McGee's partner. Kept their faces straight doing it, too. "I guess not. Where can I eat well in the town?"

The young yaller gave Lee a small smile, as if to say, 'nowhere but here, Rube.' Then shrugged and said, "Tillbury's is supposed to serve good eats, Mister Morgan." Implying he wouldn't eat there, even if it weren't a white man's resort.

"Tillbury's then." Lee was tired of standing in the lobby gabbing with this fellow while the bar looked on. "Where in hell is it?"

"Down the hill to Main, sir—then four blocks east to Altamount. The Tillbury's is up on Altamount, left side of the street."

Lee flipped him two bits, turned, and walked out the double doors into a fine blaze of sunlight. The narrow alley glowed with the brightness of it. The air, rich and fresh and cool, still held a hint of clay, a drift of odor from the workings at the top of the town. The sun's heat seemed to search through the cool air to fall on Lee's back and shoulders as he walked out through the alley's mouth, reached the street, and turned down toward Main. The heat, and the walking, soaked a comfort into his sore back and left shoulder. It felt as though a warm medicine were being poured into him; he felt his muscles loosen . . . ease, as he walked.

Plenty of people out on the streets today. Lee had the pleasure of tipping his Stetson to two handsome women—respectable women—out walking without escort, lugging a bushel shopping basket between them. Odd how like hunting a woman's shopping was. Only a different sort of go-out-and-get, when you came down to it.

He saw one of the uniformed police officers—big, wide-shouldered fellow—across the street, walking his beat. Not much use against real hard-cases, Lee supposed; the officer's pistol was buttoned under his coat. Good enough to keep street trash clear, though. Good enough so that respectable women could walk the boards and do their shopping without some drunkard unfastening his trousers to show his wares.

No children in the street yet; school must still be sessioning for the town kids. The miners' brats would be at the pits, choring and picking up, and likely happy not to have to 'A-B-C'.

A lot of dogs, though. Lee couldn't remember seeing so many dogs in a town street. Mongrels and fices most of them, scurrying around lifting their legs, hunting for scraps beneath the high boardwalks.

The sun had nearly dried the mud down there. The streets were turning from wet to dusty dry; by tomorrow, the dust would be rolling up in clouds, settling like fine wheat flour on everything. Something to be said for paved streets, after all. Someday, Lee supposed, when they got around to it, even towns like the Hill would have their streets paved as solid as San Francisco's. Just a question of when they decided to spend the money.

Main street was even more crowded—the drays and wagons as before, and many people on the walks, going in and out of the shops with packages in their hands, delivering or buying goods, he supposed. Had to be many who made their living off the mines without owning them or going down to work them, either.

These people—merchants and storekeepers, clerks and workmen—stayed off the streets at night like good Christians, then came crowding out in the day-time to make their money. Appeared a lot like ants, to Lee, the way they scurried about with their small burdens, their sleeves rolled up like lumberjacks so they could carry their notebooks and receipt books, their grocery baskets and boxes, their small kegs of nails and tacks, their rolls of canvas and finer cloth.

Ducked in and out of those shops like ants—with only a quick sidelong glance at women walking by, or at occasional fine polished rigs behind high-steppers in the street.

They walked like water birds, Lee noticed, their toes turned out.

Townspeople.

These were the ones, he figured. These clerks and merchants and lawyers. It wasn't the farmers would inherit the west from the cattlemen, the fading Indians; it was these men, with their bank accounts and ledger books and law books. In time, they'd take it all.

And had a beautiful day for their start at it. The sky, the bright light blue of blue-and-white paint mixed, set with clouds shaped like long, long feathers, and a breeze, warm with the afternoon sun—warm, too, from the heat of the wide plains beneath the Hill—drifting through the streets of the town, blowing the stink of cave clay, lamp-oil, and sweat away.

A good day to be alive on. And to hell with the two he'd killed.

Lee turned up on Altamount, and saw the *Tillbury's* sign half-way up the block on the left. It was a fancy sign—the name of the place limned out in copper and black, the top of the sign scrolled like a piece of furniture.

The place, once he walked up to it, didn't look quite as fancy as its sign. A few wide steps down into what appeared to be some sort of storage cellar.

Below there, Lee found himself in the doorway to a kitchen—no doubt about that from the noise of pots and pans, the smells and harried curses. Stoves' heat, as well. Wrong way in, apparently.

But as Lee turned to climb back up the steps, a short, fat man in a broadcloth suit came out the kitchen door and stopped him.

"Sir! Welcome to Otto Tillbury's place!" As if a cellar kitchen was the finest chow-station short of Delmonico's in New York. The fellow, who had a wart on his nose the size of an aggie marble, commenced plucking and picking at Lee's jacket sleeve to persuade him in. "Now, come in! Come in! If you regret it, sir. I'll swear right here to pay your meal price myself!" *Pluck, pluck, pluck* . . .

The man was shouting out loud, and people walking by above were grinning and staring down at the two of them. Lee planned to kill that damn yellow nigger at the Coffee Club.

"*Will you come in, now? Will you?*" Man was yelling right in Lee's ear. Lee heard people laughing up on the boardwalk.

It was a choice of knocking the man down, or going into that eating place and take his chances on ptomaine poisoning.

Pluck, pluck, pluck . . . Damn fellow was going to tug that jacket sleeve right off!

123

Lee walked inside.

Wart-nose came inside with him, quiet at last, and led Lee through a labyrinth of steam tables, stoves, chopping blocks, stacks of pans—dirty or clean was hard to tell—and a swarm of shouting cooks and scrubbers. Looked to be Indians, Negroes, Irish—you name it. A tower of Babel, cooking. The smell was not so bad, though. Some of the stuff boiling or frying or baking didn't smell all that bad . . .

Lee had just decided some of these shouting people must be customers—and he, like them, expected to eat in the kitchen on the run—when Wart-nose pushed him gently down a narrow passage with one or two inches deep of greasy water on the floor, on out a spring-door made of frame and fly-netting, and into one of the prettiest garden places that Lee had ever seen.

It was a garden in a town—walled on its sides by brick buildings and wood-sided buildings—and as full of spring flowers and blossoming fruit trees as any nabob's yard. Forty-foot on a side at most, with vines and green what-not trellised overhead, and perhaps twenty or thirty tables spaced on flagstone walks. Crowded with people, too—some of them grinning at Lee as Wart-nose herded him out, seeing him for a greenhorn surprised at this pleasantry.

"Figured you was goin' to eat in that kitchen?" a man called to him from a table near the wall. Man had his family with him, it appeared, seated around a platter piled high

124

with pan-fried chicken. They all had big red-checked napkins tied 'round their necks, to save their duds from the chicken grease.

Lee smiled to show he'd been fooled, and was glad of it, and a number of people eating there smiled back at him, proud of the place, it seemed. And for looks, they were right to be. Restaurant looked like one of those fine St. Louis beer-gardens Lee'd read about. And in a town as plain and hard as Hangfire Hill, would likely be an ease to the eyes, as well as the belly.

Wart-nose—the owner, probably, playing character for all he was worth—was guiding Lee toward a small two-chair table under a fine little crab-apple tree in a pot, when someone called out *"Idaho!"* across the garden.

Lee looked, and saw a ruddy-cheeked young man in a bottle-green velvet coat, half-standing by a table under the far wall, waving to him. A lady was sitting at the table as well.

Lee thought he'd been miscalled, and turned to follow the proprietor to his own table, when the man in the velvet coat waved and called to him again. "Say, Idaho! Come lunch with us!"

"You a friend of Ned Bierce's?" Wart-nose looked worried.

"I suppose I must be, ready or not," Lee said, and walked away toward that table, thinking that he'd seen the lady somewhere before. As he edged past a long table lined with some sort of European people—Bohemian mine people, maybe, foremen and their families, all chattering away at a great rate in whatever language they spoke—Lee saw the lady at the velvet-coated man's table more clearly.

It was the fine whore from the stage coach.

Out without her Indian woman today. And sitting bold as brass alongside respectable women and their kids. Something of the manners of a mining camp, still, in Hangfire Hill. The decent women and the churches hadn't clamped down full, yet.

The man with her waved to Lee in a very friendly fashion. "Come sit with us, Mister—?"

"Morgan. Lee Morgan."

"What did I tell you?" the man said to the handsome whore. And to Lee: "I told her I'd picked you out—fresh out of the kitchen with Otto." He stood up all the way, and pulled out a chair for Lee across from the woman. "You come sit and have your tummy full, Mister Lee Morgan; you'll never find better eats, not even in Chicago."

He was a pleasant mannered man, but odd-looking. Medium-sized and slightly plump, with vague, mild-gray eyes. He wore, beside his bottle-green coat, a pair of dark yellow trousers, which also looked to be made of velvet cloth, and he wore a silk tie, wide as a bandana, knotted softly about his neck, and thrust through with a pearl stick-pin.

Lee took the offered chair, nodded, smiled, said "Good day," to the whore, and said to the man, "I don't believe we've met, have we, before now?"

There was a bright green carpet of vine

against the brick wall behind the woman. That green set off the coolness, the clarity and smoothness of her skin. Set off her fine eyes.

She wore no veil today.

She smiled at Lee, but said nothing, bent her head, and picked at an omelette with her fork.

"No, we haven't met," the gray-eyed man said, "but we have now. I'm Ned Bierce." And stretched out a soft hand for Lee to shake.

Lee saw that Bierce had rouged his cheeks. His eyes were outlined with kohl or some such. His lips were rouged, as well.

The gray eyes were not so vague as they had seemed. "Ah, you notice my *maquillage!* The rouge and stuff!" He patted Lee's arm in a confiding way. "Well, don't be alarmed. I know it's unusual in this barbaric place, these barbaric times. But it is really—like all matters, I believe—a question of taste, and therefore, of beauty. Not so?"

A big, bony Irish girl in a black dress and white apron, had come to stand beside Lee with a pad and lead pencil in her hand. It appeared Tillbury aped Fred Harvey, using women waiters. This one seemed to be some Irish miner's daughter, by her red hands and raw complexion.

"Have the knockwurst, Lee—do have that, and fried potatoes, and scrambled eggs! Otto's people do the best eggs you've had, I guarantee it!" Bierce said.

Lee noticed the casual "Lee," and noticed something else: Bierce, who seemed at sight to be a great sissy, had, as he spoke, cut a casual hot glance at the big Irish girl, as randy as any buck's ogle might be. The fellow might like his pretties—but not the boys. Ladies were Bierce's meat; Lee wondered how well he did at gashing, what with his rouge-pot and fancy airs.

"I suppose I'll have that sausage, then," Lee said to the girl, who nodded, silent, dumb as a stone. "And the rest of it—and some cold beer."

Nod. And she wet the lead pencil tip with a long tongue, Bierce, Lee noticed, watched that with attention—and laboriously wrote the order down.

"Pie?" she said.

"It's apple, and very good," the woman said to him across the table. Her throat was like a slim, peeled stalk. White, white against the ivy green.

"I'll take your word," Lee said, and nodded to the Irish girl, who slowly wrote it down, then swung around and marched away, stumping like a soldier.

"Ever had one of those?" Bierce said, something startling Lee with that rough talk, so lady-like the whore was, sitting with them.

"I guess not."

"Well, they're surprising," Bierce said. He had a plateful of beef-steak and new potatoes, and was busily spreading horseradish on it. "Very, very clean. Very strong. And they hate it; that's the pleasure of the thing with them. They hate it; think it a sin; can't bear even the notion of fucking! And the pleasure of the thing is to persuade them different." He took a neat bite of beef-steak, cut a potato in half, and ate both halves, one-two. "Once you've done that, *if* you can do that, they present the rut like doe goats. Can't get enough of it." He cut at another piece of beef steak, spoke to the whore. "Is that your experience of them, Mercy? Irish girls—of the common sort, of course."

The woman looked up from her lunch. She had a glass of wine by her, and sipped from it. "My experience of Irish girls is that they drink, and then drink more," she said, demurely as if butter wouldn't melt in her mouth. "They will cat— but my clients say it takes a great deal of doing."

"Worth it, I say," Bierce said. "Oh, excuse me, my dear, I should have presented you in form. Mister Morgan—Miss Mercy Phillips."

"Miss Phillips," Lee said, with a small sitting bow.

She nodded and smiled. "Mister Morgan."

"I think you two will be friends," Bierce said, "and here's your lunch, Lee."

And so it was, the big Irish girl smelling faintly of starch and fresh sweat as she set the dishes down: a huge brown sausage, boiled to bursting its casing, a heap of golden fried potatoes, and, nested in parsley, a mound of scrambled eggs as yellow as butter.

It looked like heaven on a plate.

"I'll be bringin' your beer, Sorr," the Irish girl said, and stumped away.

"Ugly walk," Bierce said. "That's the worst

of that type; no fine way of moving. Now, you, my dear, amble like an Arab mare."

"Oh, I do thank you for the compliment, Ned," Mercy Phillips said, and took another sip of wine.

"And what about that lunch?" Bierce said to Lee. "Isn't that fine?"

"It seems fine," Lee said, and took a bite of egg. "And tastes damn fine."

"There you are," Bierce said. "Old Otto has the damnedest collection of folks in that kitchen —but, fact is, they cook together the way a fine hotel orchestra plays. Take those eggs, you know how a fine chef tests a new cook in his kitchen? Well, I'll tell you how; he has the fellow cook him an omelette! The fellow either shows the touch there or he doesn't." Bierce paused to cut up more beef-steak. "Out here," he said, "most people are content to *feed*, like livestock; but dining, as Oscar said, should be more than that!"

"Oscar?"

"Yes, Mister Morgan—Oscar. Oscar Wilde."

"Oh, not him again," Mercy Phillips said.

"Yes," Bierce said, "and you could do a great deal worse than to try to apply some of Oscar Wilde's taste to that dreadful decor current at your galloping-shed, my dear."

"My clients like a vulgar house."

"You mean your vulgar clients like a vulgar house! Oscar said it, and it's true: *There is no need for ugliness.*" Bierce pointed at Lee's scrambled eggs (what was left of them; Otto

Tillbury's people could indeed cook up a storm.) "Now, look at that fine mess of eggs; butter in there, and cream, too. Some herbs; of course. And it's *pretty*, all that softness, that smoothness (so like your perfect skin, my dear) and that wonderful daffodil yellow! Really perfect. And yet, such small differences can make it quite the other sort of thing!" Bierce paused while the Irish girl set down Lee's mug of beer. "You take *brains*, now (and I'm not speaking of the dish, which is a different shade altogether), you take a fellow's brains fresh shot out of his head; now there's a naughty sight, and yet not so much different from a plate of eggs, not that much different at all!" He took a bite of steak, and chewed it, considering. "More white than yellow, for one thing. That fine rich sweet yellow turned to pasty white, all lumps and curds and running in red in little threads. And yet, in consistency, not that different. More of a jelly thing to it, perhaps. Of course, the consistency is less—more busted, more watery and wormy at once—due, I suppose, to the force of ejection, whether a bullet drove them out, or a blow." Bierce took a small round roll from under a napkin covering a basket at the center of the table. "Try one of these," he said to Lee. "Just butter 'em and pop 'em in."

Lee finished the last bite of his eggs, salted his sausage and potatoes, then reached for a roll. It had, after all, taken a little effort to finish the eggs, but he did not believe he'd showed it. His hunger had helped bury the memory of that chunk of soft white showing through the round-faced man's broken skull.

Hadn't had to beat the man's brains out; had just *done* it, natural as breathing.

What in the world was this strange fellow after? To shake him? To have a joke? Some friend of McGee's, set on him to show they knew who killed those hoodlums?

"You're being rude, Ned," Mercy Phillips said, finishing her wine.

Bierce laughed. "Yes, I was—and, I suppose, Oscar would say that rudeness is also ugly, in its way." He reached over and put his hand on Lee's arm, smiling. "You were a good sport, Lee, sitting still for my little lecture on eggs and scrambled brains. I apologize." He reached for another roll. "Fact is, the Hill is really better off without Mister Jacobs—and certainly better off without his friend, Carson. As for Jacob's brains, I doubt they could have been nastier out of his head than they were in it!" He buttered his roll. "We're all much better off without them; dreadful bullies, really."

"That so?" Lee said, and took another bite of the sausage—it was delicious. Some people, the Bohemians, it sounded like, had had enough beer aboard to start to sing. Some good voices there, Lee thought, even if you couldn't understand the words. A very friendly place, altogether, or so it seemed. Hard to believe any beer-garden in Saint Louis could be more agreeable, or fix up better sausage and potatoes.

"A civilized spot," Bierce said, sitting back

from his plate with a sigh. "Think I was reading your thoughts, Lee? Well, I wasn't, but I can read pleasure on a man's face, even under his guard. Not, to be sure, as well as our dear Mercy can read pleasure on a man's face; isn't that so, lovely?"

"That's true," the handsome whore said, smiling at Lee across the table. The afternoon sun poured its white-yellow heat down into the garden, so that everything Lee saw seemed outlined in crystal light. Looking at Mercy Phillips, he saw not only the fine turn of her throat, the deep lake-blue of her eyes, centered with perfect tiny spots of black; he saw also the fine lines carved delicately into the white silk of her skin at the corners of her mouth, the corners of her eyes. Game-tracks of years-old laughter . . . tears, too, perhaps, though she didn't seem the crying kind.

"Whatever else you are," Lee said to her, since frankness seemed the order of the day at Tillbury's garden restaurant, "whatever else you are, you're as lovely as hedge-roses blossoming."

"Oh, God—she's blushing!" Bierce cried—and she was. "Now, then, my dear, we see this harsh horse-man has more parts to him than killing! Damn! Look at her blush like a Boston convent girl, as if she'd never had a cock up her!"

"Shut up, Ned," Mercy Phillips said. "And thank you, Mister Morgan, for a pretty compliment."

"A compliment meant," Lee said.

"Whatever else I may be?"

"I wasn't referring to your profession."

"By God," Bierce said, reaching over to Lee's plate with his fork to steal a fried potato, "you two are conducting a damn love affair at lunch! Mercy, my dear, I thought I was to be your chosen for the day. I have a twenty-dollar piece, my *hedge-rose*, with your name written on it."

The lady-whore smiled, and yawned delicately, covering her mouth with a white-gloved hand. "I don't know that I'm in the mood for business," she said.

Bierce said, "May I?" and reached over to Lee's plate for another piece of fried potato. "You may well wonder," he said, "where I received my notions of propriety, Lee Morgan— as well as my concern with beauty, in and of itself." He chewed the potato piece, and swallowed it.

"Oh, God," Mercy Phillips said. The Irish girl came with Lee's apple pie.

"Yes, dear—I know you've heard of my encounter on the road to Damascus, but our friend hasn't." He reached behind him to a pot of tall daisies standing behind the table, twisted one of the flowers away by its stem, and sat back comfortably, twirling the blossom, watching the play of sunlight on its color.

"Some time ago—three years, in fact—I was in Cheyenne, on business. It came to my attention that Oscar Wilde (of whom I assume you've heard) was actually lecturing that evening in that benighted town, part of his grand tour of the West. I went to that lecture, expecting nothing but the usual sissified foreigner out to astound us American rubes with culture and verbal cow manure." He leaned over to tap Lee's sleeve with the flower. "Imagine my astonishment, then—just imagine it—to discover that Mister Wilde (foreign to be sure—in fact, Irish, which is worse, and very likely a sissy as well), that this Mister Wilde was also a prophet. A prophet of beauty, of the singular *importance* of beauty. 'It is a way,' he said, 'it is a way of enriching, lengthening, *perfecting* our short lives.' " Bierce stared at Lee, his gray eyes soft as smoke. "He said: 'Why exist with ugliness? Why dwell in a prison, when the glories of palaces lie on every side?' Well, sir, I sat there in that intolorably stuffy hall, transfixed. 'Leave ugliness,' Oscar said, 'to those it comforts—bankers, politicians, and priests.' "

Bierce sighed in reminiscence. "That lecture—Oscar Wilde in black velvet with a lily in his hands," Bierce waved his daisy back and forth, "changed my life. When I walked out of there, I *saw* Cheyenne, I saw the whole damned kit and kaboodle plain. And they were ugly as toad heaven!"

"Hard to say he was wrong, at that," Lee said, and took a swig at his beer. Otto Tillbury's beer was as good as his food. Then, Lee started on his pie.

"*Impossible* to say he was wrong!" Bierce said. "I attended his lecture again—drinking in every word—and then went back stage to speak to the great man myself. And what do you think I found? Some prancing *poseur?* Some flashy tin-horn? No sir! I found a big, merry, charming fellow, down to earth as any man, with a professor's brain, Eddie Foy's wit, and a hollow leg for whiskey. In short, we became—(I won't say friends)—we became companions for the evening. And if I, in my way, taught him a thing or two about cards, say, or bones, or trouble, well, I was more than amply repaid. You see—the fellow civilized me."

Bierce reached over to Lee's lunch plate. "May I?" and forked up the last piece of potato. "I'm not saying, mind, that he made a peaceful man of me, a perfectly law-abiding man. I doubt if a *man* can be perfectly law-abiding. No, I mean that he gave me the gift of *taste*—of fine and refined judgment on matters of charm and beauty. In doing that, that big long-faced Irishman gave me more than gold."

Mercy Phillips yawned again.

"You see," Bierce said, smiling at her, "at once the strength and weakness of women— their indomitable practicality—which ever rewards them with the lumber of life, but never with the fruit of the tree of dreams." He tapped at the bread basket with the daisy. "Not my phrase, I hasten to add; but Oscar's."

"You were lucky," Lee said, "to meet up with that fellow. I met up with a man once who taught a different lesson. A little man with a big nose, who wore fine-cut suits."

136

"A lesson of death, I assume, rather than the tastes of life."

"Just so."

"Well," Bierce sighed, "that lesson has its place. You've met my father . . . ?"

"I don't think I have."

"Oh, yes—the old man. The big old preacher. I assure you he remembers you. Daddy never forgets a sinner."

Lee said nothing.

" 'A devil come leaping from the pit,' was how he described you."

"Ned, I want to be getting home."

"In a moment dear. My father frightens Mercy—frightens most people, come to think of it. Did you ever hear of the Pottawattomy massacre?"

"John Brown?"

"Well, my father was one of John Brown's men in that. Wielded a broadsword himself. And, after that (something of a come-down, I've always thought) became a Border Ruffian and enjoyed the war, killing." Bierce raised his hand and snapped his fingers for the girl waiter. "You're my guest," he said, as Lee reached for his billfold. Then, as Lee pulled his cash out, said, "*I mean it.*"

Lee put his money back, surprised at that sudden, unpleasant vehemence. "Thank you," he said. "It was a prime lunch; perhaps I can return the favor."

"Don't see why not," Bierce said, as suddenly

merry as he had been grim.

"Which of you gentlemen is going to walk a very well-fed lady to her door?" Mercy Phillips inquired.

"Why, both of us are, my dear," Bierce said, and tickled her chin with the daisy, as the big Irish girl came with her smudged accounting to get their money.

"You understand, I believe, the difficulty with fathers," Bierce said to Lee, raising his voice above the noise as they threaded their way back through the thunderous kitchen, following Mercy Phillip's light and swaying walk. Both Lee and Ned Bierce had their eyes to her haunches as they talked. "Not even Oscar could give me much of comfort, there—had trouble with his own, I believe."

"I understand that difficulty," Lee said, "for damn sure."

"Wouldn't be here without them, but would just as soon," Bierce said, and they followed Mercy Phillips up the steps from the restaurant to the boardwalk and street, all glaring and hammered bright by the sun. On the boardwalk, less crowded now, in the mid-afternoon heat, they waited while the woman shook out her parasol and opened it. Then, with Bierce and Lee lowering their hat-brims against the glare, (Bierce's a handsome straw, precisely the yellow of his velvet trousers—the same yellow as his daisy) the three of them, Mercy in the middle, began to stroll down Altamount Street toward

Main, Bierce chatting all the way about the quality of light in the Dakotas, and about the uses of natural light by the new painters in France. "Naturalists," he called them. "Impressioners."

Lee supposed that his paid-for lunch had been no whim of this eccentric's, likely not the pressure of the whore, either. Whether or not McGee had had a hand in the two roughs coming for him last night, his hand seemed likely in this odd lunch—but to what end, Lee was damned if he could see. Entertainment, for sure, and perhaps some sort of threat. But all mighty subtle for a town called Hangfire Hill.

He proposed not to worry about it—proposed to forget, as well, the sound of the Bisley Colts breaking that man's skull. *Jacob.* Jacob's skull . . .

The three of them, strolling at an easy pace, Bierce nodding now and then to men he knew, had almost reached the corner, when a man called out down in the street. A hoarse voice, like a big dog's bark. Called out once, and came striding to the corner steps. Came up to them, and shouted again. Big man with a yellow eye-tooth that showed crooked when his mouth was open. He wore a long-barrel Peacemaker in a right-hand hoster set forward. Muddy long-tail coat. Muddy boots.

"Hold on there, fancy-pants!" the man said, and came stomping up onto the boardwalk.

Looking for some kind of trouble, and talking to Ned Bierce beyond doubt. Lee felt a sudden embarrassment for Bierce, to be braced in this fashion in the street. All his fine talk to be put to shame by this rough fellow.

"Yes, it's you I'm talkin' to, girly-boy!" the man said, and stood in front of them, blocking the way. "An' a fine dick-sucker you look!"

Stay out of this, Lee said to himself. You don't have to draw on this fellow because Bierce bought you lunch.

But Bierce spoke right up.

"Where, in God's name," he said to the man, "did you get that *coat?*"

"My . . . what?" The rough looked puzzled.

"That coat—if you can call it a coat. Looks like something the cat dragged in!"

Mercy Phillips stepped away from between Bierce and Lee, and stood against the building wall.

"You never mind my coat," the man said. "You dig down an' come up with one hundred fifteen dollars! An' right now, dick-sucker, or I'll put one through yore guts fer you to think about!"

Lee had seen a score of them. Rough cobs. Half-drunk, usually, and hard to hurt in a fight. Doubtful he'd be very quick with the revolver, though.

Strange he'd brace alone, though. Damned if he could see how to stand by and let the fellow savage Bierce.

"*You heard him!*"

Not alone, then.

Lee turned half-way. A tall man, young, no more than a boy. A lank jaw.

"You heard him. You come up with that cash, or we're gonna kill yuh!"

Plain enough. The boy had a cheap pistol stuck in his belt, and would consider the work all but over, having Bierce and his drover friend boxed front and back.

The man standing in front had his way out, his crooked tooth showing as he talked. "You took one hundred and fifteen dollars off my cousin, Ron, on Tuesday. That money warn't his to lose!" He took a long step to Bierce. "Now— *get it up!*" And reached out to take Bierce by the throat.

It would have to be the boy, first. Lee braced himself to make his move.

The man who reached for Bierce shouted. Something shone bright, stuck through and through his outstretched hand. The three-inch steel stick pin, Bierce's pearl soft white against the man's dirt-blackened palm.

The fellow goggled at it for an instant, just beginning to feel the pain, and this time Lee almost caught the move that Bierce made at the lapel of his green velvet coat, saw a silver-mounted double-barrel Derringer instantly in Bierce's hand, and Bierce swinging half-around as fast as a bat-wing door to cover the boy, as well.

"Oh, dear," Bierce said, "a sad pair of hooligans." He looked annoyed, but not angry.

It came to Lee with some force that he had played the fool with this man, taking him for nothing but his mouth. Hadn't even occured to him to look the fellow over for some weapon beneath that green velvet coat of his. Should have paid more attention to Ned Bierce, less to the sausage and eggs, potatoes and pie. He'd said he'd taught Wilde something about trouble.

Lee saw people ducking into store fronts behind them. A man pulled a woman away across the street. Mercy Phillips stared at Bierce, her back against the building wall, her face white as paste.

"First things first," Ned Bierce said, and smiled as Lee took a step back, away from Bierce and the other two. "First, I don't owe you a cent," he said to the man with the crooked tooth. "I don't even know your name."

"Bledsoe," the man said, not yet very frightened by the Derringer.

"Well, Mister Bledsoe, I'd say your quarrel was with your cousin—Ron Crow?"

"He's the one you took the money off, ain't he? An' you owe me my damn money back!" Less and less afraid of the Derringer. Seemed to Lee the fellow was nerving himself to draw.

"You go on to Crow for you money," Bierce said, "if it was yours he played with, and lost for you." He gave each of them a hard look. "So much for that. Now—on to another, more important matter: your clothes. Both of you are dressed more like pigs than men, and you are offenses to the eye of any well-judging man."

142

The shadow of the brim of his straw hat fell dark across Bierce's face. It was hard to see any expression in his eyes.

"Even so, on the matter of your clothes, I would give you the benefit of the doubt. Poverty, and, I suppose, invincible ignorance must be your excuse." As he spoke, Lee saw that the two men's eyes were now following the slow, swaying motion of his hand, the bright sun-glinting steel of the Derringer, as if it were the head of a rattle-snake, ready to strike. The time of their drawing against him had passed. He had them held to stillness.

"Alas, there is a third matter, and the most serious. You have accosted me in the street, in a very vulgar fashion." Here, Bierce suddenly reached out with his free hand and neatly plucked the transfixing stick-pin out of the man's hand. That fellow didn't make a sound, and the tall boy stood as still as before.

"Accosted me in the street, and embarrassed and troubled my luncheon guests." He shook his head, slowly, the shadow of his hat brim swaying across his face. "To bad," he said. "Too bad."

"Mister—" the man with the crooked tooth started to say, but Bierce spoke right over him. "I am going to give you two a choice—a chance to act out a proper apology."

Where in hell were those peacekeeping uniformed police? Lee saw nothing and no one in the street, save a dray left standing, its team restless, where the teamster had jumped off the box and gone for cover. There was a man standing in a shop doorway across the street, watching. Didn't seem likely he intended to interfere.

"You may," Bierce said to the two, "either crawl on your hands and knees down this street and out of sight (you may keep your weapons with you while you do so)—or, if you prefer, I will kill you here."

All said in the most conversational style, as easy as his table-talk had been.

"Now, listen . . ." the man with the bad tooth said, but when Bierce stood silent, listening, he seemed to have no more to say. The fellow's size, his roughness, the large revolver holstered at his belt, all seemed insubstantial as the air. No help to him at all.

Lee could hear his own heart thumping. The sunlight seemed to pulse with it.

Bierce turned a little toward the lanky boy. "Have you something I should listen to—or would you prefer simply to begin your crawling?"

The boy's face was red with anger and humiliation. He was young, Lee thought. Maybe eighteen years old, and likely had always been tough enough to see other boys back away. Lee realized—just before it happened—what would happen, because he saw the tall kid glance at Mercy Phillips, standing up against the building wall, and knew the boy could not do his crawling in her sight.

"Bierce . . ." Lee said, and might have done

some good, but the boy burst out, *"Not even fuckin' God-almighty makes me crawl down a street!"*

"Your choice," Bierce said. And shot him through the heart.

Lee jumped at the blast of the shot, heard in that much louder sound the thump of the .44 short slamming into the kid, and saw the boy, looking suddenly younger, take a long, shaky step backward, both bony hands slowly raised to press against the center of his chest. He steadied himself, his fingers turning slowly red, and turned to look at Lee, or perhaps past him to the woman. Looking for help if ever a man or boy looked for help; then bent suddenly at the knees and sat down awkwardly on the sidewalk planking.

He moved his lips just as if he were speaking, but no breath, no sound came out of him. A red bubble appeared at his right nostril, and clung, bright in the sunshine, as he fell over onto his side. He lay there, blinking his eyes for a moment, as if the daylight troubled him, then left them open, and empty as the street.

"And . . . you?" Bierce said, looking out from under his hat brim at the man with the bad tooth. A wisp of smoke eddied from the Derringer's top barrel.

Lee's heart was pounding as if he'd shot the boy. He regretted every bite of that damn fine lunch.

The man with the bad tooth bent, and then carefully got down onto his hands and knees. He stayed there for a moment, as if that might be all that was required of him. Two, three drops of wet fell to the planks beneath his bowed head. Sweat, or tears.

"Well," Bierce said, "off you go!"

The bad tooth man slowly turned on hands and knees, and slowly made his way to the steps he had thundered up so confidently such a short time ago, and slowly clambered down them to the street, almost losing his balance on the steps, his buttocks high in the air as he descended.

When he reached the street, the man paused again, perhaps hoping this was, after all, only a dream, and he would soon awake. He paused there, his hands and knees in the mud, the big revolver dangling useless from his belt.

"Giddy-up!"

At Bierce's call, the man began to crawl—steady as a baby crossing a carpet—out toward the middle of the street. Lee watched him go, saw others across the street come out to watch, now that the shooting was over. Watched him go, broken as the spring on a dollar watch, with not even the gumption to wait for opening range on Bierce's short-barrelled Derringer, then turn and make a fight of it with the Peacemaker.

That ruined man had no fight left in him. Not now, nor, Lee supposed, ever. It would be boozing and begging, swamping and cleaning the gaboons from now on.

The man reached the middle of the street and paused again, uncertain, Lee supposed, which way to go. There were a number of people watching now. They were all coming out to see.

Lee looked over at the dead body and saw that he had bled out near a quart from his nose, likely drained out; certainly not pumped. Bierce's bullet had taken him square in his heart.

"*Gee!*" Bierce shouted, and the crawling man turned to the left, obedient as any team, and slowly crawled up Altamount Street, through mud and horse manure, while everyone watched.

Better, Lee thought, to be the boy on the boardwalk, shot through, and dead.

"I simply don't know how to apologize to you two," Bierce said, and the Derringer twinkled and was gone beneath the lapel of his bottle green coat. "I am profoundly humiliated, that actions of mine, though in a last week's card game, should have provoked this embarrassment and mess!" He stepped across the boardwalk, offered his arm to Mercy Phillips—and held it cocked until she reached out and took it. Then, gesturing for Lee to come along, he stepped out with the woman as easy as may be.

"A good example of what I was saying," he said. The three of them walked through a last breath of gun powder hanging in the heated air.

"Ugliness (some of this last, I confess, my doing) can be judged by anyone with sensibility."

Lee walked beside Bierce, considering the quickness of that draw, that neat little snatching reach beneath the coat lapel. Quick with that stick-pin, too. Bierce, having polished that item on a snowy handkerchief, was now replacing it in his cravat as he walked and talked. "One might ask oneself whether a battle of angels might be less grim—less *grimy*—than a mortal fight must be. I believe that that would be so. The beauty of the contestants must render the contest more than murder—don't you think?"

"A damaged angel might be an ugly sight," Lee said.

"Yes," Bierce said, thinking about that for a moment. "I catch your drift, and I believe you're right. The dead boy more beautiful than the crawling man. Yes, I do believe you're right." He reached up to pat Lee on the shoulder. "And I've lost my daisy!"

Mercy Phillip's place was on the edge of town. A long walk.

Bierce kept up an easy relaxed run of conversation, asking Lee about the horse-business in Idaho, the Rocky Mountains, his business with Sean McGee.

"It is possible that McGee hired those toughs who attacked you, Lee, (odd how our troubles seem to come in 'two's'—mine as well), if, that is, Sean had cooked his books to cover past profits. Can't think of another reason for it, seeing that the Penny's worn out. Nothing there to kill about. As far as I'm concerned, little enough to kill about in a rich copper mine! Went down in one once—Owen Maxwell's 'Golconda,' —and a wetter, nastier place you never imagined. Air, everything in it stunk of rusty small change."

And he went on, talking about gardens—they were passing some lady's garden at the time—and of the superior appearance of long-cultivated plants.

Lee glanced back, from time to time, during this performance, but saw no policemen on their trail, no one following them at all.

Bierce noticed these backward glances and reached up again to pat Lee's shoulder. "The 'coppers' don't much trouble me," he said. "Do they, Mercy? Don't much trouble either of us. We have our uses to Franklin, Billings, McGee and the rest of them. Their 'coppers' don't much trouble us . . ." And he sauntered along.

Mercy Phillips had little to say. Lee saw her hands trembling as she clutched her reticule, and the handle of her parasol. She had very little to say.

Tender, for a whore, Lee thought. Still, a killing and a crawling didn't exactly settle a man's lunch. Much less a woman's.

The three of them strolled out to the edge of town, past the boardwalks and street signs, where the only passers-by were children just let out from school, and their attendant dogs, frogs, and sling-shots. None of the older boys trotting past them on this or that lane or track paused or had anything to call out to Mercy Phillips. Odd, since whores and madams were fair game for kids' japes in the street. Lee supposed that the boys knew Bierce and shied off because of that—

perhaps had heard of the shooting, already . . .

These lanes were pretty, with hardly any houses on them except here or there a little miner's shack with chickens in the muddy yard and wash out back. Wildflowers lined the way, and the tracks began to peter out to only trails through fields of prairie grass, buzzing with green-hoppers in the heat of sun.

Mercy Phillip's house was big—a two storey clapboard place, like a rich farmer's house. It was painted the color of dairy cream, with shutters painted green. There was a little yard in front, with a swept dirt walk going up it. A lot of white washing on the lines behind this house, sheets and towels blowing gently in what slight breeze there was.

"A handsome place, my dear," Bierce said. "A dove-cot—and all the doves asleep."

They walked up through the yard, up onto the broad front porch. "Now," Bierce said, "I believe I'll take my leave of you two. I could not help, now, but be a reminder to you both of the spoiling of our afternoon."

"Oh, come in, Ned, and have some coffee."

"No, my dear, I won't, though I thank you for the invitation." He shook hands with Lee. "I suppose I dropped my daisy when I stuck that fellow with my pin. Be a lesson to me for robbing Tillbury of his potted flower; stolen goods don't stay!"

"Thank you for that meal," Lee said. "It was prime."

"Glad you enjoyed it," Bierce said, pausing on

the house steps. "I hope you don't think I'm a bully."

"No ordinary bully, Mister Bierce; that's for sure."

Bierce laughed at that, turned and trotted down the steps. His yellow straw hat, his yellow trousers, were very bright in the sunlight.

"Good luck with Sean McGee," he called back. "Try and settle your business with him without trouble—much the best plan." Turned again, and went strolling down the walk and out of the yard.

Lee and Mercy Phillips stood on the porch watching, until, well along the track, Bierce turned and waved to them, then suddenly stooped, picked up what appeared a wildflower, flourished that triumphantly, and went on his way, twirling it in his hand.

"Come on in," Mercy said to Lee, digging in her reticule for the latch key, and unlocking the door with it. "It's too damned hot out here."

"No need," Lee said, "I'll be on my way."

"Oh, don't be a damn fool—come on in."

Lee followed her inside, into coolness, dimness. It was a handsome house, a little out of place here on the edge of Hangfire Hill. Belonged in some more settled town, some more civilized town. High-ceilinged hallway, wide stairs up to the second floor. A fine Turkey carpet in what he could see of the parlor.

"Everyone's asleep," she started to say, and Lee saw her servant, the tall Indian woman, come out of the parlor. The woman looked mad

151

as thunder.

"Why you go eat with that sick-in-head?"

"He's a friend, Ellen—he wouldn't harm me."

"Then why you shake in your hands—he wouldn't harm you?" She hadn't even glanced at Lee.

"There was trouble in town . . ."

"A shooting," Lee said, wondering why Mercy Phillips let her help get so out of hand.

The woman glanced at him then—a savage look out of black and savage eyes. Then she went up and took her mistress's purse and parasol from her. *"You are fool!"* she said, turned and walked across the hall, back into the parlor, carrying the things like trophies.

Mercy Phillips looked at Lee, saw the expression on his face, and laughed. Some color was coming back into her cheeks. "Ellen Early Evening is . . . a friend, as much as a servant, to me. We've been together a long time."

"I see," Lee said.

Mercy Phillips unpinned her hat, hung it on a stand by the door, and walked to the foot of the stairs. "Come up," she said, and Lee climbed the stairs behind her.

"I suppose," she said as they turned the landing, "you imagine us to be Sapphics."

"I guess so," Lee said, "at some time—unless you use a baseball bat to fend her off."

She laughed at that, then turned and put her finger to her lips. "The girls are asleep."

One of them wasn't, though—a plump, dark-skinned breed came ambling down the second floor hall, wrapped in a green silk robe. *"Reba!"* Mercy Phillips said, forgetting to keep her voice down, "if you're heading for the kitchen, you damn well turn around and get back to bed! You're already fat as a pig."

The breed pouted and rolled a cow's eye at Lee, then shrugged, turned, and ambled back the way she came, leaving a drift of attar-of-roses behind her.

"Fat bitch. She doesn't give a damn what she looks like for the clients, as long as she can eat a ton, free!" Mercy opened a door just off the head of the stairs, and Lee followed her in.

He'd expected a richly decorated whore's chamber—horse-hair and plush—but this was nothing of the kind. The walls were painted white, a white-painted wood bedstead, two easy chairs with cloth covers, a dresser, and two vases with flowers in them. Hollyhocks in a yellow vase on the dresser, blue flowers he didn't know in a glass vase by the bed.

"Sit down," she said, and went behind a folding screen. As she talked, Lee heard the rustling, unpinning sounds of her undressing.

"Ellen will bring us some iced tea in a while . . . after a few minutes of being angry. She thinks I should stay clear of Ned Bierce."

"It might be a good idea to do that," Lee said, sat up in the easy chair to slip his jacket off, then tossed it over to drape across the end of the bed.

"Ned is . . . a good friend."

"After today?"

"Yes." Lee heard the material of her dress crumple as she took it off. "Yes, even after today. This isn't the first time Ned Bierce has killed a man in the streets of this town."

"First time in front of you, I'll wager." It was pleasant to talk to an invisible woman, undressing.

"Yes, that's true. But they didn't give Ned much choice."

"Find the crawling man—see what he says about choices."

"You don't know. You don't understand. You've killed men—more than those two hoodlums last night. Ned said you'd shot men. . ."

"I have; he's right. But I never made a man crawl."

Some silken stuff whispered behind the screen.

"Ned is not a well man. He's . . . *touched.* His father, that dreadful old creature—do you know what his father used to do to him? When Ned was five, six years old? He used to chain that little boy to a tree, like a dog. Chain him for days —the neighbors too frightened to do anything about it. He used to chain that little boy, and burn him with a hot iron. 'Burning the sin out of him!' A five-year old boy . . ."

Lee had nothing to say to that.

"Ned is touched. He's an insane man. But he has always been kind to me." She came out from behind the screen, wrapped in a silk dressing gown the color of roses. Her slender ankles and feet were bare. "I wish Ellen would hurry with

154

that tea—she knows how the heat troubles me."
She sat in the easy chair across from Lee's.
"How do you think," she said, "that I got this
house? Did you think I bought it or was able to
borrow the money from Billing's bank to buy
it?"

"I wouldn't know," Lee said. "But I suppose
you earned it the hard way." She threw back her
head and laughed like a girl. The line of her
throat was very fine to see.

" 'The hard way' is right." She stopped laughing, and gave Lee a look. "Ned likes you; I can
tell. Do you know that you're the only man—
except for Sean McGee—who Ned can talk to at
all? Most men are afraid of him because
Franklin, Billings—McGee too—use him and his
father to frighten people, to keep the miners in
line. If their police can't do it, then Ned and his
father do it. That's why he wasn't worried about
the police." She crossed her legs, and Lee saw
smoothness and softness, whiteness whiter than
fresh paint. "Most men, when Ned tries to talk
to them, get frightened, or just sit there with
their mouths open. But you *talked* with him."

"I had four years of very good schooling," Lee
said, "there's nothing much more to me than
that."

"No, Ned likes you, and he's terribly lonely."

"And insane."

"Yes. Ned is as mad as his dreadful father is,
only he always talks of beauty. His father
always talks of God. Don't misunderstand Ned
Bierce; he loves his father and, I suppose, the

155

old man loves Ned, too, in a way."

Lee saw there were tears in this handsome whore's blue eyes. *Friends* . . . A stately whore and a dude gunman mad as a hatter.

"Would you like to know how I got this house?" she said. "*Where in the world is that woman with our tea?*"

"Yes," Lee said, seeing that the shooting was still shaking her. Odd, how women could look at men's true insides, seeing as clear as almighty god might see, and then go sick at the simple sight of the blood and meat of them.

"I came to this town with a man named Dace. Horace Dace. We gambled, dealt faro. And we did well, too. Women dealers weren't so common, then. Horrie was a nice man, and he loved me. He was a brave man, too, and carried a gun, and didn't let anyone harm me." Her blue eyes had gone dull with memory. "We were here in the Hill for just a few months, when Horrie got sick. The cholera. They said it was the cholera. I nursed him . . . I nursed him. But he died.

"You can't know, no man can ever know what it's like to be a woman and alone. With no family, no friends. No money. No man can ever understand what that's like. It's so frightening that you want to die; that you'll do *anything* not to be so frightened . . .

"The woman who owned the house where Horrie died. She must have spoken to a friend of Franklin's. To one of their friends. She . . . she threw me out of her house. There was two

156

dollars owing on the rent, and she threw me out of her house." The blue eyes were dead as painted china, remembering. "I was in the streets for two days and nights. I was very hungry. I went to the church, and the man there refused to help me. I was a gambler and fallen away, and he wouldn't help me.

"I went to a house a woman named Page ran, on Freeman Street. I told her I would do anything. She said she had no place for me. *No place!* With the diseased creatures she sold for two-bits for twenty minutes! No place for me ...

"Then I begged in the streets. I went up to decent women in the streets, and I begged them for something to eat. For doing that, those fine policemen—so out-of-sight when shooting happens—arrested me. And I was put into the jail, in a cell there, and given dreadful stuff to eat. Stuff that made me sick to smell.

Lee saw her hands were shaking.

"I was in there, in that place, for four days. Then Charles Franklin came into the jail, and talked to me in the cell. Now I know, I've been told! that they did it—saw to it I wasn't helped. Charles Franklin had an offer for me. The owners of the Hill wanted a fine resort, and what had been a lady—or something like a lady—to run it. They were tired of crib pleasures.

"You say Ned was cruel to make that fellow crawl? Well, I crawled! I crawled across the cell floor, smeared with dirty water, with my own waste, I crawled to Charley Franklin's feet, and I told him: '*Anything,* I will do *anything.*'"

She was gripping her hands together to still their shaking.

"They took me to the Coffee Club, and let me clean myself and rest. And they fed me.

"That night, they had a . . . dinner, there. And I sat at the table with them. Then, after dinner, they sent the servants away, and a man named Montgomery brought his dog. *Tiger*, they called him, though he wasn't really fierce. A big, gentle dog, really.

"Tod Billings asked me to take off my clothes. I remember my dress was still a little damp, from washing. And I did that. Then they made me sit down on the carpet with the dog."

Her eyes . . . Lee looked away from her.

"They told me what they wanted me to do. And I did it. The poor dog; I don't think he cared for it at all. I did whatever they told me. I did everything.

"There was a man with a photographic camera; they'd had him come all the way from Sioux Falls. He had flash-powder, on a stick, and he took pictures of me, of what I was doing. Many men in this town have seen those pictures."

She looked up and tried to smile at Lee. "And that is how I earned my house. They were all there . . . Sean McGee was there.

"I'm told they planned on doing that again. That sort of dinner . . . with me. I'm told they invited people, some of the governer's friends.

"And it was Ned Bierce who stopped them! My poor mad Ned. He'd heard about it the time

158

before. And he told Charley Franklin that that was too ugly to bear—that if they wanted to see something like that, then, he said, they should 'couple her with an eagle.' That, he told them, would be beautiful. He said he'd kill Charley Franklin, if it was the dog again.''

Still weeping, Mercy Phillips began to laugh. "It all sounds so terribly funny now, in a way." She wiped her eyes with the sleeve of her gown. "And now, I've made a fool of myself. If there's anything men hate, it's women feeling sorry for themselves!" She drew in a deep breath. "I suppose that shooting upset me—I don't usually turn on the watch works." She smiled at Lee. "At least you're still awake."

"Wide awake," Lee said, stood up and went to her, and kissed her on the forehead. Her skin was smooth as glass. As cool as glass.

"Well," she said, and stroked his cheek, "that was a damn good cry. And you do see why Ned Bierce will always be dear to me, has always been dear to me, though he's not much of a lover, poor sweet. He always pays me—feels he should, I suppose—and is never happy when he goes.

"So—that's my sad story. And so I got my house, and made a business out of my misfortune, and found Ellen Early Evening drunk in the street in Shivaree, and so found my second friend. Or she *would* be my friend, if she'd bring us something cool!"

"You might sell out and move out," Lee said.

"I might," she said, and reached up for him.

"Listener." And kissed him on the mouth. "A handsome young man who's not afraid of Ned Bierce or Sean McGee either." She kissed him again, and her tongue slid into his mouth like a snake. "Do you want me to tell you what I did with the dog?" she said. "They cheered and yelled at first, and sat drinking. But after a while, they stood up and came closer, and were quiet . . ."

"Shut up," Lee said, bent, picked her up out of the easy chair, and carried her to the bed.

"What do you think of this meat?" she said, lying there, and pulled the silk wrapper open to show him her breasts. Her breasts were full, and soft, her nipples and their bases soft and brown as a pregnant girl's.

"And what do you think of this meat?" she said in her lady's voice, and brought her knees up and then spread them wide, to show him her secret place. Her nest of hair there was black as the hair on her head, but soft, and neat, and curled like lamb's wool. She had a grown woman's split, deep and long, furl-lipped and wet, red as roses.

When Lee was stripped, standing hard as iron by the bed, Mercy Phillips rolled to him and gripped his cock like a line to life, bent her head to gently bite and lick at it, then tugged him over and onto her, guided him, and finally heaved up with a grunt to socket him home.

"Oh, thank you," she said. "Oh, thank you." She kept her eyes wide open as he labored on

160

her, and only closed them as Lee heard the room door swing open.

He roused himself as if from a drowning pool, turned, and saw the Indian woman standing, expressionless, watching, a tray with glasses, a pitcher of iced tea in her hands. The door stood open behind her.

Mercy felt him going, and clutched him to her. "Oh Jesus! Oh, never mind, never mind, never mind . . . She likes it. Oh. *Oh! She likes it.* She likes to watch me being happy."

Lee half-turned his head again, and saw the Indian woman set the tray down on the dresser. And straighten up to stare him in the eye. (Her own as black, glittering, and depthless as a hawk's eyes, or a snake's.)

She stood, staring down at them, and Lee, resting in a gasping cradle of muscle and wet and cream, felt suddenly that it was both women he was at. Having both, at once. The pleasure of it was so great that he cried out, moaning to the Indian woman even more, perhaps, than to Mercy Phillips as he fucked her, drove deep into her, rode her down.

He thought of nothing at all for a while, until the pleasure became too much to bear. Then he shouted with it, with the pain of it. And it came out of him . . . spurting . . . spurting into her. Into both of them.

When he was finished, his heart still hammering, the muscles of his belly aching, still lying on her, Lee heard the rustle of skirts. He felt the

161

sudden hard hands of the Indian woman on his shoulder, his arm—prying at him, tugging at him. Lee rolled with their grip, heaved himself off the woman beneath him, lay sprawled and weary of joy, watching the tall Cheyenne, bent over Mercy Phillips, cooing and chirping to her as to a child, her long, thin, dark-skinned hands fluttering and soothing over that sighing, dreamy, sperm-sticky, sweat-slick whiteness.

CHAPTER SEVEN

Lee sat with her by moonlight after baths, and introductions to the girls, after a supper in the house's big kitchen (sweet potatoes, fricasseed chicken, dumplings and greens), sat for a time with Mercy on the side porch as the clients came stepping smartly up the front.

"Don't tell me, if you don't want to," she said, swinging in a squeaking rocker beside him, watching the fireflies flicker through the hedges. "Don't tell me if you don't want, but will you be leaving town, or staying?"

"Staying, for a while."

"For a run-out mine?"

"I think the Penny's rich," Lee said. "McGee tried too hard to prove it not so. And there's another thing. After lunch, Bierce said something about going down into a rich mine, something about the *taste* of it. 'Like rusty small change,' he said. Well, the Golden Penny smells just that way; the water running in it tastes that way."

"But didn't you see any veins?"

"No," Lee planted his boots on the porch planking, pushed back a little to keep the swing moving, "but I saw a damn big fall of fresh rock, could have hidden a lot of copper."

"And you'll tell McGee you're sticking— you'll stay in the Hill?"

"I'll stay for a while. I believe I may sell out my share to one of McGee's own. That will make him trot! Maybe to that banker, Billings . . ."

Mercy leaned over and kissed him. "My listener," she said. "If McGee finds out you're playing him, he will certainly have you killed." She stared out into the night. The moon was rising far over the dark country, the dips and swells of the prairie. It looked like the sea, with the moon rising above it. "If you would do what I ask," she said, "you'd leave McGee all his mine, and leave this vile town as well." She turned to look at him. "If you need money, I can give you some money."

"I'd thought you'd want me to stay," Lee said, and kissed her on the nose. "At least for a while."

"I want you to live," Mercy Phillips said. "I want you and Ned Bierce both to live."

"I have no quarrel with him."

"If you have a quarrel with McGee, with him or his friends, then you will surely have a quarrel with Ned Bierce. Do you understand? They will hire him. It's how Ned makes his living—that, and gambling."

Lee smiled. "Then I'll leave McGee guessing

166

as long as I can. Keep the sale quiet. Be time then, to iron out troubles."

She said nothing, for a while, and they sat together on the swing, watching the fire flies.

Then it was late. Time for her to work her girls along, to see they kept catering to the sports.

It was not something Lee cared to see, Mercy playing the whore and madam for a crew of cake-eaters and mine-foremen. Had no wish to sit yarning with them, either, and be admired as Mercy Phillip's fancy-man for the night.

He handed her up off the swing, and kissed her there, in the moonlight shadows. The piano was strumming inside the house. "Lorena."

"I'm older than you by four or five years, I expect," she said.

"I'll take a walk, and brood on it," Lee said, saw her in through the side porch door, went back to the steps, walked down, and went for a stroll by moonlight.

There was, after all, enough to brood on. And not Mercy's extra years.

McGee and The Golden Penny. Lee was sure as he could be that the Penny was rich with copper. The taste of drip water on his tongue and that fresh fall of rock nearly blocking a main tunnel.

And if he were wrong? And went in with McGee on a bust? It would cost him, that was certain sure. Could cost him thousands . . .

But the Penny was no busted flush. Lee felt it in his bones. McGee, for all his poor-mouthing, hadn't *acted* like a businessman in deep trouble. He'd acted like a rich man confident of growing richer. And another thing, a small matter, but it told. The men at the Coffee Club had still treated McGee as an equal. They'd joked about his mine, and called jovial insults from the bar. But they'd not treated him as a bankrupt is treated. They'd treated him as an equal—and maybe more than an equal. And those men knew the worth of every mine on Hangfire Hill.

They'd been running McGee's game with him for Lee's benefit. But hadn't done it well enough.

The Penny was rich—perhaps had been found richer than expected. And that meant that McGee wouldn't share, whatever he might say, whatever he might promise. He *couldn't* cut his fortune in half, forget all his great schemes for the wheat country—and all for a young horse-rancher, come out of the blue to claim his share.

In McGee's place, Lee might not do it either.

Lee strolled a narrow track in the moonlight, heading slightly upslope of the house. He could still hear the piano, hear men laughing, the sounds of pleasure on the cool night air. On either side the track, the prairie grass grew tall as Lee's elbows. Odd how some of the wildflowers showed their colors in the moonlight, and others didn't. Blues and greens showed well enough. Reds didn't show at all. Occurred to Lee that people might do well to have two gardens by their houses: a garden for day, and one for night. Made sense.

He was walking over a mounded shelf of shale —the low ridge of shale being, more than likely, why the track was running here at all—was walking over the broken rock, watching his step, when he thought he heard the soft, dry whir of a rattler.

Lee drew the Bisley Colts, stood still, listening. Listening. Damn fool thing to get snake-bit. And heard only a breeze, risen with the darkness, combing softly through moonlit grass.

Lee scuffed at the rock with his boot a time or two, to scare any rattler off, then holstered the revolver and walked on his way. There was a thin, sweet odor in the air, some night-blooming flower or other.

And there was Bierce. Lee had seen the advantage of a small pistol for a draw. Ned Bierce was eye-blink quick, producing that Derringer. Fast enough so that two roughs, both armed, had not even the option of drawing against him. They'd been covered cold, and the ball just opened. No weapon for range, of course—but what hand gun was? Must have a little glove-leather holster sewn just under his lapel. Lee'd seen a gambler named Smithers, Five-jacks Smithers, who had that arrangement. Doubted if Smithers had been in Bierce's class, though. A neat draw didn't make a killer. Far from it. Far from it. Sometimes not even killing made a man a killer, not deep into his heart and bones.

Bierce was a dangerous man, all the more dangerous because of his quick wit. Lee doubted if he could beat Bierce on the draw. Doubted it.

Not much behind, of course, and might get lucky. Bierce had not *that* much of an edge, little pistol or not.

But he had an edge.

Only two shots, of course. Didn't seem likely to waste them, though. He'd shot that boy through the heart as neatly as a man might slap a beer-drunk fly on a bar room table. And made no fuss about the doing.

In a crowded place, more distance, he might have trouble.

If McGee decided to have Lee killed. If Bierce agreed to do it.

Lee waded through a patch of high grass; the track had about dwindled out. He kicked his way through the tangle, remembering that soft whirring, rattling sound he'd thought he heard. Patch could be crawling with the damn worms.

He supposed that Bierce would take the job, if offered. First, it was Bierce's living; and it would be a tougher living to make if word got out he'd shied away from some fellow known as hard-cased. So, he'd likely do it for that reason. And even more likely do it for another.

Do it because he liked Lee. Because that would make it more difficult for him, sadder for him. So, more enjoyable. Poor, mad fellow.

Lee saw he'd come out above the path back to town, and thought a moment of walking back to the Club. A whiskey and bed would be well enough. No tar-eyed Indian woman staring at him, no sad and lovely lady, lost as the Seven Cities of Cibola. No kisses and regrets. Mercy

Phillips would shrug, and smile, and let it go.

McGee would be back in town tomorrow, or soon after—and Lee'd already had his ashes collected and hauled away. The Club—whiskey and bed—and business tomorrow. Sensible thing.

He climbed down to the path, grass-stains on his tan trousers for sure, then turned up the way, back toward Mercy Phillip's whore house.

A damn fool, perhaps, but would please himself with it. See if he could lock that bedroom door. Had enough of Pocohontas and her staring.

Gravel crunched beneath his boots. Lee heard an owl, hunting over in the brush, utter its soft, trilling scream. Little animals hid close and silent now.

Billings. "Billings and his bank," Mercy had said. One of the movers and shakers in the town. A man, among others, who enjoyed a dog's confusion, attended by a weeping woman. Banker Billings would likely be very willing to buy Lee's half-share in The Golden Penny, very willing, indeed. Then, let the rich vinegaroons and spiders of Hangfire Hill fight it out in their little bottle, and Lee well out of it, with cash in his pocket.

The piano was silent when Lee went around the house to the side porch and swing, and through the door to the back stairs. Passed a man on the stairs. Man with a short gray beard, a little drunk. Fellow nodded at Lee as he went by. Respectable-looking man, Lee thought, getting some of what his wife wouldn't give him.

Lee went into Mercy's room, heard girls trip by, giggling, in the hall, took a drink of water at the wash stand, and sat on the edge of the bed to pull off his boots. The muscles in his back still ached from the beating the two toughs had given him. Lucky they hadn't bashed in his skull.

It was a chore just getting up to take off his clothes; as he was folding his trousers, he heard the piano starting up again downstairs. "Beautiful Dreamer," this time.

Mercy woke him, coming to bed.

"What a pleasant surprise," she said, whispering in his ear. The first, lighter, darkness of dawn was at the window curtains. "What a pleasant surprise," she said. "I thought my handsome young man would have run for the town."

This time, Ellen Early Evening did not come in.

Mercy kept him long in bed through the morning, and held him as firmly through noon and early afternoon, with kisses and sandwiches, pickles and beer. With peace, and remembrance talk on the side porch swing. She had rubbed his bruised back—now something scratched, as well—with ointment in the morning; and swinging on the porch, Lee felt that the last of the soreness was gone. The soreness of the killings with it.

Mercy's mother had been a circus equestrienne, and she told Lee her mother's tale of circusing; of leaping horses through great flaming hoops, lascivious ring masters, bear tamers in love with lady bears.

And in this way, talking like old friends, they spent much of the day.

But Lee still had Tod Billings and his bank at the back of his mind and, by afternoon, Mercy could hold him to her no more. Lee kissed and held her in the parlor hall while two of her girls, come down for coffee, eyed and simpered, passing by.

"Forgive me," she said to him, "for what disappointment I may be to you."

Lee kissed her again; she felt wonderful in his arms—such a contrast of cotton and smooth skin, soft meat and lean, the deeper textures of muscle and bone beneath his hands. She smelled of flesh and flowers.

"There'll be nothing to forgive."

CHAPTER EIGHT

On the long, hot walk back to town, Lee tried a leaf from Ned Bierce's book, bent and plucked a long-stemmed bachelor's button, its little blossom blue as sky, and strolled the prairie paths twirling this in as Bierce-like a fashion as might be. Truth was, it *was* pleasant to have such a pretty at hand.

Lee considered himself, for a few moments, as he walked. Fine young fellow, all in all. Handsome enough. Had his health and strength, for sure. Money enough, too—and about to get more of it. And, to top the cake, might be half in love with a lady of some complication.

"A devil of a fellow," Sean McGee might say. Might add, "and a damn fool."

Lee wished for once he might enjoy some pleasures without fearing them. It seemed a foolish thing to do, to cloud his own joys and luck. Would always be others happy to do that for him.

In which philosophical mood, still swinging the flower, he strolled past some miner's sheds, barked back at a barking dog, and walked onto Hangfire Hill, to ask the location of Tod Billing's bank.

The bank didn't look like much, from outside. Seemed to have been some sort of dry-goods warehouse. Red brick and two-story, flanked by a tin-roofer's shack and a tonsorial parlor on Craigie Street. Looked like damn little, from outside.

Inside, though, it was a bank for sure. Clean and cool, the big room lined with bar-windowed teller's cages. A big man with a chewed ear sat shotgun in the center of the room, and even he wore a three-piece suit. Tod Billings seemed to have strong notions of propriety—at least for the appearance of it. The high-ceilinged room smelled of furniture polish.

Lee waited behind a fat lady to speak to the nearest teller and then to a young man with patent-leather shoes. The young man with the shoes was a real banking article—snotty as a baby with the grippe.

"You wish to see Mister Billings?" Looking as though he could hardly believe Lee was serious.

"That's right."

"And your name again?"

"Lee Morgan."

The young man with shiny shoes seemed to find that a funny name, for he smiled a little, and said, "Wait here, Mister Morgan."

He walked away, each shoe squeaking a

slightly different note, opened a big carved wood door behind the tellers' cages, and went in. He didn't stay long, but came right out again, holding the door half open, and waved to Lee to come on.

The young man ushered Lee through the big door—leaves had been carved into the door panels; it looked like Mexican work—and stayed outside, shutting the door as Lee went in.

If the bank lobby had looked the part, so this room did, and more. Not just the fine office of a bank owner, but the richly appointed office of a very important bank owner. It looked like what pictures Lee had seen of fine library rooms in English country houses. Filled bookcases stood at every wall and where they left space, Lee could see dark walnut paneling, heavy, oiled furniture; and, above the book shelves, glowing in soft colors in lamplight (for the windows were curtained closed) were half a dozen oil paintings as fine as Lee had ever seen.

He saw all this in one sweeping glance and didn't look at it again. The man behind a massive leather-topped desk looked up and smiled.

"Sensible—but a tiny bit slow. That's you, my laddy." Sean McGee was smiling.

"Now, me, I'd have been in to see old Billings, or Steadman, or Franklin—that thief—the very first day I hit the Hill." He beckoned Lee forward. "I'd ask you to have a seat, Lee, but there's really not that much for us to discuss." McGee opened a silver cigar box on the desk, took out a smoke, rolled it in his fingers, clipped the end, and lit up.

"First things first," he said. "On hearing of your little notion of selling out your shares to one of my . . . friends (I was informed of it, by the way, by one of *your* friends—Miss Mercy), I took steps to see that the most likely men were unavailable to you, at least for a time. Billings, now," McGee leaned back in the wide swivel chair, and blew a very neat smoke ring. "Billings, now, has gone out of town a little way to examine a piece of land I offered quite cheap. The old shark loves a bargain! And the others, well, I've seen the most likely of them are engaged for the day."

McGee put the cigar down carefully into a cut glass ashtray. He had stopped smiling. "Your actions," he said, "smack of sharp practice, my young friend. I don't care for sharp practice—not, at least, when it is attempted as a practice on me." He stopped talking, waiting to see if Lee had something to say.

"No comment? No denial?"

This neatly dressed, pot-bellied little man was beginning to anger Lee—though not nearly so much as the thought of Mercy Phillips angered him. He had been made a proper jack-ass of, and by the oldest game there was. Made to spill out his guts by a sad tale, and a wet coozy.

Mister young, handsome, clever Lee Morgan. *As green a horn as ever grew.*

Even now, Lee wondered for a moment if some terrible pressure had been put upon her to spy

180

him out, to lie, to discover what he intended.

McGee read him like a book.

"It's the lady in the case that rankles, isn't it, Morgan?" He picked up his cigar, leaned back and puffed on it. "Not that I blame you for falling for that one; our Mercy's something quite past the ordinary in whores. Did you know she came to town from Saratoga, New York? And what do you think she and her ponce did there? They put on, uh, 'circuses,' I believe the French call them. Our Mercy doing the dirty with some beast or other."

The smell of the cigar was troubling Lee. It seemed a foul smell.

"Did a show for the Club with a dog—if you can believe that. Thought the lady enjoyed it rather more than the pup, come to that. Collected over three thousand dollars from us for one night's work. Not bad business, if you have the stomach for it."

Lee felt a need to shoot Sean McGee to death. A need strong as a steady wind.

Perhaps McGee understood that; perhaps he didn't.

"I went behind your back; you intended to go behind mine. It seems to me there's justice in that. I used that woman only as she offers herself to be used. And I suppose I pity her for that. No pity for you, though, boy. You were and are a damned fool and have gotten just what you deserve! Indeed, somewhat better than you deserve!"

Lee said nothing. But the wind of rage which

had seemed to push steadily at his back, slackened a little.

McGee stood up behind the desk.

"Let's get our business done with, Morgan, once and for all. The Golden Penny *is* a working dig—and there's plenty of copper left in her, but not for you. The Penny's always been mine to run. Mine, alone. I have never had a working partner and I never shall. Never! So, make your mind up to it, boy-oh! I will purchase your shares at a price of two hundred and fifty thousand dollars. Not one single nickel more!"

He stared at Lee, his gray eyes bright.

"That amount," he said. "And no more at all. Take it—or take the consequences."

Lee stood in the center of that handsome room, held his temper, and thought about it.

It was very serious money, more than he would have expected McGee to offer, once he knew, once he'd found out Lee wasn't fooled by his mined-out variety show.

Serious money. And Lee had no doubt McGee meant it, when he'd said, 'or take the consequences.' There'd be no long-drawn-out court case up in Dakota's capital. No legal trickery from one side or the other.

It would be something sooner than that, something final.

Nor did Lee fool himself about shooting the pot-bellied man. There was a great difference in killing some street thug or known gunman. A great difference between that and shooting a Sean McGee to death in a town that he and his friends owned lock, stock, and barrel.

A great difference. A hanging difference.

And it was very serious money. Lee had no doubt McGee would pay what he'd offered. To have Lee done to death would also be no light matter. He might get away with it, to be sure, in his town, in his territory. But it would be no light matter . . .

But for the woman, but for her. *"Forgive me . . . for what disappointment I may be . . ."*

"Keep your money, you little Irish pig," Lee said—and immediately felt better. "And stuff it up your ass."

Lee turned, then, and walked out of the office, and McGee said not a word as he went.

Lee looked at his watch as he left the bank. Just past four o'clock. And no stage out of Hangfire Hill 'till nearly seven. He might, of course, rent a stable plug and try riding out of town. Might do that and, an hour or so afterward, look back down the trail to see five or six roughs riding after, and on better horses.

It would be the stage, then, and late.

I have a good chance, Lee thought, of getting killed here. The notion didn't seem to make the day less beautiful to him, though somewhere, perhaps entering the bank, afraid of looking a fool, he had dropped his wildflower. He thought of Mercy Phillips, then, thought of going out and killing her, burning her fancy house down.

To throw a flower away because you are afraid of looking a fool. As cowardly, in its way, as scuttling out of McGee's town on an evening stage. Would have to lie mighty low 'till then, too. Find some barrel house with a back room, and lie very low. Out of sight of the uniformed police. Out of sight of Bierce, also, if McGee hired him.

The sensible thing to do. Lie low and get out. Then play with Sean McGee through the federal courts in Idaho—and pretend to himself that that way he would win his property.

Sensible thing.

On the other hand, Tod Billings would be back in Hangfire Hill this evening, sure. Or, if not, then those others, Steadman, or Charles Franklin. McGee's friends and competitors. Co-owners of the town.

Lee stretched his legs, walking faster, his boot heels banging on the boardwalk. Get to the Club, and get there quickly. Collect his things and out again.

Time enough, then, to find if he was the hunter, or the hunted.

The superior Yellow was on duty again. Afternoons must be his stints. He opened the door to Lee and gave him a little bow, to boot.

"I'm leaving the Club," Lee said, "see they get my bill ready."

"Won't be any bill, sir. Your charges have been placed on Mister McGee's account."

"Like hell!" Some men at the bar had turned to enjoy this by-play. Lee had the notion that they'd been enjoying his visit considerably— those in the know. *McGee's cow-boy mark, no* doubt. "Get me that damn total!"

The Yellow wasn't fazed. "I certainly am sorry, sir—but I can't do that. Mister Ridell does the accounts, and Mister Ridell don't come in until evening." Bad enough, with the bar-flies smiling at each other in the long mirror behind the bottles, but worse to come. The Yellow took pity on him. Lowered his voice in a confidential way. "Now, sir, Mister McGee is one of the Club *directors*. I believe that Mister Ridell will have to set your charges to Mister McGee's account, because that's the way that Mister McGee wanted it, sir. There's nothing can be done about it . . ." Indicating that Lee would do well to stop making a public ass of himself.

Damn the uppity son-of-a-bitch!

"Forget it, then," Lee said, and walked past the man to the stairs. He heard someone chuckle at the bar as he went by.

In his room, Lee pulled his *portmanteau* out of the closet, tossed it on the bed, opened it, and began to pack. He left the gray trousers hanging; they were ruined, no use taking them, folded the rest of his clothes roughly and stowed them in the case, then he took his razor, soap, and strop from the wash stand (had to go back for his toothbrush—it had fallen behind the mirror) and tossed those in after his clothes.

Nothing else left. Nothing of his, anyway.

He was closing the case, when he saw one of his socks on the carpet, half under the bed. Damned socks seemed to have minds of their own! He picked that up, threw it in, and was about to close and strap the case shut, when he had a notion. He dug under the mess of clothing, found the coils of his whip, and tugged the loops of braided leather free.

Might come in handy . . .

Then one last look around, to see if he'd forgotten anything, looped the whip coils over his shoulder, hoisted the suitcase off the bed, and walked out into the hall, leaving the room door open behind him.

Thought of the maid, then, and put the case down to dig fifty cents out of his vest pocket and go back in to leave that on the high-boy.

Lee was halfway down the stairs when he heard the laugh.

McGee.

For just an instant, Lee thought of going back up those stairs. For only an instant thought of not having to see those grinning faces at the bar.

McGee would be telling them about the Idaho rube and how slow he'd been on the up-take. How much of a fool he'd played with a cozzoning whore.

Lee went on down the stairs.

McGee was at the bar, with six or seven other men. And he seemed merry as a grig and not unhappy to see Lee, either.

Then, it was as if Lee'd dreamed a foul dream only to wake and find it reality.

"And here he is, boys! The lady's man supreme!"

The men at the bar turned to look at Lee. They were all smiling. One of them laughed.

186

"And a fine business head on him, to boot!"

Two of the men laughed at that.

These were men used to having their fun as they were used to having their way. They stood at their mahogany bar, solid, smart, big-bellied, silk-vested, gold watch-chained, their Burnsides and mustaches oiled and crimped like show dogs. Not a man of them carried a pistol.

They didn't need them. Others did their shooting, their beating for them. These were money men. They were as far from that gutter violence as any angel. That distance—from occasional savage pasts—was their great mark of achievement.

They had no fear at all of Lee's Bisley Colts.

"Are you going to be leaving our fair town, then?" McGee said. "I'll be hearing from your attorneys?"

The same two men who had laughed before, laughed again.

Lee set the suitcase down at the foot of the stairs, reached up to seize the handle of the black-snake whip, and slid those slender coils off his shoulder as he stepped forward.

The length of the lash lay for a moment uncoiled its full fifteen feet along the fumed-oak flooring, a dark crimson Turkey carpet.

One of the men said something. The others were silent. The bartender, a fat-faced man with big shoulders, bent down suddenly, reaching under the bar.

Lee drew.

"*Jesus,*" a man said. The bartender froze still

187

as a stone.

The whip handle in his left, the Colt in his right hand, Lee said to the bartender, "Stay just like that, or I'll kill you." Then he leaned back—far back, as if he were a baseball pitcher, drawing back his left arm—then grunted as he snapped his arm and body forward, and sent the great coils of the whip lifting and hissing through the air to cut across the group of men standing at the bar.

They broke under the blow.

Except for McGee.

The whiplash sliced into them, sent them rushing back, their fine coat-cloth slashed, spots of blood showing on their silk vests.

They huddled for an instant, shouting, then yelled and scattered away like quail as Lee sent the whip into them again, caught one man on his uplifted arm, his wrist, and hacked it like a saber.

They ran this way and that, shouting, ducking away.

But McGee stood still, staring at Lee Morgan as if he could kill him with his eyes.

Too damn proud to run.

Lee stepped in closer, poured all of his strength into his left arm, and, standing like a pillar of stone, anchored the whining circling lash of the whip as he brought it back and around, then hauled back to crack the tip of the lash across Sean McGee's face.

It chopped the Irishman's face in half.

Split it almost straight across, cheekbone to

nose to cheekbone. It cut McGee open a half-inch deep along that slender line. There, the bones of McGee's face shone white for an instant, exposed. Then, were drowned in red.

Knocked into the bar by the force of the blow, McGee clutched at the wood, missed it, and fell headlong.

His blood was bright as he crawled on the carpet. A brighter crimson than the Turks had woven into their fine carpet.

Lee was out in the alley—not running, but not loitering either. No question now, who was the hunter, who the hunted. McGee would be able to do as he pleased, now; his friends had felt the whip as well.

But it would, Lee thought, take him a little time. Just time enough to come to himself from the stroke of the lash; time for a doctor, time to send for their uniformed police or, more likely, Bierce. They would want it to look like a fight, at least. Not too official a murder.

Likely, if he could get to the stage, they'd let him go, rather than have passengers, strangers, Well's Fargo people as witnesses. Coaches carried U.S. mail; Federal marshals took dim views of station shootings.

If he could get to the stage. Damn thing wasn't pulling out 'till seven. Not even five o'clock now.

Lee cut down the boardwalk toward Main. Get his ticket, leave the suitcase. Be ready to go.

As he walked, he had a vision of Ned Bierce,

standing between the two roughs, the little pistol twinkling in the sunlight. Might beat him on the draw. *Might.*

That bitch. Lee began to laugh as he hurried along. People looked at him oddly. Truth was, he was missing her, missing her voice. A more frightening thing than being shot at. That would be over with fast, one way or another.

Loving Mercy Phillips was a more tedious proposition. It frightened him.

Lee crossed Main Street, dodged a dray, then a buck-board with a shaggy bearded farmer on it, and made it to the south side. He could see the station sign down the block.

"Forgive me ... for what disappointment ..."

Rolling on a carpet, naked. Doing practice with a dog. McGee and the others laughing, then silent, watching. She lied about all that— lied about everything but her shame.

Lee thought it must be very sad, to be ashamed of the life you led, you enjoyed. She had lied to him, and not lied to him, at the same time.

They had the Concord out at the station stable, were washing it, laying out the harness for the run. Two passengers were already waiting, sitting playing poker at a manger to the side. The usual loafers, some of whom Lee recognized from his arrival days before.

The station master knew Lee's name—likely from hearing of the scrape at Shivaree station— and took his fare money and checked his *portmanteau* with no good grace. "Seven-oh-five," he said, "is when that there coach leaves, Mister, for points south."

Almost two hours, now.

Smartest thing would be to keep still, and stay put.

He could likely join that two-hand poker game; while the time away in that fashion. Catch some sleep, perhaps, up in the hay loft. The two hours would pass. And probably, McGee would let him go, if he didn't stray back out into the town, put himself into the way of trouble. Then, he'd probably be all right, be allowed to scramble out on the stage. McGee might, in time, even consider it all a good bargain. A working half-share in a rich mine, in fair exchange for a whip-cut across the face. Might, in time, consider that a very good bargain. If Lee kept shut, and skedadled.

Lee stood clear of the loafers, the stable hands, and shook out the long lash of the blacksnake whip. He stripped it clean with his fingers, and coiled it over his shoulder. Then he reached down to check the broad blade dagger sheathed in his right boot, then touched the butt of the Bisley Colts.

He might do very well here, if he stayed put, and relied on the threat of the Federal Law— and Well's Fargo's Pinkertons—to keep McGee's people off him, at least while he coached out of Hangfire Hill.

He might do very well—despite the whipping.

On the other hand, Tod Billings would almost certainly come home for supper, from whatever goose chase McGee had sent him on. Should be home this evening, before the Concord was due to pull out. Men of the sort who ran the Hill were not the sort to miss their suppers.

Speaking of which, Lee was feeling hungry himself.

They must do a very neat supper at Tillbury's.

I am a damn fool, and will probably die for it, Lee thought, and walked out of the station stables, past the two-hand poker game, and onto the Main Street boardwalk. There was just time for a quick supper and a visit to banker Billing's house. And minutes enough left then, if he was still breathing, to catch the Concord.

A handsome young daredevil, perfect understanding of the ladies, and a most instant eye to business. *Call me a tripping jackass, for truth.*

Tillbury's was less crowded, the kitchen less frantic than it had been for luncheon the day before. Though it was barely early evening— likely too early for the supper crowd—candles in small glass lanterns flickered wanly at each white-linened table. The garden place was even prettier in sunset light than it had been hot under noon. The greens, the flowers' colors, all softer, clearer, quieter, in cooler light.

No Bohemian family this evening. Two smaller families, though, the women dressed in lawn, white and lacy, with wide-brim picture hats. Some men dining with their friends, store owners, clerks. Cutting into beef-steaks.

Lee ordered venison and mushrooms, peas and

salad, cherry iced-cream for quits. Another Irish girl-waiter, but this one small and plump. White skin. Black brows and hair. Hair was black as Mercy's . . .

The venison came in a red-berry sauce, rich as gravy, after a fifteen minute wait. Lee checked his watch twice. Time enough, though. Time enough. She'd brought the venison first, went back for the dish of peas, the salad, and oil and vinegar cruets. The peas—the first forkful tender and green-popping in Lee's mouth—were out of somebody's garden no more than an hour before. The venison was even better. Lee sliced and chewed, sliced and chewed, and perceived that McCorkle's ranch-cookery at its best had still some refinement lacking. It wasn't only the sauce—both sweet and tart at once (some mustard in there, Lee thought)—but the venison itself, moist, juicy as aged beef.

He was half through the portion and the peas, had not had time for a bite of salad, when he heard the call from across the garden.

"Say . . . Idaho!"

Ned Bierce, resplendent in a turquoise coat and midnight trousers—both apparently cut from velvet—and sporting a Panama-straw in yellow and a malacca cane to match, came striding over, threading through the tables, looking pleased as punch.

He came up to Lee's table, plump rouged face merry in a grin, patted Lee on the shoulder, said, "I suspected youthful appetite would bring you here!" And sat down with a sigh across from

Lee, hung his slender cane on the back of his chair, and set his hat carefully on the table linen in front of him. "Damned hard to get, up here," he said, "a true wedding-ring Panama. Costs like Billy-be-damned, too!"

And all this while Lee should have kicked back his chair, and drawn on him.

Jackass shows his ears again. Perhaps, also, the jackass is fond of the fellow.

Whichever—a serious blunder. Sitting, Bierce could draw his little lapel pistol quick as ever. The Bisley Colts holstered at Lee's side as he sat, would take more doing, likely, too much doing.

Bierce winked. "Silly boy," he said.

"Oh—you ordered the venison! May I?" And leaned forward, picked up Lee's fork, and speared a piece just sliced and already dabbed with sauce.

"Heaven," Bierce said, chewing. "Heaven! I've tried to get the recipe for that berry sauce out of Otto on threat of death. No dice. Otto is like iron when he guards a recipe!"

"Would you care for some peas?" Lee said, watching Bierce's right hand, though since there was a fork in it, and a second piece of venison on that, an instant draw didn't seem likely.

"No," Bierce said, devouring the second bite of venison, "it wouldn't be fair. I know those peas—they're perfect. Otto's people use no salt in the water. They simply steam the peas in plain water; *then,* a touch (and I mean a touch) of vinegar. Of course, you can't taste it. But that's the reason for the perfect crispness. And, no, Otto didn't tell me. One of the kitchen people, a scrubber named Griffin, a colored fellow, spilled the beans (or peas) over drinks at Farley's."

"They're very good," Lee said.

Bierce swallowed his second bite of venison, sighed, and reluctantly returned Lee's fork. "Imagine my distress," he said, "I was having a nap with a free whore you don't know; 'Pipestem,' we call her—and I mean a nap, because the Pipe isn't up for much romping. A lunger. Having my nap, and a kid comes whacking at my door—a really nice, sunny three rooms, a loft I suppose you'd have to call it, but very nice, over Edricson's Feed. (There is a rather constant odor of oats and timothy.) And it appeared that Sean, who has been something of a friend, while suffering under Doctor Bowdry's none-too-gentle attentions, had sent posthaste, for me, his myrmidon."

Bierce leaned foward again, his eyes on the peas. "I wonder if I might have just one bite."

Lee handed the fork over, and Bierce took his bite.

"Perfect. You taste no salt, no country water, no vinegar. Only the perfect juicy green of springtime. Green caviar, is what they are." He handed back the fork. "What is your dessert? No *double entendre* intended."

"Cherry iced-cream."

"Good God almighty," Bierce said. "A man after my own heart." He lolled back in his chair, eyeing the nape of a woman's neck as she sat with her back to him a table away. "Do you see that? That tender hair-wisped stalk they hold their heads on? I simply do not see, and never shall, how the French were able to use a dirty machine to slice those tender napes, those slender necks that supported such gentleness, such sweet silliness. Take Mercy, now—as of course you have. What blossoming generosity in bed, what richness, what beauty. Unfolding in bed like a Japanese fan. And the odors of her, harsh and pungent as near-spoiled meat, delicate as pansy flowers." He looked Lee in the eye. "And this same creature, on her feet, shallow as a pan of water. A liar, and greedy, and sorrowful. She is a most enchanting thing. I did her a favor, once."

Lee said nothing. He watched Bierce's right hand. There was no fork, no food in it now.

"Do I hurt you? Then I'll speak of it no more," Bierce said. "As to McGee, well, you have made him an ugly man. That whip-cut will heal to a thick red line, and split his face forever." Bierce looked very serious. "I don't know that you had to do that," he said. "I realize that Sean took every advantage of you that he could—but with men like McGee, one really doesn't expect more than that! They simply don't have it in them to behave in a civilized fashion. But you, Lee, I expected something better of . . ."

Bierce looked sad, then glanced up at Lee and forced a smile. "And now, here we are, in this . . . adversarial condition. No need, though, for you to look so unhappy. I'm the one's losing a friend. Friends are precious beyond price, don't you think?'' He sat up straighter in his chair. "And I believe that we *would* have been friends, very good friends . . . don't you?''

His right hand vanished. In the same instant it reappeared and the Derringer was in it.

Lee lunged across the table and hit Ned Bierce in the face with all his strength. Then heaved the table up as Bierce went over backward, drew, and fired as Bierce did, heard a something snarl past his ear, leaned further over the fallen table, and fired a second time down through the gunsmoke into Ned Bierce's chest.

It was a killing shot, and Bierce screamed as it struck into him. The sound of the shot rang off the brick wall beside them and hurt Lee's ears. He couldn't remember hearing the first shots at all.

Ned lay half under the table, his right hand empty, the Derringer sparkling on the path. He held his left hand to his face, where Lee had hit him.

Lee threw the Bisley Colts down like trash, wrestled the fallen table away, and knelt by Bierce.

"Ned . . . Ned! *Damn you!*"

Bierce's turquoise coat was ugly at the front. He looked startled out of sleep, and took his hand away from his face. His nose was bleeding.

"What a surprise," he said. His voice sounded as if he were straining, lifting a great weight as he spoke. *"What a surprise."* He looked up at

Lee, soft gray eyes squinting in the fading light. "You naughty boy," he said, "punching at me like some damn gandy-dancer . . ." The weight he was holding appeared to bear him down, and crushed his voice. He closed his eyes for a minute. That appeared to make him easier. With his eyes closed, he said, "Well, this is dying, for sure. It's an odd feeling, I can tell you . . ."

He opened his eyes, and reached up and got hold of Lee's jacket. "Is my nose . . . do I look ugly?"

"No," Lee said, and found that he was weeping over this face-painted killer. "No," he said. "You're the spit and image of Edwin Booth."

Bierce made the face of laughing, but not the sound, then he closed his eyes again, and with them closed, said, "My dreadful father . . . is almost blind. It's been . . . a secret."

"I won't hurt him," Lee said, "I promise you."

But he was talking to the evening air.

Then Otto Tillbury came up to snuff, warty nose and all. He calmed Lee when he grew angry at the frightened people standing, staring, their napkins still tucked into their collars, at Lee, at dead Ned Bierce lying bloody in his velvets.

Otto calmed Lee, saw to it that Bierce was decently covered (with a clean linen tablecloth), and took Lee into his kitchen, after announcing that his present customers had eaten free, and that the restaurant was closed for the night.

(Most proprietors would have stayed open—and raised their prices to the curious.)

In the kitchen—quiet, for once—Otto also took the sum of two-hundred and thirty-two dollars from Lee, promising not only a fine funeral for the dead fellow, but one adorned with every cut flower, of any sort, that could be obtained in the Dakotas.

He offered Lee a shot of whiskey, agreed he'd had no choice in the affray, and then being asked, told Lee the house where banker Tod Billings lived. "The one that *should* be shot," Tillbury said.

Lee shook Otto's hand, thanked him, and went out the kitchen and up the steps to the boardwalk. The walk was crowded there with a group of lookers and questioners.

They looked at him, but no one asked him questions.

Tod Billings had many questions to ask.

Billings was a big, powerful man—or had been powerful when he was younger. His thick hair was yellow-white, his face wrinkled as cotton cloth. He never looked Lee straight in the face all the time they talked.

Billings roamed his rich-appointed parlor, the room's effect somewhat spoiled by the grind and thud of mining, sounding, it seemed, just below the floor. Billings lived high in Hangfire Hill.

Billings questioned, and Lee answered—and used Mathew Dowd's name a time or two. Lee told him of the trouble at the Club; Billings had already heard of McGee's whipping, and pursed his lips and attempted to appear disapproving.

He hadn't heard of Ned Bierce's death, and only said, "Beware the old man." By which, Lee assumed, Billings meant they had a deal—and didn't want it confused by sudden death and estate lawyers.

Lee was right. They had a deal. And, behind the banker's crumpled face, Lee sensed great satisfaction, both as to price and to the impalement of Sean McGee.

The price was agreed at three hundred and fourteen thousand dollars.

Lee was rich.

Rich men are not left by coaches.

Billings sent down to have it held.

So, rich Lee Morgan, his buckskin jacket still stinking of gun powder, still stained at the sleeve where he'd held Ned Bierce's head (Billings had not introduced him to his family), walked down the dark streets of the Hill, down toward Main, to take his seat and ride away.

Catherine Dowd had left him shares in a mine, and he had whipped a clever Irishman, old enough to have been his father, when the man outsmarted him. And he had killed a talkative, half-mad fellow, who went about with a painted face.

From this, a fortune had descended on him. To be sure, Lee'd never been true dirt poor. His mother and the Rifle River ranch had seen to that, and then his work and his inheritance of Catherine Dowd's Spade Bit, past the Gap. Two mothers, was what he'd had, really. More important to him than his father's memory could ever be.

That memory left him nothing but regret—for times missed, things misunderstood, misspoken. Regret for the neatness with which he'd killed Ned Bierce. It appeared there was always a way, whether the man was clever or fast.

There seemed to be always a way, for Frank Leslie's son. But this time, with Bierce, he hadn't enjoyed it. Lee was very grateful that he hadn't enjoyed killing Ned Bierce.

It would have meant that a mad-man had killed a mad-man.

That would have been difficult to bear.

Full dark now, and Lee was glad of it. Cooler, too. Fewer people looking at him, turning their heads as someone pointed him out. Some boys had followed him all the way to Tod Billing's house, and waited outside for him, too. Lee had wanted to go chase them off when he came out, but something in him backed away from further trouble, possibility of a fight. Maybe weapons in it, too. You never knew, with strangers in the street.

He was about fought out, for today.

The street torches blazed and flickered as the light night wind ruffled them or left them alone, so the seeing varied with that wind. Lee smelled the burning pitch-pine, heard the wood's soft seething as he passed them by, walking down Main Street's boardwalks.

Supposed to be only the dead, or the dead-drunk, could sleep in a stagecoach. Well—here was one horse-raiser and mine-share seller would sleep as deep as the dead (or almost) just as soon as he hit those stone-hard horse-hair seats.

A young couple walked past him, going the other way. Fond and spooning, leaning into each other as if both had found the single sure prop of the world. Not all the people of the town cared who'd shot who, or why. Those two surely didn't give a damn, and wouldn't, that some stranger (young, but already reputationed as a troublesome fellow, quick with a weapon in a fight), had come to their hard town, and had whipped a rich man, and killed a complicated man—and now was drifting out ahead of any further trouble.

Thinking of nothing but sleep, was what this troublesome young man was doing. Well, thinking about Mercy Phillips, too, a little.

Four miners, very drunk, were down in the street, laughing, wrestling in the dirt, shoving each other, talking about some saloon girl or trickster whore. No uniformed police in sight to quiet them. No uniformed police at all, that Lee could see, ever since he killed Ned.

Police like that were worse than none at all.

Lee thought he saw the Well's Fargo sign in the shadows across the street. He went down the boardwalk steps, hit the dirt, and started across.

The people, a man and a woman, left the side of the street, came over his way, walked past him as he crossed. The man looked back, and hurried the woman on.

Then Lee looked up, and saw the old man by torch light.

Abraham Bierce, snow-haired, bearded as a prophet, child-chainer, sword-swinger, bulked huge upon the boardwalk. The old man's massive head swung slowly from side to side, his gaze a beetling glare—a dim-sighted, short-visioned stare, Lee saw now. The old man wore a rusty claw-hammer coat, and, criss-crossed at his waist, two revolver belts, each holding a holstered Colt's Dragoon, big butts forward for cross draws.

Looking for the man who'd struck his odd boy in the face, and turned a table over onto him, and shot him to death. A man the old man had seen before—killing.

Lee turned aside as he walked, turned his face slightly away, trying not to attract Bierce's attention. He started down the street at an angle, walking slowly, aiming to cross to the other side again. Face well turned away from the old man, now. Should make it clear.

It must have been his way of walking. Perhaps the Stetson's shape on his head. Every man wears his hat differently.

"You there!"

Lee kept walking, angling slightly away.

"You there!"

The old monster had a voice like the crack of doom.

"I know you, *demon!*" And the sudden rushing stomp of huge boots down the boardwalk, the boardwalk steps.

Lee stopped and spun around in the middle of the street—expecting that the old man would fire at him. No question he had Lee marked and recognized. Wasn't *that* blind.

Lee turned in darkness toward the torchlight, saw the stage-station entrance, and below it, Abraham Bierce (in silhouette, except for that white-foaming beard). Lee saw the white blast blossom and heard, in the thunder of the shot, a soft droning, just above his head. He ducked down and hard to the left, drawing the Bisley Colts as he went.

Bierce fired again. Lee couldn't hear the bullet passing. Near fifty yards, and night. The old man was shooting fairly well, though, short-sighted and all.

Too well.

Lee ducked again—hard to the right, this time —as the old man triggered his third shot. Now, as he heard the man howling some Biblical nasti-ness, Lee thumbed back the Bisley's hammer, raised the revolver, and found Abraham Bierce bulking in torchlight at his front sight.

Lee almost touched the trigger.

Found he couldn't—remembering what he'd said, too late for Ned to hear—turned again, to the sound of the old man's fourth shot, (that droned just past his side) and, still gripping the Bisley, started running down the dark street like a deer.

Abraham Bierce, in foaming rage, came lumbering after him, shooting right hand and left in a very expert way—and would, had the light, or his sight, been slightly better—have broken Lee's back with a bullet.

Might anyway, with luck.

Lee ran down the street, not trying to duck and dodge (as likely duck into a slug as away from one), but running straight on, and faster than he had since he'd grown. Been a fair enough runner as a boy by Rifle River, but had never had the . . . encouragement . . . the old man was providing.

Lee reached the corner of Altamount, turned south, and took that turn leaning at an angle inward, he was running so fast. His hat flew off his head; the old man had fired after him again, but likely it was only the wind of running that had lifted it. Lee was certainly not intending to go back to retrieve it, either way.

He ran that short block, turned right again, and galloped on, his heart thudding, his boots thumping in the dirt. He found he still had the Bisley gripped tight in his fist, and, running, managed to find the moving holster and bucket the weapon. It was during this maneuver, hearing the howls of the old man still toiling along behind him and the blast of another shot (and heard the round go by not five feet off), that Lee began to laugh.

He laughed so hard that he began to stagger as he ran, gasping for breath between whoops of laughter. Torchlights blazed and danced in his vision as he sped along, the old man's roars of rage, his Christian imprecations, fading slightly far behind.

Lee began to worry he'd laugh himself into a cramp, and be unable to move at all 'till Abraham Bierce came stumping up to put a bullet through his head.

"Oh, Ned," Lee gasped, out loud, "You should have seen this!" The thought put him into whoops again, and he had real trouble getting his breath.

A final shot cracked out far behind him as Lee rounded the block of line out in an unsteady run toward the Well's Fargo station. Should take old Bierce a good minute and more to make the distance—and that, with a Concord already held waiting, and a fat tip for speed, should get him clear. Two couples in the street, not shy of distant gunfire, of a hatless man come running, winded, down the street (laughing to beat the band, and staggering in his stride), stood, amused, to watch Lee go hustling by them.

"My money's on this drover," one of the men said, "No matter what's chasing!" and they laughed.

It set Lee off again, hearing that. And, with no dignity at all, but lighter of heart than he had been, he trotted into the stage stables, and, still spluttering some odds and ends of laughter, got the driver to accept a ten dollar gold piece, jump to the box, crack his whip, and spring the team while Lee was still only half inside the rolling coach.

The Concord: passengers outside and in still grumbling over being held almost an hour past the start, passengers in not pleased with the late arrival—a drover, obviously drunk, armed to the teeth, barely able to climb in through the still-open door, swing it shut behind him, and fall roughly into a seat, laughing, not minding who he elbowed or joggled.

It was no more than they had come to expect, out here.

Buckskin Double Edition

HANGFIRE HILL /

CROSSFIRE COUNTRY

CROSSFIRE COUNTRY

Chapter One

In the fall, an old Red-nigger trespassed onto Spade Bit.

Bud Bent, nearly as old as the Indian, saw him riding down from the breaks on a little spotted pony. Bent saw the man was an Indian at more than a half-mile distance; he had the slouching, hump-shouldered way of riding. And when Bent had his Volcanic out of the saddle-bucket, and levered, he was close enough to see the Indian was old, and riding wrapped in a red-stripe Canadian blanket against the cold. Bud looked sharp for other savages—the Redmen were almost done, now, and rotting on reservations, but those few wild bucks still prone to breaking out, drunk and dressed in white man's castoff clothing, were men to beware of.

Bent looked, but the broad sweep of

grassland seared here and there with brown from early-season frosts showed no rider but one. Might be some much higher, trotting the slopes of the Old Man, but Bent doubted it. They'd hardly show their hand by having this old one come fumbling down so near the horse-herds, the Spade Bit hands.

The old Indian was riding as if his ass was sore. Was riding as if all his bones were sore, come to that—and, closer now, Bent saw the old man was worn to a frazzle, his pinched face as seamed and brown as a ragged old pocket wallet. Bent was no Spring chicken himself, however, and had learned long ago that age doesn't necessarily mellow a man. Hadn't, after all, mellowed him.

He kept the Volcanic, cocked, across his saddle-bow, pulled Sally up, and waited for the savage to come on.

It was something to Bent's credit that he rested calm since, as a young boy, he had lost his mother to Blackfeet Indians during a river-stop on the Oregon Trace. The savages, a small bunch led by a war shaman named Bear-eyes, had lifted the woman when she went into the reeds to make water, had taken her away screaming amid gunfire, made a getaway clean, and had, in the next few days, outraged the poor creature, penetrated her with sticks and such, and had, wearying of her, sliced off her breasts and torn her eyes out. She had died then—thankful, no doubt, to go.

All this young Bud, his father and brothers had heard of later—after they'd gotten to Oregon, in fact—in the manner in which such tales became current. The revelations of drunken Blackfeet at wintering Forts, fur trades, squaw trades, and camp gossips.

The Bents, thereafter, in amends perhaps at being just too late getting to the river-bank that hot afternoon with their rifles—the Bents, little Bud among them, though too young to blame, became for a while killers of Indians, and Blackfeet in particular, with a vision of Mrs. Bent's exposure and suffering always in their minds. The Bents killed a number of Blackfeet Indians, men, women, and cubs, until the smallpox did their work for them, and better.

Bud Bent was the last to stop Rednigger hunting, but did so finally, wearying of it. Bear-eyes, in any case, had died, drowned crossing the Snake in 1873.

Something to old Bud's credit, therefore or to the credit of those wearying Indians long ago slain that he did not take the casual opportunity to empty the old Indian's saddle without parley.

Times had changed, of course—though not enough to allow a savage to ride across ranch land and not be injured for it if caught—and, after all, the Redman was old. So was Bud Bent. Some fellow feeling there, perhaps, of aching joints in icy weather.

The Indian, who must have seen Bent as soon as or sooner than Bent had seen him, rode slowly up to him and stopped. Bent saw the old man had a shotgun with a busted stock hanging from his saddle-bow on a length of twine. No other arms apparent.

The Indian had a rheumy and wrinkled eye, but sharp enough. He sat his pony, a rack-ribbed pinto, and very small, and gave Bent a considerable and detailed study.

Then, "*Je cherche Mohr-gonne,*" he said, or something like it.

Bent had heard Canuck French before and grunted Indian, too, but he was not the Idaho wrangler to play any talk but plain American.

"If you're askin' for Lee Morgan, then by God say it in English—an' tell me why the hell I should bother."

The old man gave Bent another hard look. If looks could kill, Bent would have at least felt poorly. Then he slowly said, in English plain enough, though it creaked, "I look . . . for . . . Morgan."

"Do you now?" Bent said. "And what for?"

But the old man had done his talking, apparently satisfied that he'd found the right place at any rate, and content enough to wait Bent out . . . to wait 'till his silence brought him to the man he'd come to see.

The thin-lipped mouth, brown and wrinkled, without much in the way of teeth to obstruct it, clamped tight shut. His gaze drifted away from Bud Bent as if the wrangler had turned to campfire smoke, and the old man sat deeper into his rawhide saddle, ready, it seemed, to sit through the winter.

Bud gave a good try at waiting him out.

An hour and more later, some disgruntled, he led the old man, sitting his saddle slouched and seeming asleep, into the Spade Bit timber camp.

Lee Morgan was there—had come up from headquarters two days before to see what was delaying the cut on corral timbers and shed planks and trough boxes. Had come up and snarled some, then had taken his fine fringed buckskin jacket off, rolled up his shirt sleeves, and taken his turn down in the saw-pit.

He was sitting up on a stack of clean cut posts, taking a cup of hot-coal coffee, when Bent and the Red man came riding in. Bud Bent had known Lee Morgan for more than ten years, ever since a quiet kid with a wicked fast revolver-draw had ridden into the mountains to fetch a vengeance on his own father—and that father a legend among the great killers of the west.

That quiet boy had changed considerably. The blond hair was darker, now—almost brown. The boy's eyes, amber-colored then, had turned darker, too. And harder. Hard as clay-stained granite. The man, a boy no longer, had sized up and filled out. Bigger now than his father had been. And grimly quick with a revolver—the natural fast draw had slicked, smoothed out. Perhaps with not quite the inhuman quickness that had been Buckskin Frank Leslie's gift (and curse) but terribly fast all the same. Terribly fast and with a target-shooter's accuracy at the finish.

"A holy terror in this country, if he chose to be," a sheriff named Berman said about him once, speculating what Lee Morgan might get up to were he not a ranch owner, rich and respectable. And the sheriff had been surely right. But what capabilities, what currents of violence had run in the boy turning man, had been for the most part dammed, suppressed, buried under the endless chores and duties, business and responsibilities that went with high-mountain horse-ranching. Lee Morgan had his anchors buried in the Rocky Mountain pastureland—and, up to two years before, those anchors of duty and labor had kept him a peaceful man, bar some sprees of trouble in San Francisco, some difficulty in the Dakotas.

Up to two years before.

Then, he'd come back from the Dakotas. Rich. Rich on copper shares or some such mining stuff, and happy as a bull buffalo in grassland. Happy for two or three weeks.

The diptheria throat had come to Parker, first, and killed a few kids. Then, in weeks, had moved on down to Grover and struck at the ranches around the small town. Killed another kid or two, an old man named Claude Anstruther, and made some other people sick.

When the disease had run its course in the country, or had seemed to, Lee Morgan's Chinese girl up in Parker had come down with it. At first, she'd rallied fine, and Lee had gone up twice to help her Chinese woman-friend with the nursing. It had not, at first, seemed too serious. S'ien was a strong young woman, no sickly, croupy kid, and she had sand to spare. It had, at first, seemed only some time to spend sick, as most people had to spend, one month or another.

But she got no better. No better at all. Slowly . . . very slowly, the disease began to bring her down, as chasing wolves in deep snow will run and run and weary a stag elk to his end. S'ien got no better. For days, and then weeks, the tissue of corruption stuck in her slender throat, swollen, fiery, leaking its pus and spoiling blood.

After the third week, early one morning, her heart began to labor, to flutter like a wild bird caught in a house, like a bird that's flown in during spring cleaning and can find no open window.

Her friend had sent down-country for Lee to return,—and Lee, who raised horses and loved them, rode a fine mare named Sunshine to death, and so rode up from Grover faster than had ever been done.

He'd left the mare dying on Parker's main

street, and run all the way to the far edge of town, to the cottage he'd given his Chinese girl. A slave girl she'd been, years before, when he'd bought her in San Francisco . . .

S'ien was dying.

The diptheria had run and run her. It had wearied her as through deep snow, until she lay worn to the bone, gasping, her black eyes fever bright. The small heart, red and richly brave, that had beat for her through a childhood, a girlhood of horrors . . . that had thudded with her pleasures in Lee's embrace . . . had tapped as sweetly as a drum in the warmth of his protection, his unspoken love, this small, strong heart now failed and failed.

The Chinese girl, her slender throat on fire, lay still, and pale, and dying. She looked up at Lee from her white bed, with eyes as bright with pleasure as fever. Love joined them in that look, as with a rope of gold.

The doctor in Parker then was a man named Pauly, Amos Pauly. A physician from Baltimore, a large, fat, bulky man, and believed to be a good and scientific doctor. It was thought that he had saved several children from the diptheria that might have otherwise died. He had put a silver tube down into their rotting throats, pushed it deep into the mass, then had himself sucked the matter out, spitting it away in a basin. Had done this until the scraps of membrane, the lumps of pus were cleared way. Then had had the child held gasping, trying to scream, upside down by its feet, while with an India rubber bulb, Doctor Pauly had squirted high-proofed spirits of whiskey up into their raw and bleeding throats.

The children had screamed then right enough, and some said that Pauly had killed Michael Patterson's little girl with that treatment. And so he might have, but he saved six others, and in a manner that no one else cared to attempt.

It was this man that Lee Morgan came for that evening, Morgan cursing himself for ever going back down to the Bit at all while S'ien was sick. Morgan came onto the Paulys' front porch, struck hard at the door, and told Pauly to get his gear and come damn quick.

Pauly now was a tired man and just roused from his dinner. And he was a Southerner as well, born and bred. He came to the door, heard Lee out, and told him civilly enough and to his face that he treated no coloreds, and no yellow people either. He suggested that the girl might do better doctored by her own people in the town.

From what Mrs. Pauly later said—and it was generally, and with good reason, believed—Lee Morgan changed right then from a reasonable man, though occasionally violent, to a person of an altogether diffrent sort.

"Doctor," Mrs. Pauly said he said, "if you don't go get your things and medicines and come with me right now as hard as you can, I am going to kill every human person in your house. I will blow out their brains over your dinner table.''

This said in a voice as light and easy as a preacher's at a wedding.

Mrs. Pauly had crouched silent as a rabbit, and as still, in her dining room doorway, as if by being so still and silent she might prevent Morgan from walking into the room from the entrance hall, having killed her husband, to stand easy while firing his heavy revolver at her children, Jake and little Ivy, who sat in their chairs (Ivy's a high-chair that Mister Ferguson had made special for the Paulys after the doctor had set his leg) who sat in their chairs white in the face, waiting for that man to do what he'd just said he would do.

Doctor Pauly was a man grown and no coward. But he was no fool, either.

"Very well," he said. "Upon that threat, I must come." He gave Lee the look a man might give some poisonous mindless creature, then turned and went to get his medicines.

All that night, the doctor labored over the dying girl, and did not, for hate, hold back any skill. Lee Morgan and his revolver faded to inconsequence in that night-long struggle between Doctor Pauly and the diptheria.

He very nearly saved her.

It was thought, in fact, that he *had* saved her, when morning came. But just as the sun came full up, while Lee bent over her, whispering something to her, the girl's small heart stuttered suddenly and stopped.

Doctor Pauly left the house soon after that —and was likely glad enough to get out, though Morgan had not, apparently, threatened him or his family again. The Chinese woman, a woman named Ma Ling, left with the doctor. Left Lee Morgan alone with his dead girl.

It may have been this incident—shame, or anger over it—it may have been something else altogether, but Amos Pauly moved away from Parker not two months after, he and his family, bag and baggage. It was known that Morgan sent a wrangler to the doctor's house with a bank draft for one thousand dollars just three days after the girl's death. An apology, that great sum must have been.

The doctor tore the draft to bits in front of the wrangler that brought it, then closed the door in his face. Two months later, Amos Pauly was gone from Parker, and never returned. It left the town a good doctor short, since the only other physician was George Fipps, and he was not well thought of.

Lee Morgan left Parker the same day the girl died; he left the town in a rented buckboard. In the back of that rig, wrapped in silk clothes, and lying buried in a glittering drift of ice out of Swenson's ice-house, lay the girl, S'ien.

That was an odd enough thing to hear about, and Parker was a long-nosed town, but no one came out to see it as Lee Morgan tooled the buckboard down a deserted Main Street, and out onto the southern road. A sight to hear about, but felt unwise to view except from behind curtains, or shop shutters.

Early on the next morning, having driven all night, Lee Morgan returned to Spade Bit with his dead girl. He returned a different man than he had been riding out.

He tooled the buckboard up into the pine grove above the headquarters house, took the girl from her shroud of melting ice, and laid her out in her soaked silks on the soft, rich pine straw of the grove. Left her there in tree shadows while he went back down the slope for a pick and shovel, two wool blankets, Catherine Dowd's silver-backed set of comb and brush, a small sheath knife that McCorkle had made from a hoof-rasp (which sharpened into wicked edges), a package, which he made up himself, of sliced cold elk, that morning's biscuits, and a jar of blackberry preserves Mrs. Summers had brought over weeks before.

He carried these things back up to the grave, and then commenced to dig. No man on the Bit went near him. Sid Sefton had seen Lee driving in, saw him rattling up the track at sunrise. Had seen the shadow of the girl under the drift of ice.

Morgan had said nothing to Sid, but drove

on, and, later that morning, dug the girl's grave just the other side of his father's. Near side, Catherine Dowd was buried.

When the grave was dug, Morgan had come down again, gone to the corrals, and roped out a little spotted mare called Dandy. He filled a two-quart canteen with fresh water, tacked the mare out, slung the canteen cord on the saddle horn, and led the horse away, up into the grove.

Men down at headquarters heard a shot some time later from up in the pines, and one of the men, a new hand called Spots (from his array of freckles) was curious enough to go up the next day to see what was what. He found the girl's narrow grave, and, at her feet, the bigger burial of the mare—thought that considerable quaint (he was a merry, joking man) and would have mentioned it for fun had Bud Bent and the others not warned him.

From that day, Lee Morgan tended to be a solemn man. He would still laugh but the laugh was shorter, usually, than it would have been. He was harder in his dealings with other men, and his look weighed upon them and bore them down, as if by that he said: Who are you . . . that I should take much notice of you?

Men, always somewhat wary of him for his reputation, became still more uneasy with him, as if he threatened them just standing, looking at them.

Still, in the ways of his work, nothing much changed. If anything, he worked harder and drove the men harder. There were stories of the hoof-and-mouth sickness coming north out of Mexico, and he organized the ranchers and horse-people around Grover to patrol against that, to ban buying of that sort of southern stock, to swear to cull their herds of any sickly beasts.

This, and the daily work from an hour before sun-rise, to five hours after dark, chousing, berating, timber cutting, hay binding, nursing cankers, blow-flies, breaks, strains, glanders, splints, bird-ear, thrush. Hunting high-country wolves, low-country coyotes and occasional rustlers and thieves. These last, very unlucky men.

This work, and moving, breeding, marketing, grain-feeding, maintaining gear and buildings, and ordering and paying from six to a dozen violent and cranky men (the number varying with the season) appeared sufficient to smother whatever fire burned in Lee Morgan over the girl's death. The work—and the unlucky horse-thieves were sufficient, up to almost a year after S'ien died.

There was a man named Huffman, a miller and feed merchant who had a place on the Big Chicken, well south of the Old Man. This Huffman was a decent respectable sort of a man, thin, scanty-haired, and not tall. He had an illness of fits, however, which may or may not have been the cause of his bad temper.

He had an ungovernable temper which, though it struck him infrequently, was dangerous enough for people to beware of him.

Huffman had killed a man named Roger Parks after a discussion—not really a quarrel—over a price on feed. They had had their disagreement, and nothing much to that, and Parks had walked out of the mill and over to his wagon. Without calling out, or saying a word, Huffman had suddenly rushed out of the mill building, out along the loading dock, and come up behind Parks with a small revolver in his hand. He had shot Roger Parks in the back without warning, and, when Parks fell, bent down to shoot him again in the side of the head; Parks' wife, Betsy, sitting screaming on the wagon seat during this murder.

It was a measure of Huffman's standing in the community, (he had been a selectman at Grover two years running) and a measure as well of the long record of his being law-abiding and a respectable citizen, that he was not taken out and hanged forthwith for this killing, which was a murder and no mistake.

But Huffman was not hanged and, after some in-and-out at the County court, was not even tried over the affair, it being alleged that his illness fits were likely responsible for that violence.

This judgment, of course, left open the possibility of those brain fits causing further danger to anyone who crossed Mister Huffman, and as a result he was treated gently by the mill and feed customers, and even by his friends and family.

Huffman's temper remained uncertain, but for many months after the Parks shooting, the miller did not try to kill anyone else.

Then, one Tuesday morning, Lee Morgan went to the Big Chicken mill with Charley Potts driving wagon, to pick up an order of twenty sacks of fine-ground wheat grain.

Huffman had only ten sacks, the full order not having been freighted down from the Parker spur, and he and Lee stood at his office door and talked about that, Lee regretting a wasted trip and time off work.

Two men, customers, were standing near Lee and Huffman and later swore that not a single angry word passed between them, though Lee was heard to say he wished Huffman had sent some notice that the grain had not arrived. When he said that though, the two men thought that Huffman did not appear to take it amiss.

Lee Morgan and Huffman had their talk, Lee deciding to take a half load back, as better than none, and walking out onto the dock to help Charlie Potts with the loading.

As he left the building, the two men heard Huffman call after him, saying, "I see that you blame me for this . . . !"

Morgan said nothing but went on to where Charlie Potts was already hauling grain sacks and stacking them down in the wagon.

Huffman then went to the door of the building, and called out, "I take no blame for any matter!"

Morgan turned and looked at him but said nothing.

The two men in the building then saw Huffman come back inside, looking odd—"Looked like he was half-asleep . . ." He walked into his office, fumbled at his work-desk, and then, with a small nickel-plated revolver in his hand, went back outside.

Charlie Potts saw Huffman across the dock, saw the pistol in his hand and shouted, "*Lee!*"

As Lee turned, Huffman called out to him, "No man gives me the lie!" and stepped out onto the dock planking raising the small revolver to fire.

Lee Morgan drew and shot Mister Huffman center and low, through his guts.

Huffman's small revolver went off as he fell back, the bullet shining away through the summer trees, and Huffman sat down hard on the dock planking, his white shirt already red above his buckle. "Why . . . you've shot me!" he said, like a child awakening, and looked up at Lee as if expecting some explanation.

Lee Morgan's face was still as dark water in a rain barrel. He cocked his piece again, and firing off-hand, without appearing to take an aim, he let off a second shot that struck Huffman through his jaw and blew the bone at the side of his head away.

A man named Sundersen was sitting his wagon alongside that edge of the dock at the timee, and later swore that he could see near through Huffman's ruined head—the earhole, revealed and pouring blood, seeming to funnel into Huffman's spoiled brain deep enough to come out the other side.

So Sundersen later said, but others said he bent and vomited off his wagon seat and could have seen no such detail.

Then, with revolver-smoke still eddying in the dusty air, Lee had reholstered his Bisley Colt's and stooped to continue loading his horse-grain.

"Jumpin' Jesus," Charlie Potts had said. *"Jumpin' Jesus!"* And he bent again to help him.

This was the Lee Morgan, different and darker than he had been, to whom Bud Bent led the old Indian up at the Spade Bit timber camp.

Morgan, sitting up on a pile of cut rough planks, glanced at them as they rode in, then looked away to say something to a hand named Bob Pete, then to take another drink of his coffee. His flannel shirt was sweated black from buck-sawing.

Bud Bent rode up to him, the old Indian slouching along behind on his rackety paint, and said, "Here's a nigger wants a word with you, Lee. Won't tell me what the fuck it's all about."

"Won't, huh?" Morgan said, and tossed his cup dregs aside and handed the cup to Bob Pete. Then he turned a little as he sat, and laid his still, heavy gaze on the old man.

These two looked at each other for a while, the old Redman seeming sleepy enough to slide off and conk right there. After that short while was over though, the Indian spoke up.

"The small man is killed," he said in his rusty voice.

Lee Morgan sat looking at the old man, and said nothing. Bud Bent, watching, was amused, figuring that Lee was going to get the lesson in outwaiting that the old man had handed him—but not so. After a minute or two, the old Indian said, "Dowd."

Matthew Dowd. A little midget of a man. . . a great cattle-king and financier . . . husband to Catherine. A husband who had lost his wife to a legend, to Lee's father, Buckskin Frank Leslie.

And on her death, for whatever reason, the little man had befriended Lee, had helped him to a fortune, then sold Lee all the land of the Roughs in exchange for that fortune. Had helped him triple the size of Spade Bit.

Dead.

Killed.

A man too small to reach the floor with his feet while sitting in a chair.

Killed.

"Who killed Mister Dowd?" Lee said to the Indian.

"A white chief," the old Indian said, "and another man." He pronounced "another" the way a Frenchman might. *"Anozzer . . ."*

Lee had noted the old man's blanket.

"In Canada?"

"Canada . . . yes!" The Indian nodded vigorously. The old man had a powerful aroma to him; he smelled like a dog fox to the wranglers standing 'round.

Little Matthew Dowd had been a Canadian himself . . . had been up in the Canadian Rockies looking for pastureland on the grand scale. "Fourteen, fifteen thousand acres," he'd said to Lee six months before. "And that owned hard and fast. Ten times that land in leases and rights of way . . ."

A great deal of land for a small man to own, to control. Land all mountainous, all wild. Trappers' land, if anyone's at all.

"I feel," Dowd had said to Lee, both of them out at the yearling corral, looking at the young animals, considering a colt named Pompey as a possible stakes racer, "I feel that those wild lands in Saskatchewan hold much of the future for the cattle business . . . other businesses, as well."

"Furs?"

"No, son," Dowd had said, squinting behind his spectacles across the sun-struck corral (hazed now with kicked-up dust from the yearlings' play), "no, son—the fur trade is

232

a tenth of the trade it was. Good enough for the odd trapper, not for great concerns. Beaver's done in big business." The little man had stood awkwardly, one small shoe-shod foot propped high on the fence's lowest rail (Lee had never seen Dowd at physical ease) stood stiffly propped thus, watching the horses. "Brute land is the ticket," Dowd said. "Great miles and miles of land—for cattle, for timber, for metals."

"Fierce weather further up," Lee said. "Even fiercer than Idaho's."

"The colder the sea, the richer the fishery," the little man said, squinting, smiling up at Lee as if that tall, dangerous fellow, son of the killer who had taken Dowd's wife, were in some odd fashion a true son of Matthew Dowd as well.

"Well, it's your country, after all," Lee had said, as they turned away to walk back to the headquarters house and Sunday dinner.

"No," Dowd said to him, tripping along as well as he could to keep pace with Lee's shortened strides. "No, my country was Victoria—warm and on the sea. Those mountains up there might as well be on the moon, for my familiarity. I have my reports, of course; I mean from my personal knowledge . . ."

They'd had a lamb stew for dinner, an oddity Lee had bought from a herder past the Old Man, butchered-out and cooked by McCorkle in a gentle style. It had tasted well enough, cooked with wild onions, mint and thyme. The lamb, roasted potatoes, and lima beans. Iced cream made with fine-ground vanilla for their dessert.

The little man had enjoyed it and had jokingly offered McCorkle a hundred dollars a week to come and cook for him.

"I hear you got a sissy Frenchman already, making you sauce messes, Mister Dowd," McCorkle said, spooning out the iced cream. "I'll not be taking another man's place, and him a poor foreigner without the gift."

That afternoon, little Dowd had buggied out and off of Spade Bit, sided by a Chicago gunman named Harrison, a pleasant, dangerous fat man, and a friend to Dowd, as well as a servant.

Lee had never seen the little man again—would never see him, now—and had had no word from him, either.

The loss he felt was surprising, Dowd having, after all, been not that much to him . . . had, it was true, done Lee favors, though never to his own loss. Had, it was also true, called Lee "son," and appeared in some sort to mean it. Had, most of all, been someone who had *known* . . . . had known Catherine as his wife, had known Lee's father, had hired that gentle man-killer on as some sort of regulator.

Had *known* them.

Had met S'ien too, once, up in Parker. Had seen Lee walking with her down Corduroy

Street, arm in arm, laughing, just as if she were white, paying no heed to the looks they were getting . . .

Dowd had seen them from his carriage—he was in Parker on railroad shipping business—had had his Jehu pull the horses up, had jumped down into the dust and come trotting over to the boardwalk and up the steps to say "good day" to them both, take the Chinese girl's hand, and bow his snappy little bow to her like a small boy's at a dancing class.

For that notice, that kindness, amid a street of stares—for that small, snappy bow to her, Lee felt some considerable loss.

Some . . . duty.

He sat on the pile of sawn timber, watching the old Indian as the old Indian was watching him.

"Are you a Cree? That your tribe?"

The old man nodded slowly as a turtle might have. Lee saw that the Redman was near done in for all his sturdy dignity, his silences, his scornful airs. It would have been a long, long ride down into this country. A dangerous ride for a Redman . . . And likely no great ease before, in whatever violence had finally come to little Matthew Dowd and killed him.

The old man stunk of campfire smoke, animal grease, and sweat. The pee-stink of an old man was in there, too. But most of all, he smelled of tired.

There'd be time enough to hear how Dowd

235

had died. To decide what to do about it—if anything there was to be done.

"What's your name? The one any man can say?"

The old man pursed his withered lips, deciding whether to answer this personal a question. It took him a while, deciding.

"I called by 'Stone-Made-Shining-by-Water.' "

Lee spoke to Bud Bent. "Take old Pebble here down to headquarters; let him wash in a horse trough if he's a mind, tell McCorkle to feed him, and bunk him down in the stable. Keep him put. I'll be down and talk with him tomorrow."

The hands listening grinned at the sight of Bud Bent in the role of nursemaid to a nasty old Red nigger, nudged each other, and waited to see what Bent would say to that order.

And he might have said plenty, have said that he killed Indians (when they crossed him), and didn't wipe their dirty butts for them no matter what, no matter who said "hop!" Might have said that and had more than enough sand to say it but, annoyed that the other wranglers expected some such noise, decided to disappoint them.

"Shit," he said. And to the Cree, "Come on along with me, you old shite-poke." Then reined his horse around and trotted off, not waiting to see if the old man followed. But Pebble, (known as that from then on) had caught the drift and kicked up his little nag and shambled after, a shriveled satellite to burly old Bent and his fine deep-chested bay.

With Bud and his Indian gone, the wranglers were eager to remark on the matter—on Dowd's death, particularly. Wasn't every day a cattle king worth millions of dollars got himself snuffed like some ragged-ass drover drunk and shot behind a whorehouse.

They would liked to have discussed it, just for a time, before getting back to sawing and stacking (poor work for a horse-man, in any case), but Lee turned a cold face and a colder eye on the first remark or two, and the hands sighed and ambled back to the saw-pit, plank piles, and lumber wagon, reflecting that the Bit was getting to be a fierce horse ranch to work.

The next day at midmorning, Lee rode into headquarters and found the old Indian sitting singing on the cook-shack steps. The song was a toneless Indian thing, but the old man quavered it with considerable feeling and didn't appear abashed at Lee's pulling up his big grey by the steps to listen.

The old Cree, McCorkle later informed Lee, had taken a scrub and wash in a corral horse trough (and had rolled and splashed and spouted with pleasure while doing it). He had also, both the evening before and this morning, eaten enough food for any two young men. "Swallowed like a snake," McCorkle said, "and kept every bit of it down."

Lee sat his grey listening to the old man for a while, then dug into his buckskin jacket pocket for a Grover House cheroot, broke it in half, tossed one half to the old Redskin, and scratched a lucifer on his boot sole to light up the other for himself. Old Pebble broke off his singing abruptly, on neatly catching the tossed butt, and stood up to stand at the grey's shoulder for a light. The old man then sucked on the cigar end like a child with candy drop. Smoke wreathed his head in a moment, appearing to come out of his ears.

Lee swung down off the grey, dropping the reins to ground-tie, and hunkered down beside the old man on the steps, to sit quiet and smoke.

They both had smoked their cigar halves down to stubs and no word spoken, when the old man turned to Lee and said, "You know this Lake Leboarde?" For a moment, Lee didn't understand him; ('*Lac Leboorduh*' it sounded like.) Then, he did.

"It's up in the 'Tooths?' Up in Saskatchewan?"

"Yes!" the old man said, pleased. "It is in *Les Dents*, the Tooth Mountains." He pinched out the last embers of his cigar stub, popped the wad of tabacco into his mouth, chewed and swallowed it. "There is big

238

woods there, in the mountains. Son-of-bitch big woods. Son-of-bitch big mountains!" He burped, mouth wide and innocent. It was a long, satisfying burp, with nothing of civilization in it. Then the old man sat quiet.

Lee sat quiet as well. Bent to grind out his cigar butt, and sat still, content to let the old Indian's story come leaking out as it would.

It was some time before Pebble said anything more. Time enough for them to watch the stable hand, a boy named William Lerfer, drive the manure wagon past them, park it at the stables, get down, and commence shoveling out the dung heap beside the stable's west doorway.

They watched for a while, then the old Indian said, "I old. Old man. I have no strength not to be afraid to die." Lee said nothing, and the old man didn't either, for some time. Then he said, "White Chief Surrey come and argue with the Small Man at Lake Leboarde. Then he go away."

Lee was considerable surprised to see that the old Cree had begun to cry. Indians cried, of course, like any people, and had more reason than most. But it was unusual all the same.

"I no young man," the old Cree said. His cheeks were so deeply scored by weather-lines and wrinkles that the tears perforce ran down these channels. "Too old to fight." He shook his head, looking more shriveled than ever. "Too old to fight." Looked up at Lee.

"For to guide! Small Man pay me for to guide
—not fight!"

Lee said nothing.

"At night, owl call three times. Chief
Surrey come into camp with slave. Then,
Jacques Forge come.

"Small Man come out, speak to them.
Chief Surrey shoot in his heart . . ." Here,
Pebble rubbed his stomach, where Indians
believed the heart to lie, until the fear of
death raised it higher. "Shoot him and say
'You be long time dying for that.' "

No more tears now; the old man had run
out of them.

"I too old to fight," the Cree said. "I crawl
away like old dog. Crawl on belly away like
old dog . . ."

"Harrison," Lee said. "What of Harrison?"

The old man didn't appear to know the
name.

"The fat man, with the round hat and the
big revolver."

The old Cree wiped his nose on his right
wrist, and nodded mournfully. "Mister
Biscuit Man. He was good man—he would
fight." The old man made a clicking sound
with his tongue against his toothless gums.
"That Forge went first into Biscuit Man's
tent—" the Cree made a swift gesture across
his throat. "Kill him. Then, when White
Chief Surrey go—Forge, he put Biscuit Man
into fire. Cook him. Eat him."

Lee took the last with more than a grain of

salt. Indians told the truth as children told it, sometimes. The truth as they wished it to be. He'd heard of cannibals right enough, trappers wintered in and starving . . . Liver-eatin' Johnson, a few others. Likely, though, the old man was making monsters out of murderers to excuse his crawling out of camp when the trouble came.

Surrey . . . and *Jacques Forge*. Seemed to him he'd heard something of a trapper up in Canada named Forge. Someone up in Spring Fork talking about the man . . .

In any case, Lee doubted Pebble was lying about those names. Names were important to Indians.

Surrey . . . and Jacques Forge. Must be some punkin's, to think they could kill Matthew Dowd and step out untouched. Millionaires didn't die quietly. Their funerals were followed by a parade of police and lawyers and politicians. Some punkin's, to murder Matthew Dowd . . . And to cut Harrison's throat for him, in the bargain. That fat Chicago hoodlum had been getting on, but he'd still been tough as a nail-keg and quick with a revolver, for all his fat.

"The Small Man breathed for a day and a night. I saw. I watch. He lie in the grass. Call for water to drink. White Chief is gone . . . and by next time night come, Small Man does not call for water to drink, but he still breathes. Forge stays; he cooks; he eats; then he take big piece of Biscuit Man—" the old man patted his left leg; "—and he go away."

Lee thought that perhaps the old man hadn't lied about Jacques Forge after all.

"I come out from big woods. Get water. But Small Man cannot drink no more. He go 'psss-psss-psss.' " The old man made the sound of whispering.

"He tell me go get Morgan from Spade Bit, in States Idaho, and now I do it. Men do shit to me when I ride down! They throw rock— say *dirty nigger, go away!* But I am no son-of-bitch dog! I come here where Small Man say to come!" Darker color had flushed into the old man's face.

"You did well, Pebble," Lee said. "You are a good Indian."

"Yes, I am! I am a good Cree Indian. I am a Squirrel!"

Lee supposed that was his clan.

"Small Man was taking too long dying, and was unhappy. It was I hit him on his head with a stick so that he died."

"That . . . was well done," Lee said, after a moment.

"I am old but I am still a man," the Indian said.

Lee said nothing more for a while, but sat and thought, the Indian silent beside him. Lee thought about what was to be done on the ranch—the timbering, and building-work, the yearlings to be sold, the hoof-and-mouth theatening from the south.

His small place in Montana, the Rifle

River, could use a visit. A good little place . . . but could use a visit.

"I'll be riding north to Canada," he said to the old man. "You may stay here, if you wish, or come with me." A fool for sure, on a fool's errand . . .

"Not stay!" the Indian said. "Cree is Canada Indians! Not States' Indians! Our father is across the sea!"

"All right, then," Lee said, "we ride together—and likely to set both of our asses in a brace."

The old Cree appeared pleased at this, and smacked his lips to indicate agreement.

"An old fool and a young fool," Lee said. "That seems to suit."

CHAPTER TWO

They rode out the morning of the next day early, at still dark.

Ford, the wiry, pint-sized little tough who stood as Lee's foreman on the place, had not seemed surprised when Lee'd told him he was traveling north. "Want company?" he'd said. "Sefton?" Sid Sefton—black-haired, sleek and handsome, fast with his revolver. Good with the horses, too. Gentle.

"No, I'll take no man. Just go back up with the Cree."

"That old nigger'll be no more use than a fart in a high wind."

"I don't figure on much trouble."

Ford had stood straight in his fancy high-top Texan boots, full five-and-a-half feet in them if he was an inch. He had a face like a fighting rooster's, brown and beaked. Lee had always felt the wrangler had owl-hooted something considerable in his time. "You're a damn liar," Ford said, "but it's your look-out."

"That's right," Lee said. "My look-out. You just take care of the place for me. And for Christ's sake, watch for that hoof-and-mouth!"

In the cool darkness of morning, Lee rose in the headquarters house, empty but for him, dressed, packed his war-bag, buckled on the Bisley Colt's, and slid his broad-bladed dagger down into its sheath in his right boot. "You're a damn liar . . ." Ford had said.

True enough. True enough . . .

Making little Dowd's death his excuse to go killing?

Lee hoped to God that that was not so. He was surely not so much a beast as that . . .

He shouldered his war-bag and walked out onto the back porch to the ice-box, raised the thick oak lid, and fished down into the cold water, the drifting chunks of ice, for the corked stone jug of buttermilk. Opened it, took a long drink of the frigid sour sweetness. Plugged the jug and put it back. And remembered, for an instant, S'ien dead in her glittering shroud of ice.

Never had thought for a moment that she would die . . . it had never occurred to him. Never occurred to him . . .

He walked back through the house, took the big Sharps down from above the fireplace, and went on out the front door. The moon was down . . . no stars at all. Wouldn't be long now, maybe an hour before the sun came up. A chill on the morning, too. Winter on its way . . . would be winter pretty soon up in those Canadian mountains.

That cold, that deep snow, might have kept her looking alive.

Forever . . . ?

The old Cree was sitting his horse just past the porch, waiting.

No rackety little pinto, now; Lee had traded him even for a big-barrelled paint named Patches. A stayer, if not much of a goer. Patches was twice the horse the other had been, but old Pebble had muttered darkly about the trade, and made half-hearted gestures of refusal. Not trusting bargains with whites, apparently. Not even very good bargains.

Lee had intended tacking out his big grey, but the old Indian was already working guide, it seemed. The grey shifted restless at the rail, Lee's Brazos double-rig already cinched on, tacked from noise to tail with Lee's leather. The old man had kept his eyes open, his two days at Spade Bit.

A big brown named Butch was lead-roped behind the Cree's paint, packed up in neat diamond-hitches. The old man appeared to know his business.

Lee went down the steps to his horse, checked the girth—the grey would wind, if he got the chance—then slid the Sharps into the rifle-boot, tied his war-bag on behind the cantle, slipped the reins from the rail, and swung up into the saddle.

Lamps were lit in the bunk-house out past the yearling corral. Hands would be up and doing, heading to the cook-shack for fried steak and eggs, biscuits and molasses. Spade Bit breakfasted big and suppered small.

No need for fare-thee-wells.

"Pebble," Lee said, "you lead the packy," and turned the grey's head north.

Some fare-thee-well, after all. As they jog-trotted out past the tool shed, McCorkle came hot-footing it through the fading dark with a tied up bundle—burlap over oiled paper it felt like, as he handed it up to Lee—and said, "Some chow-chow an' shit for the trail," turned at that, and went hot-footing back up to the path to his cooking. There, at the lamplit door of the cook-shack, Lee saw Charlie Potts and Sid Sefton standing, tin coffee cups in their hands. They raised the cups to him, and Lee saw Sefton grin.

Some fare-thee-well, after all.

Lee lifted his hand to them, and spurred the grey out.

They passed the wire store, with its stink of spoiled grease and rust, then jogged on into the north field, pasture for the brood mares and colts in season. Fallow now, the last of the moonlight frosting the dew-wet grass. The morning smelled clean as new paper—if that paper had been cold pressed out of green pine, green willow, the yellow-brown grass of autumn. Cold pressed and riffled out still cold in the moonlight.

Lee felt a little better than he had felt in some time. Felt as if the weight that had borne down upon him, that had lain across his shoulders like a ox yoke since the girl had died, was easing, was easing just the least little bit.

"I pray to God," Lee said to himself, "that it might be so." He moved his shoulders as a man might under the lessening of a true weight of stone or timber or metal. "I have been sick in grief," he thought, "but I will be getting better." And thought that he would have been better already if he had been man enough to have told her what she meant to him . . . to have married her in church like a Christian person, instead of visiting her like a whore . . . fucking her like a whore. He could have married her, brought her to Spade Bit, and God help the man who had a word to say about it but "congratulations."

Then, she would have been down here, not in Parker, when the diptheria came.

Down here. Back at the house still asleep, likely, curled naked . . . soft ivory. Warm as toast. Would have wished him a quiet farewell last night, hugged him hard enough to break a rib.

Loved him. Quimmed all the lonely out of him, then slept in the circle of his arms. He would be riding out now, thinking only of riding back.

That was the way it would have been.

Oh, yes . . . that was the way it would have been.

The grey was showing his fault—shying at dawn breezes come rustling from the dark. He was a tall, knacky creature, late cut, powerful and fast. But the possession of his balls quite late had left him discontented somewhat, nervous, ill-at-ease at sudden motions, sounds.

Lee let him sidle here and there for a few moments, then slid his crop out of his left boot-top and batted the grey smartly between the ears. The horse crow-hopped, farted, and settled down to its swinging, reaching stride. Lee heard the old Cree's paint break into a fast trot behind him, the pack-horse trotting as well to keep up.

Past the pine grove . . . a good-bye of pine scent, of wind whispers. Then up beyond the north meadow, the horses' withers heaving at the climb. Steep country, every which way a man traveled. Could be steep country for a man sometimes even on the flats.

They nooned in the Roughs. Spade Bit land now, damn few squatters left, and those only shadows of men drifting across the country to hole up in a brake, to slaughter a beef or colt for feasting before starvation swung in again. Drifters who drifted mighty light, who flitted like fair-tale creatures, ducking the weight of Spade Bit's strong arm. The rope ends, the boots—and the whip.

Only a man already more than half mad could dream through a beating at the hands of the wranglers—or worse, a beating at Lee Morgan's hands—and men that mad, that dreamy with drifting, were usually left alone, only shoved on their way.

The Roughs were tamed.

Old Pebble cooked up coffee about as quick as Lee had ever seen it done, and though it wasn't any equal of McCorkle's brew, still a man could drink it and find some satisfaction.

The Cree had cooked it to almost a boil in a cracked tin pot on a handful of busted twigs, caught the loose grounds with the heel of his hand as he poured the hot stuff out into cups as poorly founded as the pot, then had hunkered back with a grunt to drink his portion, toothless jaws champing, wrinkled lips sputtering as he sipped.

The morning had wakened bright as a penny, and now noon was as hot and full of light as autumn permitted, always allowing for the steady, slow, cool flood of air that rolled forever down the granite slopes of the Old Man to flow as steadily as a river might down the mountain pastures, the steep meadows stitched now with every dark yellow, every light brown that dying grass could show.

Lee hunkered as the old Indian did, drank his coffee, and looked out over the country. Nothing to be seen but mountains and mountain country, steeps and slides, the rich borders of willow and dwarf oak. The air and its light were clear as clear water, dotted in one place only by the distant hanging of a hawk. No sounds but the slow wind through the grass . . . the distant whistle of a marmot, doubtless warning any marmot fool of the shadow of that hawk.

Lee found he felt better than he had for some time.

"Say, you Pebble—this is prime coffee."

The old Indian glanced at him, surprised. Such praise of a man (for doing well what he ought to do well) was so white-skinned a thing that he never knew how to reply to it. It occurred to him, by no means for the first time, that a people who could so waste words must be very rich in them and need telegraph wires and heliographs to bear their burden.

Lee finished his coffee, waited impatiently for the old man to finish his, then stood, caught up the grey, mounted and rode, riding as a man does from unpleasantness to pleasure, however odd that seemed in the circumstances. An observer sitting his horse higher on the mountain slope would, even at some distance, have seen that horseman eager to travel, light in the saddle and leaning forward as he rode. That same observer could then have seen how quickly an old

Indian could break a noon-day camp, toss out grounds, tap out the cups, thrust pot and cups under a canvas flap in the pack-horse's diamond hitch, stride bow-legged to a barrel-chested paint, scramble aboard, and kick on out after the white man's lead—the pack horse, shaking it heavy head to shift a late season fly, trailing along at the end of its painter.

As they threaded the brakes through the afternoon stopping once for pissing, Lee and the old Cree passed two small horse-herds, Spade Bit range stock, hard and wiry as any Texas mustangs but showing their breeding, the Morgan blood, the strains of Barb and Thoroughbred, in deep, broad chests, short backs, haunches bunched with muscle. Their legs were fine as foxes.

Two hands, Shoenfeldt and Hardy, were duty wranglers in this section, and Lee would have been happier to have seen hide or hair of them as he and Pebble rode through. Still, they might well be off about their duties—heading strays, shooting wolves . . . doctoring. They might be, and they had better be. The Bit didn't pay top wages to loafers. Time enough when he got back to check the style of Shoenfeldt and Hardy. If these high herds were short-count in the tally, then those two would pay the difference one way or another.

Lee would certainly have liked to have seen at least one of those boys working. Hated to think he'd fallen so in despondency that he'd hire or let Ford hire two lame ducks instead of prime hands.

Still . . . might not be so. Might be away chousing or hunting for the pot. Doctoring.

Be fair . . . that might be so.

The riding now was as rough as maybe—no sooner lunging up a steep, than a break-away would present itself fit to snap a horse's fores. Tangles were dense enough up here to claw a rider half off his mount, then strike him across the face as he straightened. It was harsh, tiring work for men and horses, and, mindful of the Cree's age, Lee would from time to time look behind him to see how old Pebble was faring. Each such look was returned by the old man directly—the pitch-black eyes, sunk deep in wrinkled sockets, as alert, untiring, incurious as ever. So far, the old man was well. How well he would remain after another day's riding, and then a week's riding and then *another* week's riding (and all these retracing the long journey he had already accomplished) was yet to be seen.

Up into the mountains of Canada. A fair piece of fine weather . . . something less than fair in foul. They were riding into winter, and winter coming down to meet them.

That night, at dusk, when the light had become leg-break, Lee pulled the weary grey up beside a stand of fir midway down a long, long ridge of such pines that flanked a mountain called The Grand, standing seventeen miles west of Parker, and looming over the horse-shoe loop of track the Northern Pacific had laid through Pashoka Pass.

Lee could see far below the glimmer of steel where the twin threads went snaking through the gorge. Supposed to have lost a number of dancers and layers to slides and faults, putting the line through. Hard to see how that was much of a shame . . .

Railroads were good for shipping stock. Good for business in general. Difficult to like that machinery, though. Unpleasant (except for the fine Harvey dinners) to ride those close and sweat-smelling cars, all coal smoke, and grease-spotted velvet . . . stranger's voices . . . opinions . . . their farts.

Bad memories for railroading. Perhaps those memories had spoiled these wonders for him. That mad Indian sometimes still loomed in dreams, his eyes bitten out by the whip. A merry little man in a banker's suit stood by smiling, killing Lee's father.

Dreams with the sound of locomotives in them. Gunshots . . .

It seemed to Lee, beside all that, that the railroads, like cavalry sabers, were slicing the country apart, wounding it.

He and the old Cree had ridden near a passenger train late that afternoon, one of those Northern Pacific trains, heading into Parker. They'd met it on wide flat, riding through deep, dry, and dying grass. The first

255

breath of winter's cold seemed to flow across that flat, drifting down from the north.

They hadn't seen the tracks, the grass had been too deep, but the line of telegraph poles and wire marked where the tracks must run. Blackbirds had been perched on the wires in long rows, their feathers ruffling slightly in the wind gusts—the yellow-brown grass bending to those same gusts as if they, too, were feathers, the feathers of the round earth itself.

Lee had dug into his war-bag, pulled the coils of the blacksnake whip free, shook them out, and practiced swinging the long, slim, braided lash, sending the whip loops out to snap off withered blossoms among the sedge with reports as sharp as pistol fire. This whipwork had impressed the Cree as nothing else had, and he watched from the saddle as his paint trotted along, and now and then, at some particularly acute stroke, had stretched his mouth wide open in astonishment, like a child, and covered it with a dark brown, veiny, and wire-muscled hand.

They had seen the train's smoke before they heard its engine, the rumble of its wheels on steel; the wind had carried the sounds away from them as it stretched the stack smoke out to the south, blowing it down almost to the level of the grass.

Lee and the Cree had pulled up, eased their reins for their horses' gazing, and waited to see the monster pass.

It rolled by close enough to smell. Hot steel, coal smoke, dark, friction-heated oil. As the small square windows shuttled past, Lee saw the passengers—the men in small round-brimmed hats, suit coats or shirt sleeves, the women in picture hats, white shirtwaists grey with soot. These people looked at him, and especially at old Pebble, in his dirty Canada blanket, his bent-brimmed deerhide hat, the two red feathers he had stuck in the hatband.

They looked at Lee and the old Indian as if they were something to notice in a raree show. Objects of interest . . . but not much.

It occurred to Lee that the old Rocky Mountain beaver trappers must have been looked at much that same way, sixty, seventy years before, when the toughs from Texas and Kansas—young, cruel, full of piss and vinegar—came driving their cattle through all the wild country, talking of tallies and cash.

And likely, the Blackfeet and Crow had felt the impact of that mildly interested gaze when they, years earlier, had received it from those same mountain men, come singing through the passes with their pack trains, steel traps, and iron barreled Hawkin rifles.

"I am going out," he thought, *and these people are coming in.* His father had had the best of it . . . the best of times in this country. Had died as the old wild ways were dying. What would there have been for Buckskin Frank Leslie, had he lived? Life as an aging

rancher—loved, to be sure—but the prey of every newspaper man, every curiosity seeker, every stupid bully-boy come seeking something from him.

Lee wondered, as he had wondered before, if his father had tried his fastest, that day in the Spade Bit cook-shack. If he had tried his fastest, or had not. Seeing that small madman, perhaps, as a sort of manner of bowing out, a kind of curtain call, as people in theatricals said it.

Of course, he was not the man he had been—must have been slower. Perhaps he had drawn his fastest, perhaps had held his second shot (that used, Lee had heard, to follow the first so fast no listener could tell a space between) through some miscalculation. Perhaps had done his best after all, and had not longed for death . . .

Lee and old Pebble sat their horses, watching the railroad train go by. Three men had been sitting out on the small observation deck behind the caboose, smoking their pipes; they regarded Lee and the Indian gravely as the car drew past but made no motion of greeting. It was as if, Lee, thought, he and the Cree were illustrations in *Harper's Weekly*, and not living men riding living animals. The men looked at them, puffed on their pipes, and were carried steadily past and away—seeming, so deep was the grass, to be carried magically through the prairie, the gleaming tracks lying buried under myriad wind-burned stalks.

A good reason, it seemed to Lee, for those Missouri men to have gone to robbing railroad trains. Difficult to consider a man as only landscape when he was aboard and had a long-barrel .44 presented to your head.

But rob them . . . blow the damn tracks up . . . heat the rails and twist them. All too late. Dancing of cannibal kings to conquer the rifles of the whites. Ghost dancing, and of as little use.

He swung down from the grey, loosed the cinch, heaved the saddle and his war-bag, caught the hobbles the old Indian tossed to him, and knelt to buckle them on. So fine legs this animal had—fair and fine cut. Reaching legs, for a run. Perhaps just a shade too fine for rough steep-country work.

Lee slipped the grey's bridle and slapped the horse's rump as it pranced by. Still some gumption . . .

The deep shade of the firs shadowed off into evening darkness. Far to the west, past Parker, Lee could see the last of sunlight rest red-gold along the peaks of the Rockies. The scent of the firs was rich upon the evening winds that cooled him, stirred the buckskin fringe along his jacket. Lee felt the riding sweat at the seat of his wool trousers grow cool against his butt, the heat of the day below drift away and beyond him into a chilling night.

The old Cree had already started his cook-fire—quick at trail-camp, for all his age. Appeared to be a fine hand at this sort of thing. Too bad little Dowd hadn't taken some young roughs along when he went north. The fat Chicago gunman hadn't been quick enough. This old man, nothing now but a good fire-maker, a packer, a camp cook . . .

Foolish Dowd—to go into enemy country so undefended.

Too many years spent rich, above all danger, all threat. Should have recalled that there was no perfect safety. Might not have cared, though, after Catherine died. Might not have cared enough to have regulators with him up in the north woods, when the killers came down with autumn.

Lee, feeling the riding stiffness now that he was cool (looking to see the ghost outline of the grey, the brighter-hided paint beside him gazing upslope of the firs) walked straight-legged, butt-sprung, to the Cree's fire. The old man was patting cornmeal cakes, forming them in his dirty, thin old hands and pausing now and then to add some canteen water gurgling to the mix. He'd propped a flitch of bacon on a sharp stick beside him and the tin pot was already cooking coffee in the coals.

A handy old Redskin at a campfire, no doubt about that.

Lee'd known worse traveling company. Much worse.

He hunkered across the fire feeling that bent-knee crouch pull the saddle-ache out of the long muscles of his thighs and watched across the fire as the old man worked. Pebble had made an Indian fire, small and pyramidal. Association with whites hadn't spoiled his fire-making, then.

The sparks from some damp twig went sputtering, snapping, popping up into the blackening air between them. Fountaining up, pouring up into the dark in a bright little sudden stream, as if they had a where to go.

The firs were talking where the wind came through. A cool wind, getting colder.

A pine grove, Lee thought, was no bad place to lie, asleep or dead. *Sleep well . . .* he said silently to his dead girl. *Won't be too long, surely. Not too many long years . . . and I'll be with you.*

Nine days later they crossed the line. Lee would never have known it (they were leading the horses across a confounded slope of scrub pine and shale scree) except that old Pebble, puffing and scrambling behind, suddenly called out *"En Canada!"* This was not, at the moment, great news, Lee believing that Canada scree was as likely to crack a horse's cannon as any other uncertain stone.

It had grown colder in the week and more of riding, colder and higher and thicker with trees.

In that week, Lee had seen confirmed his

good opinion of the old Cree as camper. Pebble had shot prairie hen and grouse for the pot with his crack-stocked shotgun and then cooked them near as well as McCorkle might have. He had been infallible at camp sets and horse care. He had kept still and his mouth shut, except for a few odd songs.

And he had kept up despite his age.

It was on one of the grouse shooting occasions that the old Indian had seen Lee fire the Bisley Colt's.

Pebble had sudddenly whipped his paint forward, yipping more like a Comanche than a northern forest Indian, and had stirred and started a covey of grouse up out of the autumn-bitten brush. The birds had exploded left and right, up and sideways as was their style. And rattled as they flew.

The old man had taken a going-away bird with his right barrel, missed with his left.

Lee had drawn and shot that grouse as it rose thirty feet above him and turning. The bird fell like a stone, its feathers shredding into deep brown grass. This sudden shot— most remarkable, even for the lucky shot that it surely was—did not startle the old man as Lee's whip practice had. That doing with the whip, the Cree had regarded as extraordinary. This stunning revolver draw-and-shoot, the accuracy of which surprised Lee himself —it was the odd, unlikely end result of dour months in the hills after S'ien's death . . . endless practice at pine-stobs, cones, twigs—

this the old man considered merely magic. He had seen Lee draw the pistol once before, at a sudden breaking of a high willow branch when they camped above a river whose name the Cree didn't know. It had been dark then, but Lee had turned and drawn the revolver in firelight, and Pebble had seen that action clearly. He saw it, and it was apparent to him that Lee had paid a shaman very well indeed for such a magical and enchanted weapon which leaped at his slightest motion from his holster to his hand.

At that time, of course, the old Cree believed that only the weapon was enchanted—he had, to be sure, seen many superb riflemen, had been more than a fair handler of weapons himself, and had known men very handy with revolvers. But this was in a different category. And now, after this shot that had struck the spinning grouse in midair, Pebble knew that Lee must have spent many many horses for magic bullets as well.

He was impressed by such great wealth and impressed even more that Lee should have used it only to purchase this magical weapon and its bullets and not for more serious gifts, such as the ability to turn into a crow and fly straight to heaven to roost on the arm of God.

Lee dismissed that shot for what it was—a fluke—put the Bisley away (it was a fairly new weapon, shipped from Connecticut in the spring; he had shot the screws out of the previous piece with all his practicing) and thought no more about it.

Thought no more about being in Canada, either.

Time enough for that when they got near *Eustache,* a settlement of trappers and merchants. Woods-runners. Back of beyond, from what little sense he could make out of old Pebble. Dowd had gone out from there to the mountains just west of Banf, a hopeful railroad town, apparently, and to his death.

Time enough, then, to think about being in Canada. Looking ahead, across the scree slope, the scrub pines, seemed to him that Canada looked just as rough and west and high as Idaho did and the slab of Montana they'd had to cross. Never seemed to him there was much to Canada. Furs . . . those Louis Riel people. Damned if he knew why those people were content to keep kissing England's ass—though maybe they'd gotten tired of that by now, had their own parliament or whatever.

The grey was weary of the broken shale; it danced sideways, skittering on the fractured rock. Lee kept a good hold on the reins, hauling the horse half up once when it slipped.

Heavy damned horse.

The announcement of Canada appeared to have inspired the Cree, who now commenced to sing one of his unwieldy songs, all Redskin groans and grunts.

The grey didn't like the noise, either.

"Shut up," Lee said, and Pebble shut.

Past the slope, the country fell away into a creek valley as sudden and deep as any Lee had seen. This narrow gulch was thick with trees as a wolf with fur—thick enough, it looked, to ride across the canyon on, as if it had been a plank floor—but green and fronded. It looked no more a pleasure to travel in truth than the scree slope had been. Busted knees for a rider, it looked like, if those trees grew as close as they looked.

Lee led the grey out to the level shelf, a stretch of rough gravel left by some avalanche, and swung up into the saddle. He waited until Pebble came jobbing up on his paint—the pack-horse, looking worn, head hanging, trotting heavily behind.

Lee pointed out over the creek valley. "We go through that?"

The old Cree, nodding a "no," (nodding was "no," head-wagging was "yes" among the northern tribes) said, "We go all around down there. No through."

Around was damn sure better than through, and Lee waved the old man and his led pack horse into the lead, touched the grey with his spurs to follow.

The trail down—a long, steep, notched cut was more what it was—did indeed wind "all around" as it pitched down alongside the gulch. The day's weather was chill, cloud-mottled; the sun, pale as the moon and hiding. No wind, though. The air, full of the smell of cold stone and pine, was still, heavy, cold as cold water. The sounds of their horses' hooves rang and clattered off the fractured granite that sided them closely as they rode down the side of the mountain. No-Name Mountain, apparently; at least Pebble had no name for it. A measure, Lee supposed, of the wildness, the loneliness of this north country, that great mountains and considerable rivers as well went unnamed, existed only as gigantic accidents, features of a greater wilderness.

Lee heard some small animals chattering, moving through the tangled growth to their right. They had descended below the tops of the trees and staring deep into the growth, Lee saw that the stand of trees was thick enough to crowd out daylight, to drown the light in dense row on row of tight packed trunks and tangled foliage. And these were big trees, not bare-bone lodgepole. Hundreds of them—maybe thousands—all crowded into this narrow, deep cut, not more than three-quarters of a mile long.

Lee reined the grey left, closer to the rock face. Still a good hundred-foot drop to the right, the army of tall pines marching down the mountain beside them. It was possible that Dowd had been chasing the wrong rainbow up here, going for ranch land and mine-metals. Seemed to Lee that timber might have been a better bet. Need to have your stands near good running water, of course, to raft your cut logs out . . .

Certain sure he wouldn't have been the first man to have thought of that, despite all the unnamed mountains, the unnamed rivers. These might not be named, but what was of value was surely marked down on maps in Toronto or wherever. Marked down in New York City, too, and Boston. Money people in fine business offices ordering their sissy secretaries to bring them this paper or that. Odd people . . . but tougher, crueler and harder men in their way than any horn-handed wrangler could ever be.

Lee saw Pebble pull his paint up ahead and climb slowly down from the saddle. Looked to be a sudden dip there—and was; Lee saw the old Indian climb down out of sight, rein-tugging the paint and pack-horse down after him. Lee stepped down and led the grey to follow. The pack horse wasn't going well—stepping as heavy as Barnum's elephant. Hard to understand that. Most packies picked up as a trailing went along and their loads lightened. Hate to think the damn animal was wind-broken. Some humiliating, to raise fine horses and choose out a lunger to travel.

The dip was a sudden drop and slide—at least fifteen feet, and so steep a man could barely keep his footing. Littered with stones the size of steers' heads, among a few dozen more as big as baseballs. The grey came down almost sitting on his rump, eyes walled, in a tattoo of nervous farts. Lee had to skip pretty light to stay clear of the animal's fore-hooves. As he got the grey down to damn-near-level, Lee glanced up to see old Pebble, already a good way down the track, mounted, easy in his saddle, the paint and packy well in hand, gazing back at him with the satisfied expression of a man well finished with a sticky, watching a companion not quite out of it.

Lee tried to mount the grey, but the animal shied away from him and came within a step of the trail-edge, so Lee stepped back and hauled hard on the reins. This god-damned hammer-head was going to kill himself—kill both of them, if he didn't look out!

"Now, hold hard, you son-of-a-bitch!" Lee held the reins with his right hand and hit the grey between the eyes with his left fist. He hit him as hard as he could, and the grey grunted, gave slightly at the knees, and was afterward calmer.

This seen, and the hauling and scrambling that followed, (the level sank at once to another steep dip) appeared to give some satisfaction and amusement to the old Cree, who as a guide had no doubt seen many mossy-horns make fools of themselves in strange country. For one mountain was not at all like another, and a strange country was more different than that, even to the lie of its stones.

Lee persevered, dragged the reluctant grey out of the second pit, and found the true level beside the still-faced Indian. He mounted, blew out a windy breath of relief—nothing but a lightly sprained ankle, a lightly kicked leg to show for it. Damndest little slides he'd seen. Leg-break country, for sure.

"If I find," he said to the old man, "—if I find you took this track for funning, I will peel a strip of that red hide right off you."

Pebble nodded, and smiled a little smile.

Two days later, they saw a man riding.

Lee was leading up the center of a wide valley—an old river valley, it seemed—cut down its center by the stony living grass here, protected from the hard, cold north winds by mountains running north by east along the valley's side. The grass was alive, but not by much. It had the matted, burned look the plains grasses got as winter came down on them. Live enough for the horses' graze, in any case; still light green at the roots.

There were no trees in the mile-wide stretch of the valley, no thicket, no scrub. Only the cold-flattened grass, like an endless muddy carpet, lying creased, humped, folded shallowly here and there in its reach to the rising foothills, the mountains beyond.

Lee had been sewing on a shirt as he rode along—the flannel torn where the sleeve met the shoulder. He was looking to set his last few stitches, doubled at the place the sleeve had torn away, when he noticed the grey carrying his head a little high, and looked up to find the cause.

A speck on the near horizon just to the left of the line of the old river's bed. Moving speck. Moving.

Lee pulled the grey up, jammed shirt, needle, and thread into a saddle bag, and slid off, pulling the big Sharps up and out of its bucket as he went. The grass was deeper than it looked from horseback, came up to his thighs as he stood.

A rider out there. One.

Lee heard the old Cree grunt, climbing down from the paint. It might be a notion to lay the horses down; be a sight harder to spot in this grass.

"Can you see what that fellow is?"

Pebble said nothing for a moment, just making that clicking noise with his tongue. Lee looked back and saw the old man standing on one leg, the other bent-kneed as he scratched an ankle, and squinting hard at the distant rider. He stared for awhile, then curled up a hand as if it were a telescope, and peered through it.

"*Metis.*"

"What?"

"Breed!" Pebble put his fresh-scratched leg

down into the grass, then hunched over, like an Indian riding, and gestured toward the horseman.

Lee supposed the Indian knew what the was talking about—this was his country—but damned if *he* could make out how the man over there was riding, and he a third the old man's age. *"Metis . . ."* Those would be the breed trappers who had followed old Riel—to the gallows, some of them.

No reason this man would cause them trouble. No reason—but still a maybe. Traveling, it was best to avoid strangers; might do you good to meet—more likely do you harm. Only one rider, though. Let him do the running.

"Let's ride." He reached up to slide the Sharps back into its bucket, then climbed onto the grey. Heard Pebble grunt his way aboard the paint. Old man must agree with his conclusion. The grey snorted, tossing his head, still getting the scent of a strange horse on the wind as Lee spurred him out to a canter.

Fellow wouldn't miss such doings, and would most likely haul his freight thereafter.

Lee heard another somewhere as he rode, thunder off to the north, the deep sound rolling and echoing off the mountain slopes at either side of the valley. No black cloud in the sky that he could see, just long silver fish-scales marching over them, moving slowly on a high wind. Must be storming miles and miles away, the sounds of it rolling down the range.

Lee saw the distant horseman more clearly now. He wore a cap instead of a hat, it seemed. Some sort of light-colored duster. Fellow rode a black horse.

He turned that horse's head as Lee watched. Decided to run then instead of coming on to try Lee and the old man out. Might think them road-agents or simply a pair of those wandering creatures that roamed here and there, seeking any sort of trouble or profit, however small.

Turning away. Riding toward the mountains to the south.

Lee didn't fault him for it, either—would, in fact, have skedaddled himself (old Cree, pack-horse, and all) if the rider had had companions.

Behind him, Lee heard the Cree began another of his songs, this one more tuneful than most. Lee assumed the old man was singing about this encounter, likely with considerable embroidery. Give the old man credit, he'd ridden even with Lee right along —better than even, sometimes. And this, doubling back on a long, hard ride he'd already made. A more than tough old man, and a true one, to come so far with Dowd's last words. Reason enough to respect an old man . . . to let him sing. Lee thought he had been wrong to tell the old man to shut up when he sang sometimes.

Let the old man sing. He was earning it. Didn't sound as bad as it had, anyway. Lee supposed he was getting used to it.

That night, they camped by a fast fall a few miles north of the dry-grass valley. They camped high, and went to some trouble getting up to the place; it seemed to Lee to be worth it, to get a down-hill stretch fc. the morning. And there was running water—a good deal better than the drain-hole stuff they'd been drinking and watering the horses with.

The stream (no name to it, as far as Pebble knew) broke down a mountainside through a granite trench nearly blocked at a number of places by fallen slabs of stone as big as houses. These foaming steps of falls and rapids sprayed fountains of icy water where they struck those blocking boulders in a sounding, ringing roar of noise as if to answer the distant thunder that still, at night-fall, echoed through the dark mountains from some far-away storm.

Lee and the Indian made their camp, and the Cree cooked a slumgullion stew rich and hot enough to stoke them against the wind that came whistling down with the falling river.

The stew, and coffee boiled over a heap of sticks Pebble had hoarded and bundled on the packy was followed by a smoke (Lee's last cheroot) sliced in half and shared, as they hunkered. Then, a while later, smoked out and weary, they rolled into buffalo robes, tucking well down out of the wind.

One of the great pleasures of trailing—being fed in empty wilderness, keeping warm in cold winds, lying safe in dangerous country . . .

As fat, tough Harrison had lain in Dowd's lonely camp. Fed . . . warm . . . thinking himself safe. Until the edge of the knife drew smoothly through his throat.

Lee lay beneath the weight of the robe, the dusty, raw-leather stink of buffalo, and thought about seeming safety for a while—then said *"Shit,"* shoved the warm folds of fur aside, sat up to jam on his boots, reached back into the robe for the Bisley Colt's, and stood up.

The cold soaked him like a thrown bucket of water.

It took quite a while to circuit the camp, the lay of the land was so rough, so up and down. It took more time also because Lee moved as quietly as he could over ancient heaps of water-dropped gravel, beds of pounded stone. He used his eyes in the shifting dark—the moon was still hidden behind peaks—used his ears, and his nose as well. It would be an odd man or group of men who didn't have some smelly to them after a long ride.

It took Lee a while to do this, to make his circuit slowly and thoroughly in the dark, the

Colt's ready, the double-edge dagger in his other hand.

Then he checked the horses. Unhappy and hobbled close, butts turned to the ceaseless wind. No sign from them that strangers were about—man or beast.

When satisfied, Lee sat tugging his boots off, looking out absently across the small river struggling in its trough, black as pitch except for those splashing spots where the coming moonlight barely touched it, he heard the old man cough, mutter, and then subside.

Hoped to god the Cree was not going sick on him. It was nothing to contemplate with pleasure, the notion of dragging a sick old man through this country. Likely was nothing but a Cree's comment on the noisiness of white man's quiet scout 'round the camp. Lee got his left boot off (always something of a struggle; a boot clerk in Butte had once told him all men had different-sized feet, right to left) then slid into the buffalo robe with a grunt of contentment. Any bad boys who hadn't found the camp while the fire was up and the stew cooking would be unlikely to find it now, deep full dark.

Buffalo. Had some up here, was told. Woods buffalo, something of that sort. Perhaps a chance for fresh hump . . . sight a fat cow and knock her down. Try that with wild onions . . . a can of tomatoes on the side.

A can of peaches to follow that. Be better than well-enough, that would.

Never a buffalo robe yet didn't stink to high heaven.

Warm, though—no man could say they weren't . . . .

Wolves woke Lee once, just before dawn. He lay listening to that chorus. What was it that vampire Count said in Mister Stoker's book? . . . *"Listen to them—the children of the night."* That was a book-and-a-half, that one was! 'Trash and manure,' Professor Riles would have called it. Poor Riles. Coughed his lungs up . . . that decent, wise man.

There were three wolves singing . . . maybe four, the real hundred-pound, throat-ruff, silver-tip timbers from the sound of them. A clever man could imitate a coyote's call pretty well, put lots of yapping into it; but not the sounds these articles made.

Lee turned deeper into the buffalo robe and seemed to slowly turn deeper still, into sleep. He didn't dream of S'ien.

CHAPTER THREE

Seven days later, in a fine, small fall of snow, they rode into *Eustache*. It had been a hard week's ride.

Pebble was sick, swaying in his saddle like a tired old toper. Had been sick and coughing since the night of the high camp, and had gotten sicker through the mountains. The third day from the damn camp, the old man had fallen off his paint and fainted when he tried to remount. Lee had nursed him through that night, cosying him in the robes, feeding him bits of rabbit and marmot with his fingers (the old man's toothless gums nibbling and sucking much, Lee thought, as a baby's must) and cleaning the old man's manure off his scrawny buttucks, much again, he thought, as he would have done with a little child.

Then—fed, cleaned, swaddled afresh in Lee's only clean shirt, Pebble had seemed to rest easier, to be cooler to the touch. Slept and snored a bit. Muttered, and crapped in Lee's shirt.

Then Lee regretted a dry camp, and wished mightily for that icy, thundering river with its spray-dashed stones. He also began to appreciate a portion of women's labors that had not previously occurred to him. Might be the poor souls spent much of their lives in that sort of cleansing. For himself, he was tempted to shoot the old native through the head and bury him briskly.

That night was the worst night for Lee, though the old man suffered from then on, weak, coughing, querulous. But he guided, and even, in tricky places, attempted to ride first, 'till Lee set him firmly back.

So they rode their seven days—Lee made slowly stronger and stronger by the weather and riding, the vigilance and meager food (shot conies and rabbits, mostly, but a few noosed), and Pebble, baking in fever, withering as he rode, shrinking, collapsing. The long ride down into Idaho had been, it seemed, the old Cree's last great effort. This ride—the long ride back into winter—was, after the misleading vigor of the start, killing him as surely as a Chippeway lance might have in bygone days.

Lee supposed he might have given the old man more rest before the start, perhaps have left him behind altogether. Might have done that, but hadn't. Too full of himself . . . of S'ien. Too busy with thoughts of what vengeance he would (like one of Riles's hero Greeks) wreak upon Dowd's killers.

. Well, he was wreaking, all right. He was handing out death, for a start, to this old man. By carelessness. Yet, once on the trail, it was hard to see how it might have been better to hole up hungry in winter mountains. As it was, they rode through flurries for two days before they found the town. "Found," because the old man was past guiding by then and could only sit his saddle and sing a little, taking deep, gasping breaths to gain the wind to sing again.

Lee found the track to town halfway 'round a mountain to the east of it, questioned Pebble and got weary, closed-eyed nod at this unpromising path, scarcely hoof-beaten, that swung slowly through stands of pine as tall as any Lee had ever seen. These pines—hemlocks, Lee thought—were dark enough green to be black in shadows. Uncomfortable country to travel—so dark, and forested, and narrow on the track, that a man got to wondering just where along his spine a bullet might come knocking to be let in.

They rode that trail safely enough—safely enough for Lee; there was no longer any safety for the old man. He had stopped singing now and Lee had taken him down out of

the saddle poles, but had stopped when he
saw that the old man was weeping for the
shame of it. He had lifted the Cree back up
into his saddle, and run a cord around his
shrunken middle to the saddle-horn and back
to keep him there.

Just so, Lee riding lead and holding a lead
rope, the dying old man after, and the wind-
broken pack-horse lunging behind—just in
that in glorious procession they rode into
Eustache, and were observed by a considerable crowd of the curious.

Lee saw that he was not cut out to play the
Pinkerton, or Secret Agent. All that was
lacking was a brass band.

A considerable crowd, and mostly Indians
by the look of them. Round-faced, slant-eyed,
long black hair done up under caps, and knit
hats, scarfs and bright bits of cloth. They
were noisy, gabbling at each other, calling
out to the old man—his name, Lee supposed,
since they seemed to know him. Kids, most
of them, a few men holding back a bit,
staring. Some rifles among them, but no
threatening.

The old man paid no heed, didn't turn his
head to look or speak to any of the crowd.
Great deal of noise it was getting to be,
though; kids at Lee's stirrups, plucking at the
grey's tack, seeming to be talking horse-talk
with their friends, checking the grey's points
as they trotted alongside.

Lee was getting restive for the sight of at

least one white face—didn't know if he was in Red-town, or if this was it, and *Eustache* an Indian settlement. It was not that he was scared of the Indians—they seemed a peaceful enough bunch, none of the edge to them he'd noticed even with trade Sioux coming up around the Rifle River when he was a boy. Woods Indians, he supposed; harsh once, maybe. Tamed now. Crees . . . *Gros Ventres* . . . Those tribes. Chippeways, he'd heard, were still fierce occasionally.

This *Eustache*, or Indian town or whatever, was a long rutted muddy, bordered each side and close by long, low log houses or shanties, looked rather like the places the Irish laborers used to chop and tack up beside the railroad roundhouse in Parker. Except that here there were no wild flowers stuck in pickle jars at the window sills, but rather countless furs and hides nailed and stretched on every rough log wail. Seemed that furs still were a currency in this part of the Canada mountains, anyway. Stuff stunk some, too. Hard to say that trapping was a pleasure to the nose, not in curing time. Lee had done some trapping himself as a boy for pocket money. Mushrat, small beaver, rabbit and so forth. Had bought a Barlow knife that way—Barlow knife and a harmonica. Up here, however, it looked to be an industry: Bear, beaver, lynx, Fisher-cat, marten. Some white weasel, too, even this early.

Smelling the stink of the hides and not a

few other stinks as well—these Indians appeared to have scant notion of out-house and dug latrines—and still leading his noisy procession, Lee saw his first whites, two men standing on a raised walk off to the left in front of some sort of resort—hotel and saloon, it looked like. And mighty poor doings, it seemed—a nasty buck-sawed shack two stories high, with oil-papered windows, split shake roof mended here and there with patches of tarred canvas and tacked tin. Someone had painted a naked woman on the front wall between her two ground-floor windows. Not much of a painting, but he hadn't left anything out, either. Hair between her legs . . . every damn thing.

Big round titties . . . All in sulphurous yellow paint. Not much face, though. That was a circle with a line and two dots. Couldn't be a powerful lot of ladies in Eustache, not and put up with that sort of advertisement. Ladies in Parker would have had that painting scrubbed off the wall in no time flat.

This damn parade had gone on long enough. Lee turned in his saddle and called out, "Any of you people speak English?"

Sudden silence.

The crowd was quiet as be-damned—appeared startled that Lee had the power of speech at all. Lee heard one of the white men laugh, across the street. He cut a look at them. One a short, fat fellow in a knit

sweater, wore an oiled mustache like a bartender's. The second man was taller, dressed
in a dirty brown suit. He had a long forked
beard, and looked to wear a large revolver
under his coat. An armpit holster, perhaps.

"I can speak that."

It was one of the Indian men, a hard-look-
ing article with a Winchester rifle across his
arm, a white man's shirt and trousers on. He
was standing back at the edge of the crowd,
and didn't appear likely to come closer.

"You know this old man?" Pebble was
sitting silent, his head bowed, his veiny
hands knotted on the saddle horn.

The Indian with the Winchester appeared
to stare at Pebble closely, as if Lee might be
talking about another old man—perhaps one
in Montana, or Ottawa. Then he made up his
mind. "I know him." And said what seemed
to be Pebble's Indian name.

"Well, he's sick. Where's his house?"

The crowd was listening to this exchange
with the greatest interest imaginable,
whether they understood the English or not.
Lee heard one of the white men say something. The other one laughed and called to
someone else.

The Indian with the Winchester considered this question as carefully as he had considered the other, the shifted the rifle to his
other arm while he thought. Then, after the
piece was comfortably settled, said, "Up the
hill," and indicated a wretched little track a

283

few yards further along with a movement of his head. "Under big tree." He gestured with his free hand. *"Big* tree."

"Thank you." Most civil damn proceeding yet.

Lee clicked to the grey and led on out at a walk. This time the crowd didn't go with him. Either their curiosity was satisfied, or they thought more noise impolite now that one of them had seriously spoken with him. Indian ways . . . Indian reasons. They stood quiet, even the little children, and watched him lead the old man away.

Several white people and some in-between were on the hotel porch now to see the sight. Two ugly fat women with them, and those certainly breeds. No greetings or questions were called, but they talked among themselves and stared at the old man as Lee lead him past. They were as nasty a bunch as Lee ever recalled seeing, and they were talking English, though not Idaho English. Sounded a little like Scotchmen to Lee, what little he could make out. *"Some arse-hole Yank . . ."* he did hear.

Lee turned up the track, looking back to see the lead was untangled, the paint moving nicely along. The track was steep and shelved with stones. Slick, too, from a recent rain, and what seemed to be an occasional flood of garbage, waste water, and traces of human shit. Bad footing, and the old man wouldn't survive a fall . . .

Just as Lee looked back, old Pebble raised his head a little, and stared at him. Didn't seem to know him at all. The old man's nose was running like a child's. Now, away from the crowd, Lee could hear Pebble breathing. It sounded like a steam boiler cooking up. The old Cree had the pneumonia in his lungs, there was no doubt of it.

There were several miserable shacks along this steep way, but no one came stooping out to watch Lee pass. He felt eyes on him nonetheless from dark low doorways, from shutterless windows and cracks in siding planks. Two dogs came barking, but silenced and danced away when Lee slid the coils of the blacksnake whip from around his neck.

He looked back after he had passed these places, but no-one had come out to stare after him.

The track got steeper so the grey had to hunch his shoulders to the climb, and Lee looked back again to see that the paint was steady, the pack-horse shuffling along behind. When he turned 'round, Lee saw his big tree—a whopper of a hemlock, easily a hundred feet high, trunk thick enough to carve a cabin out of.

There was a hut or shanty just beneath it, half hidden in the great fringed green-black droop of its foliage. The shack looked no better or worse than any Lee had seen along this way. Guiding, then, had not paid the old man much, if he did much of it. The job with

Dowd must have come as a godsend for the old man . . .

As he drew nearer, Lee saw there'd been some sad attempt at prettying the little place. There was calico at a window—blue cloth with yellow flowers printed on it and the small planks of the narrow front door had been white washed.

Pitiful doings.

What had been in the back of Lee's mind now came to the fore. If there was no family to care for the old man, then what? Lee would have to nurse him if he couldn't get some woman and hire it done. A mighty unpleasant thought, wiping the old man's butt for him for the lord only knew how many more days and nights. Didn't seem to Lee he deserved that sort of duty as a long-term thing.

The grey stepped over a trash heap, snorting at the stink, and Lee reined him in before that paltry whitewashed door. Didn't look tall enough for a human to come in and out of.

No use waiting for bad news—might as well call it up.

"Hello the house!"

Silence.

"Hello the damn house! If anybody's home, get on out . . . I have a sick man here!"

Another patch of silence. Lee shifted his butt on the grey, seeing nothing to do but get down and get the old man down, go inside and start nursing. Likely the poor old savage had already crapped his trousers.

A latch clacked then, and the hut door swung slowly open.

A tall, big-nosed Indian boy came out and stood looking up at Lee, then over to the old man. At that glance, Lee saw it was a woman, not a boy. A girl, rather, and mighty plain even for an Indian. White man's trousers, a dirty checkered shirt, and a green Hudson's Bay blanket over her shoulders. Couldn't be more than fifteen or sixteen or so. Skinny, dark as a nigger, and a nose on her like a mould-board plow.

Pleasant eyes, though. Dark and on a slant, like S'ien's.

The girl stood staring at the old man, and put her hands up to cover her mouth. The death was plain to see in him, and must have shocked her.

"Sorry to bring . . ." But she paid Lee no heed, ran to the paint, and began talking to the old man in a rapid rattling way, patting his hands and plucking at the lashing holding him up in the saddle. Granddaughter, likely.

Lee swung down from the grey, ground-tied him, stooped to draw the knife from his right boot, and went to help her unfasten old Pebble. They worked together for a moment, Lee cutting the cord, the girl pulling the loop free of the old man's waist. Then, though she tried to help, Lee shouldered her aside and reached up to take the old man in his arms as he sagged.

The Indian was light as a child, eyes closed, sounding that same snoring, bubbling breath.

The girl danced nervously before them, leading Lee into the shack, talking Indian to the sick man in a reassuring way. The old man seemed to Lee to hear none of it. Got him home too damn late. Should have holed up, warmed and fed him instead of traveling . . .

The inside of the shack was cleaner than the out, but there was no-one else there. Lee had expected—hoped—to see some older woman, fat and strong, ready to take care of the old man. No such luck. Unless someone was away from home, it was the girl and nobody else to nurse old Pebble and ease his dying.

Lee did not expect to find a doctor in such a settlement as this even if the white section gentled-up some, but there might be a shaman or healing woman who'd look in.

He'd have to find a new guide, too. Lee thought of the Indian who'd spoken English, the one with the Winchester. Had looked tough enough, hadn't appeared a fool . . .

Someone had tacked magazine pictures to the sagging walls—white ladies in fine feathers in Philadelphia and New York. Lee laid the old man down on the shack's only excuse for a bed—a rawhide stretcher on a frame, with mouse-chewed furs piled on it. The old man screwed up his toothless face and cried when Lee laid him down, dreaming he was a babe again, maybe, and being set down out of his mother's arms.

The plain girl bent over Pebble, murmuring and cooing at him, tugging and tucking at the furs to make him more comfortable. Lee was somewhat ashamed at the relief he felt to have the Cree off his hands. Doubtless the girl could manage—and there was cash coming to her.

"Name?" Lee said to her, and pointed at her. He pointed to himself. "Lee," he said. "Name, Lee Morgan." She glanced up at him —a plain thing, and no mistake; not wonderfully clean about her person, either; he could smell her smoky scent.

"I know you," she said, talking pretty much like a Christian, but with some of the French in her speech like the old man had. "My father's father went to tell you about the little man."

Then she appeared to have no more interest in him, and went bustling about the little shack in the way all women seemed to have, getting a nearly clean rag out of a basket, dipping it in a rusty bucket of water, and going back to her grandfather to clean his face and hands, making soft noises to him all the while, then to set the rag aside and start undressing him.

Lee made a move to help her, but she took his arm in a thin, strong grip, and pushed it away, so he stood back and watched her tending Pebble, stripping him buck naked, and washing him like a lady washed her dog, chattering softly, murmuring, scrubbing gently here and there, going to the bucket for more water.

"Tell me where you get your water; I'll fetch some."

She paid him no mind, just went on with her business. It appeared to Lee that this girl was good enough of nurse. Good enough to see the old man out, certainly, and that was all that was required. He began to wish a bath for himself—hot, to clear the trail dirt off. Some whiskey, and perhaps a whore, if he could find one not actively poxed and just handsome enough to look at. Seemed to him he'd done his duty, bringing the old man home, seeing him settled in.

"Old fellow did a good job," he said. "Made a damn hard ride. I have some money due him. Suppose I should give it to you . . ." The big-nose girl gave him a glance, and went back to work. She had the old Cree's legs up like an infant's, and was mopping gently between.

Lee dug into his jacket pocket for his purse and took a gold ten-dollar piece out of it. He held it out to her, and she set the old man's leg down, draped the rag neatly over his ankle, turned to Lee and took it in one dark, narrow hand. She was tall, for a girl, but bone thin. Her throat was not much bigger around than his forearm.

She looked at the gold piece as if she hadn't seen many.

"That was for guiding me," Lee said, felt like a fool, dug for another ten and handed it over. "I suppose your grandad never got paid for doing for Mister Dowd. That is for that work."

It took no mind-reader to see the girl had never held twenty dollars in her hand at once her whole life long.

"American dollars," she said.

"Good as any up here."

"Yes." She gave him as long a look as she'd given the money. It made Lee uncomfortable.

"He had it coming. He earned it."

"Yes," she said. "I went to Roman Catholic school with Father Pirenne. *Pere Pirenne,*" she said in French, as if that would help him understand. "I went two years."

Damned if Lee could see what that had to do with the twenty dollars, but he nodded pleasantly. Not surprising she was proud of her schooling—hell, he was fairly proud of his, a sight more than two years, and at a damn fine academy, too.

"O.K.?" she said. "O.K. to give five dollars of this to Father Pirenne?"

"Your grandfather earned it; it's all right with him, it's none of my business."

The Big-nose girl nodded, and went to a splintery shelf to drop the two coins into a

291

small rusty can. There was enough left of the label for Lee to see it had held tomatoes. Girl was some trusting or had decided Lee was too rich to need to steal, to have let him see where she was putting the money.

Time to go. The old Cree had commenced to mutter on the cot, drawing slow, noisy breaths.

"What's your name?" Seemed only courteous.

"Charity," the girl said. At first, Lee thought she was being clever, making fun of the rich white man come to call—must have taken her Indian name away and given her that one.

"Pretty name," Lee said, anxious and more anxious to be gone out of this smelly little hutch. He'd done the proper. "Say," he said, "your grandfather being sick, would you know of a man who could guide for me—maybe out to Lake LaBoarde?"

The Big-nose girl, Miss Charity, stood staring at him as if he'd suddenly started talking Swedish (it was a habit these woods Indians seemed to have when asked any question at all). She looked at Lee for a fair amount of time, then shook her head up and down—"no."

"There's an Indian—fellow with a Winchester rifle—looks handy enough . . ."

A swift look of contempt on the girl's face. "Simon Fat-tongue," she said. "He is a thief."

Unfortunate news. Still, there was not much for a thief to steal out in the deep woods, and the fellow'd looked handy—maybe hard enough to be some help . . .

"He tells all secrets," the girl nodded, as if that clinched it. And maybe it did. Had to find some sort of guide, though—that, or wander the mountains following some fool's map. Something to think about and no use thinking about it here. A wash-tub full of hot water was calling. A wet tub, a wet glass, a wet cunt all calling loud and clear. And some word to get, too, on this "White Chief Surrey," and Jacques Forge.

"Do you need any help from me?" Catherine Dowd would have approved the question.

"No," she said. "I do not." It was a shame about that nose; it surely spoiled her looks.

Lee went over to the cot and bent to the old man. "Pebble," he said, down close to the old man's ear. "Do you hear me?" and was slightly surprised when the old man opened his eyes and regarded Lee with that steady, wise gaze that dogs and babies occasionally employed.

"Morgan," the old man said, in a voice out of water. Then he said, "Where have you brought me?"

"To your home, old man—with my thanks for your courage and skill in coming down to get me." Lee patted the old man's arm and straightened up to go, but the Indian made a

293

feeble clutch at him and he paused, then bent to hear what the Cree had to say. The old man muttered softly into Lee's ear, then cleared his throat and spoke more clearly. "You foolish on slide on mountain. Funny. Make my belly shake to see . . ."

"Glad you enjoyed it," Lee said, and patted the old man's arm again. "I thought you might have taken that trail a-purpose, you old son-of-a-bitch!"

He stood straight, liking the old man a good deal, and sad to see him dying. "I'll be going on," he said to the girl. "Is there a clean place to stay the night in town?"

"Rich whites stay in Albert's," she said, and stood staring at Lee as if expecting some fabulous reply.

"Thank you. Well—I'll be going, then. Hope he'll be some better in the morning. . ."

The Big-nose girl had nothing to say to that, so Lee put his hat on and turned and left, ducking deep to clear the door-top.

There was some slight trash on the packy that belonged to the old man, but damned if Lee felt like popping the pack and dumping it here to paw through it. Hell, twenty dollars gold would more than cover an old fry-pan, coffee pot with a leak to it, a second blanket (with fleas for sure) and a buffalo robe seen better days. He'd stopped long enough.

He climbed up on the grey, reined it 'round, and was surprised to see the Big-nose girl watching from her doorway. He lifted his hat to her as if she'd been a lady.

Then he spurred down-trail, the blower of a pack-horse clattering behind. A neat rain came out of the grey sky, as if to gust him on his way.

CHAPTER FOUR

Eustache turned out to be a long road, curving slowly around the foot of a mountain. Indian town had only been Indian town—there was a white section, neater, the outsides of the cabins and log shacks whitewashed. And a great deal of traffic on the road—a swarm of people afoot (a novelty to Lee, though on reflection he could see that a canoe or good pair of boots might do a man very well in river country, in thick forest, and no horse required) and a fair trundling of freight wagons, log-skidders, barrows, burthens and teams.

But the white faces showed as little joy as had the red. It was a poor settlement, for all its business in the street (called *Main*, of course). And it seemed to Lee, from the voices he heard, that the French were fading

out and the English-speakers moving in.
English voices, or at least Canadian-Scotch
voices, everywhere overpowered and out-
shouted the French. A lot of rifles—not so
many revolvers—in people's hands, or
strapped across their backs. Hunting knives
and rifles . . . Only a few revolver butts at
belts, in holsters.

Men and women, few of the women all-
the-way white, stared at Lee as he rode by,
obviously recognizing an American. One
man, a fat fellow in a yellow canvas jacket,
spit off a boardwalk as Lee passed. Might not
have meant an insult by it. Might have been
carelessness.

The rain came and went as Lee rode the
town—didn't appear to be much to the place
off this broad, muddy, wheel-trenched street.
Stores, cabins, saloons, lean-to shacks, warehouses, restaurants (these seeming pretty vil-
lainous, despite some fancy French names
painted on their sign-boards), harness-
makers, eyeglass sellers, dentists—all the
crowd of them lining this single long street.
Women hanging out their washing and
slapping their kids right next to some vicious
resort featuring a line of drunks pissing off a
porch while a squaw (even drunker) hoisted
her skirt and squatted to match them.

A hard town, and a poor one. Not one of
the businesses looked prosperous, not even
the saloons. Still, there was an air of . . . ex-
pectation. Lee had seen it once or twice else-

where. A poor, rough town, on the edge of wilderness. Everyone waiting for the bonanza, whatever that might be. Furs? Lee thought not. Lumber? Maybe. Mining? Cattle?

Something. These people were sure of something; they just weren't sure what.

The rain was coming down steadily now, light, constant, chill drizzle. The sky over the bulk of the mountain above was grey as a dirty shirt—would have looked to threaten snow, if it had covered Idaho. Lee suspected that it threatened snow in Canada just as surely.

He was anxious, and the grey was anxious, and the wind-popped packy was anxious to find someplace warm and dry. Lee asked a man who looked like an English-speaker about Albert's. Fellow spoke French at Lee for some time, then turned and walked away. Had been wearing a fine wolf parka, though —might be handier in thick forest than Lee's long, heavy buffalo coat which was about as heavy as his sleeping robe.

Lee asked two other people. One, a pleasant looking white woman with a market basket, was new in town, visiting her son, and didn't know of the place. The other was a teamster, who looked sober as a parson as Lee approached him, and turned out to be dead drunk, though sitting upright on his dray, flourishing his whip and cursing like the Jehu of Jehus. Could curse, but couldn't speak, he was that drunk.

Leaving the fellow cursing in the middle of the street, Lee kicked the weary grey into a trot splashing and squelching through the mud and reached up to strike the soaked brim of his Stetson clear of water; the thing was drooping down like a cut flower and draining rain down Lee's jacket collar. Having made this adjustment, Lee looked out across Main Street (now a waste of water wet as any lake) and saw a neat sign in black and yellow—*ALBERT'S*, fronting a handsome whitewashed house two stories high. This looked to be a prime lodging, and was the most welcome sight Lee had seen in some time.

He was not disappointed.

There was, in turned out, no Albert, but there was a Mister Gruen, a tall, stately old sissy in a neat set of trousers (pale grey) and a black swallow-tail coat.

Mister Gruen was not daunted by Lee's trail dirt or two weeks' worth of beard. Was happy to see him, in fact, because two mineral men from Toronto had just checked out and left him a vacancy—a small room behind the house, over the back porch. It was two dollars a night (room and partial board— Mister Gruen's celebrated sour-dough flap-jack breakfast). A little steep, Lee thought, but worth it.

Mister Gruen helped him unsaddle the

300

grey and take off the horse-pack, chatting all the while about the hardships of life on the Canadian frontier, particularly the hardships of dealing with the French who thought they knew everything about everything, and particularly about cooking.

That done, Mister Gruen led Lee to the bath-house, drew him a steaming tub—"I fire this awful boiler myself, morning and evening. It's one of the trials of inn-keeping" —and stayed for a moment to see that Lee had the soap he required, and that the water was not too hot. Then, with a murmured "You're certainly a well-set-up young fellow," and he strolled out and left Lee in peace and contentment, parboiling the trail muck off in a haze of soap-smell and steam.

He bathed and soaked for more than half an hour, then climbed out of the tub, toweled dry except for his face, dug his razor out of his war-bag, lathered up, and shaved. Then clean socks; a fresh long-john shirt (his last outerwear one was still with old Pebble) a clean pair of Levi tent-cloth trousers; his buckskin jacket—worn and not warm enough for this weather—and he was ready to walk out on the town, after buckling on the Colt's and slipping his knife down into his right boot.

There was a stop to be made beforehand, however, and Lee sat enthroned upon Mister Gruen's back-yard crapper (a three-holer) and read from the Sear's and Roebuck catalogue while listening to the last few skirmishes of rain tapping on the out-house tin.

"Where to go for a jolly time?" had been the question he then had for Mister Gruen, finding that gent at work in his kitchen. There'd been another boarder there as well sitting at the deal table, puffing on a long-stem pipe. A solid built old man with a bushy beard just run to salt, and one wise and one wandering eye. McReedy, he called himself, and spoke with the same Scotch accent Lee had heard in the streets and from Mister Gruen. They said *"aboot"* instead of about, and spoke a little more formally than Americans might.

"A jolly time?" the old man said, butting in without apology. "Would you be wanting a smooth time, now? Or rougher?"

"Now, Bob . . ." said Mister Gruen.

"I'm ashamed to say . . . rougher," Lee said, and the other two laughed.

"There's the Fine Canteen, in Skin-town," the old man said.

"God," said Mister Gruen. "Don't send the boy there!"

"Then there's Barney Barkley's place . . ."

"Even worse," said Mister Gruen. "The two nastiest joints in the town."

"Boy said 'Rougher.' "

"Which is closer?" Lee said, shaking his head at Mister Gruen, who was indicating in

302

dumb show that he was making roast beef sandwiches, and asking if Lee wanted one.

"Barney's," the old man said, and paused to relight his pipe. "You would be a tough customer, wouldn't you?" (Puff, puff.)

Lee thought about it for a moment, then smiled and said that he supposed that he was.

"In that case," McReedy said, "you might enjoy Barney's. You might also get into trouble there."

"The two often go together, I've found," Lee said. And McReedy laughed, and turned to Mister Gruen at the kitchen counter. "A philosophical Yankee—what next?"

Barney Barkley's didn't look too fierce, not from the outside. The rain had stopped but a cold wind was hauling in the night to replace it. Lee had followed directions down two blocks of sagging boardwalk and across Main Street in knee-deep mud to arrive at the place.

Barney's was a cluster of split-log cabins all, like most of the white section's buildings, whitewashed. Some music was leaking out of a half shuttered window, and Lee could see the bouncing shadows of dancers against a section of lamplit wall inside.

Inviting enough, though the plank sign outside featured a hanged man holding another sign in his hands.

"BARNEY'S."

Lee climbed the boardwalk steps, scraped

some of the mud off his boots on a splintered stoop, pushed open the door, and walked in.

This was the dancing room, and no-one paid him a bit of heed.

An accordian and a fiddle were being worked in a far corner—worked about as well as Lee had ever heard—and the puncheon floor of the small cabin was being pounded like a drum by the boots and moccasins of a dozen big men and an equal number of Indian women considerably shorter but just as wide. Likely about as strong, too, Lee thought, seeing one of them, a fat and greasy creature with hams like a four-year steer, lift her partner up in the dance (and him not small and light as a daisy) and twirl him as if he were a debutante girl at a Boston cotillion.

The noise was terrific and continuous, and the stink was the same—bear oil, neat's foot oil, Macassar oil, sweat and still more sweat, stale beer and raw whiskey (a touch of vomit, too), and over all the stench of curing hides and rain-soaked wool.

Most of the dancers were too busy to notice him, but Lee saw one squaw, broad in the beam as San Franciso smack, giving him the eye as she spun. The fellow spinning her looked French—dark as she was, round as a barrel, hands like baseball catcher's mitts. For so big a woman, the Indian danced light as a gas balloon, fairly tripping back and forth in her fringed moccasins, prancing here and there, out-wrestling her partner where need be. Fellow kept grappling at her breasts, but she elbowed him away every time, and used these occasions to roll a roguish eye in Lee's direction.

A down whore, and charming in her way, Lee thought her. Likely a terror as so many Indians were in her cups, but a thunderous ride and good company, if an eye was kept on her knife-hand . . .

Lee blew her a kiss for keepers, then turned and waded his way to the inside door to find the bar.

The bar-room was larger than the dance-hall, and less crowded—a long, narrow two-log-length space with the plank ceiling no more than a foot or so over a man's head as he walked. The bar was a stretch of planed timber braced on saw horses, the bottles and kegs ranked along the log wall behind.

Two bartenders, both small men with fine mustaches, were busy serving out the gut and suds. The room wasn't crowded—not surprising, since there was no place to sit down, no tables, no chairs, not even benches. The bar *was* crowded, with a quiet crowd of hard drinkers, or Lee had never seen one. Same gopher-looking bunch as dancing, he thought, likely some hard-cases amongst them . . .

Two men looked 'round as Lee walked to the bar, then went back to minding their drinks and their business.

"What'll it be?" The bartender was wearing a clean shirt, as near as Lee could tell in the lamplight. Must be a particular fellow —or it be Wednesday and wash-day.

"Double whiskey."

"House or the Bay's?" By which Lee supposed he meant a choice of Hudson's Bay Company liquor.

"House," he said, and the bartender smiled, reached behind him (without looking), pulled a grimy looking bottle out of the row on the wall shelf, then brought it around, thumbed it open, and produced a big chip-rimmed glass mug to pour into.

"I can see you're a sport," the bartender said, and slid the mug over to him.

"Just curious," Lee said, and drank the stuff down.

"Well, Yank," the bartender said, watching Lee's face. "And is your curiosity satisfied?"

"I've had worse," Lee said—and he had, but not much worse.

"Another?" A noisy three or four were stomping into the place for the dancing.

"Once was fair," Lee said, "and once was enough. I'll try the other."

The bartender nodded. Lee saw that his shirt was clean, but his neck was dirty. "You're a sensible fella," he said, and reached behind him for a different bottle, without looking. "The Bay makes decent drink."

He might have said more, but Lee didn't hear it—one of the men in from the dancing had stepped up to the bar beside him, shouldered Lee roughly, not gotten enough room, then, half turning, put out an arm like a hickory branch, planted his hand on Lee's chest, and shoved him a yard down the bar.

Lee's mug went to the sawdust and he tripped going back and had to catch himself on the bar edge. Felt a fool, not being ready for it and having heard them come in noisy.

The man who'd pushed him didn't even look 'round. The bartender glanced at Lee, amused. It had been a considerable shove. Hard to let it pass. The bully's back was wide as a door. He wore a brown wool shirt, and had clusters of hair as golden as a girl's at the back of his head. Was a couple of inches taller than Lee.

Lee took a breath, and decided to let it pass. The fellow was big, and with friends, and it wasn't enough to be a killing matter. Not in a strange country.

The noise at the bar had increased with these men coming into it. The music and dancing in the room next door sounded louder now, too.

Lee stepped back up to the bar, well away from the big man with the yellow hair, and signaled the barkeep for his whiskey. The barman came down smiling, and slid a fresh mug across. This one had no chips out of the rim, and Lee counted himself lucky.

"Very reasonable of you, Yank," the bartender said, and nodded in the direction of the big man's back. "Very reasonable."

No sooner were the words said, than—perhaps joined by another friend, perhaps to make mischief—the big man half turned, took a long step down the bar, and put his shoulder hard into Lee's. The whiskey was jolted out of the mug, splashing down Lee's long-john shirt and he saw, over the blond man's massive shoulder, the profile of his face, watching. The man, who by his pretty hair might have been expected handsome, was a dish-face thing, with a swollen jaw and brows. Blue eyes bulging as shallow as painted china.

"Make more room, Yankee," he said to Lee. Someone had hit the fellow in his throat once, and spoiled it. His voice was broken and had a squeak to it.

"Yes, I will," Lee said to that half-turned face—and swung full-armed overhand and hit the fellow on his left ear with the edge of the glass mug. The blow made a sharp *chunk* sound as it struck.

"Shit!" the bartender said, and jumped back against the wall. And Lee stepped back, too, a long fast step as the big man turned like a swinging door and reached out for Lee with both hands. He wore no revolver. Had a sheath-knife on his hip.

Lee stepped back again, and when the blond man leaned forward, reaching, his eyes showing no particular emotion, nothing of pain or anger, Lee lunged suddenly in, swung the mug overhand again, and hit the man down across the bridge of his nose. The bone in it cracked with a small delicate snapping sound, and blood came out, just a little.

The blond man shook his head as if he recognized that pain, and very quickly got his hand onto his knife hilt, drew the weapon, and swung it very hard at Lee's right side. Lee got his arm down in time to block the stab—down, but not strongly enough; the dish-faced man was powerful as a horse. His wrist hit Lee's arm and knocked it back into him with the knife coming along in that massive clenched fist.

Lee twisted left, felt the trickling as the blade slid and sliced so quickly across some skin of his belly—kept turning as fast as he could, smashed the mug against the bar-planks and twisted back to slam the handle and a handful of splintered glass into the big man's face.

It struck and stuck there, driven into the bone of the man's cheek and jaw, and Lee had to tear it away and jump back for his life as the big man swung his knife again, crowding him, bulling him back. The blood was running like rain water all over the blond man's face.

He didn't seem to mind it.

Lee was standing out in the middle of the floor glad of the room and the man came loping after him like an ape. Lee still had a piece of the mug handle in his hand, and he dropped it, stooped, and drew the double-edged dagger from his right boot. Blond fellow didn't hesitate—came right in, shaking his head, spattering blood.

Lee danced backward, trying to keep away —saw roaring bearded faces along the bar. Couldn't hear any noise, though. Just like a dream. He wished to God he could use his pistol on this man without these people stringing him up.

The big man was following fast . . . but it seemed to Lee now that it was all moving slowly, both the big man and he, moving as if they were both dreaming about this fight . . .

The man came swinging, and Lee felt the snag as the fellow's blade caught the cloth of his shirt. Son of a bitch was ruining the only clean shirt Lee had to his name!

Saw a woman watching. Fat, sweaty round Indian face.

The big man came again—rushing in, blank-eyed, swinging that mighty arm. The hunting knife.

Lee ducked inside the swing and jumped away, felt the impact of the boot soles on the puncheon floor as he leaped. Not many more of those in him before the fellow caught him fairly and they wrestled and chopped, looking for a final stab into the gut. Lee felt he couldn't be badly hurt—couldn't afford it, somehow, win or lose.

He decided to kill this big, hurrying man.

When the blond man rushed again, Lee turned and ran halfway down the length of the room—heard the howling, the noise of the watchers seeing a finish, then spun as the dish-faced man came galloping, drew back his knife-hand underarm—then shoveled the double-edged blade up from under and out. The border toss, Lee's heard it called. Not much power to the throw, compared to an overhand pitch. Not enough power for a throw into the chest.

The needle point of the dagger took the blond man neatly under his great chin and slid on in as if sheathed, the leather-wrapped handle jutting out like some enormous stick-pin thrust out of his throat.

The man kept taking swift, pounding strides, his shallow eyes fixed on Lee as they had been since the fight began. He seemed not to realize what had happened for several seconds, and Lee backed away as if from death coming in woodsman's boots.

There was not a sound in the bar room now except for Lee's harsh breathing, his boot-steps, the echoing strides of the man with the knife in his throat.

It was no air to breathe that slowed and

stopped him. Then the dish-faced man stood puzzled for a few seconds, trying to find a breath. He dropped his knife onto the floor in his confusion, and reached up with both hands to touch at the dagger handle, to tug at it gently.

Then the china blue eyes showed something, and he grasped the dagger handle and pulled at it, but not too strongly. Some of the flat, gleaming blade slid out of his throat a little, greasy with blood, and letting more blood out. The big man, his golden curly hair all dank and dark with sweat, sank to his knees in the sawdust, still fingering at the dagger's handle, but not gripping it with full strength, not tearing it out of him.

The big man's face was turning darker in the lamp light. He lay down on his side then, turned to his back, his chest heaving as he tried to breathe. His china blue eyes had rolled up and back into his head. Only the whites showed now.

Slowly . . . slowly . . . the heavy boots began to lift and fall, kicking left, then right, the boot-heels drumming a slow tattoo on the puncheon floor. The man's tongue was out of his mouth now like a blue snake's head, seeking air.

Lee felt as tired as he could remember feeling. Felt as if he must get to sleep or would die of being so tired. He forced himself to the effort of walking to the dying man, forced himself to the effort of bending over him, and grunted with effort as he pulled the dagger free, gripped the strangling man by his fine hair, and cut his damaged throat from one ear to the other.

Stood up from that, to a room of silence.

The dancing had stopped in the other room; the music had stopped. No-one was even talking. Lee looked around at them, something dismayed by the silence. Certainly they had seen that bully or other bullies fight. Certainly had seen some of those hard-cases killed. Why such silence then? He'd cut the man's throat as a favòr and any sensible man would have seen it so.

"Don't be so damn quiet," he said to them. "It was only a fight and he got the worst of it." And he found his Stetson, picked it up, and put it on.

"That's right," a woman said, and stood by the dance-hall door, looking at him. It was the fat whore who'd eyed him in the dance-hall. Lee saw her round, beaming, dark, dirt-smudged face more clearly than any other in the place. It may have been the flickering, smoky lamplight, it may have only been that hers was the best face to see. The other people were looking at him with an odd look, every one of them. They wouldn't meet his eyes—it was like looking into the faces of cattle or horses.

Only the fat Indian woman looked straight at him.

"Is there any sort of law here?" Lee said.

None of them said a word. Two men slid out the dance-hall door, and went. Others were standing staring down at the dead man. The dish-faced man lay in a tremendous spreading pool of blood black as tar, reflecting the bar-room's lights. The big man looked shrunken . . . his pretty hair would be soaked, glued into the puddle of blood under the back of his head. Wouldn't have imagined anything like this could have happened to him just coming into a favorite ken for a drink . . . have a shove at a cowboy Yank . . .

And look what happened.

Shrunken and shorter, lighter in weight, narrower in the shoulder . . . now that he was dead.

"I suppose I look smaller now . . . They always looked smaller to me." His father, lying on that cook-shack floor, looking up at him. With not much left to say and not much time to say it.

Lee felt tired of the way they were looking at him. "I asked you people a question. There some law in this town should know about this?"

The bartender—man with the clean shirt— called across the room to him as some more men slid out the dance-hall door, not wanting any part of more trouble, apparently—not wanting to see any more, either, "There's a Mountie post in town, Yank. One riding officer. He's gone off to catch a thief."

314

That was good news, Lee supposed. He'd heard the Mounted Police were nasty customers, snotty, and pleased to use steel handcuffs on people when they arrested them. Couldn't see himself bound in steel handcuffs. And wouldn't care to have to kill a Canadian policeman about it.

"You come here," the fat Indian woman said. She came to him and put her broad brown hand gently on his arm, as if he were a restive horse, a stallion who had just injured someone.

"You come here with me, Pretty-boots," the Indian woman said, and gripped his arm tighter and began to lead him away, back through the door into the dance-hall whre the two musicians and a few others stood against the wall, drinking mugs of beer and watching Lee and the whore walk through. A difference, Lee thought, between these people and Americans. In such a harsh town in the States, in such a circumstance, the musicians would already be back to playing, the little room roaring, jumping, pounding under the dancers' feet.

A solemn bunch, up here. Came, no doubt, from not having kicked the British out.

She led him out a back door, and down a log walled corridor just wide enough to pass, his shoulders brushing as they walked. The Indian woman was in front of him, shorter than she had seemed out in the saloon. Stocky work-horse haunches on her . . . that

315

pigeon-toed walk all Indians seemed to have. She smelled of beer and sweat and campfires.

Wonderful hair, though, black and gleaming as oil-tar. The woman wore it twisted into a knot at the back of her head. Looked like S'ien's, was the truth of the matter. Lee supposed there was something to the Indians being some sort of Orientals after all. That rich, shining black hair was very like S'ien's.

The woman came to a rough plank door and pushed it open. Lee followed her inside not concerned some badger might be there, seeking his purse. If there was such a crimp in prey at Barney Barkley's and he troubled Lee, then so much the worse for him.

The crib was empty and no larger than a coal bin.

The pitch pine walls had been white-washed, though, and decorated with pictures of white ladies from the *roto gravures*— handsome women with curls at their fore-heads, stepping in and out of carriages in some Eastern cities, always with tall men, mustachioed and in silk high hats standing at their elbows to support them. Very like the pictures that old Pebble's grandaughter had tacked up in her shanty.

Lee supposed that the Indian women, seeing the white men had beaten their men at every point, and seeing that white ladies nevertheless ruled those same conquerors, sought in these pictures from the East some notion of what white women's secret power might be.

"Put away?"

The fat whore stood looking up at him, something reticent, an inquiring expression on her face.

"Put away . . . ?"

Lee had no idea what she was talking about.

"Put *what* the hell away?"

The woman pointed down to his right hand and Lee saw that he still gripped the dagger, the broad blade bared, smeared with reddish black in a thick way, as if he had been slicing a chocolate cake with it. His fist was still clenched around the weapon as if it had not yet received any news of victory, any permit for ease.

Lee felt a fool, knowing why the people had stared so, been so odd in dealing with him after the fight. He smiled at the woman to reassure her, then unclenched his fist— or tried to—that grip was reluctant to relax— but did unclench it, wiped the knife, before he thought, on his only clean trousers, and stooped to slide the blade into the sheath in his right boot.

Folks must have thought he'd run mad, lounging around with the knife out in that fashion, and the fight over and done with.

"I forgot," he said to the whore, and

wondered if they'd gotten that bully up off the floor and out of the place. Damned if he wanted to go out and see the fellow still lying there. There was no reason to be seeing that again. Over and done with, and that was that. He took off his jacket, hung it on one of a row of nails beside the door, unbuckled his gun-belt and hung that up as well.

The woman, some easier now, apparently —and sturdy of her, after all, to have brought him back, and him with that knife still fisted —now came up to cuddle in a pleasant whorish way, making him familiar of her softness and heat. She smelled of sweat and wood smoke. Pleasant . . . a pleasant smell.

Nothing in the crib by way of furniture except for cot and a nailed-up table with a water basin and kerosene lamp on it.

"You good fighter," the woman said. She was unbuttoning him, shirt and trousers, as smoothly as any mother might her child's.

"Don't talk about that," Lee said. "I don't need to hear about that."

She smiled and nodded, and said, "You deal horses? You buy—you sell horses?" She knelt before him easily, for all her flash, and tugged his trousers down. "You sit."

Lee sat down on her bed, feeling tired out, and she pulled off his boots, then took off his socks, then slid his trousers off. "I do sell horses," Lee said. "I raise them."

"So," the Indian woman said. "Strong horses? Fast horses?" She reached up and Lee raised his buttocks so she could pull his underpants down.

"Strong *and* fast. The best."

The fat woman smiled and shook her head. She put both plump hands on him and began to knead and stroke his cock. "Not so," she said. *"Nez Perce* make horses strong and fast. White mens do not."

"My father had a stallion from them," Lee said.

"You have a nice thing," the Indian woman said, stroking gently at him. She squeezed it as it stood swollen in her hands. Knelt up a little, and kissed the tip of it—a wet, affectionate, smacking kiss. She smiled up at Lee. "Not so big, though, as stallion has!" and giggled.

"Take your clothes off," Lee said, "and get up on the bed."

She let go of him, and stood up with a grunt, her round, dark face shining in the lamp light. Held out her hand.

"Two dollar," she said.

Lee sat up, reached down his jacket, dug into a pocket for his purse, took out five dollars and handed the money to her.

She looked down at it without any expression, though Lee doubted she usually received so much and more than she'd asked, then tucked up her flower print calico and stuffed the cash down into the top of her black cotton stocking. A folded straight razor was lying under a frilled garter on the fat, muscular thigh of her other leg.

Then she let her hem fall, and commenced to unbutton the dress, opened it down the front, and took it off.

Except for her stockings and her garter, she was stark naked. Dark, dark brown all over—her skin the color of wet clay-dirt, and smooth as panelled wood. She was round and fat and powerful looking as a skinned bear, with broad dark brown settings for her nipples—small breasts, plump with fat, big broad belly and hips, and flanks like a pony's. Her cunt was shaved quite clean of hair—to keep off lice and such, Lee supposed —and was left as small and simple as a child's. Dimpled and closed up tight. No sign of pink meat showing.

She smiled under Lee's gaze as if she were Lillian Russell herself, stripped for Brady or the Commodore, and turned slowly 'round to show her ass—round brown melons shining in the lamp light. Her back looked narrow above those rounds, but wasn't; she had a back as broad as a man's, and likely as strong. Her backbone was sunk in fat and muscle.

She looked back over her shoulder at him, smiling with pleasure and pride at the display of herself—her simple, fat, sturdy body. It made Lee feel tender toward her.

"Come here," he said, and when she came to stand before him at the cot, put his hands

320

on her naked hips, leaned forward, kissed her brown belly, and blew gently into her belly button, making a soft farting sound.

She gave a little jump, as if startled, then threw back her head and laughed like a man, imitated the same sound with her lips, and laughed some more.

Lee supposed people in the place must think something odd, to hear child's play through the walls of a whore's crib.

"What's your name?" he said to the fat woman smiling down at him.

"Mary."

"Your real name . . . your Indian name."

But she shook her head, and wouldn't tell it. It was her secret.

Lee reached out and stroked her small, fat mound . . . slid a finger up the crease . . . probed her with it, gently, and found her hole—narrow, tight, slippery with her oils.

"Good," she said, and climbed up onto his lap, her strong, fat legs astraddle. She hiked herself up higher, holding his cock like a handle to steady herself, raised her loins, and then carefully fitted him into her . . . just the head of his cock wedging into the small heat and slickness.

"O.K.?" she said and sat down on him a little deeper.

"O.K." Lee said, shrugged off his opened shirt so as to feel her fully against him, put his arms around her—felt all her weight and strength and softness—hugged her hard, and slowly began to drive his cock up into her.

She murmured against his throat and he felt her tense as he held her. Then she eased and opened, and he slid up into her all the way. There were things at play within her—shifting, wet, hot passages gripping him as hard as ever he'd gripped his knife. He felt wet at the hairs of his crotch; she was running liquid down him as they moved, as he thrust up and into her. She moved on him as if she were riding a horse in the Eastern style, posting.

She smelled of fish now, as the oil came out of her cunt, that smell so much richer than any that came from the body of a man. A rich fish stink to grow a baby in.

In his enjoyment, Lee still felt what a foolish thing it was to pay a woman to pretend at baby making only so the man could work his cock to sneeze and then go off well satisfied.

The whore clung to him sturdily now, thrusting herself up and down his pole, working hard enough so that Lee thought she might be getting pleasure from it. He took her shoulders and pushed her back a little so that he could see her face—round, flushed, contorted with effort. Her eyes were squinted almost shut.

They made wet sounds where they joined. The fat woman began to grunt each time she sat down fully on him, each time his cock went up her all the way. She grunted, and Lee felt her strong fingers gripping at his shoulders, squeezing and pinching at him.

He slid his hands down to her ass, took each large buttock in a grip, and commenced to help her where she wished to go—lifting her high, almost off him, then hauling her down onto it again. All the way. Her long black hair was coming down, streaming over her shoulders.

She muttered something to him in Indian and leaned forward to bite at the side of his neck. That bite—nervous, tentative, delicate —as if she were speaking to him in a manner more personal than cries, began to force from Lee a sweetness that he could no longer hold. He hugged her to him as if he loved her, as if he knew her better than something bought. They hugged each other like friends in pursuit of some great prize. They galloped together, her round face furious with concentration, shiny with sweat, her plump, small breasts shaking as she rode.

Lee felt the jissom rising from his stones, and the fat woman felt the change in him as it happened. She crowed, and bounced on him like an India-rubber ball, all sweaty and beaming, and her cunt held him, and wrung him, and worked the cum out of him in long, long spurts.

It felt as if he'd turned to honey and was

melting out.

"Ooooh . . ." she said, and pursed her lips in a little "O." "*Oooooohh* . . ." Lee felt her cunt contract around him, clenching, soaked and soft.

They stopped moving slowly, together, much as Lee had seen a railroad locomotive wheel slowly, slowly turn to a stop. The high wheel, the drive-shafts . . . the pistons moving slowly to a stop.

She lay against him, lay in his arms like a wife, her face buried in his shoulder, her fat, round belly warm against his.

Lee leaned back against the rough blank wall, holding her as she held him. To have made a down whore come was no small thing and he was proud of it.

Of course, to have made a blood-sick man a lover was no small thing either.

They sat together for a little while, then Lee felt her cunt slowly contracting, slowly recovering its privacy as his wet, limp cock slid out of her into cool air.

She sat back in his arms and looked at him. There'd been a wet sound as their sweaty skins had parted.

"Good fight. Good fuck," she said, and smiled at him.

Lee grieved his last for the slain bully, seeing that this woman had good sense. He leaned forward and kissed the whore on her lips. She stared, astonished at his doing such a thing, and Lee gently eased her off his lap, stood up, and gathered his clothes.

It was time to walk back to Albert's through the cold night air.

Time for a long, sweet sleep.

CHAPTER FIVE

"Well, you've certainly blotted *your* copy-book, Mister Morgan." Mister Gruen had waited until his other guests had left the breakfast table—two fur buyers from Victoria, a lumber man, and old McReedy—before giving Lee a small piece of his mind. Which was all right with Lee—he had some questions to ask the inn-keeper.

"I don't know," Mister Gruen said, pouring Lee a second cup of coffee, "I don't know the state of the law down in your country, but I can assure you that the Mounted Police take a *very* dim view of killings up here! Not that the fellow you bumped was an exemplary citizen—no one thinks that . . ."

He put the coffee pot down and sat down himself. It had been a rather quiet breakfast; McReedy and the others had had nothing much to say, had kept their faces to their plates for the most part.

"The constable here," Gruen said, "providentially out of town now, is a sergeant named Ferguson. An extremely severe young man who takes no nonsense, I assure you." Gruen took a cold biscuit from the bread plate, and buttered it. "It would be very wise —*very* wise of you, to scoot back over the border without delay. Ferguson might not . . ."

"Have you heard of a man named Surrey?" Lee said. "And a man named Jacques Forge?"

"Did you hear a word that I said?"

"Certainly did," Lee said, "and I appreciate it. Good advice and I'll certainly follow it just as quick as I can. A fellow named Surrey? Jacques Forge?"

Mister Gruen sat nibbling at his biscuit, regarding Lee with some discouragement.

"Is this about the Dowd affair? Is this about that?"

"You bet."

Mister Gruen finished his biscuit. "Don't let anybody tell you that beaten biscuits are superior. It's nonsense. Simply nonsense."

Lee nodded though he didn't entirely agree. He'd had beaten biscuits and they definitely had the edge over straight baked.

"Mister Dowd," Gruen said, "attempted the life of Lord Surrey, and in the ensuing struggle was wounded and died." He sat back in his chair, fixing Lee with a schoolmaster's look. "That was the tale that Lord Surrey told; that was the tale that Surrey's man, Robins, told. Dowd—whose reputation in the Provinces was not of the best—was dead, and had no story to tell. As to Forge, the man had an evil reputation, lives deep in the mountains, and as far as I know, has never even been seen in *Eustache* or near it."

"Dowd's guide came down to get me," Lee said. "Mister Dowd was a good friend; the guide said he was murdered with no chance at all."

"An Indian guide?"

"That's right," Lee said.

"Good lord, young man—Indians have their own notion of fact. Surely you know that—you're a westerner!"

"It sounded true to me."

Mister Gruen got up from the table and began collecting the dishes to wash. "I've never heard of such foolishness—not, I suppose, that it's any of my business. I *do* feel responsible for old McReedy's advisory to you on local entertainment. I notice he had the grace to keep his mouth shut this morning!"

"Tell me about this Lord Surrey," Lee said. "Is he a real English lord or posing?"

"Oh, the genuine article, I can assure you of that," Gruen said from the sink. "And if you think that doesn't mean something in this country, young man, you have another think coming! Surrey is a handsome boy, very, very rich—and *very* well connected, in the mother country of course, and in Ottawa.''

Lee finished his coffee. Well into the morning. Time to get moving. ''And what's such a precious article doing out here?''

''The 'precious article' is out here representing his family—their investments, in any case. His father is the Duke of Morne, if that means anything to you. The boy is an Earl.''

''They might be a greedy bunch,'' Lee said, and Gruen laughed, drying a plate with a small striped towel. ''Well,'' he said, ''I suppose that they are and have been for some centuries. Doesn't mean the boy murdered Mister Dowd.'' He picked up another plate.

''How in hell you people put up with those English aristrocrats, I'll never understand. We kicked their butts out long ago!''

Gruen turned from the sink, towel in one hand, wet cup in the other.

''Did you really? I understand that you people are very ready to welcome investments from those 'English aristocrats.' And I would add that when we meet such a person, whatever we might think of the individual we *are* impressed by the history they represent. Something Americans would not understand.'' Turned back to his sink, looking mighty stiff, and said, with his back turned,

"You'd be very wise, Mister Morgan, to concern yourself with constable Ferguson and leave Lord Surrey to his explorations."

"I meant no offense, Mister Gruen," Lee said, getting up from the table. "When in Rome . . ."

"Just so," Gruen said, from the sink.

"Quite right about those biscuits, too," Lee said. "Doubt I've ever had better."

"It's the dough," Mister Gruen said, and hung up his dish towel. "It's all in the dough. Most people knead their dough to death and their biscuits taste it."

"If you'll tote up the bill," Lee said, "I'll be paying and on my way."

"Oh," said Mister Gruen, holding out his hand to shake, "bed and breakfast'll run you the two dollars—unless you're strapped." He looked some concerned. "If you're caught short, seeing that you're a guest in the country, and in some difficulty—and seeing that it was in my kitchen that fool McReedy gave you ill advice—I'll knock that down to a dollar, if necessary."

"It isn't necessary," Lee said, and took out his purse to pay. "But I thank you for the thought."

"Sorry if I spoke out of turn there," Mister Gruen said, "but you young men get into the damndest fixes sometimes. I hate to see it. This sort of country can be rough enough without a fine-looking young fellow going to seek out trouble he needn't."

"You have a point, certainly," Lee said, and had turned to the stairs to get his war-bag, Stetson, and rifle from his room, when someone came scratching at Gruen's back door.

Lee was starting up the stairs, when Gruen called to him.

"You have a visitor, Mister Lee!" He sounded amused.

When Lee came back downstairs, he saw an ugly Indian boy standing in Mister Gruen's kitchen—then saw that it was old Pebble's grandaughter, dressed in white man's trousers belted with a length of cord, a cheap flour sack shirt, knee-length moccasins, and a double thickness blanket coat that had been dark green when new.

The girl's brown face, narrow and big-nosed, was blank as the side of a wall—but perhaps from the way she stood, Lee knew the old man had died. She stood very lonely.

"He's dead?"

An abrupt head-shake. "Yes."

The girl said nothing more but stood looking up at Lee, as if waiting for something.

"I'll just leave you two alone," Mister Gruen said, and left his kitchen smiling and saying "Good lord," under his breath.

Lee realized Gruen thought the girl was some whore he'd met at Barkley's, come all the way to white-town to call. The girl had paid no mind to Gruen, only stood in the kitchen looking up at Lee, and seeming solitary as a prairie tree. Lee hoped this was no invitation to an Indian funeral. He'd been fond of the old man and had respected him, but he had neither the time nor the inclination to spend two or three days listening to Cree songs and eating dog stew.

Lee came down the stairs, took the girl by an arm wiry as telegraph line even through the thickness of her coat, and guided her out the kitchen door onto the back porch. There, she didn't try to pull away from him, but stood docile as a well-broken horse, looking at him sideways.

"Did the old man die well?" Lee said. "Did it hurt him badly to die?"

"It did not," the girl said, in her incongruous English. Seemed somewhat like a fox suddenly speaking. "He sing; he sleep; he die."

It sounded well enough. The old brave would enjoy no more amusements trailing with white men. Would have to obey no more last wishes of white men. Take no more journeys, too long, too difficult to survive, for white men.

Well enough.

"What do you do now?" Lee asked her. She seemed dressed to travel, and Pebble's paint stood rein-tied to Gruen's back porch.

"You have no guide," the girl said. She had white, slightly pointed teeth. Her breath frosted as she spoke, clouding for an instant before her face. It was a cold morning; the smell of snow weighed on the air. "You have no guide, now—but you have a guide again."

"You, I suppose," Lee said, and she shook her head briskly, "Yes."

Lee started to shake his head, too, then remembered, and nodded a "No." "The hell you are," he said, and meant it. "You need a stake, I'll give you one—within reason." (He wasn't sure she understand the "within reason" part of that, and amended it.) "I'll give you some money but not much."

The big-nose girl stared at him with that by now familiar alert dog look; then she said, "I want a ten dollars for guiding you into mountain. I want a ten dollars for guiding you out. I know where is the river where Big White Chief Surrey camps." Then she shut her mouth and watched Lee closely to see what he would say to that.

Lee said nothing for a moment, but reflected that in a fever or not, old Pebble had chattered what he shouldn't and been heard. Possible this girl saw only a chance to make some money guiding—some Indian women had done that job before. Possible also that if he refused her, she would go to that river where the White Chief camped and tell Surrey that Lee was coming.

"Do you know that country?" Lee said.

She held out two skinny brown fingers. "I go twice, with Papa." Meaning God knew

334

who, her father or grandfather, Lee supposed. Truth was, he could certainly do better, *would* do better, to hire some Indian who really knew the country, had trapped it and hunted over it, and preferably a man who might back him in a fight, at least might if his own butt was in the pickling, too.

This girl filled no bill that way.

But she knew about Surrey. She knew about Lee. And what she knew, she might well go and tell.

"You're hired," Lee said. "Go to the stable, get my grey, and tack him out. We're leaving now." Then he went back into Albert's to get his possibles and ask Mister Gruen if he could board the wind-broke pack horse. Creature'd be of no use at a long fast run, and Lee had the notion he was due for some very swift running, him and a female guide, alone in quite unfriendly mountains.

Mister Gruen proving agreeable for a very small sum, Lee said his farewell, went out to the stable with his war-bag and rifle, and plundered the pack for anything handy and light to carry—the fry-pan, sack of coffee, sack of salt, sack of sugar, side of bacon, sack of corn meal. Had no good shirts, no clean trousers, no clean socks, no underwear.

Have to buy all that.

Lee looked at the girl, bending over the pack canvas by the last stall in a row, restowing Lee's goods fairly neatly. That stuff would be safe enough with Gruen . . ..

nothing much to it for a happenstance thief.

A few minutes later, Lee and the girl rode out of Gruen's stable yard in fairly fine fettle —the grey prancing from his rest and three feeds of timothy and grain—cost to be added to the packy's board, and paid upon return. "Though I doubt Constable Ferguson will allow a prisoner's debts," Gruen had said, arranging his parlor antimacassars when Lee went in to say good-bye. Mister Gruen obviously thought Lee a fool not to be hopping to the border, and added, "I suspect your young 'friend,' beside being a terribly *ugly* savage, has fleas."

Lee laughed, shook Mister Gruen's hand, promised to return nevertheless, and asked him to look out for someone foolish enough to buy the pack-horse.

Lee and the girl rode out into a cold morning. By the time she'd led him to the town's prime dry goods, haberdashery, and sundry shop, it had begun to snow. Little swirling clouds of it blew past them as they rode. Lee stuck out his tongue and felt the faintest bite of tiny flakes. He glanced to the right and saw the Indian girl (What in God's name was her name? Patience? Hope? Some damn thing like that . . .) saw her watching him riding along with his tongue sticking out like a little boy with an all-day sucker in his mitt. In defiance, Lee kept his tongue out for a while longer. It was going to be tedious, traveling for days with a girl who stared at you as if she'd never seen the like before.

Lee suspected he was affording this skinny little squaw considerable amusement.

Patience? Not Patience . . . .

The dry goods was prime.

A big store, one of the biggest Lee had seen outside a good-sized town. Must be, he supposed, to service all the woods runners up here. Likely they came in once a year, traded their furs, and then bought the place out. Traps, whiskey, fire arms . . .

The proprietor, a burly French Jew named DuPont, was shifting stock when Lee and the girl came in, set down a keg of nails that must have weighed considerable, and came over to shake hands with Lee, introduce himself, and nod to the Indian girl. "Good morning, Miss Charity," he said to her, as nicely as if she was white, thus supplying Lee her name.

Lee caught the notion that DuPont knew of the trouble the night before at Barney Barkley's, but the store keeper said nothing of it, only ask what it was Lee needed.

"A whole damn fit-out of clothes," Lee said, already regretting he'd only brought two hundred dollars up in gold, and wondering if DuPont might be able to cash a draft on the Republican Bank of Boise, if it came to that. Lee'd seen the prices charged for soft goods in boom towns, and though *Eustache* didn't appear to be that flush, he was ready to be shocked by twenty-dollar pants and ten-dollar coffee pots, if those were the prices going.

But, no such.

DuPont's charges were much the same they would have been in Parker for the same goods—lower, some of them.

The store was divided into long, back-stretch halves shadowy as any cave toward the back, and two stories high, the goods packed and stacked and hung and piled in good order right along and up and down. Appeared to Lee a fellow if he had the cash could walk into DuPont's and walk out with anything at all he might require. There were barrels of long-handled tools at the front, and, by the cash-box, a case of firearms twenty feet long.

Place smelled of grease and gun oil, dyed cottons, cut wool, fur, sawn wood, and ready-mixed paints and wash. Fellow had himself a topper of a store—and, Lee noticed as DuPont led them down the aisle where the clothing (ready made) was hangered, folded, and stacked, that the store-keep carried a revolver tucked into his back trouser pocket, the better, no doubt, to discourage any drunken trappers from getting gay with his merchandise.

"I'll need two good wool shirts . . . set of underthings . . . two pairs of wool trousers. Some socks. A wool scarf—lamb's wool, if you have it. Sharpening stone . . . small hand ax . . . (Going into deep woods, would need that, sure.)

DuPont listened to Lee, took a single sharp look at him for sizes, then went straight to the proper stack, picked up the clothng, and laid it out for Lee to choose his colors. Lee chose dark, every time. No bright reds and yellows in the shirts, no white or stripes in the lamb's wool scarf.

Nothing to show up sharply in dark forest.

"You want those trousers tuck-sewed here and there?"

"No, thanks," Lee said. "I'm handy enough with a needle, if need be."

The shirts and trousers, the scarf, and a heavy pair of knit wool gloves to wear under his leather ones. Two pairs of washed-wool long johns. Three pairs of fine wool socks, double-knit. His boots would take a two-pair fit—be only a little tight, and the extra layer would keep him warmer. All these goods were of quality, and reasonable price.

The Indian girl stood by, watching Lee. She didn't finger any of the goods around her, didn't sort through anything, or window-shop them.

"I'll need a good match safe and the best sure-fire Lucifers you've got. A small coffee pot, a big fry pan, a tin kettle—very small, if you have one of those. Tin cup . . . two tin cups. Need one hundred rounds of forty-

339

four-forty, little can of gun oil . . ."

"Graphite'd be better in this weather," DuPont said, and Lee agreed to take the powdered graphite rather than the oil.

"Neat's foot oil—little can. Two candles. Bar of soap . . . (Though heaven knew where he'd find water warm enough to wash in.) "And do you have ammunition for a fifty-caliber Sharp's?"

"I do," DuPont said, "and fine quality, too, though not much call for it."

"I'll take a box of forty, for extras," Lee said, and DuPont went behind the long gun case, pulled open a drawer back there, and was right out with just the ticket—Volcanic's Best Rifle Cartridge and Shot, Combined.

No saying there was not a pleasure, spending money. There was.

"I suppose I'll have new bandanna, too," Lee said. "Brown, if you stock that color—blue, if you don't." And some trail sweets . . . "Take a little sack of bull's eyes. Little sack of jaw-breakers. And I'll have two cans of peaches, two cans of tomatoes, and two cans of sardine fish."

"That be it?" DuPont said, still gathering the canned goods.

"No. I'll need a fur parka."

DuPont had the canned goods already out and stacked on his counter, was scooping the candies. "Wolf? Beaver? Mink?"

"What's warmest?"

"Wolf."

"Wolf it is—best you've got, please." No use freezing to death to save Surrey the necessity of killing him.

DuPont finished sacking the candy, took another hard look at Lee for size, and went off into the back for a minute or two. He returned carrying the handsomest parka Lee had ever seen—a soft heap of silver wolf fur, bone-toggled and hooded, lay over his arm.

"It's dear," DuPont said. "Thirty dollars. I have cheaper, and nearly as good."

"Hell, I'll take it," said the sport and big spender from the States. Occurred to Lee that he might be making a show of himself with this fancy a coat . . .

And that was that, for the buying.

Seventy-two dollars and change. A lot of horse-sale money to be going at once.

Lee sent the girl out for his saddle-bags, and DuPont was able to pack most of the stuff away, but had to provide an extra possibles sack for the canned goods and ammunition.

Lee shook the store keeper's hand—DuPont had a blacksmith's grip on him—then took the goods on out, the parka over his arm, the long silver fur stirring, shifting slightly in the faint breeze of his walking. A hell of a coat, and no mistake!

It was snowing harder when they got outside, and Lee made certain the girl tied the goods on tight behind the saddle-cantles. Didn't buy it, to lose it trailing.

He slipped the grey's reins from the hitch-post and swung on up—looked back to see the girl lashing the fry pan and coffee pot to the side of her saddle. Her bare hands looked thinner and darker than ever as she looped the rawhide and knotted it through a slow white swirl of falling snow. Coming down heavier and bigger flakes. Cold enough so that the flakes lay unmelted on the thin, worn wool of her coat.

Lee waited 'till she was done, and mounted on the paint, then led out down the rutted street at a jog trot. No use actually *waiting* for their damn constable.

He rode along two blocks and more, the girl (Charity) jogging along behind. Then he pulled the grey up and sat the saddle, considering. The snow was coming down like sixty now. Not much traffic on Main Street. A couple of lumber drays . . .

Sat the saddle a few moments more, the girl pulled up behind, waiting—then said "Shit!" Turned the grey's head, and rode right back the way he'd come.

Mister DuPont didn't look surprised to see him.

They rode out half an hour later. The Indian girl was fitted out with wool skirt, wool trousers (to be shortened on the trail) two wool shirts, cotton underthings ("They don't itch the ladies near as much," DuPont had said), wool socks, lamb's wool scarf, mittens, new moccasins, her own bar of soap, a tortoise shell comb, a fine hunting knife with a seven-inch blade, and—Lee figured he'd better arm her, or blame himself later for not—a brand new Winchester lever-action rifle. A thirty caliber. Too light a piece for Lee's liking, but about right for a girl Indian weighed about a hundred pounds.

All that cost him a sight of money, and Lee was relieved that DuPont had no wolf parkas small enough to fit her. Had to make do with beaver, wool-lined.

By God, I hope you're satisfied! Lee said to himself as they rode up-slope and out of town, the grey farting his morning farts. *I hope you're satisfied, spending that sort of money, and for what? So a goddamn Cree Indian will think you're a jackass—that's for what!*

Now was that all. A fat and sleepy whore had been roused out into the alley behind Barney Barkley's (Charity had gone in to wake her and call her out) to receive a rock crystal necklace as a gift, a rock crystal necklace that had cost Lee nine dollars and fifty cents at DuPont's.

Riding out of that alley leaving a fat, red-skinned, sateen-wrapped whore weeping, clutching her bauble, Lee determined that he was single-handed keeping the store keeper in business, and commencing the enrichment of the Cree nation as well.

By midafternoon the snow had stopped, and Lee followed Charity's lead along the timber line of a mountain twice the size of the Old Man at home. It was high country, and cold, and they rode into a wind that stung at Lee's face huddled into his fine new scarf like a swarm of bees.

To their left, the land fell away in great steep swoops, stairways for a race of giants who might, in hundred-yard strides, go thundering down that deep. To Lee's right, the cliffs rose up granite grey and sheer as hanging curtains, higher than a rifle shot, to still more cliffs above, lifting into the sky's haze, as cold and granite colored as the stone. These huge faces had fractured here and there and spired into pinnacles and towers, then sunk at some distant heights into deep and sudden caverns, gaping like the roosts of owls big as houses high on wide rock walls.

The wind came buffeting and gave no rest; twice, both the grey and paint had tried to stop and turn their butts to it for poor shelter.

Lee, feeling that if this was the start of winter in this country, then the rest of that season would be something to behold, had second and third thoughts about the big-nosed girl as guide. She had insisted on riding high, rather than following the river road through the forests.

"Too many," she'd said, when Lee had asked her why. "Too many." Meaning, he had supposed, that too many travelers took that road. Too many travelers who might notice and talk about a Yankee out riding after Lord Surrey's camp. Perhaps, also, too many woods-runners who might back-shoot and murder venturers with good horses under them and warm clothes on their backs.

She might have meant that. Or she might have meant evil spirits—way too many of those—or ghosts of ancestors, or unappeased animal souls, hunted and not apologized to. There was no way of telling what went on behind those anthracite eyes, that beak of a nose, that narrow brow. Homely as a hedge fence and, more than likely, no proper guide at all.

Lee booted the grey a tad to the right—the fool beast was curious, it seemed, and leaned between wind gusts to look down into the pitchy valley below. A hard trail, but the girl had seemed to know it and did not appear to be frightened by it. She rode ahead, back straight as a cavalryman's—fine saddle-sitting for a woods Indian—and seemed unworried by the uncertainty of the trail, or by the weather either. Not, of course, that she had need to be, considering the fine woolens and furs she was wearing. Truth was, far as clothing went, they were both snug as bugs in rugs.

It was the possibility of a fall and a busted horse leg that worried Lee. That happen, they would be in sore straits . . .

The girl had paused on the first steep rise hours before, pulled the stocky paint to a halt, and pointed back and down.

Lee, turning in his sasddle, had seen far, far below them the short, thin, little black worm of *Eustache*, where the town straggled for its quarter mile along the merest slight section of the mountain's skirt.

A far piece.

Ahead, the girl and paint horse turned a rock-shelf corner to the right and disappeared. Lee touched the grey with his left-side spur to quicken him and keep him to the right. Occurred to him that Surrey might already know of some such likelihood as Dowd's friend coming north. It was possible that Dowd's dying babble had been heard and noted. Possible, too, that Surrey or his cannibal Frenchman had caught old Pebble in his brush hidey and squeezed out of him the tale they'd let him carry south.

Lee had no notion of believing he knew all that had happened at Dowd's camp. No notion, either, that this big-nosed girl was as simple as she seemed.

It was a question of choice, that was all.

He had chosen, first, to come up—on the fact of Dowd's death, most of all.

Surrey was a cause in that for sure. The cannibal Frenchman, too. And if old Pebble or this stick of a girl happened to be a bait—

346

so be it. Time would tell whether the trap would hold the bear.

CHAPTER SIX

That night and the night thereafter they camped high. The first night, the girl found a fallen pine weathered more than half to punk, and wedged down in a rock crack ten feet deep.

The new winter wind poured over that ditch like a river, and if either Lee or the girl stood up, they were buffeted, the girl sent staggering. But the punk wood burned to a fine red-crusted roar, heating the cleft to hot at least where it was deepest.

Difficult to think of a finer trail camp in such weather. Would have been no good at all in rain, no good in hard heat—but for a bitter, raw wind, salted with snow, none better.

The girl had set to shifting for supper right away—had sliced the bacon and after that, discovered in the possibles sack a gift of a dozen of last morning's biscuits from Mister Gruen tucked in, likely, while Lee spoke to the Indian girl on Gruen's back porch. Lee's lie about not preferring beaten biscuits had produced its reward. The bacon sliced, the biscuits tucked down near the coals to warm, the girl had shaken canteen water—no need to conserve what the sky was flurrying down —over a tin plate of corn meal, and commenced to mix corn cakes into a frying batter. Then, the bacon into the pan, sizzling until half-cooked and shoved aside for the corn cakes to fry in the fat. Poked and prodded, then tested and tasted from the gleaming point and edge of her new knife.

When it was done—bacon crisp, with an edge of popping fat to line each slice, corn cakes puffed and browning, smelling like summer—the girl parceled it out on tin pie plates (salvaged by her from the horse-pack), and set the coffee in the fire to rumble to a ready boil and be yanked as swiftly out. She pulled a can of peaches from Lee's saddle-bags, hacked off the top of it, and set it out to be drunk and eaten from.

After that dinner, Lee no longer regretted the spree at DuPont's store, or resented the clothes and parka he had felt he must buy the girl. The Big-nose girl threw a better camp than Pebble had, and Pebble had been no slouch at trailing.

The heat of the burning fallen log was such

that neither had to wrap in a buffalo robe, but only stretch out on it, like a gentleman and lady in back garden hammocks. Through the night, just above their heads, the bitter wind went blowing, but not upon them.

One of the best camps Lee had known.

The second high camp was a different kettle of fish.

It came, for one thing, after a longer day's riding and a day's riding higher than the day before, so that the horses panted as they climbed, and Lee found his mouth and throat so dry that he had to drink water time and again to ease that dryness. The girl drank a good deal of water, too, and Lee heard her cough a time or two when she rode short in the lead.

Still, she seemed to know her way and, unlike her grandfather, appeared to take no delight in finding rough ways out to test Lee's riding, or his fine grey's carrying. She guided for the smoothest way, and precious little there was of smoothness on that no-name mountain's shoulder.

By the second evening, Lee and the girl were both dismounted, leading their horses skidding and clattering along a ledge barely wide enough. The light was leaving them—the last of the day barely bright enough to reveal the miles on miles of dark green forest stretching out from the western slopes of the mountains. There was, or seemed to be, a break in that expanse, the fading mirror-

gleam of a lake two, three days ride away—
and that only after the edge forest was
reached.

There were darker lines coiling through the
distant woods. Rivers, apparently, but not
wide enough to show as more than dark
partings in the wilderness of trees.

Earlier, Charity had pointed out one of
those leagues-away oxbows, said,
"Sansakootch," or something like it for the
river's name, and added that White Chief
Surrey was encamped there, measuring out
the land. Surveying, Lee assumed.

It looked to be a hell of a far piece.

The ledge they were leading along now
looked to be too long a piece itself. Lee
wondered if Big-nose had lost her way and
was scared to admit it. Soon enough, it would
be too dark to try and turn the horses, get
back to wider ground. The wind was down,
which was a mercy, but if anything it was
even colder than it had been the day before
. . . cold that worked and pried at a man, to
weary him and bite into his bones.

Lee heard a dim thundering—seemed to
rise and fall to some sort of rhythm—not like
weather thunder at all. He looked sharp and
looked up, thinking that an avalanche might
be coming down on them. But the cliffs
above were clear, as well as he could see in
the failing light. If the light dimmed much
more, he was liable—and the girl that much

more liable—to lead his horse straight over the shelf's edge into empty air.

That thundering . . . it stirred the mass of rock under his feet, vibrated and shook it. Perhaps an avalanche ahead—and if so, the squaw appeared willing to lead on into it.

"Say! SAY—GOD-DAMNIT!" He saw her stop walking, turn, and look back at him past the paint's shoulder. Could barely make that out, it was getting so dark.

Lee dropped the grey's reins rather than crowd him forward into the paint's butt, trusting the horse to stay ground-tied for a minute without going to try and fly off the ledge, and edged his way up alongside the paint to the Cree girl.

"What in hell's that noise?" He cupped his hand to his ear to demonstrate "noise."

The skinny thing gave him that look of hers, a stare made odder from under the hood of the beaver parka, shrugged, and said, "Water . . . falling." She made a graceful falling gesture with her free hand, the other fast to the paint's rein.

"Waterfall."

She shook her head. "Yes."

Lee shook his head, too, but meant no "Yes" by it. He walked carefully back to the grey, which had had the smarts to stay put, and gathered up its reins.

When he looked back, the girl was still watching him, apparently for instructions, and Lee waved her on. It was too late and too dark now to be turning back. Night might catch them on the ledge ahead or under that falls but it would certain sure catch them on the ledge if they turned back now.

One thing, though—the girl knew the trail, had been on it before. "Falling water . . ." And a graceful wrist to go with it. Damn shame about that nose. Gave her a proud look, though, if a man could get used to the *size* of the thing.

Lee saw her up ahead tugging at the paint's leather to get him moving, then turning to lead the animal on. Lee hauled the reluctant grey on after. The big horse was pleased enough to be ridden. Didn't care to be led. As they moved, creeping along the rock shelf as cautious as maiden aunts, the horses snorting and trembling, clattering uneasily along, Lee heard the thundering of the falls grow louder. The stone vibrated under his boot soles as it were being struck with great hammers. Thing must run close . . .

Ahead, Charity led the pinto up a shallow fall, then on. Lee saw the pinto's tail switching, the white splotches on its butt just visible. Going to be time to camp up, and soon. Time you can't see a half-white horse not twenty feet from you is the time to get off a mountain sheer and camp up. Trouble was, Lee saw no sign of the ledge widening, not in an hour and more of leading along it.

No sign of the pinto at all now, and Lee

stepped out a little, but carefully, keeping his eye to the left, following the line of the shelf edge there. Not in that much of a hurry that he wanted to sail on down two thousand feet and more to light hard at the tree-line.

No sign of the pinto—and he stepped a little faster, guiding, before he realized it, by the gleam of wet on the granite ledge.

Led around a ragged corner of stone, a corner a foot to his right that rose straight up and out of sight in darkness. It was night now and no mistake.

As he cleared that corner, the grey shaking his head, holding back, Lee was struck by a cloud of ice water spray that soaked him ass to tea kettle in a flash.

With it, a crash of sound.

Already wet, and too late to worry about that, Lee saw the pinto's light colored hide huddled against the mountain wall a yard or two ahead, and past the horse (and Indian girl holding its halter) saw a blacker blackness than the night had to offer, arching up and out over their heads—and farther, twenty feet out from the ledge. A black river, gleaming as poured oil, launched itself from high above, and poured in that terrific torrent over them . . . and far out . . . and down and down and down through the air. It thundered and struck the mountain's stone as it leaped . . . and was so black. Not any trace of foam marred its blackness once it was launched out, arching over them. A black, rushing

355

river, falling away into black night air. It was impossible to see or hear where it fell down there, or if it fell and struck at all short of those empty thousands of feet.

It was the damndest thing . . .

And they were soaked through—furs, clothes, sacks and saddle-bags. The horses were soaked.

And this on a mountain height, and that colder than the Seventh Circle. The Redskin bitch had blundered enough to freeze them dead. His fault, though. He'd let her lead too long, tired, and she'd remembered the falls being still another turn ahead, been surprised and soaked in iced water before she knew it.

Wouldn't matter who was at fault, though. Get out of this quick or die for the error.

Lee hauled the grey up closer, reached out to seize the girl's sopping furs and dragged her to him to shout in her ear over the smashing of the falls above.

"WHAT'S AHEAD? WHAT'S PAST THIS FALL?"

The girl—he could barely make out her face—shouted back, "SAME!" meaning, Lee devoutly hoped, more ledge, and not more falling water. He felt her trembling under his hand—freezing and tired, and out of grit— and so would he be if he stood drenched under that river for long.

Lee gave the Cree a savage shake to stir her. "COME ON AFTER ME!" Without waiting to see if she understood or would follow, he yanked the grey's rein and towed the tall horse along after him beneath that over-arching flood, slipping and stumbling through icy showers over heaps of rubble on that dark and narrow way. He kept his right shoulder to the rock wall, hauled the grey's head down when the animal whinnied and made to rear in the darkness, and threatened to shoot the beast there and then—a promise unheard in the appalling freight train noise of the river that ran overhead.

It seemed a long run in the dark.

Lee tripped over a low rock-shelf, fell to his knees, and staggered to his feet fast, not wanting the grey to lunge over him, kick him. A few more steps, the horse coming along pretty well, scared quiet by the dark and noise, and Lee climbed up another shallow shelf, the grey coming up right behind him—and found himself out of the freezing spray. The crashing noise was muffled to a grinding roar. Turned some sort of a corner there and he was thankful for it.

He held the grey close and turned to try and see the girl. Would have been easy enough for her to walk straight over that edge or be yanked over by the paint in panic.

Nothing. Nothing coming along the narrow ledge out of the dark.

He'd have to leave the grey. Leave him standing, and go back for that damn squaw.

Lee dropped the horse's reins, put his left and out to find the side of the mountain, and started walking back along the ledge, back into the thunder of the torrent. He could see nothing . . . feel the wet stone wall under his left hand, the rough stones and rubble under his boots. *Keep left, or fall.*

The girl walked into him out of the dark. Didn't know she was there 'till she smacked into him, soaked fur, skinny arms, big nose and all. The paint loomed shadowy-light behind.

The grey was waiting where he'd been left, too frightened to move off in the dark, likely. Lee picked up his reins, and led out. It was get clear of that icy water misting down, spraying the ledge from side to side from the falls, or freeze in the night and die.

Not more than a hundred feet further down the ledge, Lee found the shelf just slightly wider, near as he could tell probing out to the edge with the Sharp's long barrel. Dark as the inside of a sack. Back of this stretch, in the mountain wall, was a long, shallow niche, not more than a foot or two high, the same in depth.

It wasn't much. Maybe not enough, if the night got even colder. Ice rimmed the fur of Lee's parka; he had felt it with his fingers, crusted down the mountain's stone. *Maybe not enough . . .* But no choice at all about it. Try leading on out across this ledge in pitch dark, and freezing—they'd go over. They'd fall or die of the cold.

No choice left on that. Camp in here or say good-bye.

It was no slice of pie, even so. The only dry things they had were the buffalo robes still rolled under the slickers behind their saddles. Lee reached out for the girl in the dark—she was stumbling on the ledge as if she were drunk—got a hold of her, and shouted into her ear what he wanted her to do. The sounds of the river were lower now, but still rumbled through the air like drums.

Together in the dark, keeping as near the mountain wall as they could, Lee and the girl hauled the two horses in close to that long niche in the stone, found Lee's lariat-coil at his saddle-bow, slipped the line through both animals' halters, and knotted it short to hold them close together. Then Lee hobbled them, stripped the saddles, cut the frozen rawhide lashings on the slicker rolls, and tugged out the buffalo robes to spread out along the niche's shallow length. Lee's hands lost all feeling as he worked; he had to put his face down to them once in the dark to feel where he held his knife . . . where the blade was. The steel burned his face like fire.

When he'd finished, Lee had to search for the girl again, stumbling over the stones, yelling for her. He thought she might have gone over the edge, and was crouching, feeling his way to out across the ledge, when he found her lying curled on her side, shaking. He stood, pulled her to her feet, slapped her across the face, and shoved her back toward the mountain wall. He followed her there, took hold of her, dragged her stumbling in behind the hobbled horses, and stripped the ice-stiff clothing off her. He stripped her naked—she was narrow-built as a child—then pushed her down into the stone niche, into the folds of the buffalo robes. Her skin had seemed cold as the stone itself to him.

Then he pulled his own clothes off. Wet to the skin and trembling, barely able to bend his fingers. It took a time to do. The furs, the wool shirt and trousers, his underwear, socks and boots were all frozen stiff as cardboard and crackled with ice as he dragged them off.

If there were any wind at all up here, he and the girl would be dead as doornails already. No wind (and that unusual, so high) and the robes kept dry in their slicker rolls. . . These gave them their only chance.

Lee managed to get most of the girl's clothes together with his own, and spread the parkas and other pieces he could find across the horses' backs as they shifted together in the dark, snorting. He got the stuff on them, and he found the possibles sack, got out lashing line, and corded the clothes across the horses' backs.

He did it stark naked, and freezing, and in the dark—and it was the hardest thing to do that he had ever done. The only chance, though, to get those goods dry by morning. And those goods had better be dry by morning, or dry enough to wear, or God Almighty help them!

CHAPTER SEVEN

The next day, they led the horses over the mountain's hump and on down to the tree-line—still very high, but not as high as before.

They were both tired as trolley-horses. Lee's bones felt like hollow sticks, stumping along. Only good thing was, the grey was weary too, too tired to act up. The country around them was slowly leveling out, thank God. Lee had always loved the mountains and had ridden high in them many times, but never had gotten into such a fix as last night's.

That one had damn near killed him. Still felt cold and every stitch he had on felt nearly damp as a dish-rag but just dry enough to wear.

The girl had perked up fine, though, as far

as you could tell with Indians. Had spent the night wrapped around him, buck naked and skinny as a San Francisco organ grinder's monkey. Cold as a dish of iced-cream, too. Creature didn't ever seem to warm up. Then, bright and early in the dawn, damned if she didn't wake up and get up, bright as a new penny (about the same color, too) and set to doing the horses, and then a foul cold breakfast that Lee was grateful to eat.

That ledge, in daylight, was enough to frighten a general—not more than five or six feet wide and paved with sharp stone trash, and this their refuge and safety in the night.

The big-nose girl—*what the hell was her name?* Charity. Charity'd picked right up, hadn't made any excuse for guiding them into that tight, for not stopping well short of the falls—had just picked right up and gone to guiding. Taken them over the rest of the mountain.

Lee'd stepped to the lead then—any fool could see the way past timberline. He was pleased the manner the grey and paint had come through that cold night and done some clothes drying while they were at it. Poor as that packy had been—a sad representative of Spade Bit stock—poor as he'd been, the grey and paint were fine and better than fine. Couldn't ask for sweeter stayers than these horses.

The distant river that marked the forest in its dark, winding line, was closer now.

Looked to be no more than two, three day's ride away. Then . . . then it would be time to skin the cat. Lee had been wondering how it was that little Dowd got caught so short . . . had not gone better guarded to do his land-buying business against the interests of the young English Lord, it seemed. Been thinking about that, climbing down the steeps—seeing some shrub and mosses, now, the dwarf pines beginning a few hundred feet further down. (Nice hot day—damn cold, was the truth—but *seemed* hot as biscuits after a night on that ledge!)

Lee'd been thinking about it—why the little man had been so incautious—and now thought he knew. Old Gruen had given him the hint, with all that about history. Dowd had been Canadian, had been raised to respect those ancient English families. Lord Surrey. Son of a Duke! A real English Earl.

What fellow raised more British-than-not would think that an Earl would as quick to kill for his profit as any back-alley bully for a five-dollar piece?

Little Dowd should have remembered his history better and recalled just how those fine families had gotten their lands and noble titles. With what play of swords and axes. What knives in the dark . . .

So there'd be no long parley at Surrey's camp. The boy would likely be as quick to take Lee's measure as Dowd's and come to the same conclusion of killing—or trying to.

No delay with that cannibal trapper, either. The English boy would keep that creature close to guard him, might suspect—if he didn't know—that some friend of Dowd's might come calling. Charity had called the trapper a *loup-garou*, some sort of werewolf, she thought, near as Lee could make out. Scared her, that was for sure. Lee'd heard it took silver bullets to kill those creatures. In this case, steel or lead would have to do.

Surprise wouldn't be in it, that was for sure. Lee had no notion of coming close through a trapper's forest without the trapper knowing.

They'd know he was coming, the last day or so.

As well, though, they didn't know earlier—know soon enough to set a dead-fall of some kind for him. Meant no hunting, no gunshots to echo from the mountains. Could snare some early snowshoes, likely, roast them on sticks with some bacon stuffed into them. That would be about it for the hunting, next two or three days.

Not a bad day for weather, either. Cold but clear enough for good seeing, and still none of that hard, steady wind that had shoved at them first night out. A few clouds like sailing ships, way off to the west. Silver-white. No look of rain to them.

No. Not much use of playing French detective—the Lupin fellow. No use playing him or a Pinkerton with this fine young Lord and his

cannibal friend. Sure to be quick doings . . .
Lee felt satisfied enough with that. Wasn't
frightened by the notion, in any case. Likely
had all the scare scared out of him by that
brute in Barney Barkley's. If that underhand
throw had missed, the man might well have
carved Lee to a Sunday roast. Big enough.
Tough enough, too.

Not a bad day, if he'd had more sleep and
less shivering. Woke with a hard-on, too,
right smack up against the Indian girl's
skinny belly. She hadn't appeared to take
notice of it, and he'd turned away from her.
Whoever said a boner had no conscience?
One of the Latin authors, Lee thought. Professor Riles had quoted the man to him once,
in his cups. Damned if he could remember
which one . . . Catullus, maybe, though that
seemed too pat.

Some advantage, Lee supposed, to even an
incompleted education.

He was walking, leading down among
thick-grown scrub pine now. The true
timberline beginning. It felt good to be away
from only rock and stones, to be back among
green growing things again, even these short,
dense, paltry trees. Lee heard a marmot
whistle in some alarm up ahead. Likely the
shadow of a hawk had frightened it. Be time
soon for the marmots to start sleeping in for
the winter.

Lee stopped walking, held the grey's halter
for a moment to steady him, then set his

boot toe in the stirrup and swung up. "Time for you to do some of the work . . ." Safe enough riding from here—the track was gentle, at least what could be seen of it through the small crowded pines.

Lee looked back and saw the girl leading down; the paint was behaving well. No reason she shouldn't mount up, too. The lord only knew they'd walked their share.

Lee dug into his war-bag for the coils of his whip, pulled the black-snake out, shook out the fine, black braided leather, and commenced, with easy swings of his arm, to shake out the lash, and then, for practice and while thinking, to pop the leather at the stands of little trees he passed snipping morsels off here and there.

He had not thought of S'ien for a day and more.

He had just realized that, and was wondering what it meant when the grey screamed, reared straight up, whirled, and threw Lee ass over tea-cup into the greenery.

The pines were growing thick at this height, and they were there in plenty but there was no brushy ground beneath them. Lee hit stony soil, and he hit it hard. Heard the grey galloping as he lay there, heard the Indian girl—Charity—heard Charity shouting. Lee thought if his neck was broken, he'd know it, so thought it wasn't. He was lying on his face—felt marked up there more than a little—and said "God damnit!" turned over, and got up onto his knees. Still had the whip clutched in his hand. Damn nothing else. His hat had flown off. Revolver gone. Lee didn't try to stand up for a moment, afraid he'd find he'd broken a leg, at least, if not his neck. One of the worst falls he'd even taken off a horse—*That wood-headed grey son-of-a-bitch! Better be the biggest rattler in the world scared him or the biggest wasp bit him in the ass. Better be!*

Lee wiggled his feet in his boots; legs seemed all right. He was starting to feel a fool, on his knees here. The girl would think he was a damn fool.

Lee stood up but he took his time about it. A rattling fall, and no mistake.

He looked up-trail, and saw that Charity had managed to catch the grey when he ran by her—still having a hard time holding him, though; paint jumping around up there, too. Girl was staring at Lee with her mouth wide open. Looked like a baby bird, with that big beak. Guess she never saw a fellow flying before!

Lee heard a grunt, turned and saw a grizzly bear—a big bear the color of cinnamon. It was up on its hinds not forty feet away, its paws folded to its chest, and was looking at him, weaving its head slowly from side to side like a near-sighted man trying to make something out.

The girl shouted, and Lee knew what she would do next. He turned just as she was hauling her brand new Winchester repeater out of its scabbard at the paint's shoulder. Hard doings, too; both horses were dancing around her, trying to get her between them and the bear.

We'll get out of this, Lee thought, if that squaw doesn't start shooting. Might as well send Surrey a telegraph message as start firing rifle shots in these mountains!

He gestured "No"—couldn't remember to nod or shake his head, and finally shouted, "No shooting, God damnit!"

The bear didn't care for that shouting— likely had been out on the mountain hunting marmots for his winter sleep. Didn't like the shouting at all.

Lee heard the bear squeal—exactly the sound a huge pig might have made—turned, and saw the animal drop suddenly to all fours, almost out of sight in the dwarf pines, and come for him.

Lee was astonished how fast that huge beast moved. It came galloping, crashing through the little pines as if they'd been prairie grass. It looked like a great gold-brown rug, suddenly animated and made furious and given the power to charge, fronted with a gaping, wrinkled black muzzle packed with yellow teeth.

The bear champed its jaws, squealed like the father of all pigs and came for him.

Lee spun and ran to the right, conscious as he did it that he was running faster than he ever had—much faster than most men could run. Right after that, he wished the girl would disobey him, and shoot at the thing. . .

He heard the dense little pines smash right behind him, spun again with the whip still in his hand, and threw out a desperate coil to lash at the beast.

It was great good luck, and only luck, that he struck the creature's muzzle a sharp *crack* of the lash. The bear must have jerked its head aside at the sting of that, though so quickly that Lee didn't see it. Perhaps the sharp snapping sound so close to its ear threw it off its balance. But whichever, it shifted in its stride, struck Lee a glancing blow with a paw, too quick a movement for Lee to clearly see, and knocked him away ten feet, his left arm dead as mutton.

He thought he heard the girl scream.

Rooting sounds . . . snorting, rooting sounds. *Now . . . what in hell?* Lee woke up all the way as if from a terrible dream and heard the girl screaming in earnest and the sounds the bear made a few yards away. Damn animal!

Lee got to his feet and stood steady enough. He didn't feel so bad. Left arm was gone— Lee glanced down—was numb. Still had the whip.

The bear was making no noise. How could such a big animal get out of sight in the pine thickets? Lee took a slow, careful step back. Might be able to run. Might do that, and get clear . . . call to the girl from further down in the trees . . .

Lee took another slow, careful step back. Was sorry the moment he did it. It made a noise.

The bear stood up out of the pine scrub not much more than fifteen feet away and stared down at Lee. Its head was huge, looking two feet wide. The eyes were very small. They didn't look like a dog's eyes. They looked like a stupid person's eyes, set in an awful head.

Lee was so frightened he felt sick. The girl had stopped screaming.

Do something! Do something—or run like a rabbit, and listen to the bear catch up.

Lee drew back his right arm, yelled with the effort, and lashed at the bear with all his strength, the long coil of the whip leaping out, the tiny, lead-weighted tip striking the animal straight across the snout.

The beast snorted and shook its head and then took two rolling steps forward on its hind legs, its massive weight swaying from side to side. There was foam on the side of its muzzle.

Lee struck at it again. Long whip-lash whined through the air and caught the bear alongside its head, just below its ear.

The beast bawled at that, and shook its head again, suddenly snapping to the side, as if at an insect that had bitten it. But it watched Lee's right arm. Lee could smell the thing; it smelled of rotten meat.

Lee felt the bear would kill him, sure; and more in anger over this than out of courage, he drew back his arm and whipped at the animal again. But this time, in a wonderfully quick way, the bear, even awkward on its hind legs, swayed away from the flickering lash, and was not touched.

The whip, all Lee's strength behind it, cracked on empty air.

That sound appeared to frighten the animal as the slicing stroke of the lash had not. The grizzly looked down at Lee a moment more, its great head cocked to the side as if to inquire about that sharp and sudden sound.

Lee stood and looked back—hadn't the strength to do a damn thing more. Was run out of sand. Out of piss, too. Lee felt the wetness of his crotch.

The bear went to all fours more gracefully than any human could do anything and disappeared, sunk into the green thicket of stunted pines only fifteen feet away.

Lee thought he heard him . . . was certain he heard him coming. Coming slowly . . .

It seemed to take a very long time. Lee would have preferred the bear come standing, where he could see him. It was tiring, waiting to be killed, and not seeing anything.

Lee stood there, stood still, until the Indian girl called to him. He'd been staring into the thick growth of pines and was reluctant to raise his eyes from the green to look for her.

He didn't want the bear to surprise him. He wanted to see it coming.

The Indian girl called to him again.

Slowly . . . slowly, Lee looked up, and saw her perhaps a hundred yards away. She stood with the two horses. They still pranced around her, sidling and tugging at the reins. Nothing seemed to have changed over there at all. It was as if the bear had faced Lee only for an instant.

The girl pointed away, down the mountain. Pointed again, and made a swift, rippling, traveling sign with her fingers.

Lee heard himself breathing in and out . . . in and out. It appeared that the grizzly was gone.

The first thing he felt was a terrible anger at the girl for not shooting at it. That seemed for a few moments to be something unforgiveable. Lee felt like killing her for it. He remembered very well telling her not to fire and he remembered very well why that was important, but all that seemed beside the point.

The point was, she should have shot that bear—should certainly have shot *at* it.

He was too angry to talk to her for some time. He waded through the shoulder-high stand of pines to catch up the grey's reins from her, and, despite his left arm which felt asleep, numb and full of prickles, he managed to climb aboard the horse, and after a moment was able to spur it slightly and make it walk down toward the trail. He didn't care a damn if she'd seen he'd pissed his pants.

There, where the grey had reared, Lee rode in small circles, looking for his Stetson and the Bisley Colt's. He didn't trouble to take the Sharp's out of the rifle boot. He wasn't thinking of the bear, but only about the girl's stupidity in not shooting at it.

He found the revolver first—a piece of luck, because it had fallen under one of the pines, and was hard to see. The Stetson took longer and he was about to give up on it, when he saw a particular shade of grey within some green, and that turned out to be the hat. It had sailed a ways. Lee picked up both revolver and hat by leaning down from the saddle. He didn't feel like getting off the horse, and mounting up again. Seemed like too much work.

He put on his hat, set it firmly on his head, and turned the grey downhill again. To hell with the girl—she could follow on or not. Stupid savage, standing there with that Winchester in her hands. Damned if he knew what he had bought her the rifle for if she was too dumb to use it.

He found, as he rode, that he had a headache that got worse instead of better. Seemed to be cracking his head wide open . . . hurt so bad, it made him sick to his stomach.

More than a mile down the trail with the Indian girl riding well behind Lee felt too sick to stay on the horse. He pulled the grey up, climbed down, stood bent over, his hands braced on his knees, and vomited up his breakfast. He thought as he did it that maybe his heart was coming up as well, he felt that bad.

When he was finished, he stayed bent over a little longer, trying to get a true deep breath. His heart was running like a locomotive on a track. Damn hard to get a deep breath into him.

Stayed right there for a while. Seemed as though that bear had been a bad dream, fast as it had happened. Just a bad dream, and that was all . . .

The girl, Charity, rode up and sat her horse, watching him. Lee knew she was there but didn't care to look at her. Having her fun, he supposed, to see a white man had pissed his pants from fear and lost his breakfast from it, too.

"Bear-whipper," the girl said, from the paint's saddle. "No man has been so brave as that . . ."

Lee heard that stuff and didn't think much of it, but he stood up straight, at the least. Showed what a fool the girl was—how young she was—to be spouting horse-shit like that. He unknotted his bandanna and wiped his mouth with it. Wouldn't be much of a Roland with vomit on his chin.

"Don't be a damn fool," he said to the Indian girl. " That animal scared me half to death, and you know it." He went to the grey, shaking his left arm to get more life into it. It still stung and prickled, felt more than half asleep.

"Yes," the Indian girl said, "one side scared; other side, brave."

"Why don't you be quiet?" Lee said and using his right hand and arm, hauled himself up into the saddle. It occurred to him that if the bear had hit his right shoulder, he'd be out of the revolver-drawing business, maybe forever. As it was, a sad left arm would be of little help down in that forest, little help against Surrey and his French friend.

He spurred the grey on out through the dwarf pines, feeling a little better than he had. Better for the vomiting, likely.

CHAPTER EIGHT

That night at last they camped off the mountain.

They rode down off the stone in early evening, down through fields of autumn-browned brush, into the first big trees. The evening was cold, and now, as if it had waited until they were off the mountain, the wind sprang up and came whistling through the hemlocks and great pines to ruffle the horses' manes, tug at the brim of Lee's Stetson. A cold wind, with the colder smell of snow on it.

These trees, even at the mountain's foot, were big enough, tall enough, for each to have cleared around itself a space bare of other growth or brush, carpeted with soft needles deep enough to muffle the sounds of the horses' hooves. It made for quiet riding—

and all the better, Lee thought. The quieter, the better. He rubbed his left arm as they rode through dusky tree-shade. The cold wind made his left shoulder ache.

Riding into these trees was easy enough. Perhaps riding out would be more difficult.

Charity cooked bacon and sugar-flour for him for supper—refused that dainty sweet herself. Had candy, then, the two of them. Sitting in a forest as lost as Atlantis, he still stiff from a monster's paw, they gobbled bull's eyes and jaw breakers like kids.

The wind died again by full dark, and the still, silent cold came settling down through the trees.

Lee lay in his buffalo robe, trying to ease the ache in his left shoulder, in the muscle of his back. Felt as if he'd gone full rounds with the Champion. This forest air smelled better than good—the odor of pine as rich as toilet-water, but cleaner by the nostrils, somehow. Cleaner. Odd, how after such a fright by a great wild creature he felt no fear at all of this forest dark. It was as if a man had only so much fear in him and could exhaust it, run out of fear as men sometimes ran out of courage. If that was true, then sure as God made little green apples, he had scraped the bottom of his barrel of that commodity. The bear had taken all fear from him—at least for a while.

Lee lay thinking of other times, sunnier country. Other people, too. Some living.

Most of them, dead. Didn't make him sad, though, thinking of the dead ones. His father . . . and Harvey Logan. That small pimp, out behind Blackie's in San Francisco. Catherine Dowd . . . S'ien.

Didn't make him sad. It made him . . . consider matters. Appeared that being near eaten by a bear made for philosophy. Life and the puzzles of life. Jig-saw puzzles, was what they were . . .

He was just slipping into sleep when the Big-nosed girl came to him in the dark.

She woke him when she left her robe across the fire's embers. He heard her getting up, stepping softly over the pine needle carpet. She came to him around the fire. He turned his head and saw her in the embers' glow, buck naked and skinny as a grass stalk in the faint, warm light. Shame about her nose . . . Slanted eyes, much like S'ien's, really. No question at all those people were relatives of some sort—the Indians and Orientals. Too like not to be.

Little fur on her narrow cunt that he could see—almost bare, and soft, the slit pouted tight shut as any child's. Her tender breasts, in ember-light, were delicate, barely budded, but tipped with the fat, brown nipples of a woman.

"Go on back over there," Lee said to her. "Get in that robe there or you'll freeze your butt."

She said nothing to that, but came to him,

bent down and drew back his cover and slid in beside him bare as a nut. Her skin was smooth as glass and icy cold from only that short walk.

"You're not much comfort," Lee said, "cold as that. I was more comfortable without you." She turned on her side to him under the buffalo robe and commenced to rub at his sore left arm and shoulder. Her hand was cold, too. "More comfortable by a damn sight." But she continued that rubbing, and it felt well enough, seemed to help the arm a bit, being rubbed like that. His shoulder ached more than a little, though. She was digging her fingers into the muscles there, felt like she was trying to dig the ache right out of him.

Felt all right. Felt pretty good, really . . . Hurt sometimes, when she gripped too hard but all in all, felt pretty good. He turned a little so that she could get at his shoulder-blade and she slid her fingers up his back there, drew the line of the blade-bone with her fingertips, then pressed harder, as if she could push the pain out of him, force the stiffness and soreness out.

"Not so hard."

She eased off then but only for a while, then began stroking harder, pressing harder. This time it felt all right. Pleasant, to have her so close, to have the arm and shoulder rubbed to warmth in that way. Must have learned the trick of it rubbing at her grandfather's aches and pains. Old rheumatics . . .

He stretched out under the buffalo robe, easing under the girl's thin, strong hands. Rubbing, stroking, pressing the stiffness away, drawing out the ache of it.

"You're a good girl," Lee said. "I told you not to shoot at that damn bear and you didn't do it.

"Good girl."

He turned on his back in the warmth of the buffalo robes, and the girl slid a skinny leg across his belly, and sat half up the better to lean her weight onto his arm and shoulder. She had strong hands for such a slight girl. Warmer now, too. Her skin was warm from the shelter of the robe, from the heat of their bodies together.

She dug her thumbs into the joint of Lee's shoulder where the pain, the stiffness seemed to be set, and seemed to search the discomfort out. Hurt as much as the ache itself at first, then slowly made it better.

Big nose or not, Lee was becoming mighty fond. *Charity* . . . in no way misnamed.

She shifted, stroking Lee's bruised shoulder, his arm, more lightly. Lee began to consider that the Cree Indians had a value considerably above other Redskins, if this sort of Swedish rubbing was a habit among them. Never heard that the Sioux or Comanche did such—the Blackfeet either. It seemed a greater gift than the artful scalping of white land agents and troopers had proved to be for those southern tribes.

"I want to thank you for this," Lee said, and surely meant it. He could clench his left hand now and feel only a shadow of pain up through his shoulder. Much better. The grizzly had clubbed him as a great baseball player might have done wielding a bat of stone. Felt a lot better. And here was Lee Morgan, sport and horse-rancher (and try not to think of chores left uncompleted on the Bit. Try not to think of the Mexican fever, the hoof-and-mouth. Not that far north, please God!) "Thank you," Lee said into the dark to an invisible girl, tall and scrawny, naked and mirror-smooth, boney as a bunch of sticks. Her shaggy, rough-cut hair smelled like a fox's pelt; her body smelled, too—a sharp, rich, animal smell. Dirt and sweat, campfire smoke. Slightly, the creamy scent of girl . . . the faint fish-stink of her privates.

Comforting . . . No saying it wasn't.

"That was pleasing . . . Charity."

No answer from the Indian girl. Silence from the Big-nose Cree.

Lee felt her thin leg shift against him . . . thought he could hear her breathing, just barely, above the soft sea-sounds of the wind through the hemlocks overhead. The wind through those tree tops sounded as it had sounded years before, off Seal Rock. Almost the same soft, heavy, insistent whispering.

"That was pleasing . . ."

He felt her shift her slight weight, start to

draw away from him under the robe. Lee reached up and took hold of her thin arm to hold her still—did it with his left hand, too. He slid his other hand up under the buffalo hide, found her skinny, smooth-skinned thigh (his hand reached halfway 'round it, she was so meager) and held it.

Charity made no further move to try and draw away; she stayed, half over, half beside him and was quiet under the shelter of the robe. Still beside him in that close and narrow place of warmth, so fragile in the circling leagues of forest, the freezing night.

Lee felt his cock stir, slowly rise against her narrow flank.

She was young—damn young. An Indian, though . . . had likely grunted under some drunken buck well before now. Must have, to come sashaying stark naked over to a man's bed roll. Young, though, and may have meant only to ease the aches . . .

She was quiet under his hands as a young rabbit might have been, frozen in terror, lifted by its nape from a trap. Lee likely should take his hands from her, let her go, let her walk back to her buffalo robe.

Surely should do that.

He caressed her thigh, stroking it gently, sliding his hand up along that smooth length slowly up to her ass. The Indian girl had hardly any ass at all—her little rounds of butt were almost as flat and muscular as a boy's. Lee fitted his hand to her small ass-cheek. It filled his hand nicely as if it had been made for just that purpose. He gripped and squeezed it, squeezed it hard enough to make her murmur in the darkness. She moved slightly so the skin of her hip rubbed smoothly against the heat and swelling of his cock.

Lee let go of her arm, put his hand to her throat, and slid it down her thin, tendon-corded neck to her chest, again, near flat as a boy's except where the small, surprising breasts grew like soft lemons with harder tips. She made to pull away when Lee touched her there, when he began to squeeze one of her breasts, took the nipple between his thumb and forefinger and pinched it lightly. Then barely touched it, his fingertip tapping it, brushing it . . . feeling, after a while, the small nipple fatten under his moving finger.

He began to tickle at her with his other hand, cupping the round of her ass that he had squeezed to hurting before and tracing the glossy smoothness of her skin there with his fingers. He slowly curled his fingers under her buttock cheek . . . felt the soft little button of her asshole . . . stroked it gently . . .

Lee felt the girl relax in his hands. It was a slight and subtle thing, a sagging into him . . . letting him bear her weight.

He reached further up under her, his fingers searching from her ass along the slight, downy rise of her cunt . . . found the tight, narrow little slot, and gently touched it, searched along it with his fingertips. Found a small damp place. Pushed harder with his finger.

The girl said something to him, twisted in his arms, but Lee held her hard, got his finger up into her, and pushed it deeper.

Felt something there. Something. Knew what it was, and didn't stop.

Lee rolled the girl over and under him, felt the night's hard cold fall across his shoulders where the robe slid away. The Cree girl clutched at him, strong, skinny fingers biting into the muscle of his arms, his shoulders. Lee's left arm ached as he leaned on it above her. He wished he could see her face, her eyes.

He bent over her, and, something to his own surprise, kissed her on the lips. Charity must not have done much white-style kissing; he felt her start when he kissed her, touched her half-parted lips with his tongue.

She tasted rich. Soft and sweet and rich.

Lee, braced over her, bent his head again and began to lick slowly along the thin plains of her face, her lips, her closed eyelids. He kissed the proud little beak of her nose, licked gently at her lips again, nuzzled her head to one side so that he could trace the delicate whorls of her ear with his tongue tip.

No question the missionary Cree was getting a lesson in the white man's mouth ways . . .

. . . And liking it.

Lee heard her sigh, felt her turn slightly beneath him as he kissed and sucked at her throat. It was startling, how good she tasted. Apparently it was the best sort of flavoring for a young girl, to have ridden high country for two or three days sweating or chilled, weary and unbathed. Gave this big-nosed little girl a fine high flavor . . .

Lee used his tongue along the lines of her slender throat, kissed her softly under the angle of her jaw. She had turned her small head in the dark, to present that place to him. *"The Colonel's lady, and Rosie O'Grady . . ."*

Lee found one of her breasts with his mouth, tongued the nipple, then sucked strongly on it. That pleased the girl very much, pleased her so that she cried out something in Indian. Then he pleased her at her other little breast and bit that nipple lightly, tugging at it.

He felt one of her hands then drifting slowly down between them. Slowly . . . slowly. Then her fingers found him. Lee would have known even if he hadn't already felt the evidence of it, that she was virgin. Would have known by the delicate, searching way she touched it, traced the swollen size of his cock, then lightly gripped it.

Her other hand slid down, and she held

him and gently squeezed at it, as if to test its hardness, its heat.

Lee had intended to lick her from armpits to toes, and all dark, sweet stops in between, but that gentle, faintly trembling grip changed his mind.

He crowded her under the buffalo robe, reached down to tug her knees apart, reached down between them when she spread them wide, obedient as a child. Touched her, found that small in-folded spot, wetter now under his fingertips. Slippery.

The Cree girl panted under him; her grip on his cock was not so gentle now. Her breathing was harsh as a dog's—Lee felt the touch of it on his cheeks. She was holding his cock, rubbing it, the tip of it, against her cunt. He felt the smooth heat against his, heard the faint sticky sound as she used him. Had done the like before, no doubt, used something long and hard to play with in that fashion . . .

She murmured something in the dark, pulled at him, thrust up just a little.

Time—and past time.

Lee sat back, reached down to her narrow hips to lift them up, then with one hand brushed her tentative hands away, gripped his cock, set it to the soft fork of her crotch, searched with it for that little oily place . . .

He found it, put the head of his cock hard against it. And pushed.

She grunted then tried to twist away, but Lee had her and meant to keep her. He thrust again—felt that veil of tissue snagging at his cock-head—and thrust into her with all his strength.

Charity screamed one short, sharp cry, then was silent, struggling. She kicked out, trying to escape the pain, her skinny legs tangled in the buffalo robe. Silent wrestling—Lee was careful to hold his head up, away from a bite. Set his hands to her hips and held her down with all his weight.

He gritted his teeth against the squeezing pressure of her narrow passage (hurt him a little, tell the truth) then thrust again, hard as he could. Fiery hot for all the cold night against his uncovered back, and didn't, for that moment, care if he killed her.

His cock drove into her like a great greased pole, opening her up, spreading her, shoving up inside her. It drove up into her all the way and she screamed again, and twisted on it as if it was killing her, as if it had entered the chambers of her heart.

Once there, Lee rested, lying on her, bearing her down with his weight, feeling the wonderful sensations of it—of being at once inside her, and in a way, within a new country, too. Her screams, her weeping—she was sobbing under him as any white girl might—meant very little to him.

Nothing but that entrance into her living guts meant much to Lee immediately.

It seemed a long time he lay with the thin Indian girl in their robe in the dark. Lay on her, and in her, and was very well pleased. She wept for a while, quieter and quieter, and Lee bent to kiss her, kiss the tears.

He was still buried deep inside her, and hard as any stone.

It was still a while after that before he slowly began to move, over her murmured protests, her fluttering, staying hands. He moved slowly, slowly, deeper and then almost out of her, and took great care in doing it.

It took a long time before, still crying out softly at the pain now and again, the Big-nose girl commenced to dance with him the oldest dance of all.

Until, gasping, her small cunt and ass soaked with her juices, trembling as she received the long, pumping stokes, Big-nose Charity, grandaughter of Stones-Made-Shiny-By-Water, threw back her head in the cold night dark, kicked out in desperation at her pleasure, and screamed with delight.

Lee groaned and filled her—spurted his heart right out into her, so that the jissom leaked in blurts where they joined. It was so sweet, it made him shake, gasp for breath . . .

He loved her, then, for the while. Loved everything about her. "Sweetheart . . ." he called her then, and the girl heard him.

Lee woke late, after dawn, to a dark and

windy morning. There was the barest tracery of snow laced across the forest floor—damned if he knew when it had fallen. Touches of it still decorated the spreading fronds of the hemlocks overhead.

Must have slept like an Irishman on a work day to have missed the fall of snow.

Lee rolled over in the buffalo robe, and saw Charity at the morning fire, setting the coffee pot on. She worked with her head lowered, not looking at him. Ashamed, likely, of what they'd done last night. Could thank the missionaries for that. Roman Catholics as bad as the Protestants. Same superstitious nonsense.

"Good morning . . ."

She glanced up, murmured a "Good morning" back, then went on with her work, feeding the fire more fallen wood, working it up despite the wind that gusted through the camp. She did it well—that would be a good cooking fire.

Hadn't noticed the snow—hadn't wakened to it. Hadn't felt the girl getting up, either. Seemed that a scramble with a bear made for deep sleeping.

Lee lay back, stretching, trying his left shoulder, the sore arm. Better. Both were better. The rubbing—and the other—had eased the hurt considerably. Cold day, cold enough to snow again, more heavily. He wouldn't miss that one. Wind was hissing through these trees like snakes, fluttering the fire.

Time to roll out and get doing, and Lee started to do just that.

"I believe that I could pink this Yankee nicely through the skull—would you say so, Robins?"

"I would indeed, m'Lord. Sittin'—or in flight."

Lee held still—made no move at all. They had come up into the wind, likely smelling camp smoke all the way. Must have canoed down the river to the mountain's base, quartered the forest, and waited for Lee to make a mistake. Something foolish, like building fires in strange country just so as to be warm and have a hot breakfast.

Lee looked across at Charity and saw she was startled. Not from her, then, nor with her. Poor little Dowd must have cried out too particularly as he lay dying.

They'd expected him.

CHAPTER NINE

Very slowly, Lee turned to see the men. He was up on one elbow, still half in the buffalo robe, and naked. The Bisley Colt's was an arms-reach away to the side, holstered, resting neatly on folds of cartridge belt, protected from the snow by a flap of slicker.

Just an arm's reach away—and distant from use as a shotgun in Brady's hardware in Parker, Idaho.

The English boy was beautiful even in his furs and gaiters. Looked like a fine blonde woman, a tall and merry one, but for a fair breadth of shoulder and the size of his hands. He held a heavy Webley revolver in his right hand, and the revolver was not too big for his grip.

"Good morning to you, Mister . . . ?" The boy had bright blue eyes; his silver hair curled like fine sheep's wool. His voice was pitched so high, so musically, that it sounded like singing.

He seemed to be a proper English lord, Lee thought. Proper enough to have played one on the stage.

"Morgan," Lee said. "Lee Morgan."

The beautiful boy nodded and strolled over to the fire. He kept his eyes, and the muzzle of the big Webley, directed where Lee lay like a cadet surprised in bed with the sheriff's wife. Caught like a jackass, and like to be dealt with accordingly. Lee had no doubts the boy intended to kill him, though he appeared to enjoy taking his time about it, and hunkered by the fire like an old mossy horn, warming his elegant bottom by the fire's heat, facing Lee, watching him, smiling. He was only a little farther from the holstered Colt's then Lee was, and Lee knew that the boy knew all the thoughts being thought about that weapon.

"I shouldn't if I were you," Lord Surrey said, indicating the Colt's with a raised eyebrow. "Simply too far from you, dear fellow. Too far."

Couldn't argue with the sissy son-of-a-bitch on that.

"You—girl." Surrey turned his head just a little toward her. "If that's coffee—and I suppose it must be, despite its odor—you may pour me a cup, and bring it to me."

Charity kept her eyes lowered, as though she didn't want to see any of them, as though she didn't want to see anything at all.

She picked the pot up out of the coals, poured a measure into a tin cup, and came around the fire at a slow half-crouch, looking scared to death.

Lee didn't blame her. But he didn't feel afraid, himself. Felt angry at dying a fool's death but did not feel afraid.

He looked slowly 'round again and saw "Robins." The Earl's man was a small, neat, well-set-up fellow, with a pale, pinched face. Looked like a game keeper, by his stance, the easy way he cradled a double-barrelled shotgun. He appeared to know how to use a shotgun. He seemed very easy with it.

Lee saw no way. There was a chance, of course, that he might get to the Bisley and take only one round from the smiling boy's revolver in doing it. Might be fit then, to draw and shoot the holstered Colt's—or might not. There was a chance of his doing that, though more than likely Surrey would have put two or more rounds into him. More than likely would have blown his fool head off, as it deserved.

Still there was a *slight* chance of using the Colt's. Except for Robins. Surrey's man would certainly not miss with that shotgun at this range even if his master did.

Charity handed the pretty boy his coffee,

serving carefully, and from her decorous crouch, a servant born, a savage well tamed and trained.

The boy sipped his coffee and regarded Lee. He seemed amused. "It was, I believe, a social solecism to have come upon you in such a . . . state of nature, my dear fellow." He sipped again. "Your friend, the minute Mister Dowd, though greedy and a trespasser, had at least the fortune of facing us in his night-shirt. An extraordinary sight he was, too. That shirt, Robins—was it yellow-striped, or puce?"

The servant's voice came back over Lee's shoulder. "Puce, m'lord." That voice, fat with satisfaction at its subordination to this murdering rich pup, made Lee's skin crawl. To be done by such a pair as this, and all his own fault! His own fault . . . lying out in soogins like a drunken Paddy . . . toasting himself at a damned bonfire . . .

Close to, the earl wasn't quite as beautiful a boy as he'd seemed. Had a trace too much jaw . . . a length too much nose to match it.

"To go to one's Maker in such a state," the young lord said, "is to compound one's stupidity in going at all, in such a cause." He'd stopped smiling. "The theft of another man's land is the one unforgivable crime." Boy sounded as if he meant it. The smile was as distant as the season of Spring, now. Lord Surrey looked like a hangman, one of the fortunate that enjoyed that work. "You," the handsome boy added, and took a third sip of coffee, "I consider to be an aider and abettor of Mister Dowd's attempted theft." He'd had enough coffee now or simply wished both hands free and handed the cup to Charity to take away. "And I intend to deal with you as appropriately . . ." Charity went crouching away behind him to the fire, the cup held as if the boy's lips had plated it with gold.

The Webley came level.

It seemed to Lee that it was a very large-bored weapon. Forty-five caliber or over, it looked to him . . . Lee took a deep breath.

"Head-shot, Robins?"

"Oh, I should think so, m'lord, at that range . . ."

Lee saw Charity, obscured behind the boy, slowly stand up, appear to draw back both her hands. Then, as if she were swinging a baseball bat, in a swift, hard sideways motion, she stepped closer to Lord Surrey and hit him hard in the back.

"What the devil did you *do?!*" The boy stood straight up, his voice going high as a girl's, astonished. He turned 'round on her, one hand a fist to strike her down—and Lee saw the hunting knife handle, the blade sunk deep beside his spine.

Lee rolled for the holstered Colt's and took that infernal buffalo robe with him, tangled at his legs.

The movement of turning must have stirred the steel and sliced inside what

399

shouldn't be cut, for the boy who must have felt at first only the thump of impact as she struck him, suddenly strained up on his toes —up and then arching back so far that Lee thought his back must break from the posture.

"Oh!" the boy shouted. "Oh, dear—oh, *dear!*" He spun on his toes like a dancer, the knife hilt sticking like a long peg from his back, then fell face first into the fire.

Lee had the buffalo robe kicked free, had the Bisley out and cocked and saw Charity, her narrow beaky face well pleased, suddenly struck in the throat by a shotgun charge. Blood blew from her slight neck in a furious spray, and Lee rolled to his belly, half turned to fire over his left shoulder, and placed his first round into the servant's groin.

Even shot so and hard hit, Robins re-shouldered the shotgun and swung it smooth as a safe door down at Lee, the pinched, pale face as set as bread pudding.

Lee shot him again, through the stomach, and in spasm, the man pulled his second trigger. The buckshot hissed across the clearing and rattled into a tree, and Lee fired at the son-of-a-bitch a third time (hasty and despairing, Charity on his mind) aimed poorly and shot the falling man's lower jaw away, leaving a bright white splinter under the servant's sprouting tongue as he fell stretched out beneath a great green fan of hemlock branches.

Lee got to his feet naked in the freezing air, which he felt not at all, and saw Charity dying on the other side of the fire where the young lord crawled and muttered, his fine hair burning, his face frying, combing the seething còals.

When Lee reached her she was all but bled completely out, lying on her back, her thin, dark hands held half above her as if to ward off some terrible descending blow. Her hands, her whole slight body was slowly clenching into spasm, then relaxing, after. Her slender neck was hacked wide open, torn away by the shotgun charge. She was so drenched in blood she looked made of bronze —a statue memorial of a dying Indian girl.

She smelled of salt from all the blood when Lee took her in his arms—a dead girl, near as might be.

"I love you," the horse-rancher said, and meant it. She might have heard it, but likely not.

It took Lee more time than he'd thought to put her away.

He'd dressed himself, put her fine beaver parka on her, then wrapped her in the robe they'd shared, corded that around her, tight and then, burdened by her, had carefully climbed up through the thick low branches of the largest hemlock over the camp, to lash her high in the air, safe near the trunk of the tree.

Then he'd gone into the forest a way to find the hobbled horses, and brought them into camp (they'd shied at the stink of the handsome young Earl who, still and silent at last, crouched in the bed of dying fire, his roasted buttocks in the air, his face an eyeless char, Charity's knife still stuck in his back.

Lee tacked the animals out, and struck camp.

He had ridden less than a mile, perhaps a good deal less in this forest, (umbrella'd by such trees, distance was a chancy thing to tell) when he heard a man laughing behind him.

It was a faint sound and a good distance back, but it was laughter right enough, and a kind to set a chill down Lee's back. Nothing mad or loony about it—no inhumanity.

Simply the free and open laughter of a man who'd come upon something very funny.

A fellow with his jaw shot off, say. And a well-cooked Earl.

Lee wondered if the Frenchman would try a slice of Surrey, so providentially prepared. Wondered, too, why the trapper had not been with the others when they took the camp. Forge had loitered for some reason— perhaps weary of the young Lord's company, peerhaps the other way 'round, and the Englishmen had found the cannibal's company unsettling—and so had arrived too late for that fight. Lee had no illusions that he

402

might have survived if the Frenchman had joined the others earlier.

He was only alive now because the Indian girl had felt a duty to him—out of love, perhaps, or out of gratitude for the pleasures he had shared with her the night before, or, and most likely, out of duty as his guide. She, a meager girl, had not failed where her grandfather had failed.

Lee did not care to think where he had failed in his duty to her. He built a wall of seasoned timber in his mind against those thoughts and rode the tall grey and led the sturdy, ambling paint down dark aisles of forest, slowly circling back toward that distant, merry sound of laughter.

Poor chance, of course, against such a woodsman in such a wood, but a chance to be taken just the same. This was the last fellow Lee had come to see, and there was no riding south without.

Did not care to think . . .

The Frenchman, after all, would not be killing much, should he do Lee down. Dowd at least had brought a gunman with him into danger when he went hunting land and grants and leases.

Lee had brought a big-nosed girl, fifteen years old, perhaps. Maybe sixteen . . .

The Frenchman, if he was lucky enough, and clever, would be killing a fellow looked like a man, was tall, and strong. Was fierce and quick with weapons. Looked like a man, sure enough, but rang hollow in the clinch. Had, in the past, brought home death to his father. Had now brought another here to death.

Sill, even such a person as that will "try the last."

Lee dug spurs to the grey and that fine horse went galloping. They threaded at speed through stands of rough-barked trunks, the grey dashing past in quick curves or in between so close and so fast that Lee's stirrup irons struck the trees at times to one side or the other as he leaned with the horse on the turns. The paint pounded after.

No use trying to sneak a march on a master trapper. The Frenchman would duck and dodge, hide and conceal and laugh that ringing merry laugh of his as Lee came stumbling after, clumsy on horseback.

Only chance was to rush him—to come in fast and at a run, to hasty the man (or anger him) into a present fight. Lee bent low over the saddle-bow as the grey drove headlong into a rare clump of brush—bulled and battered through, and ran reaching out the other side. Branches were striking like spade handles at Lee as he galloped past. His Stetson went at one, and a second and third branch hit out at him and almost clubbed him from the saddle. There was no bending low enough in that tangle at a run to keep from being scraped and lashed at, keep from being beaten.

He was almost back at camp—was sure he was almost at it, when the grey was shot at and hit and killed all in a single stride.

Lee never heard the shot—wouldn't have above the horses' slamming hooves that shook even this soft forest floor, the crash and crackle of the greenery as they went galloping through. Never heard the shot, but felt the grey falter as the jolt went through it —felt the animal's legs fold beneath it like a duck's wing as it is shot—felt the grey pitching headlong into its fall.

Lee unstirruped, rolled out of his saddle to the right, struck soft ground and not, by good luck, a tree, and was up and running, Bisley Colt's in his hand, toward the camp now no more than some yards away, and the place for sure where a rifle round must have started, to have caught the grey so neatly at his right shoulder. Lee'd felt that jolt in his right leg as it lay along the grey's barrel.

Lee ran through the last of the low hemlock branches and got a smart cut along his left cheek-bone doing it, then charged into the camp clearing (matters now seeming to move slowly, as if in a dream, as if he had time and enough to spare for any action).

The clearing was empty.

Silence.

No bird sounds. The sun, in this almost

open spot, came dappling down in small splashes on the dark pine straw underfoot.

No sign of the Frenchman at all—not even the faintest smell of gun-powder, either. Or haze of it.

Lee heard the paint, deprived of its customary companion and trail lead, blundering about in the woods beyond.

Otherwise, silence.

Lee stood in the camp's center, armed. Where he looked, the muzzle of the Bisley Colt's turned also, a bright, vacant, inquiring eye. Forge had not taken his opportunity of cooked meat. Neither dead man had been disturbed, only laughed at. Lee wondered if the Frenchman was a big man; he surely was a swift one.

Perhaps had had some fun or other with the girl's body. Signs of climbing and scrape and fuss would have led Forge there as surely as a street sign would a city clerk.

Lee, stopping once to watch behind him, stepped over to that hemlock, under it, and peered up into the branches.

He saw the darker shape of the girl's wrapped corpse, undisturbed.

And beside it, crouching, smiling down at him, a bulky man with a rosy, merry face, clean-shaven as a Catholic monk. The man, in the instant Lee had to look, was dressed in a fringed fur coat and had upon his head a round fur hat with a sprig of green tucked into it.

The Frenchman dropped down onto Lee like a stooping hawk, and as he fell, brought down a bright-bladed hatchet as Lee brought his revolver up, and struck the Colt's clean out of Lee's hand as the man himself struck Lee and drove him to the ground.

They rolled there for an instant, Lee managing by great luck to grip the trapper's hatchet-arm at the wrist. It was luck, and only of the moment, because the Frenchman was sickeningly strong. Now Lee knew the man was mad, no matter how healthy his laughter. Forge was too strong not to be mad.

Lee could do that range-country strong man's trick of bending horse shoes . . . could loop an iron poker, too. And had won bets more than once, arm or Indian wrestling iron-muscled drovers and wranglers and teamsters. Was, in fact, reckoned a dangerously strong man and of course, wonderfully quick. Little use, now.

Forge rolled with Lee on the pine needle carpet, beaming with apparent great pleasure all the while, pulled his wrist from Lee's grip with no seeming effort at all and struck with the hatchet again.

The edge of the blade sliced a small piece of Lee's cheek away—about as much as could have been covered by a silver dollar—and then buried itself in the forest floor.

Forge had it out and struck again as Lee threw himself back and away. The blade caught him lightly across his left forearm, and Lee felt and heard the faint *snick* as it nicked the bone there. Lee leaped up and backward for his life. Forge, still pleasant in the face, came up and after him faster than a man should have been able and Lee stepped back into the charred dead branches of the fire, tripped, tripped again as he tried to balance, and fell full back into the crouched corpse of the English boy.

The Frenchman chuckled, or made that sort of sound, and drove across the ashes to seize Lee and butcher him just as he rolled clear of the toppled corpse.

The Frenchman drove down, seized Lee by his hair, hauled him up to his knees, and held him close. The hatchet went swinging up and back.

Lee stabbed the Frenchman in the balls with Charity's hunting knife, wrenched it out, and stabbed the man again.

The hatchet's bright blade hung still in the air, as if Forge had been turned to stone. Stabbing a third time, driving the long blade deep, deep up into the trapper's privates, up into his bowels, Lee still felt that dreadful grip clenched upon his hair, still saw, high over the Frenchman's head, his raised arm, the gleaming hatchet head.

The cannibal stood seeming frozen as stone, either by the mortal wounds, or the agony of them, or by the sudden knowledge of death present.

The man stood stock still in that fashion—

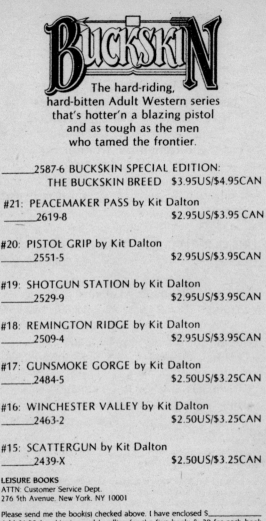

BUCKSKIN

The hard-riding,
hard-bitten Adult Western series
that's hotter'n a blazing pistol
and as tough as the men
who tamed the frontier.

_____2587-6 BUCKSKIN SPECIAL EDITION:
       THE BUCKSKIN BREED $3.95US/$4.95CAN

#21: PEACEMAKER PASS by Kit Dalton
_____2619-8 $2.95US/$3.95 CAN

#20: PISTOL GRIP by Kit Dalton
_____2551-5 $2.95US/$3.95CAN

#19: SHOTGUN STATION by Kit Dalton
_____2529-9 $2.95US/$3.95CAN

#18: REMINGTON RIDGE by Kit Dalton
_____2509-4 $2.95US/$3.95CAN

#17: GUNSMOKE GORGE by Kit Dalton
_____2484-5 $2.50US/$3.25CAN

#16: WINCHESTER VALLEY by Kit Dalton
_____2463-2 $2.50US/$3.25CAN

#15: SCATTERGUN by Kit Dalton
_____2439-X $2.50US/$3.25CAN

LEISURE BOOKS
ATTN: Customer Service Dept.
276 5th Avenue, New York, NY 10001

Please send me the book(s) checked above. I have enclosed $_____
Add $1.25 for shipping and handling for the first book; $ .30 for each book
thereafter. No cash, stamps, or C.O.D.s. All orders shipped within 6 weeks.
Canadian orders please add $1.00 extra postage.

Name _____

Address _____

City_____State_____Zip_____

Canadian orders must be paid in U.S. dollars payable through a New York banking facility.   ☐ Please send a free catalogue.

The hard-riding,
hard-bitten Adult Western series
that's hotter'n a blazing pistol
and as tough as the men
who tamed the frontier.

#12: RECOIL by Roy LeBeau $2.50US/$2.95CAN
_____2355-5

#11: TRIGGER GUARD by Roy LeBeau
_____2336-9 $2.50US/$2.95CAN

#10: BOLT ACTION by Roy LeBeau
_____2315-6 $2.50US/$2.95CAN

#8: HANGFIRE HILL by Roy LeBeau
_____2271-0 $2.50US/$2.95CAN

#5: GUNSIGHT GAP by Roy LeBeau
_____2189-7 $2.75US/$2.95CAN

PONY SOLDIERS

They were a dirty, undisciplined rabble, but they were the only chance a thousand settlers had to see another sunrise. Killing was their profession and they took pride in their work—they were too fierce to live, too damn mean to die.

_____2620-1   #5: SIOUX SHOWDOWN
$2.75 US/$3.75 CAN

_____2598-1   #4: CHEYENNE BLOOD STORM
$2.75US/$3.75CAN

_____2565-5   #3: COMANCHE MOON
$2.75US/$3.75CAN

_____2541-8   #2: COMANCHE MASSACRE
$2.75US/$3.75CAN

_____2518-3   #1: SLAUGHTER AT BUFFALO
CREEK $2.75US/$3.75CAN

The World's Greatest Western Writer

ZANE GREY

Classic tales of action and adventure
set in the Old West
and penned with blistering authority
by America's Master Story Teller

THE BUFFALO HUNTER. Rugged, dangerous men and the
beasts they hunted to the point of extinction.

_____2599-X $2.75 US/$3.75 CAN

SPIRIT OF THE BORDER. The settlers were doomed unless a
few grizzled veterans of the Indian Wars, scalphunters as
mean and vicious as the renegades, could stop them.

_____2564-7 $2.75 US/$3.75 CAN

THE RUSTLERS OF PECOS COUNTY. Although out-
numbered a thousand to one, the Texas Rangers were the
last chance the settlers had. It had to be enough.

_____2498-5 $2.75 US/$3.50 CAN

THE LAST RANGER. The classic frontier tale of a brutal Indian fighter and a shrewd beauty who struggled to make a
heaven of the hell on earth they pioneered.

_____2447-0 $2.95 US/$3.75 CAN

THE LAST TRAIL. White renegades stir up the hostile Indian
tribes surrounding the little settlement of Fort Henry.

_____2636-8 $2.95 US/$3.95 CAN

JIM STEEL MEANS GOLD, GUNS, WOMEN & BLOOD

The rip-roaring Western series that blasts off the page like a runaway train.

_____2485-3 #6: AZTEC GOLD
$2.50 US/$3.25 CAN

_____2464-0 #5: GOLD TRAIN
$2.50 US/$3.25 CAN

_____2440-3 #4: DEVIL'S GOLD
$2.50 US/$3.25 CAN

_____2421-7 #3: BLOODY GOLD
$2.50 US/$3.25 CAN

_____2399-7 #2: DIE OF GOLD
$2.50 US/$3.25 CAN